Emile Zola

His Excellency

French Literature
published by Mondial:

Emile Zola: The Fortune of the Rougons
(ISBN 1595690107 / 9781595690104)

Emile Zola: A Love Episode
(ISBN 1595690271 / ISBN 9781595690272)

Emile Zola: The Fat and the Thin (The Belly of Paris)
(ISBN 1595690522 / ISBN 9781595690524)

Emile Zola: Abbé Mouret's Transgression (The Sin of the Abbé Mouret)
(ISBN 1595690506 / ISBN 9781595690500)

Emile Zola: The Dream
(ISBN 1595690492 / ISBN 9781595690494)

Emile Zola: A Love Episode
(ISBN 1595690271 / ISBN 9781595690272)

Emile Zola: The Conquest of Plassans
(ISBN 1595690484 / ISBN 9781595690487)

Emile Zola: The Joy of Life (Zest for Life)
(ISBN 1595690476 / ISBN 9781595690470)

Emile Zola: Doctor Pascal
(ISBN 1595690514 / ISBN 9781595690517)

Emile Zola: Fruitfulness
(ISBN 1595690182 / 9781595690180)

Victor Hugo: The Man Who Laughs (By Order of the King)
(ISBN 1595690131 / 9781595690135)

Victor Hugo: History of a Crime
(ISBN 1595690204 / 9781595690203)

Honoré de Balzac: Ursula (Ursule Mirouët)
(ISBN 1595690530 / 9781595690531)

Honoré de Balzac: Maître Cornelius
(ISBN 1595690174 / 9781595690173)

Anatole France: Penguin Island
(ISBN 1595690298 / 9781595690296)

Gustave Flaubert: Salammbo (Salambo)
(ISBN 1595690352 / 9781595690357)

Jules Verne: An Antarctic Mystery (The Sphinx of the Ice Fields)
(ISBN 1595690549 / 9781595690548)

Emile Zola

HIS EXCELLENCY

Edited, with a preface, by:
Ernest Alfred Vizetelly

Mondial

Mondial
New York · Berlin

The Rougon-Macquart:
Emile Zola: His Excellency
(French original title: "Son Excellence Eugène Rougon")
Reprint of the English edition of 1897

Edited, with a preface, by:
Ernest Alfred Vizetelly

Copyright © 2006 Mondial
(for this edition of "His Excellency")
Editor (Mondial, 2006): Andrew Moore
All rights reserved.

ISBN 1595690557
ISBN 9781595690555

Library of Congress Control Number: 2006935433

Cover painting: Uday K. Dhar

www.mondialbooks.com

CONTENTS

PREFACE

WE live at such high speed nowadays, and the Second French Empire is already so far behind us, that I am inclined to place *Son Excellence Eugène Rougon* in the category of historical novels. In some degree it certainly belongs to another class of fiction, the political novel, which in Great Britain sprouted, blossomed, and faded away contemporaneously with the career of Benjamin Disraeli. But, unlike Disraeli's work, it does not deal with theories or possibilities. Whatever political matter it may contain is a record of incidents which really occurred, of intrigues which were matured, of opinions which were more or less publicly expressed while the third Napoléon was ruling France. In my opinion, with all due allowance for its somewhat limited range of subject, *Son Excellence Eugène Rougon* is the one existing French novel which gives the reader a fair general idea of what occurred in political spheres at an important period of the Empire. It is a book for foreigners and particularly Englishmen to read with profit, for there are yet many among them who cherish the delusion that Napoléon III. was not only a good and true friend of England, but also a wise and beneficent ruler of France; and this, although his reign began with bloodshed and trickery, was prolonged by means of innumerable subterfuges, and ended in woe, horror, and disgrace.

The present translation of M. Zola's book was not made by me, but I have revised it somewhat severely with the object of ensuring greater accuracy in all the more important passages, and of improving the work generally. And, subject to those limitations which deference for the opinion of the majority of English-speaking readers has imposed on the translator and myself, I consider that this rendering fully conveys the purport of the original. During the work of revision I was struck by the great care shown by M. Zola in the handling of his subject. There is, of course, some fiction in the book; but, again and again, page after page, I have found a simple record of fact, just deftly adapted to suit the requirements of the narrative. The history of the Second Empire is probably as familiar to me as it is to M. Zola himself—for, like him, I grew to manhood in its midst, with better opportunities, too, than he had of observing certain of its distinguishing features—and thus I have been able to identify innumerable incidents and allusions, and trace to their very source some of the most curious passages in the book. And it is for this reason, and by virtue of my own knowledge and experience, that I claim for *His Excellency* the merit of reflecting things as they really were in the earlier years of the Imperial *régime.*

Against one surmise the reader must be cautioned. Napoléon III. and the Empress Eugénie figure in the following pages without disguise; and wherever the name of the Count de Marsy appears, that of the infamous Duke de Morny—whom Sir Robert Peel, in one of his most slashing speeches, did not scruple to call the greatest jobber in Europe—may be read without a moment's hesitation. But his Excellency Eugène Rougon is not, as many critics and others have supposed, a mere portrait or caricature of his Excellency Eugène Rouher, the famous Vice-Emperor of history. Symbolism is to be found in every one of M. Zola's novels, and Rougon, in his main lines, is but the symbol of a principle, or, to be accurate, the symbol of a certain form of the principle of authority. His face is Rouher's, like his build and his favourite gesture; but with Rouher's words, actions, opinions, and experiences are blended those of half-a-dozen other personages. The forgotten ones! the men whose names were once a terror, but who are as little remembered, as little known, in France to-day, as the satraps of the vanished Eastern realms, as the eunuchs who ruled the civilised world on behalf of effete Emperors when Byzantium, amidst all her splendour, was, like Paris, tottering to ruin. Baroche, Billault, Delangle, Fialin *alias* Persigny, Espinasse—there is something of each of these, as well as something of Rouher, in the career of Eugène Rougon as narrated by M. Zola. Words which one or another of these men wrote or uttered, things which one or another of them actually did, are fathered upon Rougon. He embodies them all: he is the incarnation of that craving, that lust for power which impelled so many men of ability to throw all principle to the winds and become the instruments of an abominable system of government. And his transformation at the close of the story is in strict accordance with historical facts. He salutes the rise of the so-called 'Liberal' Empire in the very words of Billault—the most tyrannical of all the third Napoléon's 'band.'

Rougon has a band of his own—they all had hands in those days, like the Emperor himself; and since that time we have in a similar way seen Gambetta and his *queue* and Boulanger and his *clique.* And, curiously enough, as in Rougon's case, those historic coteries were in each instance the prime factors in their leader's overthrow.

Thus we have only to turn to the recorded incidents of history to realise the full truth of M. Zola's account of the Rougon gang. It is a masterly account, instinct with accuracy, as real as life itself.

And Rougon, on whatever patchwork basis he may have been built, is a living figure, one of a nature so direct, so free from intricacy, that few ignorant of the truth would imagine him to be a patchwork creation at all. Surely, to have so fully assimilated in one personage the characteristics of half-a-dozen known men in such wise that, without any clashing of individual proclivities, the whole six are truthfully embodied in one, is a signal proof of that form of genius which lies in the infinite capacity for taking pains.

If we pass from Rougon to Marsy we find another embodiment of that principle of authority which both help to represent. Rougon, as M. Zola says, is the shaggy fist which deals the knockdown blow, while Marsy is the gloved hand which stabs or throttles. Years ago, when I was unacquainted with this comparison, and was contrasting the rising genius of Emile Zola with that of his great and splendid rival, Alphonse Daudet, I likened M. Zola to the fist and M. Daudet to the rapier. A French critic had previously called the former a cactus and the latter an Arab steed. The cactus comparison, as applied to M. Zola, was a very happy one; for I defy anybody, even the smuggest of hypocrites, to read M. Zola's works without some prickings of conscience. And verily I believe that most of the opposition to the author of the Rougon-Macquart series arises from that very cause.

But I must return to Marsy, though he need not detain me long, for he only flits across the following pages with his regal air and sardonic smile. For a fuller and, in some degree, a more favourable portrait, one must turn to the pages of Daudet, who of course could not write ill of the man to whom he owed his start in life. In the present work, slight as is the sketch, Marsy, or Morny, the name signifies little, is shown as he really was—venal, immoral, witty, and exquisitely polite. Then there is Delestang, who, physically, represents M. Magne; while in like way Beulin d'Orchère, the judge whose sister marries Rougon, is copied from Delangle, whose bulldog face is alluded to by most of the *anecdotiers* of the Empire. La Rouquette is, by name at all events, a connection of Forcade de la Roquette—a stepbrother of Marshal St. Arnaud—who rose to influence and power in the latter days of the Empire; and M. de Plouguern, the profligate old senator, reminds me in some respects of that cynical and eccentric Anglomaniac, the Marquis de

Boissy. The various members of Rougon's band are sketched from less-known people. Kahn I cannot quite identify, but I suspect him to be the deputy who was mixed up in the scandal of the Graissesac railway line, to which M. Zola refers as the line from Niort to Angers. However, there is no member of the band that I like better than Béjuin, the silent deputy, who never asks a favour, and yet has favours continually showered upon him. I have known a man of that character connected with English public life.

To return to those of M. Zola's masculine characters who may be identified with real personages, none is more genially, more truthfully, portrayed than Chevalier Rusconi, the Italian or, more correctly, Sardinian, Minister in Paris. Here we have that most amiable of men, Chevalier Nigra, of whom Prosper Mérimée once said in my presence: 'C'est un bohème tombé dans la diplomatie.' Withal, Chevalier Nigra—who, though very aged, still serves his country, I believe, with distinction at Vienna—was a very good diplomatist indeed; one of Cavour's right-hand men, one of those to whom Italy owes union and liberty. And what a career was his in France, and what memoirs might he not write! Few diplomatists ever had stranger experiences: from all the secret plotting which so largely helped to make Victor Emmanuel King of Italy to the surveillance so adroitly practised over the Empress Eugénie, whose support of Pope Pius IX. was ever an obstacle to Italian aspirations. For her Nigra-Rusconi became the handsome, gallant courtier; he was a musician, could sing and dance, was proficient in every society accomplishment, and before long the Empress's Monday receptions at the Tuileries, those *petits Lundis* enlivened by the wit of Mérimée, were never complete without him. Yet, all the time, a stern duel was being fought between him and the consort of Napoléon III. And so long as her husband ruled France she kept her adversary at bay. Rome, capital of Italy, was but the fruit of Sedan. Yet Nigra was chivalrous. When the hitter hour of reckoning arrived, he stood by the woman who had so long thwarted him. He and Prince Richard Metternich smuggled her out of the Tuileries in order that she might escape to England, beyond the reach of the infuriated Parisians.

We catch a few glimpses of the Empress in the pages of *His Excellency.* We find her at Compiègne surrounded by the ladies of her Court; we also see her riding in state to Notre Dame to attend the baptism of her infant son. A great day it was, when the Empire reached its zenith: a gorgeous ceremony, too, attended by every

VI

pomp. On referring to the newspapers of the time I have found M. Zola's description of the function to be remarkably accurate. We espy the Man of December raising the Prince Impérial in his arms, presenting the heir of the Napoléons to the assembled multitude—even as once before, and in the same cathedral, the victor of Austerlitz presented the infant King of Rome to the homage of France. But neither the son of Marie-Louise nor the son of Eugénie de Montijo was destined to reign. And what a mockery now seems that grand baptismal ceremony, as well as all the previous discussion in the Corps Législatif, of which M. Zola gives such an animated account. What a lesson, too, for human pride, and, in the sequel, what a punishment for human perversity! I often read, I often hear, words of compassion for the Prince Impérial's widowed mother, but they cannot move me to pity, for I think of all the hundreds, all the thousands, of mothers who lost their sons in that most wicked and abominable of wars in the declaration of which the Empress Eugénie played so prominent a part. Her evil influence triumphed in that hour of indecision which came upon her ailing husband; and her war—*ma guerre à moi*—ensued, with fatal consequences, which even yet disturb the world. And so, however great, however bitter, her punishment, who will dare to say that it was undeserved?

But whilst I consider the Empress to have been, in more than one momentous circumstance, the evil genius of France, even as Marie Antoinette was the evil genius of the crumbling Legitimate monarchy, I am not one of those who believe in all the malicious reports of her to be found in *la chronique scandaleuse*. That she threw herself at the Emperor's head and compelled him to marry her, may be true, but that is all that can be alleged against her with any show of reason. She undoubtedly proved a faithful wife to a man who was notoriously a most unfaithful husband. There are those who may yet remember how one November morning in the year 1860 the Empress arrived in London, scarcely attended, drove in a growler to Claridge's Hôtel, and thence hurried off to Scotland. Her flight from the Tuileries had caused consternation there. For four days the *Moniteur* remained ominously silent, and when it at last spoke out it was to announce with the utmost brevity that her Majesty was in very delicate health, and had betaken herself to Scotland—in November!—for a change of air. This ridiculous explanation deceived nobody. The simple truth was that the Empress had obtained proof positive of another of her husband's infidelities.

It is needless for me to enlarge upon the subject; I have only mentioned it in corroboration of the portrait of Napoléon III. which M. Zola traces in *His Excellency*. The Emperor was an immoral man—the Beauharnais if not the Bonaparte blood coursed in his veins—and the names of several of his mistresses are perfectly well known. For the rest, M. Zola pictures him very accurately: moody, reserved, with vague humanitarian notions, and as great a predilection for secret police spying as was evinced by Louis XV. The intrigue between him and M. Zola's heroine, Clorinde, is no extravagant notion. Here again a large amount of actual fact is skilfully blended with a little fiction. Clorinde Balbi at once suggests the beautiful Countess de Castiglione; but in the account of her earlier career one finds a suggestion of the behaviour which innumerable scandalmongers impute—wrongly, I believe—to the Empress Eugénie. In Clorinde's mother, the Contessa Balbi, there is more than a suggestion of Madame de Montijo, who was undoubtedly an adventuress of good birth. Both the Balbis are very cleverly drawn; they typify a class of women that has long flourished in France, where it still has some notorious representatives. It is a class of great popularity with novelists and playwrights, possibly because contemporary history has furnished so many examples of it, from the aforementioned Countess de Castiglione who laid siege to Napoléon III. in order to induce him to further the designs of Cavour and Victor Emmanuel, to the Baroness de Kaulla, who ensnared poor General de Cissey that she might extract from him the military and Foreign Office secrets of France. And with half-a-dozen historical instances in my mind, I find no exaggeration in the character of Clorinde as portrayed in *His Excellency*.

Having thus passed M. Zola's personages in review, I would now refer to the actual scenes which he describes. The account of the sitting of the Corps Législatif, given in the opening chapter, is as accurate as the official report in the *Moniteur* of that time. The report on the estimates for the baptism of the Prince Impérial is taken from the *Moniteur* verbatim. In Chapter III., when the Balbis are shown at home, the description of the house in the Champs Elysées is assuredly that of the famous *niche à Fidèle*. The baptism, described in Chapter IV., is, as I have already mentioned, very faithfully dealt with. I have by me an account of the day's proceedings written for the *Illustrated Times* by my uncle, the late Frank Vizetelly, who was killed in the Soudan; and I find him laying stress on the very points which M. Zola brings into prominence, often indeed using almost the same words. However, this is but one of the curious coincidences on which malicious critics found ridiculous charges of plagiarism; for I am convinced that M. Zola never saw the *Illustrated Times* in his life, and moreover he knows no English. Passing to Chapter V., which narrates the horsewhipping administered by Clorinde to Rougon—an incident which it has been necessary to 'tone down' in this English version—I may remark that this is founded on contemporary scandal, according to which the true scene of the affair would be the Imperial stables at Compiègne, and the recipient of the whipping none other than Napoléon III. himself. In Chapter VI., the scheme for reclaiming the waste Landes of Gascony is well-known matter of history. Suggested to the Emperor, this scheme was ultimately taken up by him with considerable vigour, and though it was never fully carried out it may rank as one of the few really beneficent enterprises of the Imperial *régime.*

In the ensuing chapter we come to Compiègne, and here I have found nothing to call in question. I was twice at Compiègne myself under the Empire, of course not as a guest, but in connection with work for the *Illustrated London News,* which brought my father and myself into constant intercourse with the Imperial Court over a term of years. And, judging by my personal recollections, I consider M. Zola's picture of life at Compiègne to be a very true one. He has been attacked, however, for having based his descriptions on a work called *Les Confidences d'un Valet de Chambre.* Some few years ago Mr. Andrew Lang, in criticising the French original of *His Excellency* in an English review, sternly reproved M. Zola for relying, in any degree, upon such back-stairs gossip. But a little knowledge is a dangerous thing. Whatever its title may be, *Les Confidences d'un Valet de Chambre* was not written by a *valet de chambre* at all. I have a copy of it among my collection of books relating to the Empire. It is brimful of information, bald in style, but severely accurate. As for its authorship, these are the facts: The Court's sojourn at Compiègne, which lasted for a month or six weeks every autumn—having been suggested in part by the *Voyages à Fontainebleau* of the *ancien régime,* and in part by the Empress's partiality for the place where she had been wooed and won by Napoléon—had long been the subject of tittle-tattle among the Parisians. The newspapers dared not publish any of the current scandal for fear of being immediately suppressed; however, the impression prevailed, especially among the lower classes, that the Court only betook itself to

Compiègne to indulge in a month's orgie far from such prying eyes as might have spied upon any similar excesses at the Tuileries. So many reports circulated, that it was at last deemed expedient to give the *entree* to the château to a Court chronicler, who should report what actually took place there, and in this way show the Parisians how foolish were the stories circulated through the cafés and wine-shops. The *soi-disant valet de chambre* was then, purely and simply, a journalist recommended by Théophile Gautier; and his accounts of the Court at Compiègne were published, in part at all events, by the Paris *Figaro,* and were subsequently collected in volume form. There is no scandal of any kind in the book: it simply chronicles the day's doings, with descriptions of the various rooms of the château, and accounts of certain Court customs thrown in here and there. Nobody desirous of describing life in Imperial circles at second-hand could do without this little volume, and it is only natural that M. Zola should have consulted it. Its general accuracy I can, by personal knowledge, fully confirm. Among the various incidents which M. Zola has adapted from it I may mention that of the aged dignitary who fondles first the Prince Impérial and afterwards the Emperor's dog Nero. This aged dignitary is a little bit of invention, the real hero of the incident having been a certain M. Leciel, an *adjoint* to the Mayor of Compiègne, who subsequently got into hot water with the Empress owing to his partiality for irreverent witticisms which usually turned upon his own name. In English we might have called him Mr. Heaven. His residence at Compiègne adjoined the somewhat dirty little inn of the Holy Ghost, which it was at one time proposed to demolish in order to build a new theatre, which was to have been connected with the château by means of a suspension bridge. This gave M. Leciel an opportunity for a most deplorable pun concerning himself and the inn, which he calmly repeated to the Empress, who was considerably incensed thereat. And in the result M. Leciel received no further invitations to the château.

But I must pass from Compiègne to M. Zola's next chapter, in which he deals, indirectly, with the famous Orsini conspiracy. Here we find a story of how the authorities were warned of the approaching attempt at assassination—a story which I have heard told by M. Claude, the famous ex-chief of the detective police, when I was his neighbour at Vincennes in 1881. Something similar, I believe, figures in the so-called *Mémoires de M. Claude,* but these, based on Claude's papers, which were 'worked up' after his death by

X

an imaginative penny-a-liner, are worthy of little or no credence. It is, however, certain that the French authorities were not only warned from London about the Orsini plot, but obtained additional information in the manner described by M. Zola, and that the incident became the stepping-stone of Claude's subsequent fortune. In *His Excellency* the Orsini affair is followed by Rougon's return to power. For Rougon one should here read General Espinasse, to whom the Emperor undoubtedly addressed the words: 'No moderation; you must make yourself feared.' All that M. Zola says of the wholesale arrests of French Republicans at that time is quite true. Even the brief interview of the Prefect of the Somme with Rougon is based on historical documents; while that in which figures the editor whose newspaper publishes a story of feminine infidelity is derived from the autobiography of Henri de Villemessant.

In Chapter X., which deals with Rougon's experiences at Niort, we have the story of the arrest of the old notary Martineau. This, again, is true, line for line, almost word for word; but the incident really occurred at Charost, not Coulonges, and the notary's real name was Lebrun. He was a cousin of the illustrious parliamentarian, Michel of Bourges. And once again, fact is piled upon fact in Chapter XI, which describes the Ministerial Council at St. Cloud. The project for the creation of a new nobility emanated from Persigny and Magne; numerous documents concerning it were discovered in the Emperor's study after Sedan; and I may here remark *en passant* that M. Zola has frequently and rightly availed himself of those *Papiers trouvés aux Tuileries* as published by the Government of National Defence. And he carries accuracy to such a point that in Chapter XIII., when he is describing Rougon's resignation, he dates the Emperor's acceptance of it from Fontainebleau, as actually happened in the case of Espinasse; and gives us a charity fair at the orangery of the Tuileries as the scene of the minister's receipt of that acceptance—again an historical incident. And finally, in the last chapter, which, like the opening one, deals with the Corps Législatif, we read the very words of Jules Favre and Billault. Moreover, when we here find a clerical deputy exclaiming, 'It displeases me that proud Venice, the Queen of the Adriatic, should become the obscure vassal of Turin,' we must not attribute the remark to M. Zola's imagination; for those words were spoken in that very debate by Kolb. Bernard, who, with Vicomte Lemercier, led the parliamentary group which opposed the Emperor's liberal policy in Italy.

XI

Some raiders and some reviewers may think that I have acted somewhat unkindly to M. Zola in thus partially dissecting *Son Excellence Eugène Rougon,* in showing how little it is a work of imagination and how much a work based upon fact. I could have given many more instances than those I have quoted, but this preface has already stretched to such length that I must stay my hand. I would mention, however, that I could in a similar way dissect most volumes of the Rougon-Macquart series, for these books are novels in their arrangement only. Even when they do not deal with historical personages and publicly recorded facts, they are based on incidents which really happened, and more frequently than otherwise portray people who really lived. The whole series constitutes a truthful, lifelike synthesis of a period; and if certain readers recoil from some of the portraits contained in it, this is simply because they will not face the monstrosities of human life. And far from doing my good and dear friend, the author of this imperishable literary edifice, an unkindness by pointing out where and how he has borrowed and adapted, I conceive that I am rendering him a service, for how often has not his accuracy been impugned! Moreover, it is not upon power of imagination that he particularly prides himself—though imagination, and of a high order, is undoubtedly a feature of his genius—he claims rank chiefly by reason of his power of delineation, his power of analysing, blending and grouping facts and characteristics. In one word, he is a Realist. And if he is to describe people as they have lived, incidents as they have really occurred, how can he do otherwise than turn to the records of actual experience, to the unchallenged descriptions of historical episodes? Plagiarism forsooth! When every situation, every dilemma, every experience, every characteristic and every emotion that can enter into the history of the human race have been dealt with time without number by thousands of writers of fiction, either in the form of the novel or the drama! How, then, is it possible for anybody, however great his genius, to be absolutely and perfectly original? Such originality is dead. Let us bow to its grave; we shall never see it more. The only genius in literature which can remain to the writers of to-day and to-morrow is that genius which may lie in the handling of one's materials. The human range of ideas is limited; even madmen—so closely allied to men of genius—cannot carry their fancy beyond certain bounds; and thus the old saws must crop up again and again, distinguished one from another simply by mode of treatment. And as for such charges of plagiarism that may have been brought against M. Zola, I apply to him the words which Molière applied to himself: *Il prend son bien où il le trouve.* And I will add that he does well in following this course, for over all he casts the magnificent mantle of powers which none of his contemporaries can equal.

E. A. V.
Merton, Surrey, April 1897

I

THE CORPS LÉGISLATIF

FOR a moment the President remained standing amidst the slight commotion which his entrance had caused. Then he took his seat, saying carelessly and in an undertone: 'The sitting has commenced.'

He next began to arrange the Législative bills lying upon the desk in front of him. On his left, a short-sighted clerk, with his nose close to the paper he held, read the minutes of the previous sitting in a rapid and confused manner, none of the deputies paying attention to him. In the buzzing noise that filled the Chamber, these minutes were only heard by the ushers, who maintained a very dignified and decorous bearing which contrasted with the lounging attitudes of the deputies.

There were not a hundred members present. Some were reclining in their red velvet-covered seats, with listless eyes, already half-asleep. Others, leaning over their desks, as though wearied by the compulsory labour of a public sitting, were beating a gentle tattoo on the mahogany with their finger-tips. Through the ceiling-window, which revealed a crescent of grey sky, the light of a rainy May afternoon streamed down perpendicularly upon the pompous severity of the Chamber. It spread over the desks in a sheet of gloomy ruddiness, brightening into a rosy glow here and there where some seat remained unoccupied; while, behind the President, the statues and sculpture-work showed in clear white patches.

One of the deputies on the third row to the right still remained standing in the narrow passage between the seats. He was rubbing his rough fringe of grizzly beard with a thoughtful air, but as an usher came by, he stopped him and asked a question in an undertone.

'No, Monsieur Kahn,' replied the usher, 'the President of the Council of State has not yet arrived.'

M. Kahn thereupon sat down, and, abruptly turning to his neighbour on the left, inquired, 'Tell me, Béjuin, have you seen Rougon this morning?'

M. Béjuin, a small, thin man of dark complexion and silent demeanour, raised his head nervously as though his thoughts were altogether elsewhere. He had drawn out the slide of his desk, and was writing a letter on some blue paper with a business heading formed of these words: 'Béjuin and Co. The Saint-Florent Cut-Glass Works.'

'Rougon?' he repeated. 'No, I haven't seen him. I did not have time to go over to the State Council.'

Then he quietly reverted to his work, consulting a memorandum-book, and beginning a second letter, amidst the confused buzzing murmur of the clerk, who was finishing his reading of the minutes.

M. Kahn leant back in his seat and crossed his arms. He had a face with strongly marked features, and his big but well-shaped nose testified to a Jewish descent. He seemed out of sorts. He gazed upwards at the gilt rose-work on the ceiling and listened to the plashing of a shower which at that moment burst down upon the skylight; and then with vaguely wondering eyes he seemed to be examining the intricate ornamentation of the great wall in front of him. His glance lingered for a few seconds upon two panels hung with green velvet and decked with gilt borders and emblems. Then, after he had scanned the columns between which allegorical statues of Liberty and Public Order showed their marble faces and pupilless eyes, his attention was turned to a curtain of green silk which concealed a fresco representing King Louis Philippe taking the oath to the Constitution.

By this time the clerk had sat down; nevertheless, the scene remained one of noisy confusion. The President was still leisurely arranging his papers. He again and again pressed his hand on his bell, but its loud ringing failed to check any of the private conversations that were going on. However, he at last stood up amidst all the hubbub and for a moment remained waiting and silent.

'Gentlemen,' he began, 'I have received a letter—' Then he stopped short to ring his bell again, and once more kept silent, his grave, bored face looking down from the monumental desk which spread out beneath him with panels of red marble bordered with white. His frock-coat, which was buttoned up, showed conspicuously against the bas-relief behind him, rising like a black bar between the peplum-robed figures of Agriculture and Industry with antique profiles.

'Gentlemen,' he resumed, when he had succeeded in obtaining something like silence, 'I have received a letter from Monsieur de Lamberthon, in which he apologises for not being able to attend to-day's sitting.'

At this a laugh resounded on the sixth row of seats in front of the desk. It came from a deputy who could not have been more than twenty-eight years old. He was fair and effeminately pretty, and was trying with his white hands to stifle an outburst of girlish rippling laughter. One of his colleagues, a man of huge build, came up to him and whispered in his ear: 'Is it really true that Lamberthon has found his wife? Tell me all about it, La Rouquette.'

The President, however, had taken up a handful of papers. He was speaking in monotonous tones, and stray fragments of sentences reached the far end of the Chamber. 'There are applications for leave of absence from Monsieur Blachet, Monsieur Buquin-Lecomte, Monsieur de la Villardière—'

While the Chamber was granting these different requests, M. Kahn, who had probably grown weary of examining the green silk curtain stretched before the seditious portrait of Louis Philippe, turned to glance at the galleries. Above the wall of yellow marble veined with lake red, there was a gallery with hand-rests of amaranthine velvet spanning the spaces from one column to another; and higher up a mantle of embossed leather failed to conceal the gaps left by the suppression of a second tier of seats which had been assigned to journalists and the general public previous to the Empire. The narrow, gloomy boxes between the massive yellowish marble pillars, which stood in somewhat heavy splendour round the semicircle, were for the most part empty, although here and there they were brightened by the light-tinted toilettes of some ladies.

'Ah! so Colonel Jobelin has come!' murmured M. Kahn.

And forthwith he smiled at the colonel, who had perceived him. Colonel Jobelin was wearing the dark-blue frock-coat which he had adopted as a kind of civilian uniform ever since his retirement from the service. He sat quite alone in the questors' gallery, and his rosette as an officer of the Legion of Honour was so large as to look almost like the bow of a cravat.

But M. Kahn's eyes had already strayed to a young man and woman who were nestling in a corner of the gallery of the Council of State. The young man was continually bending his head and whispering to the young woman, who smiled with a gentle air, but did not turn to look at him, her eyes being fixed upon the allegorical figure of Public Order.

'I say, Béjuin,' M. Kahn remarked, nudging his colleague with his knee.

M. Béjuin, who was now busy with his fifth letter, again raised his head with an expression of absent-mindedness.

'Look up there,' continued M. Kahn, 'don't you see little Escorailles and pretty Madame Bouchard? I'll be bound he's making love to her. What eyes she's got! All Rougon's friends seem to have made a point of coming to-day. There's Madame Correur and the Charbonnels up there in the public gallery.'

However, the bell sounded again for some moments, and an usher called out in a fine bass voice: 'Silence, gentlemen!'

Then the deputies began to listen, and the President spoke the following words, not a syllable of which was lost: 'Monsieur Kahn asks permission to publish the speech which he delivered on the bill for the establishment of a municipal tax upon vehicles and horses in Paris.'

A murmur ran along the benches, and then the different conversations were resumed. Quitting his own place, M. La Rouquette came and sat down near M. Kahn. 'So you work for the people, eh?' he said playfully, and, without waiting for a reply, he added: 'You haven't seen or heard anything of Rougon, have you? Everyone is talking about the matter, but it seems that nothing is definitely settled yet.' Then he turned round and glanced at the clock. 'Twenty minutes past two already!' he exclaimed. 'Well, I should certainly be off now, if it were not for the reading of that confounded report. Is it really to come off to-day?'

'We have all been notified to that effect,' M. Kahn replied, 'and I have heard nothing of any change of plans. You had better remain. The 400,000 francs for the baptism will be voted straight off.'

'No doubt,' said La Rouquette. 'Old General Legrain, who has lost the use of both legs, has had himself carried here by his servant, and is now in the Conference Hall waiting till the vote comes on. The Emperor is quite right in reckoning upon the devotion of the whole Corps Législatif. All our votes ought to be given him upon this solemn occasion.'

While speaking the young deputy did his utmost to assume the expression of a serious politician. His doll-like face, which was ornamented by a few pale hairs, wagged gravely over his collar, and he seemed to be relishing the flavour of the two last sentences he had uttered—sentences which he had remembered from somebody else's speech. Then he suddenly broke into a laugh. 'Good gracious!' he exclaimed, 'what frights those Charbonnels are!'

4

M. Kahn and himself thereupon began to make merry at the Charbonnels' expense. The wife was wearing an outrageous yellow shawl, and her husband sported a country-cut frock-coat which looked as though it had been hewn into shape with an axe. They were both very short, stout and red, and were eagerly pressing forward, with their chins almost resting upon the balustrade of the gallery in order to get a better view of the proceedings, which, judging by their blank, staring eyes, were utterly unintelligible to them.

'If Rougon gets the sack,' said La Rouquette, 'I wouldn't give a couple of sous for the Charbonnels' case. It will be just the same with Madame Correur.' Then he inclined his head towards M. Kahn's ear, and continued in a very low tone: 'You, now, who know Rougon, just tell me who and what that Madame Correur is. She formerly kept a lodging-house, didn't she? Rougon used to lodge with her, and it is even said that she lent him money. What does she do now?'

M. Kahn assumed a very grave expression and slowly rubbed his beard. 'Madame Correur is a highly respectable lady,' he replied curtly.

This answer checked La Rouquette's curiosity. He bit his lips with the expression of a schoolboy who has just been lectured. For a moment they both looked in silence at Madame Correur, who was sitting near the Charbonnels. She was wearing a very showy dress of mauve silk, with a profusion of lace and ornaments. Her face showed too much colour, her forehead was covered with little fair dollish curls, and her plump neck, still very comely in spite of her eight-and-forty years, was fully exposed to view.

Just at this moment, however, the sudden sound of a door opening and a rustle of skirts at the far end of the Chamber caused all heads to turn. A tall girl exquisitely beautiful, but strangely dressed in an ill-made sea-green satin gown, had entered the box assigned to the diplomatic body, followed by an elderly lady in black.

'Ah! there's the fair Clorinde!' said M. La Rouquette, who had risen to bow at random.

M. Kahn had also risen; but he stooped towards M. Béjuin, who was now enclosing his letters in envelopes: 'Countess Balbi and her daughter are there,' he said. 'I am going up to ask them if they have seen Rougon.'

The President meanwhile had taken a fresh handful of papers from his desk. Without ceasing his perusal of them he cast a glance at the beautiful Clorinde Balbi, whose arrival had given rise to a buzz of comments in the Chamber. Then, while he passed the papers one by one to a clerk, he said in monotonous tones, never even pausing to punctuate his words: 'Presentation of a bill to continue certain extra duties in the town of Lille... of a bill to unite into one single commune the communes of Doulevant-le-Petit and Ville-en-Blaisais (Haute-Marne)—'

When M. Kahn came back again he seemed quite disconsolate. 'Really, no one appears to have seen anything of him,' he said to his colleagues, Béjuin and La Rouquette, whom he met at the foot of the semicircle. 'I hear that the Emperor sent for him yesterday evening, but I haven't been able to learn the result of their interview. There is nothing so provoking as being unable to get a satisfactory account of what happens.'

La Rouquette turned round and whispered into M. Béjuin's ear: 'Poor Kahn is terribly afraid lest Rougon should get into disfavour at the Tuileries. He might fish for his railway if that should occur.'

In reply M. Béjuin, who was of a taciturn disposition, said very gravely: 'The day when Rougon retires from the Council of State, we shall all be losers.' Then he beckoned to one of the ushers and gave him the letters which he had just written, to post.

The three deputies remained standing on the left of the President's desk, discreetly discussing the disfavour with which Rougon was threatened. It was an intricate story. A distant relation of the Empress, one Señor Rodriguez, had been claiming a sum of two million francs from the French Government since the year 1808. During the war with Spain, a vessel freighted with sugar and coffee, and belonging to this Rodriguez, who was a shipowner, had been taken in the Bay of Biscay by a French frigate, the *Vigilante,* and brought to Brest. Acting upon information received from a local commission, the administrative officials had declared the capture to be a valid one, without referring the matter to the Prize Committee. Rodriguez, however, had promptly appealed to the Council of State, and, after his death, his son, under every successive Government, had vainly tried to bring the matter to an issue until the day came when a word from his distant cousin, Eugénie de Montijo, now all-powerful, had secured the insertion of his action in the official cause list.

Of this the three deputies talked, while the President's monotonous voice still resounded above their heads: 'Presentation of a bill

authorising the department of Calvados to borrow 300,000 francs...
of a bill authorising the town of Amiens to borrow 200,000 francs
for the purpose of making new promenades... of a bill authorising
the department of Côtes-du-Nord to borrow 345,000 francs to cover
the deficiencies in the revenues of the last five years.'

'The truth is,' said M. Kahn, again lowering his voice, 'that this
Rodriguez had a very artful method of managing his business. He
and a son-in-law of his, residing at New York, were the owners of
vessels which sailed either under the American flag or the Spanish,
according as one or the other might subject them to the least risk
during their passage. Rougon told me that the captured vessel was
exclusively the property of Rodriguez, and that there is no valid
ground whatever for the claims that are made.'

'And then,' interposed M. Béjuin, 'the steps that were taken
by the officials cannot be impugned. The administrative officer at
Brest was perfectly right in declaring the capture a valid one in accordance with the customs of the port, without referring the matter
to the Prize Committee.'

Then they lapsed into silence for a moment while La Rouquette,
with his back resting against the marble wall, raised his head, and
tried to attract the attention of the fair Clorinde. 'But,' he asked
naively, 'why does Rougon object to the two millions being paid to
Rodriguez? What difference would it make to him?'

'It is a matter of conscience,' said M. Kahn solemnly.

M. La Rouquette glanced at his colleagues one after the other,
but, seeing them both so grave, he did not even venture to smile.

'Then, too,' continued M. Kahn, as though he were dwelling
upon some thought which he had not expressed aloud, 'Rougon has
had a good deal of bother since Marsy has been Minister of the Interior. They have never been able to get on together. Rougon himself
told me that, if it had not been for his attachment to the Emperor, for
whom he has already done so much, he would long ago have retired
into private life. He no longer seems welcome at the Tuileries, and
he feels that a change has become necessary for him.'

'He is acting like an honourable man.' remarked M. Béjuin.

'Yes, indeed,' said M. La Rouquette, with a wise look, 'if he
wants to retire, the opportunity is a good one. All the same, his
friends will be greatly grieved. Just look at the colonel up there,
with his anxious face! He has been hoping to fasten the ribbon of
Commander of the Legion of Honour round his neck on the 15th of

next August. And pretty Madame Bouchard, too, swore that worthy Monsieur Bouchard should be head of department at the Ministry of the Interior before six months were over. Little Escorailles, Rougon's pet, was to put the nomination under Monsieur Bouchard's napkin on Madame's birthday. But where have they got to, pretty Madame Bouchard and little Escorailles?'

The three deputies looked about for them, and at last discovered them ensconced at the back of the gallery, in the front part of which they had been seated at the opening of the sitting. They had taken refuge in the gloom there behind a bald old gentleman, and were both very quiet, though very red.

However, the President was now coming to the end of his reading.

'A bill,' said he, 'to sanction an increase in the rate of interest upon a loan authorised by an Act of the 9th of June, 1853, and to impose an extraordinary rate in the department of La Manche.'

Just then M. Kahn ran forward to meet a deputy who was entering the Chamber, and as he brought him along he exclaimed, 'Here is Monsieur de Combelot. He will give us some news.'

M. de Combelot, an imperial chamberlain whom the department of the Landes had chosen as deputy upon the formally expressed desire of the Emperor, bowed with a discreet air while waiting to be questioned. He was a tall, handsome man, with a very white skin, and an inky black beard which had been the means of winning him great favour among the ladies.

'Well,' asked M. Kahn, 'what do they say at the Tuileries? What has the Emperor decided upon?'

'Well, indeed,' replied M. de Combelot in a guttural tone, 'they say a good many things. The Emperor has the warmest friendship for the President of the Council of State. Their interview was undoubtedly of the most cordial nature. Yes, indeed, most cordial.'

Then he stopped, after carefully weighing his words, as it were, so as to satisfy himself that he had not said too much.

'Then the resignation is withdrawn?' asked M. Kahn, with glistening eyes.

'I did not say that,' replied the chamberlain, uneasily. 'I know nothing about it. You understand that my position is a peculiar one—'

He did not finish what he was going to say, but contented himself with smiling, and then hurried off to take his seat. M. Kahn shrugged his shoulders, and remarked to M. La Rouquette, 'But you, surely, ought to be posted on what is going on. Doesn't your sister, Madame de Llorenz, give you any information?'

'Oh, my sister is even more reserved than Monsieur de Combelot,' replied the young deputy, with a laugh. 'Since she has become one of the ladies-in-waiting, she has put on quite a minister's gravity; though yesterday, indeed, she assured me that the resignation would be accepted. By the way, I can tell you a funny story in connection with this matter. It appears that some lady was sent to Rougon to try to influence him. Now, you would never guess what Rougon did! He turned her out of doors, although she was a delicious creature!'

'Rougon is a very steady fellow,' M. Béjuin declared solemnly.

M. La Rouquette shook with laughter, and, protesting against M. Béjuin's estimate of Rougon, asserted that he could have disproved it by evidence had he chosen. 'And so, Madame Correur, for instance,' said he.

'Pooh! you don't know the truth of that story,' replied M. Kahn.

'And the fair Clorinde?'

'Nonsense, nonsense! Rougon is much too clever a fellow to forget himself with such a wild creature as that!'

Then the three men drew closer, and talked on without any mincing of words. They repeated the stories which were told about those two Italian women—-mother and daughter—who were semi-adventuresses and semi-great ladies, and were to be met everywhere, at all parties and gatherings, at the houses of state ministers, in the stage-boxes of minor theatres, on the sands at fashionable watering-places, and even in out-of-the-way hostelries. The mother, it was said, had been the mistress of a royal personage; and the daughter, with an ignorance of French customs and etiquette which had earned her the reputation of being an eccentric, badly brought-up wench, galloped about on horseback till she foundered her mounts, made a display of her dirty stockings and damaged boots on rainy days, and looked around her for a husband with the boldest of smiles. M. La Rouquette told how she had come one night to a ball at the Sardinian Minister's, in the character of the huntress Diana, with so scanty a costume that she had been all but asked in marriage the next morning by old Monsieur de Nougarède, a profligate senator. During the narration of this story, the three deputies cast frequent glances at the fair Clorinde, who, in spite of the regulations, was examining the members of the Chamber one after another through a large pair of opera-glasses.

'No, no!' M. Kahn repeated, 'Rougon would never be such a fool! He says, though, that she is very intelligent, and he has nick-named her "Mademoiselle Machiavelli." She amuses him, but that's all.'

'At the same time Rougon is wrong in not marrying,' said M.Béjuin. 'It settles a man.'

Then they all three set to work to discuss the sort of woman that it was desirable Rougon should marry. She ought to be a woman of some age, thirty-five at the least, they said, rich, and competent to maintain her house on a footing of high decorum.

Hubbub still prevailed in the Chamber, and the three deputies became so absorbed in the stories they were telling, that they ceased to notice what was taking place around them. Away in the distance, the voices of ushers could be faintly heard calling out, 'To the sitting, gentlemen, to the sitting.'

Fresh deputies were entering from all sides by way of the folding doors of massive mahogany, whose panels gleamed with golden stars. The Chamber, previously half empty, was now gradually filling. The little scattered groups of members talking to each other from one row of seats to another, with an expression of weariness on their faces, or dozing, or trying to conceal their yawns, were now disappearing amid the increasing crowd and general shaking of hands. As the members took their seats, they exchanged smiles; there was a general, almost family likeness about them. By the expression of their faces one and all seemed impressed by the duties they had to fulfil. A stout man, on the last row to the left, had fallen asleep, but was awakened by his neighbour; and, when the latter whispered a few words in his ear, he hastily rubbed his eyes, and assumed a more decorous attitude. The sitting, after dragging on wearily through a series of petty tedious details, was at last about to become supremely interesting.

M. Kahn and his two colleagues were being gradually driven towards their seats by the increasing crowd, almost without being aware of it. They went on with their conversation, every now and then suppressing a laugh. M. La Rouquette began a fresh story about the fair Clorinde. She had taken a strange whim into her head one day, he said; it was to have her room hung with black, spangled with silver tears, and to hold a reception of her friends there; she herself lying in bed, covered up with black drapery which allowed scarcely anything more than her nose to appear.

As M. Kahn at last took his seat, his memory suddenly returned to him. 'La Rouquette is a foolish chatterbox,' he muttered; 'he has made me miss Rougon.' Then he turned towards his neighbour and exclaimed angrily: 'You really might have reminded me, Béjuin!'

Rougon, who had just been introduced with the customary ceremonial, had already taken his seat between two members of the Council of State on the Government bench, a sort of huge mahogany box, situated beneath the President's desk and occupying the place of the suppressed tribune. His broad shoulders tightly distended his uniform of green cloth, ornamented with gold braid at the neck and sleeve-cuffs. His face, with thick grizzly hair clustering over his square brow, was turned towards the Chamber, but his eyes were hidden by their heavy drooping lids. The commonplace plainness of his big nose, fleshy lips, and long cheeks, which his six-and-forty years had not yet furrowed with a single wrinkle, was every now and then irradiated with something like beauty by an expression of great strength. He sat perfectly quiet, leaning back with his chin resting on his coat collar, noticing nobody, and seeming quite indifferent and a little weary.

'He looks just as he does every day,' M. Béjuin remarked.

The deputies were all leaning over to observe Rougon. Whispered remarks on his appearance buzzed from ear to ear. In the galleries especially his entrance had caused lively excitement. The Charbonnels, in their desire to let their presence be known, craned their enraptured faces forward at the risk of falling over; Madame Correur coughed slightly and drew out a handkerchief which she gently waved, while pretending to carry it to her lips; Colonel Jobelin straightened himself; and pretty Madame Bouchard, after tying her bonnet-strings afresh, again hurried down to the front row of the State Council gallery, while M. d'Escorailles remained behind quite still and seemingly much annoyed. As for the fair Clorinde, she did not beat about the bush. Seeing that Rougon did not raise his eyes, she began to tap her opera-glass against the marble column beside which she was leaning, and as these tactics did not succeed in attracting his attention, she said to her mother, in such a clear ringing voice that every one in the Chamber heard her: 'He's in the sulks, the fat sly fellow!'

Several deputies looked round and smiled, and Rougon himself glanced up at the fair Clorinde. As he nodded his head almost imperceptibly towards her, she triumphantly clapped her hands, and leant back, laughing and talking quite loudly to her mother, quite careless of the men down below who were staring at her.

Before Rougon dropped his eyes again he glanced slowly round the gallery, where his comprehensive gaze at once took in Madame Bouchard, Colonel Jobelin, Madame Correur, and the Charbonnels. However, his face remained expressionless. He again let his chin drop and half-closed his eyes as he stifled a slight yawn.

'I'll go and have a word with him now,' M. Kahn whispered into M. Béjuin's ear.

But as he was rising from his seat, the President, who during the last few moments had been looking round to see if all the deputies were in their places, rang his bell authoritatively. Then all at once there was profound silence. A fair-haired member in the first row of seats now stood up, holding a large sheet of paper upon which he kept his eyes fixed as he spoke.

'I have the honour,' he said in a sing-song voice, 'to present a report upon the bill by which it is proposed to include among the estimates of the Ministry of State for 1856 a sum of 400,000 francs, to defray the expenses of the ceremonies and rejoicings connected with the baptism of the Prince Impérial.'

Then he slowly stepped forward as though about to lay the paper on the table of the Chamber, but the deputies cried out unanimously: 'Read it! Read it!'

The deputy who had prepared the report waited till the President gave his sanction. Then he commenced in a voice that seemed affected by emotion: 'Gentlemen, the bill which has been brought before us is one of those which make the customary formalities of voting seem dilatory, since they check the enthusiastic impulses of the Corps Législatif.' 'Hear! hear!' cried several members. 'In the humblest families,' continued the speaker in carefully modulated tones, 'the birth of a son and heir, with all the ideas of transmission which are attached to that title, is a source of such sweet joy that the trials of the past are forgotten, and hope alone hovers over the cradle of the new-born child. What, then, shall we say of such a happy event when it not only prompts the rejoicing of a family but that of a great nation, and is an event of European interest?'

This piece of rhetoric thrilled the Chamber with emotion. Rougon, who appeared to be asleep, could see none but beaming faces in front of him. Some deputies accentuated their attention, holding their hands to their ears so that they might lose nothing of this carefully prepared report. Its author, after a. slight pause, raised his voice as he continued, 'To-day, gentlemen, it is indeed the great family of France that invites all its members to give expression to their joy; and what pomp and circumstance would be magnificent enough if it were possible by display to express the grandeur of our legitimate hopes?' Here the reporter paused again. 'Hear! hear!' cried the deputies.

'That's very nicely put,' M. Kahn remarked; 'isn't it, Béjuin?'

M. Béjuin was wagging his head with his eyes fixed on the cut-glass chandelier which hung from the window-ceiling in front of the President's seat. He was in a state of blissful rapture.

Meanwhile in the gallery the fair Clorinde kept her opera-glass to her eyes and lost not a single expression of the reporter's face. The Charbonnels' eyes were moist, and Madame Correur had assumed a decorously attentive attitude, while the colonel expressed his approbation by nodding his head, and pretty Madame Bouchard ventured to lean against M. d'Escorailles' knees. The President and the clerk and the ushers listened solemnly, without making the slightest gesture.

'The cradle of the Prince Impérial,' resumed the reporter, 'is henceforth our security for the future; for, by perpetuating the dynasty which we have all acclaimed, it assures the prosperity of our country, its repose and stability, and, through ours, that of the rest of Europe.'

Cries of 'Hush! hush!' were necessary to subdue the burst of enthusiastic applause which broke out at this touching reference to the cradle.

'Once before a scion of this illustrious race seemed equally intended for a great destiny, but his time and our own have no similarity. Peace is the result of the wise and skilful rule of which we are now reaping the fruits, even as the genius of war dictated that epic poem which forms the story of the first Empire.

'Hailed at his birth by the guns which from north to south proclaimed the successes of our arms, the King of Rome was not even permitted to serve his country; so, indeed, Providence then decreed—'

'What's that he's saying? He's putting his foot in it,' said sceptical M. La Rouquette. 'That's very clumsy; he'll spoil his speech.'

The deputies certainly seemed uneasy. Why was this historical reference dragged in to damp their enthusiasm? Several of them blew their noses. The author of the report, however, only smiled when he saw the chilling effect of his last sentences. He raised his voice and pursued his antithesis, carefully modulating his tones, evidently quite confident that he would make his point.

'But, coming to us at one of those momentous times when the birth of a single life may be regarded as the salvation of all, the Child of France to-day gives to us and to all future generations the right and the privilege of living and dying at our ancestral firesides. Such is the promise vouchsafed to us by the divine kindness.'

This seemed exquisite. Everybody understood, and a murmur of pleasure travelled through the Chamber. The assurance of an everlasting peace was very charming. The tranquillised members once more resumed the pleased expressions of men revelling in rhetoric. There was nothing to disturb them. Europe belonged to their master.

'The Emperor,' continued the speaker with fresh vigour, 'having become the arbiter of Europe, was about to sign that noble peace which, bringing together the productive forces of the different nations, is as much an alliance of peoples as of monarchs,[1] when God was pleased to crown his happiness as well as his glory. Is it not allowable to think that, at that moment, he foresaw many fair and prosperous years while gazing upon that cradle where slumbers, though now but an infant, the heir who is destined to carry on his great policy?' This, too, was thought very pretty. Such a hope might be justifiably entertained, so the deputies said, as they nodded their heads approvingly. The report, however, was now beginning to seem a trifle long, and several members looked solemn again. Some of them even glanced at the gallery like practical matter-of-fact politicians who felt rather ashamed of being thus seen spending their time in an unbusiness-like way. Others ceased to pay attention, and reverted to their own affairs, or again tapped the mahogany of their desks with their finger-tips; while through the minds of others there flitted vague recollections of other sittings when professions of devotion had been lavished on some other cradle.

As for M. La Rouquette, he turned very frequently to look at the clock, and when the hand pointed to a quarter to three an expression

---

[1] This is a reference to the Peace of Paris after the Crimean War.—*Ed.*

of desperation passed over his face. He would miss an appointment! Meantime M. Kahn and M Béjuin sat motionless side by side, with crossed arms and blinking eyes, which wandered from the great velvet panels to the bas-relief of white marble across which the President's frock-coat stretched like a black bar. In the diplomatists' gallery the fair Clorinde was still gazing through her opera-glass, making a lengthy examination of Rougon, who preserved the majestic mien of a sleeping bull.

However, the author of the report showed no signs of hurry, but listened to himself as he read on, indulging the while in a rhythmic beatifical motion of the shoulders.

'Let us then display full and complete confidence, and may the Corps Législatif, upon this great and solemn occasion, bear in mind that the Emperor and itself have a common origin, which almost confers upon it a family-right above that which the other State bodies may possess to share in its Sovereign's joy.

'The Corps Législatif, which, like himself, is the offspring of the willing vote of the people, becomes now the mouthpiece of the nation in offering to the august child the homage, of its unchangeable respect, of its devotion which nothing can destroy, and of that boundless love which converts political faith into a religion whose duties are blessed.'

The mention of homage and religion and duties seemed to betoken that the speaker was drawing to a conclusion. The Charbonnels therefore ventured to exchange remarks in low tones, and Madame Correur stifled a slight cough in her handkerchief; while Madame Bouchard quietly returned to the rear of the Council of State gallery, and resumed her seat near M. Jules d'Escorailles.

And, indeed, the reporter suddenly changed his tone and came down from the solemn to the familiar, as he quickly gabbled out: 'We propose to you, gentlemen, the adoption of the bill, such as it has been brought forward by the Council of State.'

Then he resumed his seat amidst general applause. Shouts of 'Hear, hear!' rang out from all sides. M. de Combelot, whose smiling attention had not waned for an instant, even cried, 'Long live the Emperor!' but the exclamation was lost amid the hubbub; however, Colonel Jobelin received almost an ovation as he stood at the edge of the gallery, and clapped his withered hands, in spite of the regulations to the contrary. Everybody enthusiastically congratulated everybody else. Work was over, and from row to row kindly remarks were exchanged, while a crowd of friends thronged round the author of the report and energetically shook both his hands.

But above the confusion came a cry of 'Deliberate! deliberate!'

The President had been standing at his desk, apparently expecting this cry. He rang his bell, and as the Chamber suddenly became respectfully attentive, he said: 'Gentlemen, a large number of members desire that we should at once deliberate upon this measure.'

'Yes, yes,' cried the Chamber with one voice. But there was no deliberation. They proceeded to vote at once. The two clauses of the measure which were successively put to the Chamber were immediately passed by the deputies rising in their places. The President had scarcely finished reading each clause before all the members rose in a mass with much stamping of feet, as though under the influence of some thrill of enthusiasm. Then the urn-shaped ballot-boxes were passed round by the ushers who, threading their way between the seats, received the votes in these zinc receptacles. The 400,000 francs were voted unanimously by the 289 members present.

'That's good work done,' said M. Béjuin naively, and he began to laugh as though he had said something witty.

'It's past three o'clock; I'm off,' exclaimed M. La Rouquette, passing in front of M. Kahn.

The Chamber was emptying. The deputies were all making for the doors and seemed to vanish through the walls. The next business consisted of matters of mere local interest, and there was soon no one left on the benches except a few willing deputies who had probably nothing to do elsewhere, and these resumed either their interrupted naps or their conversation at the point where it had been broken off, the sitting concluding, as it had begun, in the midst of listless indifference. Gradually, too, the general buzzing subsided as though the Corps Législatif had dropped off to sleep in some quiet corner of Paris.

'You had better try to get a word with Delestang as you go away,' said M. Kahn to M. Béjuin. 'He came with Rougon, and must know something.'

'Yes, you are right; that's Delestang yonder,' replied M. Béjuin, gazing at the councillor who was sitting on Rougon's left; 'I never know them in those confounded uniforms.'

'I shall stop here so as to have a chance of getting hold of the great man,' added M. Kahn. 'It's necessary that we should know the truth.'

The President was putting to the vote an interminable string of bills, which were passed by the members rising in their places. They all stood up and then sat down again quite mechanically, without ceasing to converse and even without ceasing to sleep. The proceedings were becoming so wearisome that most of the spectators whom curiosity had brought to the gallery took their departure. Only Rougon's friends remained. They were still hoping that he would speak.

Suddenly, a deputy, whose correctly trimmed whiskers bespoke the provincial lawyer, arose. This at once stopped the monotonous mechanism of the voting. Surprise made all the members turn and look at the one who had risen. 'Gentlemen,' said he, standing in his place,' I ask permission to explain the reasons which, to my great regret, have compelled me to differ from the majority of the Committee.'

His voice was so shrill and comical that the fair Clorinde had to stifle a laugh with her hands. Below in the Chamber itself, the astonishment was increasing. What was the man talking about? By dint of inquiries, the others ascertained that the President had just brought before the Chamber a bill authorising the department of the Pyrénées-Orientales to borrow 250,000 francs wherewith to build a Palace of Justice at Perpignan. The speaker, who was a general councillor of the department, was opposing the bill. The matter seemed likely to be interesting, so the deputies began to listen.

The member with the correctly trimmed whiskers spoke, however, with great circumspection. He used the most guarded language, and referred with the greatest respect to all the authorities; but the expenses of the department, he said, were very heavy, and he dwelt at length upon the financial situation of the Pyrénées-Orientales. Moreover, he did not think that any necessity for a new Palace of Justice had been satisfactorily demonstrated. He continued in this strain for a quarter of an hour, and on sitting down seemed quite overcome with emotion. Then Rougon again slowly dropped his eyelids which he had temporarily raised.

However, the reporter of the Committee which had examined the bill got up. He was a little animated old man who spoke in clear, incisive tones like one who is sure of his ground. He began with a complimentary reference to his honourable colleague, with whom he regretted to find himself in disagreement. But really, he went on to say, the department of the Pyrénées-Orientales was not nearly so heavily burdened as had been alleged, and he brought forward fresh figures which showed the financial position of the department in an entirely different light. Moreover, the absolute necessity for a new Palace of Justice could not be denied. And he entered into details. The old Palace, he said, was situated in such a densely populated neighbourhood that the noise of the streets prevented the judges from hearing counsel speak. Then it was too small; and when the Assizes were being held, and there happened to be a large number of witnesses in attendance, they were obliged to remain on the landings exposed to the solicitations of interested parties who might desire to influence them. The speaker concluded by mentioning as an irresistible argument the fact that the measure had been introduced at the instigation of the Keeper of the Seals himself.

Rougon was sitting quite still, his hands clasped upon his legs and his head resting against the mahogany desk. At the outset of the discussion his shoulders had seemed to sink lower than before, but when the first speaker rose to reply, he raised his big frame without actually getting on to his feet, and said in a husky voice: 'The honourable member who reported upon this measure forgot to mention that it has also received the approval of the Minister of the Interior and the Minister of Finance.'

Then he let himself drop again and resumed the attitude of a drowsy bull. A slight murmur ran through the Chamber, and the deputy who had risen to reply sat down with a low bow. The bill was passed, and those members who had shown any interest in the debate once more assumed an expression of indifference.

Rougon had spoken. From one section of the gallery to another Colonel Jobelin exchanged glances with the Charbonnels, while Madame Correur made ready to leave her place, just as she would have quitted her box at the theatre before the fall of the curtain, if the hero of the play had delivered his last speech. M. d'Escorailles and Madame Bouchard had already taken their departure. Clorinde stood by the velvet-covered balustrade, her majestic figure showing conspicuously as she slowly wrapped her lace shawl about her, glancing round the deputies' seats as she did so. The rain was no longer beating down upon the window, but the sky remained overcast. The mahogany desks looked quite black in that sombre light, and a, shadowy mist streamed over the seats, which the bald heads of some of the deputies lighted up here and there with patches of white. Against the marble-work below the vague, pale allegorical figures, the President and the clerks and ushers, all in black and ranged in a line, showed like the stiff silhouettes of a shadow-pantomime. The whole Chamber became blurred in the suddenly waning light.

'Oh, come along!' exclaimed Clorinde, pushing her mother out of the gallery; 'it is enough to kill one in here!'

She quite startled the drowsy ushers in the corridor by the strange fashion in which she had twisted her shawl round her hips.

When they got downstairs into the hall the ladies met Colonel Jobelin and Madame Correur.

'We are waiting for him here,' said the colonel. 'Perhaps he will come out this way. But in any case I have signalled to Kahn and Béjuin to come and give me some information.'

Madame Correur stepped up to the Countess Balbi. 'Ah! it would be a great misfortune,' she said in a disconsolate voice without attempting to explain her meaning.

The colonel raised his eyes to heaven. 'The country has need of men like Rougon,' he resumed after a short pause. 'The Emperor would make a great mistake.'

Then there was another pause. Clorinde tried to peep into the 'Salle des Pas Perdus,' but an usher promptly closed the door. So she came back to her mother, who was standing silent in her black veil. 'What a bore it is having to wait like this!' she muttered.

Some soldiers now made their appearance, and Colonel Jobelin thereupon announced that the sitting was over. Next the Charbonnels came into sight at the top of the staircase, and made their way down very carefully one after the other and each clinging to the balustrade. As soon as M. Charbonnel saw the colonel he called out: 'He didn't say much, but he completely shut them up.'

'He hadn't a proper chance,' the colonel whispered when the other reached him, 'otherwise you would have heard something fine. He wants warming up.'

However, the soldiers had formed a double line from the Chamber to the gallery leading to the President's mansion. Then a procession made its appearance while the drummers beat a salute. At the head walked two ushers, dressed in black with cocked hats under their arms, chains about their necks, and swords with steel hilts at their sides. Then came the President, escorted by two officers. The clerks of the Chamber and the President's secretary followed. As the President passed the fair Clorinde he smiled at her like a *homme du monde,* notwithstanding the pomp of his procession.

'Ah, you are there!' cried M. Kahn, running up with a distracted look.

Though the public were at that time excluded from the 'Salle des Pas Perdus,' he took them all into it and conducted them to one of the large glass doors which opened upon the garden. He seemed very much annoyed. 'I have missed him again!' he cried. 'He slipped out into the Rue de Bourgogne while I was waiting for him in the General Foy gallery. But it really makes no difference; we shall get to know everything all the same. I have sent Béjuin after Delestang.'

They waited for another ten long minutes. The deputies were all coming away looking careless and unconcerned. Some of them lingered to light cigars and others stood in little groups, laughing and shaking hands. Madame Correur had stepped aside to inspect the 'Laocoon'; and while the Charbonnels threw back their heads to look at a sea-gull which a whimsical artist had painted on the frame of a fresco, as though it were flying out of the picture, the fair Clorinde, standing in front of the great bronze figure of Minerva, examined the arms and bosom of the gigantic goddess with an air of interest. Meantime in a corner by the glass door Colonel Jobelin and M. Kahn were carrying on an animated conversation in low tones.

'Ah, there's Béjuin!' suddenly exclaimed the latter. Then they all drew together with an expression of anxiety. M. Béjuin was breathing heavily. 'Well?' they asked him.

'Well! the resignation has been accepted, and Rougon retires.'

It was a crushing blow. An interval of deep silence followed. However, Clorinde, who, to employ her nervous fingers, was knotting a corner of her shawl, caught sight of pretty Madame Bouchard walking slowly along the garden, upon M. d'Escorailles' arm, with her head inclined over his shoulder. They had come down before the others, and, taking advantage of an open door, were now strolling like lovers under the lace-work of fresh young leaves, in the quiet walks usually utilised for serious meditation. Clorinde beckoned to them.

'The great man has retired!' she said to the smiling young woman.

At this Madame Bouchard abruptly dropped her cavalier's arm, and turned very pale and grave, while M. Kahn, surrounded by Rougon's alarmed friends, despairingly raised his arms to heaven, unable to say a single word.

II

RESIGNATION

In the next morning's *Moniteur* Rougon's resignation was officially announced. It was stated that he had resigned for 'reasons of health.' After his lunch, wishing to set everything in order for his successor, he went down to the Council of State, and installed himself in the spacious room hung with crimson and gold, which was assigned to the President. And there, in front of a large rosewood writing-table, he began to empty the drawers and classify the papers, which he tied up in bundles with pieces of pink tape. All at once, however, he rang the bell, and an usher entered the room—a splendidly built man who had served in the cavalry.

'Give me a lighted candle,' said Rougon.

Then as the usher was leaving the room, after placing on the table a small candlestick taken from the mantel-piece, Rougon called him back. 'Admit nobody, Merle,' he said; 'no one at all, you understand?'

'Yes, Monsieur le Président,' replied the usher, closing the door noiselessly behind him.

A faint smile played over Rougon's face. He turned towards Delestang, who stood at the other end of the room carefully examining the contents of several pasteboard boxes. 'Our friend Merle hasn't read the *Moniteur* this morning,' he muttered.

Delestang merely shook his head, unable to think of any suitable reply. He had a magnificent head, very bald, indeed, but bald after that precocious fashion which is rather pleasing to women. His bare skull greatly increased the size of his brow and gave him an expression of vast intelligence. His clean-shaven, florid, and somewhat squarely cut face recalled those perfect, pensive countenances which imaginative painters are wont to confer upon great statesmen.

'Merle is extremely devoted to you,' he remarked after a pause.

Then he lowered his head over the pasteboard box which he was examining, while Rougon crumpled up a handful of papers, and after lighting them at the taper threw them into a large bronze vase which stood at the edge of his table. He watched them burn away.

'Don't touch the boxes at the bottom, Delestang,' he said; 'there are papers in them that I must examine myself.'

21

Then, for another quarter of an hour, they both went on with their respective occupations in silence. It was a very fine day, and the sun streamed in through three large windows which overlooked the quay. Through one of them, which was half open, puffs of fresh air from the Seine were wafted in, occasionally stirring the fringe of the silk curtains, and rustling the crumpled pieces of paper which lay about the floor.

'Just look at this,' said Delestang, handing Rougon a letter which he had found.

Rougon read it and then quietly lighted it at the taper. It was a letter on a delicate matter. The two men carried on a disjointed conversation, breaking off every few moments to bury their faces afresh in the piles of old papers. Rougon thanked Delestang for having come to help him. He was the only person whom he felt that he could trust to assist him in this task of washing the dirty linen of his five years' presidency. They had been friends together in the Legislative Assembly, where they had sat side by side on the same bench. It was there that Rougon had taken a genuine fancy to this splendid-looking man, on finding that he was so delightfully foolish and shallow and proud. He often used to say with an air of conviction that 'that precious Delestang would go a long way.' He did what he could to push him on, gratitude yielding devotion, and he made use of him as a kind of strong box in which he locked up whatever he could not carry about with him.

'How foolish of me to have kept all these papers!' Rougon murmured, as he opened a fresh drawer which was crammed quite full.

'Here is a letter from a lady!' said Delestang winking.

At this Rougon broke out into a loud laugh, and his huge chest shook. He took the letter with a protest. However, as soon as his eyes had glanced over the first lines, he exclaimed: 'It was little Escorailles who let this drop here! They are pretty things those letters. With three lines from a woman, a fellow may go a long way!' Then, as he burnt the letter, he added: 'Be on your guard against women, Delestang!'

Delestang bent his head again. He was perpetually becoming the victim of some hazardous passion. In 1851 he had all but ruined his political prospects. At that time he had been madly infatuated with the wife of a socialist deputy, and to curry favour with her husband had more frequently than not voted with the opposition against the Elysée. The *coup d'état* of the second of December consequently filled him with terrible alarm, and he shut himself up for a couple of days in distraction, overwhelmed, good for nothing, trembling with fear lest he should be arrested. However, Rougon had helped him out of his awkward position, advising him not to stand at the ensuing elections and taking him down to the Elysée, where he succeeded in getting him a place in the Council of State. Delestang, whose father had been a wine-merchant at Bercy, was himself a retired attorney and the owner of a model farm near Sainte-Menehould. He was worth several millions of francs and lived in a very handsome house in the Rue du Colisée.

'Yes, beware of women,' Rougon repeated, pausing after each word so as to glance at his papers. 'When a woman does not put a crown on your head she slips a halter round your neck. At our age a man's heart wants as carefully looking after as his stomach.'

At this moment a loud noise was heard in the antechamber, and Merle's voice could be recognised refusing admission to some visitor. However, a little man suddenly rushed into the room, exclaiming, 'I really must shake hands with my dear friend!'

'Hallo! is it you, Du Poizat?' exclaimed Rougon without rising.

Merle was making sweeping gesticulations to excuse himself, but his master bade him close the door. Then he quietly said to Du Poizat: 'I thought you were at Bressuire. So you desert your subprefecture as easily as an old mistress, eh?'

Du Poizat, who was a slightly built man with a mean-looking face and very white irregular teeth, shrugged his shoulders as he replied: 'I arrived in Paris this morning on business, and I did not intend to come and see you till the evening, when I should have called upon you in the Rue Marbeuf and have asked you to give me some dinner. But when I read the *Moniteur*——' Then he broke off, pulled an easy-chair in front of the writing-table, and seated himself face to face with Rougon. 'Well now, what's been happening, eh?' he resumed. 'I've come from the depths of the Deux-Sèvres. I had heard something down there, but I had no idea of this. Why didn't you write to me?'

Rougon, in his turn, shrugged his shoulders. It was evident that tidings of his disgrace had reached Du Poizat in the country, and that he had hastened to Paris to see if he could find a means of securing stability for his own position. So Rougon gave him a keen glance as he rejoined: 'I should have written to you this evening. Send in your resignation, my good fellow.'

'That's all that I wanted to know. Well, I will resign,' replied Du Poizat quietly.

Then he rose from his seat and began to whistle. As he slowly paced the room he caught sight of Delestang kneeling on the carpet in the midst of a litter of pasteboard boxes. He approached and silently shook hands with him. Then he took a cigar out of his pocket and lighted it at the candle.

'I may smoke here, I suppose, as you are moving?' he said, again sitting down in the easy-chair. 'It's good fun is moving!'

Rougon, however, was absorbed in a bundle of papers which he read with deep attention, sorting them very carefully, burning some and preserving others. Du Poizat, with his head lolling back, and puffing light clouds of smoke from between his lips, remained watching him. They had become acquainted with each other some months before the Revolution of February, 1848. At that time they were both boarding with Madame Correur at the Hôtel Vanneau in the Rue Vanneau. Du Poizat had found himself quite at home there, for he and Madame Correur had both been born at Coulonges, a little town in the district of Niort. His father, a process-server, had sent him to study law in Paris, where he allowed him only a hundred francs a month, although he had amassed large sums by lending money for short periods at extortionate interest. The old man's wealth seemed, indeed, so inexplicably great to his country neighbours that it was said he had discovered a large treasure in an old chest of drawers upon which he had distrained. From the outset of the Bonapartist propaganda Rougon had availed himself of the services of this scraggy youth, who, chafing and fuming, made such short work of his monthly hundred francs, and they dabbled together in the most risky undertakings. Later on, when Rougon was desirous of entering the Legislative Assembly, Du Poizat worked energetically to secure his election for Deux-Sèvres. Then, after the *coup d'état,* Rougon in his turn used all his influence on behalf of Du Poizat and got him appointed sub-prefect at Brossuire. The young man, then barely thirty years of age, had desired to return in triumph to his own neighbourhood, where he would be near his father, through whose avarice he had led a life of torture ever since leaving college.

'And how is your father?' asked Rougon, without raising his eyes.

'Oh, much too well,' answered Du Poizat bluntly. 'He has sent his last remaining servant away because she ate three pounds of bread a week. Now he keeps a couple of loaded guns behind his door, and when I go to see him I have to parley with him over the wall of the yard.'

While talking, Du Poizat leaned forward and poked his fingers into the bronze vase, where some fragments of paper were lying only half-consumed. Rougon sharply raised his head as he noticed this. He had always felt somewhat distrustful of his old lieutenant, whose irregular white teeth resembled those of a young wolf. In the days when they had worked together he had always made a point of never allowing any compromising document to fall into his hands; and now, as he saw him trying to decipher some words that still remained legible on the charred fragments, he threw a handful of blazing letters into the vase. Du Poizat perfectly understood why he did so; however, he merely smiled and began to joke. 'It's a thorough cleaning you're going in for,' he said.

Then he took a large pair of scissors and began to use them as tongs. He raised the letters which were not consumed to the taper in order to relight them, held up those which had been too tightly crumpled to burn in the vase, and stirred all the flaming ashes as though he were mixing a blazing bowl of punch. The red-hot sparks danced about in the vase, and a cloud of bluish smoke arose and gently curled away towards the open window. At intervals the candle flickered and then burnt brightly again with a straight, tall flame.

'That candle looks like a funeral-taper!' said Du Poizat with a grin. 'Ah! it's really a burial, my poor friend. What a lot of skeletons that require to be reduced to ashes, eh!'

Rougon was about to reply, when a fresh commotion was heard in the ante-chamber. Merle was a second time refusing admission. As the voices grew louder, Rougon at last exclaimed: 'Will you kindly see what it is, Delestang? If I show myself we shall be quite invaded.'

Delestang cautiously opened the door and closed it behind him. But he popped his head into the room almost immediately afterwards, exclaiming: 'It's Kahn!'

'Oh, well!' replied Rougon; 'let him come in; but no one else, mind!' Then he called to Merle and reiterated his orders.

'I beg your pardon, my dear friend,' he said, turning to Kahn, as soon as the usher had left the room; 'but I am so very busy. Sit down beside Du Poizat and keep quite still or I shall be obliged to turn you both out of the room.'

The deputy did not appear in the least offended by Rougon's blunt reception. He was quite accustomed to those ways. He took an easy-chair and sat down beside Du Poizat, who was lighting a second cigar. 'It is getting very warm,' he said, after drawing breath. 'I have just been to the Rue Marbeuf; I expected to find you at home.'

Rougon made no reply, and there was an interval of silence. The ex-President crumpled up some papers and threw them into a basket which he had placed by his side. 'I want to talk to you,' resumed M. Kahn. 'Talk away!' said Rougon; 'I am listening.' Then the deputy seemed to become suddenly aware of the disorder of the room. 'What are you doing?' he asked with admirably feigned surprise. 'Are you changing your room?' His tone seemed so sincere that Delestang actually paused in what he was doing in order to hand him the *Moniteur.*

'Oh dear! Oh dear!' he cried, as soon as he had glanced at the paper. 'I thought the matter was satisfactorily arranged yesterday evening. This comes upon me like a thunderbolt. My dear friend—'

He rose and pressed Rougon's hands. The latter looked at him in silence, while two deep scoffing creases appeared on his heavy face near his under lip. As Du Poizat seemed quite unmoved, he suspected that he and Kahn had already met earlier in the morning, and he was confirmed in this opinion as the deputy had shown no surprise at seeing the sub-prefect. He surmised that one of the pair had come straight to the Council of State while the other hastened to the Rue Marbeuf, so that they might be sure to find him at the one or the other place.

'Well, there is something you want to say to me,' quietly resumed Rougon. 'What is it?'

'Oh, I won't trouble you about that now, my dear friend!' exclaimed the deputy. 'You have got sufficient to worry you as it is. I should be very sorry to bother you with my own troubles at a time like this.'

'Oh, it will be no bother, I assure you. Speak away.'

'Well, then, I wanted to speak to you about that affair of mine, that confounded grant. I am very glad that Du Poizat is here, as he may be able to give us information upon certain points.'

Then he explained at great length the exact position which the matter had reached. It was a scheme for a railway from Niort to Angers, upon which he had been engaged for the last three years. The projected line would pass through Bressuire, where he possessed some blast-furnaces, the value of which it would largely increase. At the present time there were great difficulties in the way of transport, and the business was consequently languishing. M. Kahn had some hopes, too, that he would be able to get some very profitable pickings out of the affair, and so he had greatly exerted himself in order to obtain the grant. Rougon had supported him energetically, and the grant had almost been secured when M. de Marsy, the Minister of the Interior, vexed at having no share in the affair, which he guessed would afford a superb opportunity for jobbery, and being also very desirous of doing anything that might annoy Rougon, had used all his influence to oppose the scheme. With that audacity of his which made him such a terrible opponent, he had even just persuaded the Minister of Public Works to offer the grant to the Western Railway Company, besides circulating a statement that this company alone could successfully carry out the branch line, for the satisfactory working of which some substantial guarantee was required. Thus M. Kahn seemed in great danger of losing all the advantages he had hoped to gain, and Rougon's fall appeared likely to involve him in ruin.

'I heard yesterday,' said he, 'that one of the company's engineers had been instructed to make a survey for the new line. Have you heard anything of it, Du Poizat?'

'Yes, indeed,' replied the sub-prefect. 'The survey has already commenced. They are trying to avoid the detour which you were planning in order to make the line touch Bressuire, and propose to carry it straight along past Parthenay and Thouars.'

A gesture of discouragement escaped the deputy. 'It is sheer persecution!' he exclaimed. 'What harm could it do them to let the line pass my place? But I will protest and write against their plan. I will go back with you to Bressuire.'

'No, no; you had better not wait for me,' said Du Poizat with a smile. 'It seems that I have got to resign.'

M. Kahn fell back in his chair, as though overcome by a final catastrophe. He rubbed his beard with both hands and looked at Rougon with an air of entreaty. The latter had ceased to examine his papers, and was leaning on his elbows and listening.

'I suppose,' he said, somewhat roughly, 'that you want my advice? Well, then, my good friends, just remain quiet and try to keep things as they are until we get the upper hand. Du Poizat is going to resign, because, if he didn't, he would be dismissed within a fortnight. As for you, Kahn, you had better write to the Emperor and use all available means to prevent the grant being obtained by the Western Railway Company. You won't get it for yourself at present, but as long as it is not given to any one else, there is a chance of your winning it later on.' Then, as the two men nodded, he continued: 'Well, that's all I can do for you. I am down and you must give me time to pick myself up again. You don't see me going about with a woe-begone face, do you? Well, I should be much obliged if you wouldn't look as though you were attending my funeral. For my part, I am delighted at retiring into private life again. I shall at last be able to take a little rest.'

He heaved a deep sigh, crossed his arms, and rocked his huge frame backwards and forwards. M. Kahn said nothing more about his scheme, but tried to imitate Du Poizat and appear perfectly indifferent. Delestang had opened some more pasteboard boxes, and worked away so quietly behind the chairs that the slight rustling noise which he made every now and then might have been attributed to a troop of mice flitting across the papers. Meantime the sunlight was travelling over the crimson carpet and lighting up a corner of the writing-table, paling the flame of the candle which was still burning there.

A friendly conversation sprang up amongst the men. Rougon, who was tying up some more bundles of papers, declared that he was really not cut out for politics, and smiled good-naturedly as his heavy eyelids drooped, as though with weariness, over his glistening eyes. He would have liked, he said, to have a large estate to cultivate, fields which he could dig up at his pleasure, and flocks of animals, horses, cattle, sheep, and dogs, of which he would be the one absolute monarch. He told them that in former days, when only a country lawyer at Plassans, his great pleasure had consisted in setting off in a blouse on a shooting expedition of several days through the ravines of La Seille, where he shot eagles. He said that he was a peasant; his grandfather had dug the soil. Then he assumed the air of a man disgusted with the world. Power had grown wearisome to him, and he meant to spend the summer in the country. He declared that he had never felt so light-hearted as he did that morning, and he gave a mighty shrug of his strong shoulders as though he had just thrown off some heavy burden.

'How much did yon get here as President?' asked M. Kahn; 'eighty thousand francs?'

Rougon nodded assent.

'And now you'll only have your thirty thousand as a senator.'

However, Rougon exclaimed that this change would not affect him at all. He could live upon next to nothing and indulged in no vices; which was perfectly true. He was neither a gambler, nor a glutton, nor a loose liver. His whole ambition, he declared, was to be his own master. Then he reverted to his idea of a farm, where he would be king of all sorts of animals. His ideal life was to wield a whip and be paramount; to be the master, chief both in intelligence and power. Gradually he grew animated and talked of animals as though they had been men, declaring that the mob liked to be driven, and that shepherds directed their flocks by pelting them with stones. His face seemed transfigured, his thick lips protruded scornfully, while his whole expression was instinct with strength and power. While he spoke he brandished a bundle of papers in his clenched fist, and it seemed every now and then as though he were going to throw it at the heads of M. Kahn and Du Poizat, who watched his sudden outburst of excitement with uneasy anxiety.

'The Emperor has behaved very badly,' at last muttered Du Poizat.

Then Rougon all at once became quite calm again. His face turned loamy and his body seemed to grow flabby and obese. He began to sound the Emperor's praises in an exaggerated fashion. Napoléon III. was a man of mighty intelligence, he declared, with a mind of astonishing depth. Du Poizat and Kahn exchanged a meaning look. But Rougon waxed still more lavish of his praises, and, speaking of his devotion to his master, declared with great humility that he had always been proud of being a mere instrument in the Emperor's hands. He talked on in this strain till he made Du Poizat, who was of a somewhat irritable nature, quite impatient, and they began to wrangle. The sub-prefect spoke with considerable bitterness of all that Rougon and he had done for the Empire between 1848 and 1851, when they were lodging with Madame Correur in a condition of semi-starvation. He referred to the terrible days, especially those of the first year, when they had gone splashing through the mud of Paris, recruiting partisans for the Emperor's cause. Later on they had risked their skins a score of times. And wasn't it Rougon who on the morning of the second of December

had taken possession of the Palais Bourbon at the head of a regiment of the line? That was a game at which men staked their lives!
Yet now to-day he was being sacrificed and made the victim of a
court intrigue. Rougon, however, protested against this assertion.
He was not being sacrificed—he was resigning for private reasons.
And as Du Poizat, now fully wound up, began to call the folks of
the Tuileries a set of 'pigs,' he ended by reducing him to silence by
bringing his fist down upon the rosewood writing-table with a force
which made it creak.

'That is all nonsense!' he said.

'You are, indeed, going rather far,' remarked M. Kahn.

Delestang was standing behind the chairs looking very pale. He
opened the door gently to see if any one were listening, but there
was nobody in the ante-chamber excepting Merle, whose back was
turned with an appearance of great discretion. Rougon's observation
had made Du Poizat blush, and quickly cooling down he chewed his
cigar in silent displeasure.

'There is no doubt that the Emperor is surrounded by injudicious
advisers,' Rougon resumed after a pause. 'I ventured to tell him as
much, and he smiled. He even condescended to jest about it, and
told me that my own *entourage* was no better than his own.'

Du Poizat and Kahn laughed in a constrained fashion. They
thought the reply a very good one.

'But,' continued Rougon in meaning tones, 'I repeat that I am
retiring of my own free will. If any one questions you, who are my
friends, on the matter, you can say that yesterday evening I was
quite at liberty to withdraw my resignation. You can contradict, too,
the tittle-tattle which is being circulated about Rodriguez's affair,
out of which people seem to be making a perfect romance. On this
subject no doubt I disagreed with the majority of the Council of
State, and there has certainly been a deal of friction in the matter
which has hastened my retirement. But I had weightier and earlier
reasons than that. For a long time past I had made up my mind to
resign the high position which I owed to the Emperor's kindness.'

He punctuated this speech with the gesture of the right hand, in
which he constantly indulged when addressing the Chamber. He
evidently wished that what he was saying might be made public.
M. Kahn and Du Poizat, who knew very well the kind of individual
they had to deal with, tried all kinds of stratagems to get at the real
truth. They felt quite sure that 'the great man,' as they familiarly

called him between themselves, had some formidable scheme in his head. So they turned the conversation on general politics. Rougon then began to scoff at the parliamentary system, which he called 'the dunghill of mediocrity.' The Chamber, he declared, enjoyed quite an absurd amount of liberty even now, and indulged in far too much talk. France required governing, he said, by a suitably devised machine, with the Emperor at the head, and the great state-bodies, reduced to the position of mere working gear below. He laughed, and his huge chest heaved, as he carried his theory to the point of exaggeration, displaying the while a scornful contempt for the imbeciles who demanded powerful rule.

'But,' interposed M. Kahn, 'with the Emperor at the top, and everybody else at the bottom, matters cannot be very pleasant for any one except the Emperor.'

'Those who feel bored can take themselves off,' Rougon quietly replied. He smiled, and then added: 'They can wait till things become amusing, and then they can come back.'

A long interval of silence followed. M. Kahn began to stroke his beard contentedly. He had found out what he wanted to know. He had made a correct guess at the Chamber on the previous afternoon when he had insinuated that Rougon, finding his influence at the Tuileries seriously shaken, had taken time by the forelock and resigned. Rodriguez's business had afforded him a splendid opportunity for honourable withdrawal.

'And what are people saying?' Rougon at last inquired in order to break the silence.

'Well, I've only just got here,' said Du Poizat, 'but a little while ago I heard a gentleman who wore a decoration declaring in a café that he strongly approved of your retirement.'

'Béjuin was very much affected about it yesterday,' added M. Kahn. 'Béjuin is much attached to you. He's rather slow, but he's very genuine. Little La Rouquette, too, spoke very properly, and referred to you in the kindest terms.'

Other names were mentioned as the conversation continued. Rougon asked direct questions, without showing the least embarrassment, and extracted full particulars from the deputy, who complaisantly gave him an exact account of the demeanour of the Corps Législatif towards him.

'This afternoon,' interrupted Du Poizat, who felt somewhat annoyed at having no information to impart, 'I will take a ramble through Paris, and to-morrow morning, as soon as I'm out of bed, I will come and tell you all I have heard.'

'By the way,' cried M. Kahn, with a laugh, 'I forgot to tell you about Combelot. I never saw a man in greater embarrassment.'

He stopped short on seeing Rougon glance warningly towards Delestang, who, with his back turned towards them, was at that moment standing on a chair removing an accumulation of newspapers which had been stored away atop of a bookcase. M. de Combelot had married one of Delestang's sisters. Delestang himself, since Rougon had fallen into disfavour, had felt a little down-hearted on account of his relationship with a chamberlain; and so, wishing to affect independence, he turned and said with a smile: 'Why don't you go on? Combelot is an ass. That's the long and short of it, eh?'

This ready condemnation of his brother-in-law afforded the others much amusement, and Delestang, noticing his success, continued his attack even to the extent of falling foul of Combelot's beard, that famous black beard which had such a reputation among the ladies. Then, as he threw a bundle of newspapers on to the floor, he said abruptly: 'What is a source of sorrow to some is a source of joy to others.'

This truism led to M. de Marsy's name being introduced into the conversation. Rougon bent his head and devoted himself to a searching examination of a portfolio, leaving his friends to ease their minds. They spoke of Marsy with all the rageful hostility which politicians show for an adversary. They revelled in the strongest language, bringing all kinds of abominable accusations against him, and so grossly exaggerating such stories which had a foundation of truth that they became mere lies. Du Poizat, who had known Marsy in former days, before the Empire, declared that he was kept at that time by a baroness whose diamonds he had exhausted in three months. M. Kahn asserted that there was not a single shady affair started in any part of Paris without Marsy having a hand in it. They encouraged each other in charges of this kind, and went on from worse to worse. In a mining affair Marsy had received a bribe of fifteen hundred thousand francs; during the previous month he had offered a furnished house to little Florence of the Bouffes Theatre, a trifle for which he had paid six hundred thousand francs, his share of the profits of a speculation in Morocco railway stock; finally, not a week ago, a grand scheme for constructing canals in Egypt, which had been got up by certain tools of his, had scandalously collapsed, the shareholders discovering that not a single shovelful of earth had been turned, although they had been paying out money for a couple of years or so. Then, too, they fell foul of Marsy's physical appearance, tried to depreciate his good looks, and even attacked the collection of pictures which he was getting together.

'He's a brigand in the skin of a vaudevillist,' Du Poizat ended by exclaiming.

Rougon slowly raised his head and fixed his big eyes on the two men. 'You are going it well,' he said. 'Marsy manages his affairs in his own way, as you manage yours in your way. As regards myself and him, we don't get on well together, and if ever I have a chance to crush him I shall avail myself of it without hesitation. But all that you have been saying doesn't prevent Marsy from being a very clever fellow, and, if ever the whim takes him, he will only make a mouthful of you two, I warn you of it.'

Then Rougon, tired of sitting, rose and stretched himself. He gave a great yawn, as he added: 'And he will do it all the more easily, my friends, now that I shall no longer be in a position to interfere.'

'Oh, you can lead Marsy a pretty dance if you like,' said Du Poizat, with a faint smile. 'You have some papers here which he would be glad to pay a big price for. Those yonder, I mean, the papers in the Lardenois matter, in which he played such a singular part. There's a very curious letter from him among them, which I recognise as one that I brought you myself at the time.'

Rougon went up to the grate in order to throw the papers with which he had gradually filled his basket into the fire. The bronze vase was no longer large enough. 'We must deal a skinning blow, and not give a mere scratch,' he replied, shrugging his shoulders disdainfully. 'Every one has foolish letters astray in the possession of other people.'

He then lighted the letter just spoken of at the candle, and used it to set fire to the heap of papers in the grate. He remained squatting for a moment, whilst watching the blazing pile. Some thick official documents turned black, and twisted about like sheets of lead; the letters and memoranda, scrawled over with handwriting, threw up little tongues of bluish flame, while inside the grate, amidst a swarm of sparks, half-consumed fragments still remained quite legible.

At this moment the door was thrown wide open, and a laughing voice was heard exclaiming: 'All right! I will excuse you, Merle. I belong to the house, and if you don't let me come in this way, I shall go round by the Council Chamber.'

It was M. d'Escorailles, for whom some six months previously Rougon had obtained an appointment as auditor at the Council of State. On his arm hung pretty Madame Bouchard, looking delightfully fresh in a bright spring toilette.

'Good heavens!' muttered Rougon, 'we've got women here now.'

He did not immediately leave his place by the grate, but still stooping, grasping the shovel, and pressing down the blazing papers so as to guard against an accident, he raised his big face with an air of displeasure. M. d'Escorailles, however, appeared in no way disconcerted. When he and the young woman had crossed the threshold, they ceased to smile, and assumed an expression more suited to the circumstances.

'My dear master,' said Escorailles, 'I bring a friend of yours, who insists upon coming to express her sorrow. We have seen the *Moniteur* this morning—'

'Oh, you have seen the *Moniteur,* too,' muttered Rougon, at last rising erect. Then he caught sight of some one whom he had not previously noticed. 'Ah, Monsieur Bouchard also!' he exclaimed, blinking.

It was, indeed, the husband who, silent and dignified, had just entered the room in the wake of his wife's skirts. M. Bouchard was sixty years old: his hair was quite white, his eyes were dim, and his face was worn by twenty-five years of official labour. He did not say a single word, but took Rougon's hand with an appearance of emotion, and gave it three vigorous shakes.

'It is really very kind of you all to come and see me,' said Rougon, 'only you will be terribly in my way. However, come here, will you? Du Poizat, give Madame Bouchard your chair.'

He turned as he spoke, and then saw Colonel Jobelin standing in front of him. 'What! are you here as well, colonel?' he cried.

As a matter of fact, the door had been left open, and Merle had been unable to stop the colonel, who had come up the staircase immediately behind the Bouchards. He was accompanied by his son, a tall lad of fifteen, a pupil at the Louis-le-Grand College. 'I wanted Auguste to see you,' he said. 'It is misfortune that reveals true friends. Auguste, go and give your hand—'

Rougon, however, had sprung towards the ante-room, crying:

'Shut the door, Merle! What are you thinking about? We shall have all Paris in here directly!'

With calm face the usher replied: 'It's all because they caught sight of you, Monsieur le Président.'

Even as he spoke, he was obliged to step back close to the wall, in order to allow the Charbonnels to pass. They came into the room abreast, but not arm-in-arm. They were out of breath, and looked disconsolate and amazed; and they both began to speak at once. 'We have just seen the *Moniteur*! What dreadful news! How distressed your poor mother will be! And what a sad position, too, it puts us in ourselves!'

More guileless than the others, the Charbonnels were about to enter upon their own little affairs at once, but Rougon stopped them. He shot a bolt, hidden beneath the door lock, and remarked that if any people wanted to come in now, they would have to break the door open. Then, observing that none of his visitors showed signs of leaving, he resigned himself, and tried to finish his task in the midst of these nine people who were crowding his room. The whole place was now in a state of chaotic confusion, there being such a litter of portfolios and papers on the floor that when the colonel and M. Bouchard wanted to reach a window-recess, they had to exercise the greatest care in order to avoid trampling upon some important document. All the chairs were covered with bundles of papers, excepting the one on which Madame Bouchard was now seated. She was smiling at the gallant speeches of Du Poizat and M. Kahn; while M. d'Escorailles, unable to find a hassock, pushed a thick blue portfolio, stuffed with letters, under her feet. The drawers of the writing-table, which had been pushed into a corner of the room, afforded the Charbonnels a temporary seat where they could recover their breath, while young Auguste, delighted at finding himself in the bustle of a removal, poked about till he disappeared behind the mountain of pasteboard boxes, amid which Delestang had previously entrenched himself. As the latter threw down the newspapers from the top of the bookcase, he raised considerable dust, which made Madame Bouchard cough slightly.

'I don't advise you to stay here amidst all this dirt,' said Rougon, who was now emptying the boxes which he had asked Delestang to leave unexamined.

The young woman, however, quite rosy from her fit of coughing, assured him that she was very comfortable, and that the dust would not harm her bonnet. Then all the visitors poured forth their condolences. The Emperor, they declared, must care very little about the real interests of the country to allow himself to be influenced by men so unworthy of his confidence. France was suffering a great loss. But it was ever thus, they said; a man of high intelligence always had every mediocrity leagued against him.

'Governments have no gratitude,' declared M. Kahn.

'So much the worse for them!' exclaimed the colonel; 'they strike themselves when they strike those who serve them.'

However, M. Kahn was desirous of having the last word on the subject, so he turned to Rougon, and said: 'When a man like you falls, it is a subject for public mourning.'

This met with the approval of all. 'Yes, yes,' they exclaimed, 'for public mourning, indeed!'

Rougon raised his head upon hearing this fulsome praise. His greyish cheeks flushed slightly, and his whole face was irradiated by a suppressed smile of satisfaction. He was as proud of his ability as a woman is of her beauty, and he liked to receive point-blank compliments. It was becoming evident, however, that his visitors were in each other's way. They repeatedly glanced at one another, resolving to sit one another out, unwilling as they were to say all they desired in the presence of their companions. Now that the great man had fallen, they were anxious to know if he had done anything for them while he yet had the power. The colonel was the first to take an active step. He led Rougon, who, with a portfolio under his arm, readily followed him, into one of the window-recesses.

'Have you given me a thought?' he asked with a pleasant smile.

'Yes, indeed. Your nomination as commander of the Legion of Honour was again promised me four days ago. But, of course, today it is impossible for me to say anything with certainty. I confess to you that I am afraid my friends will be made to suffer by my fall.'

The colonel's lips trembled with emotion. He stammered that they must do what they could, and then, turning suddenly round, he called out: 'Auguste!'

The lad was on his hands and knees underneath the desk, trying to decipher the inscriptions on the batches of documents. However, he hastened to his father.

'Here's this lad of mine,' resumed the colonel in an undertone. 'I shall have to find a berth for the young scamp one of these days.

I am counting upon you to help me. I haven't made up my mind yet between the law and the public service. Give your good friend your hand, Auguste, so that he may recollect you.'

While this scene was going on, Madame Bouchard, who had begun to bite her gloves impatiently, had risen from her chair and made her way to the window on the left, after giving M. d'Escorailles a look which meant that he was to follow her. Her husband was already there, leaning upon the cross-bar and gazing out upon the view. The leaves of the tall chestnut trees in the Tuileries Garden were languidly waving in the warm sunshine, and the Seine could be seen rolling blue waters, flecked with golden light, between the Royal and Concorde bridges.

Madame Bouchard suddenly turned round and exclaimed: 'Oh! Monsieur Rougon, come and look here.'

Thereupon Rougon hastily quitted the colonel, while Du Poizat, who had followed the young woman, discreetly retired, again joining M. Kahn at the middle window.

'Do you see that barge full of bricks? It nearly foundered just now,' said Madame Bouchard.

Rougon looked and obligingly lingered there in the sunshine till M. d'Escorailles, upon a fresh glance from the young woman, said to him: 'Monsieur Bouchard wants to send in his resignation. We have brought him here in order that you may try to dissuade him.'

M. Bouchard then explained that he could not endure injustice. 'Yes, Monsieur Rougon,' he continued, 'I began as a copying-clerk in the office of the Minister of the Interior, and reached the position of head clerk without owing either to favour or intrigue. I have been head clerk since 1847. Well, the post of head of department has been vacant five times—four times under the Republic and once under the Empire—and yet the Minister has not once thought of me, though I had hierarchical rights to the place. Now that you will no longer be able to fulfil the promise you gave me I think I had better retire.'

Rougon tried to soothe him. The post, said he, had not yet been bestowed upon any one else, and even if he did not get it this time, it would only be a chance lost; a chance which would certainly present itself again on some future occasion. Then he grasped Madame Bouchard's hands and complimented her in a paternal fashion. Her husband's house had been the first thrown open to him on his arrival in Paris, and it was there that he had met the colonel, who was the head clerk's cousin. Later on, when M. Bouchard had inherited his father's property and had been smitten, at fifty-four years of age, with a sudden desire to get married, Rougon had acted as witness on behalf of Madame Bouchard, then Adèle Desvignes, a well brought up young lady of a respectable family at Rambouillet. The head clerk had been anxious to marry a young lady from the provinces, because he made a point of having a steady wife. However, the fair and adorable little Adèle, with her innocent blue eyes, had in less than four years proved to be a great deal worse than a mere flirt.

'There, now, don't distress yourself,' said Rougon, who was still holding her hands in his big fists. 'You know very well that I will do my best for you.'

Then he took M. d'Escorailles aside, and told him that he had written that morning to his father to tranquillise him. The young auditor must remain quietly in his place. The Escorailles family was one of the oldest in Plassans, where it was treated with the utmost respect; and Rougon, who in former days had often dragged his worn-down boots past the old Marquis's house, took a pride in protecting and assisting the young man. The family retained an enthusiastic devotion for Henri V., though it allowed its heir to serve the Empire. This was one of the inevitable consequences of the wickedness of the times.

Meanwhile, at the middle window, which they had opened to obtain greater privacy, Kahn and Du Poizat were talking together, while gazing out upon the distant roofs of the Tuileries, which looked blue in the haze of the sunlight. They were sounding each other, dropping a few words, and then lapsing into intervals of silence. Rougon, they agreed, was too impulsive. He ought not to have allowed himself to be irritated by that Rodriguez question, which might have been very easily settled. Then M. Kahn, gazing blankly into the distance, murmured as though he were speaking to himself: 'A man knows when he falls, but never knows whether he will rise again.'

Du Poizat pretended not to hear; but, after a long pause, he said: 'Oh! he's a very clever fellow.'

Then the deputy abruptly turned, and, looking the sub-prefect full in the face, spoke to him very rapidly: 'Between ourselves, I am afraid for him. He plays with fire. We are his friends, of course, and there can be no thought of our abandoning him. But I must say that he has thought very little about us in this matter. Take my own case, for instance. I have matters of enormous importance on my hands, and he has placed them in utter jeopardy by this sudden freak of his. He would have no right to complain—would he, now?—if I were to knock at somebody else's door; for, you know, it is not I alone who suffer, there are all the townsfolk as well.'

'Yes, well, *go* and knock at some other door,' said Du Poizat, with a smile.

At this the deputy, in a sudden outburst of anger, let the truth escape him. 'But is it possible? This confounded fellow spoils you with everybody else. When you belong to his band, every one else fights shy of you.'

Then he calmed down, sighed, and looked out towards the Arc de Triomphe, which could be seen rising in a greyish mass out of the green expanse of the Champs Elysées. 'Well, well,' he continued softly, 'I'm as faithful as a dog myself.'

For the last moment or two the colonel had been standing behind the two men. 'Fidelity is the road to honour,' said he in his military voice. Then, as Du Poizat and Kahn made room for him, he added: 'Rougon is contracting a debt to us to-day. Rougon no longer belongs to himself.'

This remark met with the warmest approval. It was certainly quite true that Rougon no longer belonged to himself. What was more, it was necessary that he should be distinctly told so in order that he might know what it behoved him to do. Then the three friends chatted in whispers, forming plans and fortifying each other with hope. At intervals they turned and cast a glance into the big room to make sure that no one was monopolising the great man for too long a time.

The great man was now gathering up the portfolios, while still talking to Madame Bouchard. The Charbonnels were wrangling in the corner where they had remained silent and ill at ease ever since their arrival. They had twice attempted to get hold of Rougon, but had been anticipated by the colonel and the young woman. Now, at last, M. Charbonnel pushed his wife towards the ex-President.

'This morning,' she stammered, 'we received a letter from your mother—'

Rougon did not allow her to finish, but took her and her husband into the window-recess on the right hand, once more abandoning his portfolios without any great sign of impatience.

'We have received a letter from your mother,' repeated Madame

Charbonnel, and she was going to read the letter in question, when Rougon took it from her and glanced over it. Charbonnel was a retired oil merchant of Plassans, and he and his wife had been protected by Madame Félicité, as Rougon's mother was called in her own little town. She had given them a letter of introduction to her son on the occasion of their presenting a petition to the Council of State. A cousin of theirs, one Chevassu, a lawyer at Faverolles, the chief town of a neighbouring department, had died, leaving his fortune of five hundred thousand francs to the Sisters of the Holy Family. Originally the Charbonnels had not expected to inherit his fortune, but having suddenly become his next heirs, owing to his brother's death, they contested the will on the ground of undue influence; and the Sisterhood having petitioned the Council of State to authorise the payment of the bequest to them, they had left their old home at Plassans, hastened to Paris, and taken lodgings at the Hôtel du Périgord in the Rue Jacob in order that they might be on the spot to look after their interests. The matter had been lingering on for the past six months.

'We are feeling extremely depressed,' sighed Madame Charbonnel, while Rougon was reading the letter. 'I myself was always against bringing this action, but Monsieur Charbonnel said that with you on our side we should certainly get the money, as you had only to say a word to put the five hundred thousand francs into our pocket. Isn't that so, Monsieur Charbonnel?'

The retired oil merchant nodded his head with a hopeless air.

'And for such a sum as that,' continued Madame Charbonnel, 'it did seem worth while to make a change in our old way of life. And it has been nicely changed and disturbed, indeed. Will you believe it, Monsieur Rougon, they actually refused to change our dirty towels at the hotel yesterday? We who have five chests full of linen at home!'

She went on railing at Paris, which she detested. They had originally come thither for a week. Then, as they had always hoped to be able to return home during the following week, they had not thought it worth while to send for anything, and, their case still being unsettled, they doggedly lingered on in their furnished lodgings, eating whatever it pleased the cook to provide, short too of clean linen and almost of clothes. Madame Charbonnel was obliged to dress her hair with a broken comb. Sometimes they sat down on their little valise and wept from very weariness and indignation.

'And the hotel is frequented by such queer characters!' complained M. Charbonnel, with a shocked expression. 'A young man has the room next to ours, and the things we hear—'

But Rougon was folding up the letter. 'My mother,' said he, 'gives you excellent advice in telling you to be patient. I can only suggest to you to take fresh courage. You seem, to me, to have a good case, but now that I have resigned I dare not promise you anything.'

'Then we will leave Paris to-morrow!' cried Madame Charbonnel, in an outburst of despair.

As soon as this cry had escaped her lips, she turned very pale and her husband had to support her. For a moment they both remained speechless, looking at each other with trembling lips and feeling a great desire to burst into tears. They felt faint and dazed as though they had just seen the five hundred thousand francs dashed out of their hands.

'You have had to deal with a powerful opponent,' Rougon continued kindly. 'Monseigneur Rochart, the Bishop of Faverolles, has himself come to Paris to support the claim of the Sisters of the Holy Family. If it had not been for his intervention, you would long ago have gained your cause. Unfortunately the clergy are now very powerful. However, I am leaving friends here behind me, and I hope to bring some influence to bear in your favour, while I myself keep in the background. You have waited so long that if you go away to-morrow—'

'We will remain, we will remain!' Madame Charbonnel hastily gasped. 'Ah, Monsieur Rougon, this inheritance will have cost us very dear!'

Rougon now hastened back to his papers. He cast a glance of satisfaction round the room, delighted that there was no one else to take him off into one of the window-recesses. They had all had their say. And so for a few minutes he made great progress with his task. Then he waxed bitterly jocose and avenged himself on his visitors for the bother they had caused him by attacking them with biting satire. For a quarter of an hour he proved a perfect scourge to those friends of his to whose various stories he had just listened so obligingly. His language and manner to pretty Madame Bouchard became indeed so harsh and cutting that the young woman's eyes filled with tears, though she still continued to smile. All the others laughed, accustomed as they were to Rougon's rough ways. They knew that their prospects were never better than when he was bela-bouring them in this fashion.

However, all at once, there was a gentle knock at the door. 'No, no!' cried Rougon to Delestang, who was going to see who was there; 'don't open it! Am I never to be left in peace? My head is splitting already.' Then, as the knocking continued with greater energy, he growled between his teeth: 'Ah, if I were going to stay here, I would send Merle about his business!'

The knocking ceased, but suddenly a little door in a corner of the room was thrown back and gave entrance to a huge blue silk skirt, which came in backwards. This skirt, which was very bright and profusely ornamented with bows of ribbon, remained stationary for a moment, half inside the room and half outside, without anything further being visible. However, a soft female voice was heard speaking.

'Monsieur Rougon!' exclaimed the lady, at last showing her face.

It was Madame Correur, wearing a bonnet with a cluster of roses on it. Rougon, who had stepped angrily towards the door, with fists clenched, now bowed and grasped the newcomer's hand.

'I was asking Merle how he liked being here,' she said, casting a tender glance at the big lanky usher, who stood smiling in front of her. 'And you, Monsieur Rougon, are you satisfied with him?'

'Oh, yes, certainly,' replied Rougon pleasantly.

Merle's face still retained its sanctimonious smile, and he kept his eyes fixed upon Madame Correur's plump neck. The latter braced herself up to her full height and then brought her curls over her forehead.

'I am glad to hear that, my man,' she continued. 'When I get any one a place, I am anxious that all parties should be satisfied. If you ever want any advice, Merle, you can come and see me any morning, you know, between eight and nine. Mind you keep steady, now.'

Then she came inside the room, and said to Rougon: 'There are no servants so good as those old soldiers.'

And afterwards she took hold of him and made him cross the room, leading him with short steps to the window at the other end. There she scolded him for not having admitted her. If Merle had not allowed her to come in by the little door, she would still have been waiting outside. And it was absolutely necessary that she should see him, she said, for he really could not take himself off in that way without letting her know how her petitions were progressing. Forthwith she drew from her pocket a little memorandum-book, very richly ornamented and bound in rose-coloured watered silk.

'I did not see the *Moniteur* till after *déjeuner,*' she continued; 'and then I took a cab at once. Tell me, now, how is the matter of Madame Leturc, the captain's widow, who wants a tobacco shop, getting on? I promised her that she should have a definite answer next week. There's also the case of Herminie Billecoq, you remember, who used to be a pupil of Saint Denis. Her seducer, an officer, has consented to marry her if any charitable soul will give her the regulation dowry. We thought about applying to the Empress. Then there are all those ladies, Madame Chardon, Madame Testanière, and Madame Jalaguier, who have been waiting for months.'

Rougon quietly gave her the replies she sought, explained the various causes of the delays that had occurred, and entered into minute details. However, he gave her to understand that she must not reckon so much upon him in the future as she had done in the past. This threw her into great distress. It made her so happy, she said, to be able to be of service to any one. What would become of her with all those ladies? Then she spoke of her own affairs, with which Rougon was fully acquainted. She again reminded him that she was a Martineau, one of the Martineaus of Coulonges, a good family of La Vendée, in which fathers and sons had been notaries without a break over seven successive generations. She never clearly explained how she came to bear the name of Correur. When she was twenty-four years old she had eloped with a young journeyman butcher, and for six months her father had suffered the greatest distress from this disgraceful scandal, about which the neighbourhood still gossiped. Ever since then she had been living in Paris, utterly ignored by her family. She had written fully a dozen times to her brother, who was now at the head of the family practice, but had failed to get any reply from him. His silence, she said, was due to her sister-in-law, a woman who 'carried on with priests, and led that imbecile brother of hers by the nose.' One of her most cherished ambitions, as in Du Poizat's case, was to return to her own neighbourhood as a well-to-do and honoured woman.

'I wrote again a week ago,' she said; 'but I have no doubt she throws my letters into the fire. However, if my brother should die, she would be obliged to let me go to the house, for they have no child, and I should have interests to look after. My brother is fifteen years older than I am, and I hear that he suffers from gout.' Then she suddenly changed her tone, and continued: 'However, don't let us bother about that now. It's for you that we must use all our energies at present, Eugène. We will do our best, you shall see. It is necessary that you should be everything in order that we maybe something. You remember '51, don't you, eh?'

Rougon smiled, and as Madame Correur pressed his hands with a maternal air, he bent down and whispered into her ear: 'If you see Gilquin, tell him to be prudent. Only the other week, when he got himself locked up, he took it into his head to give my name, so that I might bail him out.'

Madame Correur promised to speak to Gilquin, one of her tenants at the time when Rougon had lodged at the Hôtel Vanneau, and withal a very useful fellow on certain occasions, though apt to be extremely compromising. 'I have a cab below, and so now I'll be off,' she said aloud with a smile as she stepped into the middle of the room.

Nevertheless, she lingered for a few minutes longer, hoping that the others would take their departure at the same time. In her desire to effect this, she offered to take one of them with her in her cab. The colonel accepted the offer, and it was settled that young Auguste should sit beside the driver. Then general hand-shaking began, Rougon took up a position by the door, which was thrown wide open; and as his visitors passed out, each gave him a parting assurance of sympathy. M. Kahn, Du Poizat, and the colonel stretched out their necks and whispered a few words in his ear, begging him not to forget them. However, when the Charbonnels had already reached the first step of the staircase, and Madame Correur was chatting with Merle at the far end of the ante-room, Madame Bouchard, for whom her husband and M. d'Escorailles waited a few paces away, still lingered smilingly before Rougon, asking him at what time she could see him privately in the Rue Marbeuf, because she felt too stupid, said she, when he had visitors with him. At this the colonel, hearing her, suddenly darted back into the room, and then the others followed, there being a general return.

'We will all come to see you,' the colonel cried.

'You mustn't hide yourself away from every one,' added several voices. But M. Kahn waved his hand to obtain silence. And then he made that famous remark of his: 'You don't belong to yourself; you belong to your friends, and to France.'

At last they all went away, and Rougon was able to close the door. He heaved a great sigh of relief. Delestang, whom he had quite forgotten, now made his appearance from behind the heap of pasteboard boxes, in the shelter of which he had just finished classifying different papers, like a conscientious friend. He was feeling a little proud of his work. He had been acting, while the others had merely been talking; so it was with genuine satisfaction that he received the great man's thanks. It was only he, so the latter said, who could have rendered him this service; he had an orderly mind, and a methodical manner of working which would carry him far. And Rougon made other flattering observations, without it being possible for one to know whether he was really in earnest or only jesting. Then, turning round, and glancing into the different corners, he said: 'There, I think we've finished everything now, thanks to you. There's nothing more to be done, except to tell Merle to have these packets carried to my house.'

He called the usher, and pointed out his private papers. And in reply to all his instructions the usher repeated: 'Yes, Monsieur le Président.'

'Don't call me Président any more, you stupid,' Rougon at last exclaimed in irritation; 'I'm one no longer.'

Merle bowed, and took a step towards the door. Then he stopped and seemed to hesitate. Finally he came back and said: 'There's a lady on horseback down below who wants to see you, sir. She laughed, and said she would come up, horse and all, if the staircase were wide enough. She declared that she only wanted to shake hands with you, sir.'

Rougon clenched his fists, thinking this to be some joke; but Delestang, who had gone to look out of the window on the landing, hastened back, exclaiming, with an expression of emotion: 'Mademoiselle Clorinde!'

Then Rougon said that he would go downstairs; and as he and Delestang took their hats, he looked at his friend, and with a frown and a suspicious air, prompted by the latter's emotion, exclaimed: 'Beware of women!'

When he reached the door, he gave a last glance round the room. The full light of day was streaming through the three open windows, illumining the open pasteboard boxes, the scattered drawers and the packets of papers, tied up and heaped together in the middle of the carpet. The apartment looked very spacious and very mournful. In the grate only a small heap of black ashes was now left of all the handfuls of burnt papers. And as Rougon closed the door behind him, the taper, which had been forgotten on the edge of the writing-table, burnt out, splitting the cut-glass socket of the candlestick to pieces amid the silence of the empty room.

III

MADEMOISELLE CLORINDE

Rougon occasionally went to Countess Balbi's for a few minutes towards four in the afternoon. He walked there in a neighbourly way, for she lived in a small house overlooking the avenue of the Champs Elysées, only a few yards from the Rue Marbeuf. She was seldom at home, and when by chance she did happen to be there she was in bed, and had to send excuses for not making her appearance. This, however, did not prevent the staircase of the little house from being crowded with noisy visitors, or the drawing-room doors from being perpetually on the swing. Her daughter Clorinde was wont to receive her friends in a gallery, something like an artist's studio, with large windows overlooking the avenue.

For nearly three months Rougon, with his blunt distaste for female wiles, had responded very coldly to the advances of these ladies, who had managed to get introduced to him at a ball given by the Minister for Foreign Affairs. He met them everywhere, both of them smiling with the same winning smile—the mother always silent, while the daughter always chattered and looked him straight in the face. However, he still went on avoiding them, lowering his eyes so as not to see them, and refusing the invitations which they sent him. Then as they continued to press him hard and pursued him even to his own house, past which Clorinde used to ride ostentatiously, he made inquiries before at last venturing to call on them.

At the Sardinian Legation the ladies were spoken of in very favourable terms. There had been a real Count Balbi, it appeared; the Countess still kept up relations with persons of high position at Turin, and the daughter, during the preceding year, had been on the point of marrying a petty German prince. But at the Duchess of Sanquirino's, where Rougon made his next inquiries, he heard a different story. There he was told that Clorinde had been born two years after the Count's death, and a very complicated history of the Balbis was retailed to him. The husband and wife had led most adventurous and dissolute lives; they had been divorced in France, but had afterwards become reconciled to each other in Italy, their subsequent cohabitation being an illicit one, in consequence of their previous divorce.

A young attaché, who was thoroughly acquainted with what went on at the court of King Victor Emmanuel, was still more explicit. According to him, whatever influence the Countess still retained in Italy was due to an old connection with a very highly placed personage there, and he hinted that she would not have left Turin had it not been for a terrible scandal into the details of which he would not enter. Rougon, whose interest in the matter was increasing with the extent of his inquiries, now went to the police authorities, but they could give him no precise information. Their entries relating to the two foreigners simply described them as women who kept up a great show without any proof that they were really in possession of a substantial fortune. They asserted that they had property in Piedmont; but, as a matter of fact, there were sudden breaks in their life of luxury, during which they abruptly disappeared, only to reappear shortly afterwards in fresh splendour. Briefly, all that the police could say was that they really knew nothing about them and would prefer to know nothing. At the same time, it was certain that the women associated with the best society, and that their house was looked upon as neutral ground, where Clorinde's eccentricities were tolerated and excused on account of her being a foreigner. And so Rougon at last made up his mind to see the ladies.

By the time he had paid his third visit, the great man's curiosity with respect to them had still further increased. He was of a cold dispassionate nature which was not easily stirred into life. What first attracted him in Clorinde was the mystery surrounding her, the story of a past-away life and the yearning for a new existence which he could read in the depths of her big goddess-like eyes. He had heard disgraceful scandal about her—an early love-affair with a coachman, and a subsequent connection with a banker who had presented her with the little house in the Champs Elysées. However, every now and then she seemed to him so child-like that he doubted the truth of what he had been told, and again and again essayed to find out the secret of this strange girl, who became to him a living enigma, the solution of which interested him as much as some intricate political problem. Until then he had felt a scornful disdain for women, and the first one who excited his interest was certainly as singular and complicated a being as could be imagined.

Upon the morrow of the day when Clorinde had gone on her hired horse to give Rougon a sympathetic shake of the hand at the door of the Council of State, Rougon himself went to pay her a visit. She had made him give a solemn promise to do so. She wanted, she said, to show him something which would brighten his gloomy moods. He laughingly called her his 'pet vice', forgot his worries when he was with her, and felt cheerful and amused. The more so as she kept his mind on the alert, for he was still seeking the key to her history, and was as yet no nearer a solution than on the first day. As he turned the corner of the Rue Marbeuf, he glanced at the house in the Rue du Colisée tenanted by Delestang, whom he fancied he had several times seen peering through the half open shutters of his study at Clorinde's window across the avenue; but to-day the shutters were closed. Delestang had probably gone off to his model-farm at La Chamade.

The door of the Balbis' house was always wide open. At the foot of the staircase Rougon met a little dark-complexioned woman, with untidy hair and a tattered yellow dress. She was biting at an orange as though it were an apple.

'Is your mistress at home, Antonia?' he asked her.

Her mouth was too full to allow her to reply, so she nodded her head energetically and smiled. Her lips were streaming with orange juice, and her little eyes, as she screwed them up, looked like drops of ink upon her dark skin. Rougon was already accustomed to the irregular ways of the Balbis' servants, so without more ado he went up the stairs. On his way he met a big lanky man-servant, with a face like a brigand's and a long black beard, who coolly stared at him without giving him the balustrade-side. When he reached the first floor, he found himself confronted by three open doors, but saw no one about. The door on his left hand was that of Clorinde's bed-room. Curiosity prompted him to peep inside. Although it was four o'clock in the afternoon, the bed had not been made or the room tidied. Upon a screen standing in front of the bed and half concealing the tumbled coverlets, some splashed petticoats which the girl had worn on the previous day had been hung to dry, while a wash-basin, full of soapy water, stood on the floor in front of the window, and the cat of the house, a grey one, slept, comfortably curled, in the midst of a heap of garments.

It was, however, upon the second floor that Clorinde was generally to be found, in the gallery which she had successively turned into a studio, a smoking-room, a hot-house, and a summer drawing-room. As Rougon ascended upwards he heard a growing uproar of voices, shrill laughter and a noise as of furniture being overturned; and when he reached the door he could distinguish the notes of a consumptive piano and sounds of singing. He knocked at the door twice without receiving any answer, and then determined to enter.

'Ah! bravo, bravo, here he is!' cried Clorinde, clapping her hands.

Rougon, whom it was generally so difficult to put out of countenance, for a moment remained timidly on the threshold. Chevalier Rusconi, the Sardinian Minister, a handsome dark-complexioned man, who, under other circumstances, was a grave diplomatist, sat in front of the piano, the keys of which he was striking furiously so as to extract a fuller sound from the instrument. In the middle of the room deputy La Rouquette was waltzing with a chair, the back of which he amorously encircled with his arms, and he was so absorbed in his amusement that he had littered the carpet with other chairs which he had overturned. Then, in the bright light of one of the window-recesses, Clorinde stood upon the centre of a table, posing, with perfect unconcern, as the huntress Diana, in front of a young man who was sketching her with charcoal upon white canvas. Finally, on a couch, three serious-looking men with their legs crossed were silently smoking big cigars and looking at Clorinde.

'Wait a moment! don't move!' cried Chevalier Rusconi to Clorinde, who was about to jump off the table. 'I am going to make the presentations.'

Then, followed by Rougon, he said playfully, as he went past M. La Rouquette, who had dropped breathless into an easy chair: 'Monsieur La Rouquette whom you know; a future minister.' And going up to the artist, he continued: 'Signor Luigi Pozzo, my secretary; diplomatist, painter, musician, and lover.'

He had overlooked the three men on the couch, but catching sight of them as he turned round, he dropped his playful tones, bowed towards them and said in a ceremonious voice: 'Signor Brambilla, Signor Staderino, Signor Viscardi, all three political refugees.'

The three Venetians bowed without removing their cigars from their lips. Chevalier Rusconi was returning to the piano when Clorinde briskly called him back and reproached him with being a very careless master of the ceremonies. Then, motioning towards Rougon, she just said, though in a very significant and flattering tone: 'Monsieur Eugène Rougon.'

Every one bowed again; and Rougon, who for a moment had been rather afraid of some compromising pleasantry, felt surprised at the unexpected tact and dignity shown by this girl, so scantily clad in gauze. He took a seat and inquired after the Contessa Balbi, as was his custom. He even pretended every time he came that his visit was intended for the mother, as this seemed more consonant with strict propriety.

'I should have been very glad to have paid my respects to her,' he said, using the formula which he always employed under the circumstances.

'But mother is there!' exclaimed Clorinde, pointing to a corner of the room with her bow of gilded wood.

The Countess was indeed there, reclining in a deep easy chair behind a variety of other furniture. This discovery came quite as a surprise. The three political refugees had evidently been unaware of her presence, for they at once rose from their couch and bowed. Rougon went up and shook hands with her, standing while she, still lying back in her chair, answered him in monosyllables with that perpetual smile of hers which never left her, even when she was ill. Then she relapsed into listless silence, glancing every now and then into the avenue along which a stream of carriages was passing. She had probably taken up her position there in order to watch the people. And so Rougon soon left her.

Chevalier Rusconi, having again taken his seat at the piano, was trying to recall a tune, gently striking the keys and humming some Italian words in a low voice. La Rouquette, meantime, was fanning himself with his handkerchief; Clorinde was again seriously impersonating Diana, and Rougon, in the sudden calm which had come upon the room, took short steps up and down while looking at the walls. The gallery was crowded with an extraordinary collection of articles; a secretaire, a chest, and several chairs and tables, all pushed into the middle of the apartment and forming a labyrinth of narrow passages. At one end of the room some hothouse plants, crowded together and neglected, were drooping and dying, their long, pendent leaves already turning yellow; and at the other end there was a great heap of dried sculptor's clay, in which one could still recognise the crumbling arms and legs of a statue which Clorinde had roughly moulded one day when seized with the whim of becoming an artist. Although the gallery was very large, there was only one unencumbered spot in it, a patch in front of one of the windows, a small square, which had been turned into a kind of little drawing-room, furnished with a couch and three odd easy chairs.

'You are at liberty to smoke,' said Clorinde to Rougon. He thanked her, but told her that he never smoked. Then, without turning round, the girl cried out: 'Chevalier, make me a cigarette. The tobacco is in front of you, on the piano.'

While the Chevalier was making the cigarette there was another interval of silence. Rougon, vexed at finding all these people present, felt inclined to take up his hat; however, he turned round and walked up to Clorinde; then raising his head, he said with a smile: 'Didn't you ask me to call because you had something to show me?'

She did not immediately reply, but maintained her serious pose; so he continued: 'What is it that you want to show me?'

'Myself,' she answered.

She spoke this word in a majestic tone, not moving a limb as she stood there on the table in her goddess-like posture. Rougon, in his turn becoming grave, took a step backward and scrutinised her. She was truly a superb creature, with her pure perfect profile, her slender neck, and admirable classic figure. She rested one hand upon her bow, and preserved all the antique huntress's expression of serene strength, regardless of the scantiness of her attire, contemptuous of the love of man, at once cold, haughty, and immortal.

'Charming, charming!' exclaimed Rougon, not knowing what else to say.

As a matter of fact he found her statuesque immobility rather disturbing. She looked so triumphant, so convinced of her classical beauty, that, if he had dared to express his thoughts, he would have criticised her like some marble statue, certain details of which displeased his unaesthetic eyes.

'Have you looked enough?' asked Clorinde, still serious and earnest. 'Wait a moment and you shall see something else.'

Then, of a sudden, she was no longer Diana. She dropped her bow and assumed another, and more syren-like posture. Her hands were thrown behind her head and clasped together in her hair; her bust bent slightly backwards, and, as she half-opened her lips and smiled, a stream of sunshine lighted up her face. And standing thus she looked like the very goddess of love.

Signor Brambilla, Signor Staderino, and Signor Viscardi broke into applause in all seriousness, never casting off their gloomy conspirator-like mien.

'Brava! brava! brava!'

On his side M. La Rouquette, was quite frantic with enthusiasm, and Chevalier Rusconi, who had stepped up to the table to hand the girl the cigarette which he had made for her, remained transfixed there, gazing at her with ecstatic eyes and slightly jogging his head as though beating time to his admiration.

Rougon said nothing, but clasped his hands so tightly together that their joints cracked. A subtle tremor had just sped through him. He no longer thought of going away, but dropped into a chair. Clorinde had already resumed her easy, natural pose, and was laughing and smoking her cigarette with a proud twist of her lips. It would have delighted her, said she, to be an actress. She could personate anger, tenderness, modesty, fright, and with a turn of her features or an attitude hit off all sorts of different people.

'Monsieur Rougon,' she asked abruptly, 'would you like to see me imitate you when you are addressing the Chamber?' And thereupon she drew herself up to her full height, puffed herself out and thrust her fists in front of her with such droll, yet truthful, mimicry, that they all nearly killed themselves with laughing. Rougon roared like a boy. He found Clorinde adorable, indeed exquisite, but also very disturbing.

'Clorinde, Clorinde!' cried Luigi, gently tapping his easel.

She was moving about so restlessly that he was obliged to desist from his work. He had now laid his charcoal aside and was putting colour on the canvas with an earnest air. He himself remained quite serious amidst all the laughter, raising his glistening eyes to the young girl and then glancing fiercely at the men with whom she was joking. It was his own idea to paint her in the character of Diana, in a costume which had been the talk of all Paris ever since the ball at the embassy. He claimed to be her cousin, as they had both been born in the same street in Florence.

'Clorinde!' he repeated almost angrily.

'Luigi is right,' she then exclaimed, 'you are not behaving properly, gentlemen. What a noise you are making! Come, let us get on with our work.'

Then she once more assumed her Olympian attitude, again presenting the semblance of a beautiful marble image. The men remained where they were, keeping perfectly still, as though rooted to the floor. La Rouquette alone ventured to beat a gentle tattoo with his finger-tips on the arms of his chair. Rougon, for his part, sat back and gazed at Clorinde, and gradually fell into a dreamy state in which the girl seemed to him to expand into gigantic proportions. A woman was certainly a wonderful piece of mechanism, he reflected. It was a matter that he had never before thought of studying; but now he began to have vague mental glimpses of extraordinary intricacies. For a moment he was filled with a distinct consciousness of the power of those bare shoulders, which seemed strong enough to shake a world. All swam before him, and Clorinde's figure seemed to grow larger and larger till it appeared gigantic, and entirely hid the window from his sight. But he blinked his eyes sharply, and then he again saw her clearly, standing upon the table and much smaller than himself. At this his face broke into a smile, and he felt surprised that he could have entertained a moment's fear of her.

At the other end of the gallery some talk was now going on in low tones. Rougon listened from force of habit, but could only distinguish a rapid murmur of Italian syllables. Chevalier Rusconi, who had just glided behind his chair, had laid one hand on the back of the Countess's seat, and, bending over her respectfully, seemed to be telling her some long story. The Countess said nothing, but nodded every now and again. Once, however, she made an energetic gesture of negation, whereupon the Chevalier bent still closer and tranquillised her with his melodious voice, the murmur of which was like the warbling of a song-bird. At last Rougon, through his knowledge of the dialect of Provence, caught a few words which made him grave.

'Mother,' Clorinde cried abruptly, 'have you shown the Chevalier the telegram you received last night?'

'A telegram!' exclaimed the Chevalier in a loud tone.

The Countess drew a bundle of letters from her pocket and began to search amongst them. Then she handed the Chevalier a much crumpled strip of blue paper.

As soon as he had glanced over it he made a gesture of anger and astonishment. 'What!' he cried in French, forgetting the presence of the others, 'you knew this yesterday! And I only learnt it this morning!'

Clorinde indulged in a fresh burst of laughter, which increased his irritation.

'And Madame la Comtesse allows me to tell her the whole story, as though she knew nothing about it!' he continued. 'Well, as the head-quarters of the legation seem to be here, I shall call every day to see the correspondence.'

The Countess smiled. She again searched in her bundle of letters and took out a second paper which she gave the Chevalier to read. This time he seemed much pleased. Then they renewed their conversation in whispers, the Chevalier's face once more wearing a respectful smile. Before he left the Countess, he kissed her hand.

'There! we've done with business,' he said in a low voice as he took his seat at the piano again.

Then he rattled off a vulgar air which was very popular in Paris that year. But having ascertained what time it was, he suddenly sprang up to get his hat.

'Are you going?' asked Clorinde. Then she beckoned him to her, and leaning on his shoulder whispered something into his ear. He nodded and smiled; and finally said: 'Capital, capital. I will write and mention it.'

At last he bowed to the company and retired. Luigi tapped Clorinde, who was squatting on the table, with his maul-stick, in order to make her stand up again. The Countess appeared to have grown tired of watching the stream of carriages in the avenue, for she pulled the bell-rope that hung behind her as soon as she lost sight of the Chevalier's brougham, which quickly disappeared among the crowd of landaus coming back from the Bois. It was the big lanky man-servant with the brigand's face who answered her summons, leaving the door wide open behind him. Leaning heavily on his arm, she slowly crossed the room, the men standing up and bowing as she passed. She acknowledged their salutations with a smiling nod. When she reached the door, she turned and said to Clorinde: 'I have got my headache again; I'm going to lie down a little.'

'Flaminio,' called the young girl to the servant who was assisting her mother, 'put a hot iron at her feet.'

The three political refugees did not sit down again. For a few moments they remained standing in a row, finishing their cigars, the stumps of which they then threw, each with the same precise gesture, behind the heap of dry clay. And afterwards they filed past Clorinde, going off in procession.

M. La Rouquette had just commenced a serious conversation with Rougon. 'Yes, indeed,' he remarked,' I know very well that this question of sugars is one of the greatest importance. It affects a whole branch of French commerce. But unfortunately nobody in the Chamber seems to have thoroughly studied the subject.'

Rougon, whom he bored, only answered with a nod. However, the young deputy drew closer to him, an expression of sudden gravity coming over his girlish face as he continued: 'I myself have an uncle in the sugar trade. He has one of the largest refining-houses at Marseilles. I went to stay with him for three months, and I took notes, very copious notes. I talked to the workmen and made myself conversant with the whole subject. I intended, you understand, to make a speech in the Chamber on the matter.'

In this wise he tried to show off before Rougon, giving himself a deal of trouble in order to talk to him on the only subjects which he thought would interest him; and, at the same time, being anxious to pass for a sound politician.

'And didn't you make a speech?' interposed Clorinde, who seemed to be growing impatient of M. La Rouquette's presence.

'No, I didn't,' he replied; 'I thought I'd better not. At the last moment I felt afraid that my figures might not be quite correct.'

Rougon eyed him keenly and then gravely asked him: 'Do you know how many pieces of sugar are consumed every day at the Café Anglais?'

For a moment La Rouquette seemed quite confused and stared at the other with a blank expression. Then he broke into a peal of laughter. 'Ah! very good! very good!' he cried. 'I understand now. You are chaffing me. But that's a question of sugar. What I was speaking about was a question of sugars. Very good that, eh? You'll let me repeat the joke, won't you?'

He wriggled on his chair with much self-satisfaction. The rosy hue came back to his cheeks and he seemed quite at his ease again, once more talking in his natural light manner. Clorinde attacked him on the subject of women. She had seen him, she said, two nights previously at the Variétés with a little fair person who was very plain and had hair like a poodle's. At first the young man denied the accusation; but, irritated by Clorinde's cruel remarks about the 'little poodle,' he at last forgot himself and began to defend her, saying that she was a highly respectable lady and not nearly so bad looking as Clorinde tried to make out. The girl, however, grew quite scathing, and finally M. La Rouquette cried out: 'She's expecting me now, and I must be off.'

As soon as he had closed the door behind him, Clorinde clapped her hands triumphantly, and exclaimed: 'There, he's gone at last. Good riddance to him.'

Then she jumped lightly from the table, ran up to Rougon, and gave him both her hands. Assuming her most winning look, she expressed her regret that he had not found her alone. What a lot of trouble she had had to get all those people to go! Some people couldn't understand anything! What a goose La Rouquette was with his sugars! Now, however, there was no one to disturb them, and they could talk. She had led Rougon to a couch as she was speaking, and he had sat down without releasing her hands, when Luigi began to tap his easel with his maul-stick, exclaiming in a tone of irritation: 'Clorinde! Clorinde!'

'Oh yes, of course, the portrait,' she cried, with a laugh.

Then she made her escape from Rougon, and bent down behind the artist with a soft caressing expression. How pretty his work looked, she cried. It was very good indeed; but, really, she felt rather tired and would much like a quarter of an hour's rest. He could go on with the dress in the meantime. There was no occasion for her to pose for the dress. Luigi, however, cast fiery glances at Rougon, and muttered disagreeable words. Thereupon Clorinde hastily said something to him in Italian, knitting her brows the while, though still continuing to smile. This reduced Luigi to silence, and he began to pass his brush over the canvas again.

'It's quite true what I say,' declared the girl as she came back and sat down beside Rougon; 'my left leg is quite numb.'

Then she slapped herself to make the blood circulate, she explained; and she was bending towards Rougon, her bare shoulder touching his coat, when she suddenly looked at herself and blushed deeply. And forthwith she sprang up and fetched a piece of black lace which she wrapped around her.

'I feel chilly,' she said, when she had wheeled an easy chair in front of Rougon and sat down in it.

Nothing but her bare wrists now peeped out from beneath her lace wrapper, which she had knotted round her neck. Her bust was completely concealed in its folds, and her face had turned pale and grave.

'Well, what is it that has happened to you?' she exclaimed. 'Tell me all about it.'

Then she questioned him about his fall from office with daughterly curiosity. She was a foreigner, she told him, and she made him again and again repeat certain details which she said she did not understand. She also kept on interrupting him with Italian ejaculations, and he could read in her dark eyes the interest she took in what he was telling her. Why had he quarrelled with the Emperor? How could he have brought himself to give up such a lofty position? Who were his enemies, that he should have allowed himself to be worsted in that way? And as he hesitated, unwilling to make the confessions which she tried to extort from him, she looked at him with an expression of such affectionate candour, that at last he threw off all reserve and told her the whole story from beginning to end. She soon seemed to have learnt all that she wanted to know, and then began to ask him questions quite unconnected with the matter which had first engaged her attention, questions so singular that Rougon was altogether surprised. But at last she clasped her hands and lapsed into silence. Closing her eyes she seemed buried in deep thought.

'Well?' said Rougon, with a smile.

'Oh, nothing,' she murmured, 'but this has made me quite sad.'

Rougon was touched, and tried to take hold of her hands again, but she hid them away in her lace wrapper, and they both sat there in silence for a minute or two, when she opened her eyes again and said: 'You have formed some plans, I suppose?'

Rougon looked at her keenly, with a touch of suspicion. But she seemed so adorable as she languidly reclined in that easy chair, as though the troubles of her 'dear friend' had broken her down, that he dismissed the chilling thought. Moreover, she plied him with flattery. She was sure, said she, that he would not long be allowed to remain aloof, but would be master again some day. She was confident that he had high ambitions and trusted hopefully in his star, for she could plainly read as much on his brow. Why wouldn't he take her for his confidante? She was very discreet, and it would make her so happy to share his hopes for the future. Rougon, quite infatuated by all this, and still trying to grasp the little hands hidden away beneath the lace, thereupon kept nothing back, but confessed everything to the girl, his hopes as well as his certainties. He required no further urging from her, and she had only to let him talk on, refraining even from a gesture for fear of checking him. She kept her eyes upon him, examining him searchingly limb by limb, fathoming his skull, weighing his shoulders and measuring his chest. He was certainly a solid, well-built man, who, with a turn of his wrist, could have tossed her, strong as she was, on to his back and have carried her without the least difficulty to whatever height she might have desired.

'Ah! my dear friend,' she exclaimed abruptly, 'it is not I who have ever felt any doubts.'

Then she sprang from her seat, and, spreading out her arms, let the lace wrapper slip off. A momentary all-alluring vision, a sort of promise and reward, appeared to Rougon.

'Ah!' she cried, 'my lace has fallen,' and quickly picking it up again, she knotted it round her more tightly than before.

'Oh!' she next exclaimed, 'there's Luigi growling.'

Then she hastened back to the artist, bent over him a second time and rapidly whispered to him. Rougon, now that she was no longer by his side, roughly rubbed his hands together, feeling almost angry. That girl had exercised a most extraordinary influence over him and he resented it. If he had been a lad of twenty he could not have acted more foolishly. She had wheedled him into a confession as though he had been a mere child; whereas he, for the last two months, had been doing his best to make her speak, but had only succeeded in extracting peals of laughter from her. She, however, had merely had to deny him her little hands for a moment, and he had foolishly forgotten all his prudence and told her everything in order to gain possession of them.

Nevertheless, Rougon smiled a smile of conscious strength. He could break her, he told himself, whenever he liked. Wasn't it she herself who was challenging him? He certainly could not go on playing the part of an imbecile with this girl who so freely showed him her shoulders. He was by no means sure that the lace wrapper had slipped off without her assistance.

'Would you say that my eyes were grey?' Clorinde now asked him, stepping towards him again.

He rose and looked at her quite closely, but she bore his inspection without even her eyelids quivering. However, when he stretched forth his hands, she gave him a tap. There was no occasion to touch her. She had become very cold, now. She wrapped herself yet more closely in her strip of lace, and her modesty seemed to take alarm at the least hole in it. In vain did Rougon joke and jest. She only covered herself the more, and even refused to sit down again.

'I prefer walking about a little,' she said; 'it stretches my legs.'

Then Rougon followed her and they paced the room together. He tried, in his turn, to extract a confession from her. As a rule, she could not be got to answer questions. Her conversation usually consisted of sudden starts and jumps, interspersed with ejaculations and snatches of stories which she never finished. When Rougon adroitly questioned her concerning the fortnight of the previous month which she and her mother had spent away from Paris, she started on an interminable string of anecdotes about her journeyings. She had been everywhere, to England, Spain, and Germany; and she had seen everything. Then she vented a series of trifling remarks upon food, and the fashions and the weather. Now and then she began some story, in which she herself figured with sundry well-known persons, whom she named; and, thereupon, Rougon listened attentively, hoping that she was at last going to make some real revelation; but she either turned the story off into some childish nonsense or stopped short and left it unfinished altogether. That day, as previously, he learnt absolutely nothing. Her face retained its impenetrable smile, and she remained full of secretive reserve amidst all her boisterous freedom. Rougon, quite confused by the different extraordinary stories he had heard of her, each of which gave the lie to the other, was utterly unable to determine whether he had before him a mere girl whose innocence extended even to foolishness, or a keenwitted woman who cunningly affected simplicity.

She was telling him of an adventure that had happened to her in a little town in Spain, and of the gallantry of a traveller who had given up his room to her, when she suddenly broke off and exclaimed: 'You mustn't go back to the Tuileries. Make yourself missed.'

'Thank you, Mademoiselle Machiavelli,' he replied, with a laugh.

She laughed louder than he did, but none the less she went on giving him excellent advice. However, as he still sportively tried to pinch her arms, she seemed to grow vexed and declared that it was impossible to talk to him seriously for a couple of minutes together. Ah! if she were a man, she said, she would know how to mount high. But men were so light-headed. 'Come now and tell me about your friends,' she continued, seating herself on the edge of the table, while Rougon remained standing in front of her.

59

Just then, however, Luigi, who had kept his eyes on them, violently closed his paint-box and exclaimed: 'I'm going!'

At this Clorinde ran up to him, and brought him back, after promising to resume her pose. Probably, however, her only motive in asking him to remain was that she felt afraid of being left alone with Rougon, for when Luigi had assented to her request, she began to make further excuses for the purpose of gaining time. 'Just let me get something to eat,' she said; 'I am dreadfully hungry. Just a couple of mouthfuls.' And then opening the door, she called out: 'Antonia! Antonia!'

She gave an order in Italian, and had just seated herself again on the edge of the table when Antonia came into the room, holding on each of her outspread hands, a slice of bread and butter. She held her hands out to Clorinde as though they had been plates, breaking into a giggle as she did so, a laugh which made her mouth look like a red gash across her dusky face. Then she went off, wiping her hands on her skirt. Clorinde, however, called her back and told her to get a glass of water.

'Will you have some?' she said to Rougon, 'I'm very fond of bread and butter. Sometimes I put sugar on it; but it doesn't always do to be so extravagant.'

She was certainly not given to extravagance, and Rougon remembered that he had found her one morning breakfasting off a fragment of cold omelet which had been left over from the previous day. He rather suspected her of avarice, which is an Italian vice.

'Three minutes, eh, Luigi?' she said, as she began her first slice of bread and butter. Then turning once more to Rougon, who was still standing in front of her, she exclaimed: 'Now there's Monsieur Kahn, for instance: tell me about him. How did he get to be a deputy?'

Rougon yielded to this fresh request, hoping that he would somehow be able to worm some information out of the girl. He knew that she was very curious about everyone, ever on the alert to gather information concerning the intrigues in the midst of which her life was passed. She always seemed particularly anxious to know the origin of any great fortune.

'Oh!' he replied, with a laugh, 'Kahn was born a deputy. He cut his teeth on the benches of the Chamber. As early as Louis Philippe's time he sat in the Right centre and supported the constitutional monarchy with youthful enthusiasm. After 1848 he went over to the Left centre, still keeping very enthusiastic. He made a confession of republican principles in magnificent style. Now, however, he has gone back to the Right centre and is a passionate supporter of the Empire. As for the rest, he's the son of a Jewish banker at Bordeaux. He has some blast furnaces at Bressuire, has made a specialty of financial and industrial questions, lives in a quiet way until he comes into the large fortune which he will one day secure, and was promoted to the rank of officer in the Legion of Honour on the fifteenth of last August—'

Rougon hesitated for a moment and seemed to be thinking. 'No,' he resumed, 'I don't think I have omitted anything. He has no children.'

'What! is he married?' exclaimed Clorinde, indicating by a gesture that she took no further interest in M. Kahn. He was an impostor: he had never let them know that he had a wife. Rougon thereupon explained to her that Madame Kahn led a very retired life in Paris; and without waiting to be questioned further, he continued: 'Would you like to hear Béjuin's biography?'

'No, no,' replied the girl.

All the same, however, he went on with it. 'He comes from the Polytechnical School. He has written pamphlets which nobody has read. He is head of the Saint-Florent cut-glass works, about seven or eight miles from Bourges. It was the prefect of the Cher who discovered him—'

'Oh, give over!' cried Clorinde.

'He is a very worthy fellow, votes straight, never speaks, is very patient and waits contentedly till you think of him, but he is always on the spot to take care that you sha'n't forget him. I got him named chevalier—'

Thereupon Clorinde impatiently placed her hand over Rougon's mouth, and exclaimed: 'Oh, he is married too! He isn't a bit interesting. I saw his wife at your house. She's a perfect bundle! She invited me to visit the works at Bourges.'

She now swallowed the last mouthful of her first slice of bread and butter, and then gulped down some water. 'And Monsieur Du Poizat?' she asked, after a pause.

'Du Poizat has been a sub-prefect,' was all that Rougon replied.

She glanced at him, surprised by the brevity of this account. 'I know that,' she said. 'What else?'

'Well, by-and-bye he will be a prefect, and then he will be decorated.'

She saw that he did not want to say anything further about Du Poizat; whose name, moreover, she herself had merely mentioned at random. However, she now began to mention other men, counting their names on her fingers. Touching her thumb, she began: 'Monsieur d'Escorailles; he's flippant and in love with every woman—Monsieur La Rouquette; he's no good, I know him only too well—Monsieur de Combelot; he's another married man—'

Then, as she stopped short at the ring-finger, unable to think of another name, Rougon, keeping his eyes on her, remarked: 'You are forgetting Delestang.'

'So I am!' she exclaimed. 'Tell me about him!'

'He's a handsome fellow,' said Rougon, still watching her attentively. 'He is very rich, and I have always prophesied a great future for him.'

He went on in this strain, exaggerating his praises and doubling his figures. The model-farm of La Chamade, said he, was worth a couple of million francs. Delestang would certainly be a minister some day. Clorinde, however, curled her lips disdainfully. 'He is a big booby,' she said at last.

'What?' cried Rougon with a subtle smile. He seemed quite charmed by her remark.

But with one of those sudden transitions which were habitual with her, she asked him a fresh question, keenly scrutinising him in her turn: 'You must know Monsieur de Marsy very well?'

'Oh yes, we know each other,' he replied unconcernedly, amused that the girl should have asked him such a question. Then he became serious, and showed himself very dignified and impartial. 'Marsy is a man of extraordinary intelligence,' he continued. 'I am honoured by having such a man for my enemy. He has filled every position. At twenty-eight years of age, he was a colonel. Later on, he was at the head of a great business. And since then, he has successively occupied himself with agriculture, finance and commerce. I hear, too, that he paints portraits and writes novels.'

Clorinde had grown thoughtful, and was forgetting her bread and butter. 'I was talking to him the other day,' she said in a low tone. 'He's perfect—a genuine queen's son.'

'In my estimation,' continued Rougon, 'it is his wit that spoils him. My idea of ability is quite different. I have heard him making puns under the gravest circumstances. Well, anyhow, he has been very successful, and is as much the sovereign as the Emperor himself. All these natural children[1] are lucky fellows. However, his greatest characteristic is his grip of iron; he has firm and resolute hands, though they are light and slender.'

Clorinde unconsciously let her eyes wander to Rougon's hands, so large and powerful. He noticed it, and with a smile continued: 'Ah, mine are mere paws, aren't they? That's why Marsy and I have never been able to get on well together. He gallantly sabres his foes without soiling his white gloves, while I knock mine down.'

Thereupon he clenched his heavy hairy fists and shook them, seemingly proud of their enormous size. Clorinde took up her second slice of bread and butter and dug her teeth into it, still absorbed in thought. At length she raised her eyes to Rougon's face. 'And now about yourself?' she asked.

'Ah, you want to hear my history, do you?' said he. 'Well, it's very easily told. My grandfather sold vegetables. I myself, till I was thirty-eight years of age, kicked up my heels as a country lawyer in the depths of the provinces. Yesterday I was unknown, for I haven't, like our friend Kahn, helped to back up every Government in turn, and I haven't come, like Béjuin, from the Polytechnical School. I can't boast of little Escorailles' fine name or poor Combelot's handsome face. I haven't even as good family connections as La Rouquette, who is indebted for his seat in the Chamber to his sister, the widow of General de Llorentz and now a lady-in-waiting. My father did not leave me five million francs gained in the wine trade, as Delestang's left him. I wasn't born on the steps of a throne, like Count de Marsy was, nor have I grown up tied to the apron-strings of a clever woman, under the favour of Talleyrand. No, I'm a self-made man; I've only my own hands—'

Then he clapped his hands together, laughing loudly, and turning what he had said into a joke. Finally he braced himself to his full height and looked as though he were crushing stones with his clenched fists. Clorinde gazed at him admiringly.

'I was nothing; I shall now be whatever I like,' he continued, as though he were speaking to himself and had forgotten the presence of others. 'I am a power. Those other fellows make me shrug my shoulders when they prate of their devotion to the Empire! Do they really care for it? Do they appreciate it? Wouldn't they conform to

[1] Morny (Marsy), it will be remembered, was the illegitimate son of Queen Hortense, the Emperor Napoléon's mother.—*Ed.*

all kinds of governments? For my own part, I have grown up with the Empire! I have made it, and it has made me! I was named a Chevalier of the Legion of Honour after the tenth of December, an officer in January 1851, a commander on the fifteenth of August 1854, and a grand officer three months ago. Under the Presidency, I was entrusted for a short time with the portfolio of Public Works; later on the Emperor gave me a mission to England, and since then I have entered the Council of State and the Senate—'

'And, to-morrow, what will you enter?' Clorinde interrupted with a laugh, by which she tried to conceal her ardent curiosity.

He stopped short and looked at her. 'You are very inquisitive, Mademoiselle Machiavelli,' he said.

Then Clorinde began to swing her legs more briskly, and there was an interval of silence. Rougon, seeing her absorbed in a fresh reverie, thought that a favourable moment had come for extorting a confession from her. 'Women—' he began.

But in a low tone she interrupted him, smiling at her own thoughts, with a vague expression in her eyes: 'Oh, women are quite different!'

This was all the confession she made. She finished her bread and butter and drained her glass of water. Then she leapt to her feet on the table, with a spring that testified to her adroitness as a horse-woman. 'Now, Luigi!' she cried.

For the last few minutes the artist, who had left his seat, had been impatiently gnawing his moustache while irritably walking up and down in front of Rougon and Clorinde. With a sigh, he now sat down again and took up his palette. The three minutes' grace which Clorinde had asked for had expanded into a quarter of an hour. Now, however, she was again standing on the table, still enveloped in her black lace. When she had set herself in the proper attitude, she uncovered herself with a light movement of the hand, and became a marble statue once more.

Fewer carriages were now rolling along the Champs Elysées, over which the declining sun cast a stream of hazy light, enveloping the trees in a ruddy haze that might almost have been taken for a coating of dust stirred up by the passing vehicles. Clorinde's shoulders gleamed as with sheeny gold in the light that fell through the lofty windows. The sky gradually became greyer.

'Is Monsieur de Marsy's intended marriage with the Wallachian princess settled yet?' asked the girl.

'Yes, I think so,' Rougon replied. 'She is very rich, and Marsy is always short of money. And they say, too, that he is madly in love with her.'

A spell of silence followed. Rougon stayed on, perfectly at his ease, without any further thought of going away. He was absorbed in meditation, and began to pace the room again. That Clorinde, he said to himself, was certainly a remarkably fascinating creature. He thought of her as though he had left her some time ago; and, as he walked up and down, with his eyes turned to the floor, his mind dwelt on dimly formulated, but very alluring thoughts, from which he derived a tender pleasure. He seemed, moreover, to be breathing some strangely perfumed atmosphere, and would have liked to throw himself upon one of the couches and drop off to sleep amidst that odorous air.

A sound of words suddenly recalled him to himself. A tall old man, whose entrance he had not observed, was kissing Clorinde on the brow, while the girl smilingly stooped over the edge of the table.

'Good-morning, my dear,' said the old gentleman. 'How pretty you look! You are exhibiting your charms, I see.' Then he gave a little snigger, and as Clorinde in confusion picked up her lace wrapper, he quickly added: 'No, no! You are very nice as you are! You needn't be afraid of us.'

Then he turned towards Rougon, whom he addressed as 'dear colleague,' as he shook his hand. 'I dandled her many a time on my knees, when she was a little thing,' he added. 'Ah! what a dazzling creature she is now!'

The new-comer was M. de Plouguern. He was seventy years of age. A representative of Finistère in the Chamber during the reign of Louis Philippe, he had been one of those Legitimist deputies who made the pilgrimage to Belgrave Square,[1] and he had resigned in consequence of the vote of censure then passed upon himself and his companions. Later on, after the Revolution of February 1848, he had manifested a sudden affection for the Republic, which he vigorously applauded from the benches of the Constituent Assembly. Now that the Emperor had granted him the well-earned refuge of the Senate, he was a Bonapartist. But he knew how to be a Bonapartist and a man of high birth and breeding at the same time.

---

[1] Charles X., the exiled king, was then living there.— *Ed.*

With all his great humility he occasionally indulged in a spice of opposition. Ingratitude amused him, and, though he was a sceptic to the backbone, he defended religion and family-life. He thought that he owed that much to his name, one of the most illustrious in Brittany. Accordingly every now and then he found the Empire immoral, and said so openly. He himself had lived a life of dissolute intrigue and elaborate pleasure-seeking, and stories were told even of his old age which set young men dreaming. It was during a journey in Italy that he had first met Countess Balbi, whose lover he had remained for nearly thirty years. After separations, which lasted sometimes for years, they would come together for a short time in some town where they happened to meet. According to some, Clorinde was his daughter; however, since the girl had grown up and had become a plump and pretty young woman, he asserted, while gazing at her with his still glistening eyes, that he had known her father well in former days. At the same time he treated her with considerable freedom as being an old friend. This tall, withered, scraggy old Plouguern bore some resemblance to Voltaire; and the likeness was the source of much secret pleasure to him.

'You don't look at my portrait, godfather,' Clorinde said to him all at once.

She called him godfather by reason of their intimacy. The old man stepped behind Luigi, and screwed up his eyes with the air of a connoisseur. 'Splendid!' he exclaimed.

Rougon also came up, and Clorinde herself jumped off the table to get a better view. All three of them were delighted. The picture was excellent, they said. The artist had already covered the entire canvas with a thin coating of pink and white and yellow, as pale as though it were a mere water-colour wash. The face was wreathed into a pretty dollish smile, the lips were curved into a bow, and the eyebrows symmetrically arched, while the cheeks glowed with soft vermilion. It was a Diana, fit for the lid of some box of sweetmeats.

'Oh, just look at that little freckle close to the eye!' cried Clorinde, clapping her hands in admiration: 'Luigi forgets nothing!'

Rougon, whom pictures generally wearied, was charmed. Just then he appreciated art, and in a tone of earnest conviction he pronounced this judgment: 'It is admirably drawn.'

'And the colouring is excellent,' added M. de Plouguern. 'Those shoulders look like real flesh. And what arms! But the dear child has really got the most wonderful arms! I admire that full roundness below the bend of the arm immensely; it is perfect.' Then, turning to the artist, he added: 'Pray accept my compliments, Monsieur Pozzo. I have already seen a picture of a woman bathing by you. But this portrait will certainly excel it. Why don't you exhibit? I knew a diplomatist who played marvellously well upon the violin, and yet it didn't prevent him from attaining great success in his profession.'

Luigi bowed, feeling highly flattered. The daylight was now fast waning, and so, saying that he wished to finish an ear, he begged Clorinde to resume her position for another ten minutes. Meantime, M. de Plouguern and Rougon went on discussing art. The latter confessed that his special studies had prevented him from following the artistic movement of recent years, but he expressed great admiration for fine productions. He went on to say that he was not much affected by colour, but preferred good drawing—drawing which was capable of elevating the soul and inspiring it with great thoughts. M. de Plouguern, on his side, only cared about the old masters. He had visited all the galleries in Europe, and could not understand, said he, how the moderns had the hardihood to go on painting. All the same, he confessed that only the previous month he had had a little room of his decorated by an artist who was quite unknown, but who certainly possessed great genius.

'He has painted me some little cupids and flowers and foliage with extraordinary skill. You might positively think you could pluck the flowers. And there are some insects on them, butterflies, cock-chafers, and flies, which you could almost swear were alive. It is very amusing. I like amusing pictures.'

'Art should not weary one,' retorted Rougon.

Just at this moment, as they were slowly pacing the room side by side, one of M. de Plouguern's boot-heels crushed something which gave out a sharp sound. 'Hallo! What's that?' he cried.

Then he picked up a chaplet, which had slipped off an arm-chair into which Clorinde had doubtless emptied her pockets. One of the glass beads near the cross had been shivered to atoms, and an arm of the cross itself, a very small silver one, was bent and flattened. The old man dangled the chaplet in his hand, and said with a slight snigger: 'My dear, why do you leave these playthings of yours lying about?'

Clorinde, however, had turned quite crimson. She sprang off the table, with swollen lips, and tears of anger welling into her eyes, and, as she rapidly covered up her shoulders, she stammered: 'Oh, the wretch! the wretch! he has broken my chaplet!'

She snatched it from him, and then burst into sobs like a child.

'There! there!' said M. de Plouguern, still laughing. 'Just look at my little devotee! The other day she nearly tore my eyes out because I noticed a branch of palm over her bed and asked her what she used that little besom for. There now, don't cry, you great goose! I haven't broken your Divinity.'

'Yes, yes,' she cried,' you have injured it.' With trembling hands she removed the fragments of the bead, and then, with a fresh outburst of sobs, she tried to put the cross right again. She wiped it with her finger tips, as though she saw drops of blood oozing through the metal.

'It was the Pope who gave me this,' she sobbed, 'the first time I went with mother to see him. He knows me very well, and he calls me his "fair apostle," because I told him one day that I should be glad to die for him. It was a chaplet that brought me good luck. But now it has lost its virtue, and it will attract the devil—'

'Here, give it to me!' interrupted M. de Plouguern, 'you will only break your nails by trying to straighten it. Silver is hard, my dear.'

He took the chaplet from her and tried to straighten the arm of the cross, using great care so as not to break it. Clorinde had ceased crying, and watched him attentively. Rougon, too, smilingly craned his head forward. He was deplorably irreligious; so much so, indeed, that the girl had twice all but broken with him on account of his ill-considered pleasantries.

'The deuce!' muttered M. de Plouguern, 'this divinity of yours isn't very tender! I'm afraid of snapping it in two, and then you would have to get another one.'

He made a fresh attempt and this time the arm of the cross broke off. 'Oh! so much the worse!' he cried; 'it is broken this time.'

At this Rougon began to laugh again. But Clorinde, with angry eyes and convulsed face, sprang back glaring at them, and then fell upon them furiously with her fists, as though she wished to drive them out of the room. She railed at them in Italian, quite beside herself.

'She's giving it us! she's giving it us!' cried M. de Plouguern gaily.

'Such are the fruits of superstition,' muttered Rougon between his teeth.

The old man ceased his jesting and suddenly assumed a grave expression; and then as Rougon continued to declaim in conventional phraseology against the detestable influence of the priesthood, the shocking training of Catholic women, and the degradation of priest-ridden Italy, the other drily exclaimed: 'Religion makes the greatness of states.'

'When it doesn't eat them away like an ulcer,' replied Rougon. 'It's matter of history. If the Emperor doesn't keep the Bishops in check, he will soon have them all on his back.'

Thereupon M. de Plouguern in his turn grew angry. He defended Rome, and talked of what had been the convictions of his whole life. Without religion, he protested, men would return to the condition of brutes. Then he went on to plead the great cause of family ties. The times were becoming full of abomination. Never before had vice been so impudently paraded; never before had impiety worked such woe in men's consciences.

'Don't talk to me of your Empire!' he ended by crying; 'it is the bastard son of the Revolution. Oh! we are quite aware that your Empire dreams of humiliating the Church. But we are wide-awake, and we shall not allow ourselves to be slaughtered like mere sheep. Just try to ventilate those doctrines of yours in the Senate, my dear Monsieur Rougon.'

'Oh, don't talk to him any more,' retorted Clorinde. 'If you push him too far, he will spit on the crucifix. He is doomed.'

Rougon bowed, quite overcome by this onset. Then there was a fresh pause, while the girl searched on the floor for the arm that had fallen from the cross. When she had found it, she carefully wrapt it with the chaplet in a piece of newspaper. She was growing calmer.

'Ah now, my dear!' M. de Plouguern suddenly exclaimed, 'I haven't told you why I came to see you. I have got a box at the Palais Royal for this evening, and I'm going to take you and your mother with me.'

'Oh, you dear godfather!' cried Clorinde, turning quite rosy again with pleasure. 'I'll send to have mother awakened.'

Then she gave the old man a kiss, by way of reward, she said; and afterwards turning to Rougon with a smile, and, offering her hand, she said with the sweetest little pout: 'You don't bear me a grudge, do you? Please don't make me angry again with your pagan talk. I lose my head when anyone makes fun of religion: I should quarrel with my best friends over it.'

Luigi had by this time pushed his easel into a corner, having lost all hope of getting the ear finished that day. He took up his hat, and tapped the girl on the shoulder to apprize her of his departure. She accompanied him on to the landing, closing the door behind her as she left the room. However, they took leave of one another very noisily, for a slight scream of Clorinde's rang out, drowned in a burst of smothered laughter. When she returned to the room, she said: 'I'll go to dress now, unless my godfather would like to take me to the Palais Royal as I am.'

They all laughed at the notion. It was now dusk. When Rougon took his leave, Clorinde went downstairs with him, leaving M. de Plouguern by himself while she went to dress. It was already dark on the staircase as Clorinde descended it in front of Rougon without speaking a word, and so slowly that he felt the rustle of her gauze costume. When she reached the door of her bedroom she took a step or two forward before turning round. Rougon had followed her to the threshold. 'You won't bear me a grudge, will you?' she repeated in a low tone, again offering him her hands.

He assured her that he would not; but as he once more took hold of her hands his grip was so rough, so threatening almost, that Clorinde made all haste to escape from him, and while he stood panting there he heard her calling through an inner door which had been left open: 'Antonia, bring a light and get me my grey dress.'

When Rougon reached the avenue of the Champs Elysées he felt dazed, and stood still for a moment to inhale the fresh breeze which was blowing down from the Arc de Triomphe. The gas-lamps of the avenue, where now not a vehicle remained, were being lighted one by one, spangling the darkness with a trail of vivid sparks. Rougon felt as if he had just had an apoplectic fit, and rubbed his face with his hands.

'Ah, no!' he suddenly exclaimed aloud, 'no, no—it would be too foolish!'

IV

AN IMPERIAL CHRISTENING

THE baptismal procession was to start from the Pavilion de l'Horloge—the central pavilion of the Tuileries palace—at five o'clock. It was to wend its way along the main avenue of the Tuileries gardens, the Place de la Concorde, the Rue de Rivoli, the Place de l'Hôtel de Ville, the Arcole bridge, the Rue d'Arcole and the Place du Parvis.

By four o'clock there was an immense crowd assembled near the Arcole bridge. There, in the breach which the river made in the midst of the city, a whole people could find accommodation. The view expanded, with the Ile Saint Louis in the distance barred by the black line of the Louis-Philippe bridge. The narrow arm of the Seine on the left vanished amid a mass of low buildings; while the broader one on the right afforded a far-reaching prospect bathed in purplish vapour, through which the trees of the Port aux Vins showed in a green patch. On both sides of the river, from the Quai Saint Paul to the Quai de la Mégisserie, from the Quai Napoléon to the Quai de l'Horloge, were long foot-pavements and roadways; while, in front of the bridge, the Place de l'Hôtel de Ville afforded a large, open, level space. And over all the wide expanse, the sky, a bright, warm June sky, spread a vault of blue.

When the half hour struck, there were people everywhere. All along the footways endless lines of eager spectators were pressed against the quay parapets. A sea of human heads, which was continually surging, filled the Place de l'Hôtel de Ville. Opposite, in the dark gaps of the open windows of the old houses on the Quai Napoléon, faces were thickly crowding, and even in the gloomy alleys leading to the river, the Rue Colombe, the Rue Saint Landry and the Rue Glatigny, women's caps, with ribbons streaming in the breeze, could be seen leaning forward. The bridge of Notre Dame displayed a serried row of sight-seers, whose elbows rested on the stone parapet, as on the balustrade of some colossal balcony. Further down, the Louis Philippe bridge swarmed with little black figures; and even the most distant windows streaking the grey and yellow house-fronts were every now and then brightened by some gay dress. There were men on the roofs among the chimney stacks.

People, who could not be distinguished, were looking through telescopes from their terraces on the Quai de la Tournelle. And the sunlight spreading over all seemed like the very quiver of the crowd; it bore afar the laughter of those surging heads, while gay, mirror-like parasols reflected the glow, showing as planets amidst all the medley of skirts and coats.

But there was one thing that was visible from every side, from the quays and bridges and windows, and that was a fresco painting of a colossal grey overcoat on the blank wall of a six-storeyed house on the isle of St. Louis. The sleeve of this coat was bent at the elbow as though the garment still retained the shape and attitude of a body that had disappeared from within it. In the bright sunshine, above all the swarming sight-seers, this gigantic advertisement presented a most conspicuous appearance.[1]

A double line of troops kept the roadway clear for the procession. National Guards were drawn up on the right hand, and infantrymen of the Line on the left. At one end, this military cordon expended to the Rue d'Arcole, which was gaudy with banners, while from the windows hung costly draperies which flapped languidly against the dingy house-fronts. The bridge, to which the crowd had not been admitted, was the only clear spot amidst the general invasion, and it presented a strange appearance, thus deserted. But, lower down, on the river banks, the crowding began again. Shopkeepers in Sunday clothes had spread out their pocket-handkerchiefs and seated themselves beside their wives to rest after a whole afternoon of lounging idleness. On the other side of the bridge, where the river expanded, showing a deep blue shot with green just where its arms united, there were some boatmen in red jackets who were working their oars to keep their boat on a level with the Port aux Fruits. By the Quai de Gèvres, too, there was a floating laundry, with wooden walls green with moisture, in which washerwomen could be heard laughing and beating their clothes. And all the teeming sight-seers, numbering from three to four hundred thousand people, now and again raised their heads to glance at the towers of Notre Dame which rose up square and massive above the houses of the Quai Napoléon. Gilded by the declining sun, so that they looked ruddy

---

[1] The idea of this clothier's advertisement—*La Redingote grise*—was derived from the circumstance that Napoléon I. wore a grey overcoat, like the one depicted, during his last campaigns.—*Ed.*

against the clear sky, the towers resounded with the clanging peals of their bells, which sent a quiver through the atmosphere.

Three or four false alarms had already caused a great deal of jostling in the crowd.

'I tell you that they won't pass before half-past five,' said a tall fellow who was sitting in front of a café on the Quai de Gèvres with M. and Madame Charbonnel.

It was Gilquin, Théodore Gilquin, Madame Mélanie Correur's old lodger, and Rougon's redoubtable friend. He was dressed that day in a complete suit of yellow duck, a cheap ready-made line, stained and creased, and here and there unsewn at the seams. His boots, too, were split, and his straw hat lacked a ribbon. However, he wore tan coloured gloves, and for that reason considered that he was in full dress. He had been acting since noon as a guide to the Charbonnels, whose acquaintance he had made one evening in the kitchen at Rougon's house.

'You shall see everything, my children,' he said to them, as he brushed aside the long black moustaches which swept across his tipsy-looking face. 'You have put yourselves in my hands, haven't you? Very well, then let me manage our little holiday.'

Gilquin had already drunk three nips of brandy and five glasses of beer. For the last two hours he had been keeping the Charbonnels prisoners at the café, whither he had brought them, on the pretext that it was absolutely necessary to be in good time. It was a little café with which he was well acquainted, and where they would be very comfortable, he assured them, and he seemed to be on most familiar terms with the waiter. The Charbonnels had resigned themselves to their fate, and listened to his talk, feeling much surprised at its abundance and variety. Madame Charbonnel had declined to take anything beyond a glass of *eau sucrée,* and M. Charbonnel had ordered for himself a glass of anisette, such as he occasionally indulged in at the Commercial Club at Plassans. Meanwhile Gilquin discoursed to them about the Baptism as explicitly as though he had spent the morning at the Tuileries for the purpose of acquiring information.

'The Empress is in very high spirits,' he said. 'She got over her delivery splendidly. She's a fine woman! You will see by-and-bye what a figure she has. The Emperor got back from Nantes on the day before yesterday. He went there on account of the floods. What a dreadful calamity those floods are!'

Madame Charbonnel pushed her chair back. She was beginning to feel rather afraid of the crowd which was streaming past her in increasing numbers. 'What a lot of people!' she muttered.

'Yes, indeed,' cried Gilquin, 'I should think so. There are more than three hundred thousand visitors in Paris. Excursion trains have been bringing them here for the last week from all parts of the country. See, over yonder there are some people from Normandy, and there are some from Gascony, and some from Franche-Comté. I can spot them at once; I've knocked about a good deal in my time.'

He next told them that the courts and the Bourse were closed, and that all the clerks in the government offices had got a holiday. The whole capital was holding festival in honour of the Baptism. Then he began to quote figures, and calculate what the ceremony and rejoicings would cost. The Corps Législatif had voted 400,000 francs, but that was a mere nothing, for a groom at the Tuileries had informed him that the procession alone would cost nearly 200,000. If the Emperor got off with a million from the civil list, he might think himself lucky. The layette alone had cost 100,000 francs.

'What, 100,000 francs!' cried Madame Charbonnel in amazement. 'Why, how can they have possibly spent all that? What can it have gone in?'

Gilquin laughed as he told her that some laces cost an enormous sum. He himself had travelled in the lace business in former days. Then he went on with his calculations: 50,000 francs had gone to the parents of children who had been born on the same day as the little prince, and of whom the Emperor and Empress had expressed their intention to be godfather and godmother respectively. Then 85,000 francs were to be spent in purchasing medals for the authors of the cantatas which were sung at the theatres. Finally, there were 120,000 commemorative medals distributed among the collegians, the pupils of the primary schools and asylums and the non-commissioned officers and privates of the army of Paris. He had got one of those medals himself, and showed it to them. It was about the size of a half-franc piece, and bore on one side the profiles of the Emperor and Empress, and on the other that of the Prince Impérial, with the date of the latter's baptism, namely, June 14, 1856.

'Would you mind selling it me?' M. Charbonnel inquired of Gilquin.

The other expressed his willingness to do so, but as Charbonnel, embarrassed as to what he should offer for it, handed him a twenty-sous-piece, he declined it, saying that the medal was not worth more than ten sous. Madame Charbonnel, meanwhile, was gazing at the profiles of the imperial couple, and seemed quite affected by emotion: 'How good they look!' she said. 'There they are, side by side, like an affectionate pair. See, Monsieur Charbonnel, you would say two heads lying on the same pillow when you look at them this way.'

Then Gilquin returned to the subject of the Empress, of whose charitable disposition he spoke in the most laudatory terms. But a short time before her delivery she had devoted whole afternoons to furthering the establishment of an educational institute for poor girls in the Faubourg Saint Antoine. Moreover, she had just refused to accept an offering of 80,000 francs which had been collected in sums of five sous amongst the poorer classes for the purpose of buying a present for the young prince; and by her express desire the money was to be devoted to the apprenticing of a hundred poor orphans. Gilquin, who was already somewhat tipsy, twisted his eyes about in the most dreadful manner as he sought for tender phrases and expressions which should combine the respect of the subject with the passionate admiration of the man. He declared that he would gladly offer up his life in sacrifice at the feet of that noble woman. And nobody protested against this. The murmur of the crowd seemed indeed like a distant echo of his praises. It was now growing into a continuous clamour, while over the house-tops from the bells of Notre Dame rolled peal on peal of clanging, tumultuous joy.

'Don't you think it time for us to go and take our places?' timidly suggested M. Charbonnel, who felt tired of sitting still.

At this Madame Charbonnel rose up and fastened her yellow shawl about her neck. 'Yes, I'm sure it is,' she said. 'You wanted to be there in good time, and we're sitting here and letting everyone go past us.'

Gilquin, however, became indignant; and, with an oath, brought his fist down on the little zinc table. Didn't he know all about Paris? he asked; and then, as Madame Charbonnel timidly dropped upon her chair again, he cried to the waiter: 'Jules, a glass of absinthe and some cigars!'

But as soon as he had dipped his big moustaches in the absinthe, he angrily called the waiter back again. 'Are you having a game with me? Just take this filth away, and give me some out of the other bottle; the same as I had on Friday. I have travelled in the liquor-trade, my fine fellow. You can't bamboozle me.'

He calmed down, however, when the waiter, who seemed afraid of him, had brought the other bottle, and then he tapped the Charbonnels on the shoulders, and called them 'old fellow' and 'old lady.' 'Ah! so you're itching to be on the move, are you, old lady?' said he. 'You'll have plenty of use for your feet between now and to-night, so you needn't be in a hurry. We're very comfortable at this café; don't you think so, old fellow? We can take our ease and watch the people go by. We've plenty of time, I assure you, so you'd better order something else.'

'Thank you, we've had all that we want,' said M. Charbonnel.

Gilquin had just lighted a cigar. He leaned back in his chair, inserted his thumbs in the arm-holes of his waistcoat, thrust out his chest, and began to rock himself backwards and forwards. His eyes glowed with an expression of perfect content. Suddenly an idea seemed to strike him. 'I'll tell you what,' he cried; 'I'll call for you at seven o'clock to-morrow morning, and take you off with me and show you all the festivities. We'll have a splendid day of it.'

The Charbonnels looked at each other very uneasily. But Gilquin proceeded to explain his programme after the manner of a strolling showman. In the morning they would lunch at the Palais Royal, and walk about the city. In the afternoon they would go to the Esplanade of the Invalides, where there would be military performances, greasy poles, three hundred balloons laden with packets of sweets, and one large balloon raining down sugared almonds. In the evening they would dine at a wineshop which he knew of, on the Quai de Billy; then they would see the fireworks, the principal set-piece of which would represent a baptistery, and afterwards they could stroll among the illuminations. And he also told them of a fiery cross which was to be fixed on the Hôtel de la Legion d'Honneur; of a fairy palace on the Place de la Concorde, in the building of which 950,000 pieces of coloured glass had been used; and of the image atop of the tower of Saint Jacques, which would look like a blazing torch in midair.

As the Charbonnels still hesitated, however, he leaned towards them and added in lower tones: 'And then, as we come back, we might look in at a creamery in the Hue de Seine where they give you such stunning onion soup with cheese.'

At this the Charbonnels no longer dared to refuse. Childish curiosity and alarm mingled in the expression of their dilated eyes. They felt that they could not escape from that terrible man, and

must do whatever he told them. Madame Charbonnel simply murmured: 'Oh! this Paris! this Paris! Well, well, since we are here,
I suppose we must see all that there is to be seen. But if you only
knew, Monsieur Gilquin, how quiet we were at Plassans! I have
a store-room full of preserves and brandied cherries and pickles
which are all mouldering away!'

'Don't alarm yourself, old lady,' replied Gilquin, who was growing more and more familiar; 'when you gain your case, you can ask
me to come and stay with you, and then we'll all have a go at the
jam-pots!'

So saying, he poured himself out another glass of absinthe. He
was now perfectly tipsy. For a moment he looked at the Charbonnels with loving affection; but, all at once, he sprang to his feet and
waved his long arms while calling: 'Eh! eh! Hallo! you there!'

Madame Mélanie Correur, arrayed in a dress of dove-coloured
silk, was just then passing on the opposite footwalk. She turned her
head and seemed extremely annoyed at seeing Gilquin. However,
she crossed over with the majestic gait of a princess, but on reaching the table required a deal of pressing before she would accept
any refreshment.

'Come now,' cried Gilquin, 'have a little glass of blackcurrant
brandy. I know you like it. You haven't forgotten the Rue Vanneau,
eh? We used to have fine times then, didn't we? Ah! that big old
stupid of a Correur!'

Just as Madame Correur was at last sitting down, a loud shouting was heard among the crowd. The promenaders scuttled off like
sheep, as though swept along by a gust of wind. The Charbonnels
had instinctively risen with the idea of following the others, but
Gilquin's heavy hand brought them to their chairs again. His face
was quite purple.'

'Just keep still and wait for orders, will you?' said he. 'Those
folks are making fools of themselves. It is only five o'clock, isn't
it? Well, then, it's the Cardinal-Legate who's coming; and we don't
want to see the Cardinal-Legate, do we? For my part, I think it's
very neglectful of the Pope not to have come himself. When a man
is a godfather he ought to behave as such, it seems to me. However,
I tell you that the youngster won't be here for another half-hour.'

His intoxication was rapidly depriving him of all sense of decorum. He had cocked his chair back and begun to smoke in people's
faces, winking the while at the women and glaring defiantly at the

men. A few yards away, near the bridge of Notre Dame, there was
now a block in the road traffic. Horses were pawing the ground with
impatience, and the uniforms of high functionaries and officers, embroidered with gold and glittering with decorations, appeared at the
windows of the passing carriages.

'There's a nice show of tinsel and pewter!' sneered Gilquin, with
the smile of a man who cares nothing for gewgaws.

However, as a brougham came along from the Quai de la Mégisserie, he almost upset the table as he sprang up and cried: 'Hallo,
Rougon!'

He saluted the great man with his gloved hand, and then, fearing that he had not been recognised, snatched off his straw hat and
began to wave it. At this, Rougon, whose senatorial uniform was
attracting a deal of notice, quickly withdrew to a corner of his
brougham. And thereupon Gilquin began to call him, raising his
hand to his mouth and using it as a speaking-trumpet. The people on
the footway stopped and turned to see what was the matter with this
strange-looking fellow dressed in yellow duck. At last, however, the
coachman was able to urge his horse forward, and the brougham
turned on to the bridge of Notre Dame.

'Do be quiet!' said Madame Correur in a low voice, while catching hold of Gilquin's arms.

But he would not at once sit down again. He remained on tip-
toes, watching the brougham as it mingled with the other carriages,
and at last he hurled a parting shout after the fleeing wheels: 'Ah!
the turn-tail! just because he wears gold lace on his coat now! All
the same, my fat fellow, you were deucedly hard up once upon a
time!'

Some middle-class citizens and their wives who were sitting at
the seven or eight tables of the little café heard this and opened their
eyes in astonishment. At one table there was a family, consisting of
the father and mother and three children, who seemed profoundly
interested in Gilquin's proceedings. The latter puffed himself out,
quite delighted to find that he had an audience. He let his eyes
travel round the customers of the café, and said in a loud voice as he
dropped into his seat again: 'Rougon! why it was I who made him
what he is!'

Then turning to Madame Correur, who was trying to quiet him,
he appealed to her for corroboration. She knew that he was speaking
the truth, he proclaimed. It had all happened at the Hôtel Vanneau in

the Rue Vanneau. She surely wouldn't deny that he had lent Rougon his boots a score of times to enable him to go to the houses of highly-placed people and mix in a lot of mysterious goings-on. Why, in those days Rougon only possessed an old pair of split shoes, which a rag-picker wouldn't have taken as a gift. Then with a triumphant air Gilquin bent towards the family at the next table, and exclaimed: 'Oh, she won't confess it, but it was she who paid for his first pair of new boots in Paris.'

Madame Correur, however, turned her chair round, so that she might no longer seem to be one of Gilquin's party. The Charbonnels had become quite pale at hearing the man who was to put half a million francs in their pockets spoken of in such a fashion. Gilquin, however, was wound up, and rattled off innumerable stories of Rougon's early days. He, Gilquin, claimed to be a philosopher, and he began to laugh, and accosted the parties at the different tables one after another, smoking, spitting, and drinking, while telling them that he was quite accustomed to the ingratitude of mankind, and was satisfied with preserving his own self-respect. And he repeated that he himself had been the making of Rougon. At that time, he said, he had been a traveller in the perfumery line, but the Republic was bad for trade. Both he and Rougon had been living on the same floor in a state of starvation. Then he was struck with the idea of getting Rougon to send for some olive-oil from a producer at Plassans, and they had both wandered about Paris in different directions till ten o'clock at night with samples of olive-oil in their pockets. Rougon was not clever at the business, but he occasionally succeeded in getting some good orders from the fine folks to whose houses he went in the evenings.

Ah! that rascal Rougon, he was a bigger booby than a goose in most things, yet all the same he was very cunning. A little later, how he had made him, Gilquin, run about to further his politics! Here Gilquin lowered his voice a little and winked, and let them know that he himself had belonged to the Bonapartist band. He had haunted the low dancing-rooms crying out 'Long live the Republic'; for it was necessary to profess Republicanism to get influence over the people. The Empire certainly owed him a big debt for what he had done; but it hadn't even thanked him. No, while Rougon and his clique shared all the prizes, he was turned out of doors like a mangy dog. Well, on the whole, he preferred that it should be so, he would rather remain independent. He had only one regret now, and that was that he had not stuck to the Republicans and made an end of all this scum with his musket.

'It's just the same, too, with little Du Poizat,' he said in conclusion. 'He pretends not to know me now; a skinny little beggar to whom I've often given a pipe of tobacco! And yet he's a sub-prefect now! Why I've often seen him with big Amélie, who used to box his ears and kick him outside the door when he didn't behave properly.'

After this he became silent for a moment as if overcome by tender recollections amidst his maudlin fit. Then, glancing round at his audience, he began again.

'Well, you've just seen Rougon. I'm as tall a man as he is, and I'm the same age, and I flatter myself that I've got a better looking head on my shoulders. Well, now, don't you think that it would be much better for everyone if I were in that carriage instead of that great fat pig, with his body covered all over with gold lace?'

However, just at this moment such a shouting arose on the Place de l'Hôtel de Ville, that the people at the café became much too excited to reply. The crowd made another rush; men's legs flew along, while women caught up their petticoats to enable themselves to run the faster. As the shouting came nearer and grew more distinct, Gilquin cried out:

'Ah! here comes the youngster! Hurry up and pay the score, old man, and then follow me all of you!'

Madame Correur grasped his yellow duck coat so as not to lose him, and Madame Charbonnel panted along close behind, while her husband was almost lost in the crowd. Gilquin, by much resolute pushing, managed to open a passage through the dense throng, making such a show of authority that people drew back even at the most crowded parts. When he at last reached the quay, he lifted the ladies with an effort, and seated them on the parapet, with their legs dangling over, on the water side, and this in spite of their little shrieks of alarm. He himself and M. Charbonnel remained standing behind.

'Well, my little dears, you're in the front boxes now,' he said, to reassure the women; 'don't be frightened, we'll take hold of your waists.'

Thereupon he slipped both arms round Madame Correur's plump figure. She smiled at him. It was impossible to get angry with such a jovial fellow. As yet, however, they could see nothing. The

Place de l'Hôtel de Ville was full of surging heads, and echoed with continuous cheering. Hats were waving in the distance, held aloft by hands which were indistinguishable, and forming a huge black billow which slowly rolled nearer and nearer. Then the occupants of the houses on the Quai Napoléon, which fronted the Place, began to show signs of excitement. They leant out of the windows, crowding against each other, with beaming faces, and arms outstretched to call attention to something in the direction of the Rue de Rivoli. For three minutes, which seemed very long, however, the bridge still remained empty. The bells of Notre Dame were ringing louder than ever, as though in some wild fit of joyful excitement.

Suddenly the anxious multitude beheld a company of trumpeters upon the empty bridge. There was a great sigh of expectation. Behind the trumpeters and the mounted band which followed them, came a general, escorted by his staff. Then, behind squadrons of carabineers, dragoons and hussars, followed the state-carriages. There were eight of them, each drawn by six horses. In those that came first sat the ladies-in-waiting, the chamberlains, the officers of the household of the Emperor and Empress, and the ladies in attendance upon the Grand Duchess of Baden, who had been deputed to represent the young prince's godmother. Gilquin, without letting go his hold of Madame Correur, told her from behind that the godmother, the Queen of Sweden, had not put herself out any more than the godfather had done. Then, as the seventh and eighth carriages went past, he told her the names of those who occupied them, with a glibness which bespoke great familiarity with court matters. Those two ladies, he said, were the Princess Mathilde and the Princess Marie. Those three gentlemen were King Jérôme, Prince Napoléon and the Crown Prince of Sweden. The lady with them was the Grand Duchess of Baden. Meanwhile, the procession swept on slowly. The equerries and aides-de-camp and gentlemen-in-waiting all rode with short reins to keep their horses at a walk.

'But where is the baby?' asked Madame Charbonnel impatiently.

'Oh! don't be frightened,' said Gilquin, with a laugh; 'they haven't put him under a seat. Wait a little and you'll see him.'

So saying, he tightened his grasp round Madame Correur, who allowed him to do so, she explained, because she was afraid of slipping into the water. Then, growing enthusiastic over the display, he continued, while his eyes glistened brightly: 'Isn't it really splendid? See how they take their ease, the rascals, in their satin-quilted coaches! And to think that I worked for all this!'

Then he began to puff himself out as though the procession, the crowd and everything that was to be seen owed their origin to him. However, after the temporary lull, caused by the appearance of the first carriages, there came a tremendous uproar. It was upon the quay itself now that hats were waving over the surging heads of the crowd. Six imperial outriders, wearing green liveries and round caps, from which dangled large gold tassels, had made their appearance on the bridge. Then at last the Empress's carriage came in sight. It was drawn by eight horses; and at each of its four corners there was a magnificent lamp. Large and rounded, panelled almost entirely with glass, this coach resembled a huge crystal casket with gold settings, mounted upon golden wheels. Inside it, amidst a cloud of snowy lace, one could clearly distinguish the rosy face of the Prince Impérial, carried upon the knees of the Governess of the Children of France, by whose side sat the wet nurse, a young, handsome, and buxom Burgundian. Then a short distance behind, following a group of mounted equerries and grooms on foot, came the Emperor's carriage, which also was drawn by eight horses, and was as magnificent as the previous one. In it sat the Emperor and Empress, who bowed to the people as they passed. Beside these two last carriages rode several marshals of France, who, without sign of impatience, let all the dust from the wheels settle on their richly broidered uniforms.

'Just fancy if the bridge were to break down!' exclaimed Gilquin with a grin. He was fond of indulging in the most awful suppositions.

Madame Correur, frightened at the thought of such a thing, tried to stop him, but he would dwell on the subject, remarking that iron bridges were never safe. He even asserted that he could see the platform oscillating when the two carriages were but half-way across. What a splash, he continued; if papa and mamma and baby went down they would get such a drink as would keep them from ever wanting another! The carriages, however, rolled softly and silently over the bridge, and the frame-work of the gently-curving arch was so light that they looked almost as though suspended in space over the river, in whose blue depths they were reflected like strange gold-fishes, carried up by the flow of the tide. The Emperor and Empress, feeling a little tired, leaned back against the buttoned satin, glad to escape the crowd for a moment and the necessity of bowing to it. The Governess, too, took advantage of the stretch of empty space to raise the little prince, who was slipping from her knees, while the nurse, leaning forward, amused him with a smile. The whole procession was steeped in bright sunshine. The uniforms, the gay gowns, and the horse-trappings shone out brilliantly, while the sparkling planet-like coaches cast tremulous beams of reflected sunlight along the fronts of the dingy houses on the Quai Napoléon. In the distance, above the bridge, the colossal advertisement of the giant grey overcoat, painted on the wall of a six-storeyed house, and now illumined with radiant splendour by the sun, formed a sort of background to the magnificent picture.

Gilquin noticed the overcoat just as it towered above the two carriages. 'Look!' he cried, 'there's the uncle[1] over yonder!'

A laugh ran through the surrounding crowd. M. Charbonnel, who did not catch the point, wanted to have it explained to him, but his request was drowned by the deafening cheering and clapping of hands that arose from the three hundred thousand people there pressed together. A mighty thrill of enthusiasm had sped through the mass of sight-seers as the little prince, followed by the Emperor and Empress, came into sight on the middle of the bridge, of which they had a full, unbroken view. Men rose on tiptoe, and set their dazed youngsters astride their necks, while women wept or stammered out expressions of love for 'the little darling,' showing a heartfelt sympathy with the happiness of the imperial parents. A storm of shouts still rolled on from the Place de l'Hôtel de Ville; and upon the quays, both up and down the river, there was a forest of waving, outstretched arms. Handkerchiefs fluttered from the windows, and men and women craned forward with glistening eyes and gaping mouths. Away in the distance the windows of the Ile Saint Louis, which looked like narrow streaks of charcoal, were lighted up with white gleams and evidences of life too far away to be clearly distinguished. However, the boatmen in red jackets stood up in the middle of the river, where the current swept them along, and shouted their loudest, while the washerwomen, leaning out of the windows of the floating laundry, waved their bare arms excitedly, and, in their desire to be heard, dealt blow after blow with their beetles till they nearly broke them.

---

[1] Napoléon I.

'There, it's all over!' exclaimed Gilquin; 'let us be off.'

The Charbonnels, however, wanted to see the end of everything. The tail of the procession—squadrons of Cent Gardes, cuirassiers and carabineers—was plunging into the Rue d'Arcole. Then there came a scene of dreadful confusion. In several places people broke through the double line of National Guards and regulars, and women began to scream.

'Come along! come along!' repeated Gilquin. 'We shall be crushed to death!'

When he had deposited the ladies on the footway, he made them cross the road in spite of the crowd. Madame Correur and the Charbonnels had wanted to keep near the parapet, so as to make their way to the bridge of Notre Dame and see what was happening on the Place du Parvis. But Gilquin would not hear of it, and dragged them after him. When they once more reached the little café, he gave them a push and made them sit down again at the table which they had recently left.

'What perverse creatures you are!' he cried, 'Do you suppose that I want to have my feet crushed by all those louts? We'll have something to drink, we will! We are much better off here than in that crush. We've had enough sight-seeing. It was beginning to get wearisome. Come, old lady, what will you drink?'

The Charbonnels, upon whom he kept his perturbing eyes, began to make timid objections. They would have liked to see the procession leave the church. But Gilquin assured them that it would be best to give the crowd time to disperse, and that he would take them to the church in a quarter of an hour, if the crush was not too thick. However, while he was telling Jules to bring a supply of cigars and beer, Madame Correur prudently made her escape. 'Well, stay and rest yourselves a little,' she said to the Charbonnels. 'You will find me over yonder by-and-bye.'

She made her way to the bridge of Notre Dame and then into the Rue de la Cité. But the crush there was still so great that it took her a good quarter of an hour to reach the Rue de Constantine. At last she made a cut through the Rue de la Licorne and the Rue des Trois Canettes, and in this way emerged upon the Place du Parvis, after losing at the ventilator of a suspicious house one of the flounces of her dove-coloured dress. Bound the square, strewn with sand and flowers, stood tall masts, from which hung banners bearing the imperial arms. In front of the church a vast tent-shaped porch draped the stone-work with curtains of crimson velvet, having fringes and tassels of gold.

Here Madame Correur was checked by a body of troops who kept back the crowd. In the middle of the space from which the public had been excluded, footmen were pacing up and down beside the carriages, which were drawn up in five rows, their coachmen still occupying their seats and holding their reins. As Madame Correur craned her head forward in the hope of finding some gap through which she might pass, she caught sight of Du Poizat quietly smoking a cigar in a corner of the square among some of the footmen.

'Don't you think you could get me in?' she asked him, when she had attracted his attention by waving her handkerchief.

Du Poizat went and spoke to an officer, and then led Madame Correur in front of the church.

'If you'll take my advice,' he said to her, 'you'll stay here with me. It's perfectly packed inside. I was nearly suffocated myself, and so I came out. See, there are Colonel Jobelin and Monsieur Bouchard, who have given up all hope of finding room.'

She looked and saw the two men on her left, near the Rue du Cloître Notre Dame. M. Bouchard was saying that he had just left his wife in charge of M. d'Escorailles, who had an excellent seat for a lady at his disposal, while the colonel's chief regret seemed to be that he was not able to explain the ceremony to his son Auguste.

'I much wished to show him the famous vase,' he said. 'It is, as you know, the genuine vase of Saint Louis—a vase of copper, damascened and ornamented with niello-work in the most perfect Persian manner. It is a relic of the times of the Crusades, and has been used at the christenings of all our kings ever since.'

'Did you see all the insignia?' M. Bouchard asked Du Poizat.

'Yes,' replied the latter. 'Madame de Llorentz was carrying the chrisom.'

Then he entered into details. The chrisom was the christening cloth, a fact of which neither of the men had been aware. But Du Poizat went on to enumerate, not only the insignia of the Prince Impérial, the chrisom, the candle and the salt-cellar, but the insignia of the godfather and godmother, the basin, the ewer and the towel, all of which were carried by ladies-in-waiting. Then there was also the little prince's mantle, a most magnificent and wonderful mantle, which was hung over an arm-chair near the font.

'Isn't there really the smallest corner where I could squeeze my-

self?' cried Madame Correur, in whom all these details had roused
a fever of curiosity.

Then they told her of all the great state bodies and high officials
and innumerable deputations that they had seen pass. It was an
almost endless procession, they said; the Diplomatic body, the Senate, the Corps Législatif, the Council of State, the Supreme Court,
the Exchequer Court, the Appeal Court, the Tribunals of Commerce
and of First Instance; to say nothing of the ministers, the prefects,
the mayors and their deputies, the academicians, the general officers, and a host of others, including even delegates from the Jewish
and Protestant consistories.

'Oh! what a splendid sight it must be!' Madame Correur exclaimed with a sigh.

Du Poizat shrugged his shoulders. He was in a very bad humour.
All those people bored him, he said, and he seemed irritated by the
length of the ceremony. How much longer would they be? They
had sung the *Veni Creator* and had censed themselves and walked
about and saluted one another. Surely the child must be christened
by this time!

Meanwhile M. Bouchard and the colonel manifested greater patience and examined the decorated windows of the square; then, as
a sudden peal of the bells shook the towers, they turned their heads
and quivered uneasily at their close proximity to the huge church,
whose summit they could not even discern in the sky. However,
Auguste had slipped towards the porch, whither Madame Correur
followed him. But when she reached the great door, which was
wide open, the magnificent sight she beheld kept her rooted to the
ground.

Between the two great curtains of the porch the church appeared
like a vision of some superhuman temple. The vaulted arches, of a
soft blue, were spangled with stars. Around this wondrous firma-
ment the stained-glass windows gleamed like mystic planets, sparkling with burning jewels. From the lofty pillars on all sides hung
drapery of crimson velvet, which still further shut the daylight out
of the usually dim nave; and in the centre of this roseate twilight
there blazed a multitude of tapers—thousands of tapers—so closely
crowded that they seemed like a great sun flaming out amidst a rain
of stars. This blaze was that of the altar, set on a platform in the
centre of the transept. Thrones were placed on the right and left of
it. Over the higher of the two thrones a spreading canopy of velvet

lined with ermine showed like a huge bird with snowy breast and purple wings. The church was filled with a glittering crowd, bright with gold and jewels. Near the altar a group of clergy, bishops with mitres and croziers, formed, as it were, a glory, one of those dazzling splendours which suggest heaven itself. Around the altar princes, princesses and great dignitaries were ranged in sovereign pomp and circumstance. Then tiers of seats had been set up in the arms of the transept, for the Diplomatic body and the Senate, on the right, and for the Corps Législatif and the Council of State on the left; while representative bodies of every kind crowded the rest of the nave, and ladies displayed their bright, variegated gowns in the galleries above. A sanguineous haze floated over everything. The heads which showed in tiers on all sides had the roseate hue of painted porcelain. The dresses, the satin and silk and velvet, glowed with a dull splendour as though they would soon burst into a blaze. Rows of people suddenly seemed to flare. The whole deep church was like some wondrous furnace.

Then Madame Correur saw an assistant master of the ceremonies advance to the centre of the choir, where he thrice shouted energetically: 'Long live the Prince Impérial! Long live the Prince Impérial! Long live the Prince Impérial!'

And as the lofty arches shook with a mighty acclamation, Madame Correur saw the Emperor standing on the altar steps overlooking the throng. He stood out black and distinct against the background of blazing gold which the bishops formed behind him. He was presenting the Prince Impérial to the people, holding the infant, who seemed a mere bundle of white lace, aloft in his upstretched arms.

But a beadle suddenly motioned to Madame Correur to retire. She took a couple of steps backwards, and the next moment saw nothing but one of the curtains of the porch. The vision had disappeared. The bright daylight made her blink, and for an instant she remained confused, half fancying that she had been gazing upon some old picture like those in the Louvre, some picture baked by age, purpled and gilded, and depicting people of a past-away time, such as one no longer met in the streets.

'Don't stop there,' Du Poizat said to her, as he led her back to the colonel and M. Bouchard.

The latter were now discussing the floods, which had caused terrible destruction in the valleys of the Rhone and the Loire. Thousands of families had been rendered homeless. The subscriptions which had been opened on all sides were insufficient for the relief of such great distress. However, they asserted that the Emperor had exhibited most admirable courage and generosity. At Lyons he had been seen fording the low parts of the inundated city, and at Tours he had spent three hours rowing in a boat through the submerged streets; and everywhere he had lavishly distributed alms.

'Ah, listen!' interrupted the colonel.

The organ was now pealing through the church, and a sonorous chant rolled through the porch, whose curtains swayed as the great gust of sound swept out.

'It is the *Te Deum!*' exclaimed M. Bouchard.

Du Poizat heaved a sigh of relief. They were getting to an end at last! M. Bouchard, however, informed him that the registers had yet to be signed, and, afterwards, the Cardinal-Legate would have to give the pontifical benediction. Some of the congregation were, however, already leaving. Rougon was one of the first to appear, giving his arm to a lady of slight build, who had a sallow complexion, and was very plainly dressed. They were accompanied by a personage who wore the dress of a president of an Appeal Court.

'Who are those?' asked Madame Correur.

Du Poizat told her their names. M. Beulin-d'Orchère, the president, had become acquainted with Rougon some time before the Coup d'état, and had manifested much esteem for him since that period, without, however, attempting to establish any close intimacy. Mademoiselle Véronique, his sister, lived with him in a house in the Rue Garancière, which she seldom left except to attend low mass at Saint Sulpice.

'Ah!' said the colonel, lowering his voice, 'that is the wife for Rougon!'

'Exactly,' assented M. Bouchard. 'She has got a suitable fortune; her family is good, and she is a steady-going woman of experience. He will never find a wife more fitted for him.'

Du Poizat, however, protested. The lady, he said, was as over-ripe as a forgotten medlar. She was at least thirty-six years of age, and looked forty. A nice broom-handle in all truth! A devotee with hair brushed smooth and smug! As faded and as washed-out as though she had been soaking her head in holy water for the last six months!

'You are young,' rejoined the head-clerk, gravely. 'Rougon ought to make a sensible marriage. I myself married for love, but that does not succeed with everyone.'

'Oh! I don't apprehend any danger from the lady herself,' continued Du Poizat; 'it's Beulin-d'Orchère's look that alarms me. He's got a regular dog's jaw. Just look at him with his heavy muzzle and forest of woolly hair, without a single silver thread in it, in spite of his fifty years. What's he thinking about, I wonder? Why does he still drive his sister into Rougon's arms now that our friend is out of favour?'

M. Bouchard and the colonel kept silent, and exchanged uneasy glances. Was 'the dog,' as the ex-sub-prefect called him, going to make Rougon his own prey?

However, Madame Correur slowly opined: 'It is a good thing to have the judicial bench on one's side.'

Meantime, Rougon was conducting Mademoiselle Véronique to her carriage, and, before she got into it, he bowed to her. Just at that moment the fair Clorinde came out of the church, leaning upon Delestang's arm. She became quite grave, and cast a fiery glance at that tall sallow creature, the door of whose carriage Rougon was gallantly closing, notwithstanding his senatorial uniform. And as soon as the carriage had gone off, Clorinde dropped Delestang's arm, and stepped straight up to the great man, breaking out into her old gay laugh. All the others followed.

'I have lost my mother!' merrily said the girl to Rougon. 'She has been carried off somewhere in the crowd. Will you give me a little corner in your brougham?'

At this Delestang, who had hoped to take her home, seemed very much annoyed. She was wearing a dress of orange silk, brocaded with such showy flowers that the very footmen stared at her. Rougon had immediately granted her request, but they had to wait for the brougham for another ten minutes. And they all remained standing where they were, even Delestang, though his carriage was in the first row, only a yard or two away. In the meanwhile the congregation continued to leave the church. M. Kahn and M. Béjuin, who were passing, came up and joined the group. And as the great man shook hands in a listless way, and looked somewhat out of sorts, M. Kahn asked with anxious concern: 'Aren't you feeling well?'

'Oh, yes,' he answered, 'but those lights inside there rather dazed me.' He remained silent for a moment, and then continued in a low voice: 'It was a splendid sight. I never saw such an expression of happiness upon a man's face before.'

He was referring to the Emperor, and, as he spoke, he slowly spread out his arms with a sweeping majestic gesture, as though he were recalling the scene in the church. But he added not a word, and the others likewise kept silence. They formed quite a little group in a corner of the square. In front of them the stream of people leaving the church grew larger; there were judges in their robes, officers and functionaries in full uniform, a crowd of belaced and bedizened and decorated personages who trod over the flowers strewing the square, amidst the calls of footmen and sudden rolling of carriage-wheels. The soaring glory of the Empire blazed, as it were, in the crimson of the setting sun; and the towers of Notre Dame, all rose-ate and musical, seemed to attest the lofty peace and greatness to which the future reign of the child, baptized beneath their shadow, would some day attain. But in Rougon's group, the splendour of the ceremony, the pealing bells, the streaming banners, and the enthu-siasm of the city only aroused feelings of envy and desire. For the first time Rougon himself felt the chilly weight of the disfavour into which he had fallen. His face was very pale, and, as he stood there deep in thought, he envied the Emperor.

'Well, good afternoon; I'm off! I can't stand it any longer!' ex-claimed Du Poizat, shaking hands with the others.

'What's the matter with you to-day?' asked the colonel, 'you seem very fractious.'

But the sub-prefect quietly replied, as he went away: 'Well, you can scarcely expect me to be in very high spirits. I saw in the *Monit-eur* this morning that that ass of a Campenon has been appointed to the prefecture which was promised to me.'

The others exchanged glances. Du Poizat was quite right. They had no share in the fête. They were all left out in the cold. Ever since the birth of the prince, Rougon had promised them a shower of presents for the day of the christening. M, Kahn was to have had his railway grant; the colonel was to have had a commander's cross, and Madame Correur was to have had the five or six tobacco-shops for which she had asked. And now they were all huddled there in a corner of the square, empty-handed. At this thought they cast such a distressful and reproachful look at Rougon, that the latter shrugged his shoulders furiously. And as his brougham at last drew up, he hastily pushed Clorinde inside, got in himself, and closed the door with a bang, never saying a word.

'There's Marsy under the porch,' muttered M. Kahn, dragging M. Béjuin on one side. 'How arrogant the rascal looks! Don't show him your face; it would only give him the opportunity of cutting us.'

Delestang had hastily got into his carriage in order to follow Rougon's brougham. M. Bouchard, however, waited for his wife, and when the church was empty he was surprised at not seeing her appear; however, he went off with the colonel, who had grown equally tired of waiting for his son Auguste. As for Madame Correur, she accepted the escort of a lieutenant of dragoons, who came from her own part of France, and who was to some extent indebted to her for his epaulets.

Meanwhile, inside the brougham, Clorinde was prattling enthusiastically about the ceremony that had just taken place; while Rougon leaned back with sleepy eyes and listened to her. She had seen the Easter solemnities at Rome, she told him, but they were not finer than what she had just beheld. And she added that, for her, religion lay in a vision of heaven with God the Father seated on His throne like a glittering sun amidst the glory of His encircling angels, a host of lovely youths and maidens. But all at once she broke off to inquire: 'Are you going to the banquet which the city is giving to their majesties to-night? It will be magnificent.'

She had got an invitation herself, and meant to wear a pink dress, brocaded with forget-me-nots. M. de Plouguern was going to take her, as her mother would not go out at night on account of the headaches to which she was so subject. However, she suddenly changed her subject again, asking abruptly: 'Who was that judge you were with just now?'

Rougon raised his head, and said all in a breath: 'Monsieur Beulin-d'Orchère, fifty years of age, of a legal family, began as public prosecutor's assessor at Montbrison, was afterwards public prosecutor at Orléans, advocate-general at Rouen, a member of a mixed commission in 1852, and then came to Paris as councillor at the Appeal Court, of which he is now the president. Oh! I was forgetting; he approved of the decree of the twenty-second of January, 1852, confiscating the property of the Orléans family. There, are you satisfied?' Clorinde began to laugh. He was making fun of her, she said, just because she asked for information; but there was nothing foolish—was there?—in asking about people whom one was liable to meet. She did not say a word about Mademoiselle Beulin-d'Orchère; but again began to talk of the banquet at the Hôtel de Ville. The grand gallery would be decorated with unheard-of magnificence, and a band would play the whole time the guests were dining. Ah! France was truly a great country! Nowhere, neither in England, nor in Germany, nor in Spain, nor in Italy, had she seen such wonderful balls, such prodigious galas. She had quite made up her mind now, she said, her face beaming with admiration; she meant to be a Frenchwoman.

'Oh, look!' she cried; 'there are some soldiers there!' The brougham, after rolling along the Rue de la Cité, had now been stopped at the end of the Pont Notre Dame by a regiment which was marching back to its quarters. It was one of the line. The soldiers, all of them little fellows, were hastening on like sheep, their march being somewhat irregular by reason of the trees planted along the roadside. They had been keeping the line for the procession; their faces were scorched by the hot afternoon sun; their feet were white with dust; and their backs bent beneath the weight of their knap-sacks and rifles. And they had felt so bored amid the jostling of the crowd that they still looked dazed and stupid.

'I adore the French army,' said Clorinde enthusiastically, as she leant forward to get a better view.

Rougon roused himself, and in his turn looked out of the window. It was the power of the Empire that was passing through the dust. A great many carriages had now gathered together on the bridge, but the coachmen respectfully waited for the soldiers to pass, and dis-tinguished personages in gala costumes smiled sympathisingly at the little fellows who were so stupefied by their long day's work.

'Do you see those in the rear?' exclaimed Clorinde. 'There's a whole row of them without a hair on their faces. How nice they look!'

Then, in her enthusiasm, she began to kiss her hands to the little soldiers from the depths of the brougham. She lay back a little so that she might not be seen. Rougon smiled in a paternal manner. He, too, had just felt a thrill of pleasure, the first he had known during the whole day.

'What's going on here?' he exclaimed, when the brougham was at last able to turn the corner of the quay.

A considerable crowd had formed on the footway and in the road, and the brougham had to stop again. A voice in the throng was heard saying: 'It's a drunken man who has insulted the soldiers. The police have just taken him into custody.'

Then, as the crowd parted, Rougon caught sight of Gilquin,

dead-drunk, and held by a couple of policemen. His yellow duck clothes were torn, and his naked flesh showed through the rents. But he still retained his garrulous joviality and scarlet face. He addressed the policemen in the most familiar fashion, calling them his little lambs. He told them that he had been quietly spending the afternoon in a neighbouring café with some very rich people, and referred them for inquiries to the Palais Royal theatre, where M. and Madame Charbonnel, who had gone to see *Les Dragées du Baptême,* would readily confirm his statement.

'Come, let me go, you jokers!' he cried, suddenly stiffening himself. 'Confound it all, the café's close at hand; come with me there, if you don't believe me. The soldiers insulted me. There was a little scamp who laughed at me, and I shut him up. But for me to insult the French army! Never! Just you mention the name of Théodore to the Emperor and hear what he says. Ah! you're a nice set, you are!'

The crowd roared with amusement, while the imperturbable policemen slowly dragged Gilquin towards the Rue Saint Martin, where the red lamp of a police-station could be seen. Rougon had hastily thrown himself back in his brougham, but Gilquin, raising his head, caught sight of him. Then, drunk though he was, he again became good-natured and prudent, and casting a glance at Rougon, exclaimed, so that the latter might hear him: 'Well, well, my friends: I might get up a scandal if I liked, but I've too much self-respect. Ah, you wouldn't lay your hands on Théodore in this way if he drove about with princesses as a citizen of my acquaintance does. All the same, however, I've worked with great people, and cleverly, too, though I don't want to boast about it, and never asked for a big reward. But I know my own worth, and that consoles me for other people's meanness. Ah, confound it, are friends no longer friends, then?'

He spoke with growing emotion, his speech impeded by hiccoughs, while Rougon quietly beckoned to a man wearing a closely buttoned coat, whom he saw standing near his brougham, and, after whispering a few words to him, gave him Gilquin's address, 17 Rue Virginie, Grenelle. And thereupon the man—a detective—stepped up to the officers as though he were about to help them with the drunkard who had begun to struggle. However, the crowd was greatly surprised to see the policemen turn to the left and bundle Gilquin into a cab, whose driver, after receiving an order, drove away along the Quai de la Mégisserie. Gilquin, however, thrust his huge unkempt head from the window, and, with a burst of triumphant laughter, shouted: 'Long live the Republic!'

When the crowd had dispersed, the quays resumed their wonted tranquillity. Paris, weary of enthusiasm, had gone off to dinner. The three hundred thousand sight-seers, who had struggled and crowded there, were now invading the restaurants by the water-side and those of the district of the Temple. None but country cousins paced the deserted pavements, quite knocked up and at a loss where to dine. Down below, in the floating laundry the washerwomen were finishing their work with vigorous blows. A last ray of sunlight still gilded the towers of Notre Dame, which now rose quite silent above the houses already dark with shadow. And through the slight mist ascending from the Seine, nothing could be distinguished among the grey mass of buildings, on the Ile Saint Louis, save the giant great-coat, that colossal advertisement hanging seemingly from some nail on the horizon, and looking like the garment of a Titan, whose body had been pulverised by the thunderbolts of Jove.

V

PASSION AND MATRIMONY

ONE morning towards eleven o'clock, Clorinde called at Rougon's house in the Rue Marbeuf. She was on her way back from the Bois, and a groom held her horse at the door. She went straight into the garden, turned to the left, and halted in front of the open window of the study in which the great man sat at work.

'Ah! I've taken you by surprise!' she exclaimed.

Rougon quickly raised his head. The girl stood laughing in the warm June sunshine. Her riding-habit of heavy blue cloth made her seem taller. She was carrying its long train over her left arm, and its tight-fitting corsage clung to her shoulders and breast and hips like skin. She wore linen wristbands and collar, and a narrow necktie of blue silk, while atop of her rolled-up hair a tall silk hat was jauntily perched with a veil of bluish gauze powdered with the golden dust of the sunlight.

'What, is it you?' cried Rougon, hastening to her. 'Pray come in!'

'No, no,' she answered; 'don't disturb yourself, I have only a word to say to you. My mother will be expecting me back to lunch.'

This was the third time that she had come in this way to Rougon's house in defiance of all propriety. She made a point, however, of remaining in the garden; and upon the previous occasions, as upon this one, she had come in her riding-habit, a costume which seemed to confer masculine privileges upon her.

'I've come to beg,' she said. 'I want you to buy some lottery tickets. We are getting up a lottery for the benefit of some poor girls.'

'Oh, indeed; well, come in,' repeated Rougon, 'you can tell me all about it.'

She had kept her whip in her hand, a slight delicate whip with a little silver handle. And on hearing him she again began to laugh while gently tapping her skirt with her whip.

'Oh, I've told you all there is to tell,' said she. 'You must take some tickets. That's all I came for. I've been looking for you for the last three days without finding you, and the drawing takes place to-morrow.' Then, as she took a little case out of her pocket, she inquired: 'How many tickets would you like?'

'Not one, if you won't come in!' cried Rougon. And he continued, playfully: 'We can't transact business at the window, you know, and I'm not going to hand you money out as though you were some beggar-woman.'—'Oh, I don't object, as long as I get it.'

But Rougon remained firm. She looked at him for a moment in silence, and then resumed: 'If I come in, will you promise to take ten tickets? They are ten francs each.'

However, she did not make up her mind without some further hesitation, and she even cast a hasty glance round the garden. There was a gardener on his knees planting a bed of geraniums. Then she smiled slightly and stepped towards the little flight of steps upon which the folding-window of the study opened. Rougon held out his hand and drew her into the middle of the room.

'Are you afraid that I shall eat you?' he asked her. 'You know very well that I am the most submissive of your slaves. What are you frightened of?'

'I! I'm not afraid of anything,' she replied again, tapping her skirts with her whip, which she then laid upon a couch in order to fumble in her little case once more. 'You'll take ten, won't you?' she asked.

'I will take twenty, if you wish it,' he replied; 'but do, please, sit down and let us have a little chat. You surely don't want to be off at once.'

'Well, then, it shall be a ticket a minute. If I stay a quarter of an hour, you will have to take fifteen tickets, and if I stay twenty minutes, you will have to take twenty tickets, and so on as long as I stay. Is that agreed?'

They laughed merrily over this arrangement, and Clorinde thereupon seated herself in an easy chair in the very embrasure of the window which remained open. Rougon, on his side, resumed his seat at his table in order to put her at her ease. Then they began to talk, taking the house for their first subject. Clorinde glanced out of the window and remarked that the garden was rather small, but very charming, with its central lawn and clumps of evergreens. Then Rougon began to describe the house to her. On the ground-floor, said he, were his study, a large drawing-room, a small one, and a very handsome dining-room. On the first-floor there were seven bedrooms, and as many on the second. Although to some people the house might seem a very small one, it was much too big for him, he declared. At the time when the Emperor had made him a present of it he had been engaged to marry a widow, chosen by his Majesty himself; but the lady had died, and now he intended to remain a bachelor.

'Why?' asked Clorinde, looking him straight in the face.

'Oh! I've other things to do than to get married. When a man reaches my age, he no longer thinks about a wife.'

'Don't be so affected,' replied Clorinde, with a shrug of her shoulders.

They had become intimate enough to talk very freely together. Clorinde declared that she believed Rougon to be amorously inclined, but he defended himself, and told her of his early times, of the years he had spent in bare rooms, which never a woman entered. Still, she went on questioning him about his lady-loves with childish curiosity, and he again and again replied with a shrug of the shoulders.

'No! no wife for me!' he cried at last, though his eyes were glistening at the sight of Clorinde's careless attitude.

A peculiar smile played on the girl's lips as she lay back in her chair. There was an expression of soft languor on her face, and her bosom gently heaved. When she replied, it was with an exaggerated

Italian accent, and in a sort of singing voice. 'Nonsense, my friend; you adore us, I know. Will you bet me that you aren't married by this time next year?'

She was really provoking, so certain did she seem to be of conquering him. For some time past she had been calmly offering herself to Rougon. She no longer attempted to disguise her snares and the clever way in which she had worked upon him before laying siege to his desires. She considered that he was now sufficiently overcome for her to bring the matter to an issue. It was a real duel that was going on between them, and although the conditions of the combat were not mentioned in actual words, there were unmistakable confessions in their glances. When they looked at each other they could not refrain from smiling. Clorinde had set her eyes upon her goal and went straight towards it, with a haughty boldness; while Rougon, infatuated though he was, resolved to play a wily game in order to prove his superiority. Their pride was engaged in the struggle quite as much as their passions were.

'With us in Italy,' resumed Clorinde in a low tone, 'love is the great business of life. Young girls of twelve already have their lovers. For myself, I have travelled about so much, that I've almost become a man. But if you could only have seen mamma when she was young! She was so lovely that people came from long distances to see her, but she seldom if ever left her house. There was a count who stayed at Milan expressly for six months without catching sight of her hair even. The fact is, that Italian women are very different from French women, who are always chattering and gadding about. An Italian woman remains with the man she has chosen. But I have travelled so much, that I really don't know whether I haven't lost that instinct or not; still I think that I could love very strongly; ah, yes, with all my heart and soul.'

She had let her eyelids fall, and her face glowed as with a voluptuous ecstasy. While she was speaking, Rougon had left his table as though attracted by some force which he could not withstand, and his hands were trembling. But when he got near to Clorinde, the girl opened her eyes again and gave him a quiet glance. Then, as she looked at the clock, she said with a smile: 'This makes ten tickets.'

'Ten tickets! what do you mean?' asked Rougon, quite confused.

When he had recovered his self-possession, she burst into a laugh. It delighted her to bewitch him and intoxicate him in this way, and when he opened his arms to clasp her, to elude him with a laugh. She seemed in high glee. At this Rougon turned very pale, and cast a furious glance at her, which only served to increase her merriment. 'Well, I think I'd better be off now,' she said. 'You're not polite enough for ladies' society. No, really, my mother will be expecting me.'

Rougon, however, had resumed his paternal manner, and told her that she must spare him another five minutes. He had got tired of the work he was doing when she came in, he said; it was a report to be presented to the Senate on certain petitions. Then he began to talk to her about the Empress, for whom she professed enthusiastic devotion. The Empress, said he, had been at Biarritz for the last week. At this the girl again leant back in her arm-chair and began to chatter. She knew Biarritz very well; she had once spent a season there, before it had become such a fashionable watering-place; and she very much regretted that she was unable to revisit it while the Court was there. Then she went on to describe a meeting of the Academy to which M. de Plouguern had taken her on the previous day. An author had been admitted as a member, and she made many jokes at the expense of his baldness. She had a horror of books, she declared. Whenever she tried to read, she had to go off to bed, suffering from terrible nervous attacks. She could not understand what she read. Then, on Rougon telling her that the author received at the Academy on the previous day was an enemy of the Emperor's, and that his discourse had swarmed with abominable allusions, she seemed quite astounded.

'Why, he looked such a nice man!' she exclaimed.

But Rougon also had begun to inveigh against books. A novel had just been published, he said, which had aroused his utmost indignation. It was a work of the most depraved kind, which, while claiming to portray the exact truth, dragged the reader through all the wild fancies of an hysterical woman.[1] The word hysterical seemed to please him, for he repeated it three times; but when Clorinde asked him to explain what he meant by it, he refused to answer, suddenly becoming very prudish.

'Everything may be said,' he continued, 'only there is a fitting way of saying it. In administrative matters, for instance, we are frequently obliged to tackle very delicate subjects. I have read,

---

[1] An allusion to M. Flaubert's 'Madame Bovary.'—*Ed.*

for example, reports upon certain matters which have been very precise, very detailed; but they have been written in a clear, simple, straightforward style, so that there was nothing unchaste or impure about the document. But our present-day novelists have adopted a style which is full of suggestiveness, a manner of describing things which makes it appear as if they were actually going on before you. They call that art. To me it seems to be simply indecency and bad taste.'

Then he went on to speak of authors, whom he had never read, but whom, like many other people, he accused of the grossest immorality. And yet while he was thus prating of virtue and denouncing vice, he was cleverly manoeuvring to get behind Clorinde's chair without her being aware of it. The girl was gazing at the ceiling with an expression of absent-mindedness. 'Oh, as for novels,' she murmured, 'I have never even opened one. They are all a pack of falsehoods. You don't know *Leonora, the Gipsy,* do you? It is a pretty book. I read it in Italian when I was quite little. It is about a young girl who ends by marrying a lord. She is captured by brigands to begin with—'

However, a slight grating sound behind her made her start and turn her head: 'What are you doing?' she asked.

'I am pulling the blind down,' replied Rougon; 'I was afraid the sun was inconveniencing you.'

The girl was, indeed, sitting in a flood of sun-light, whose dancing dust gilded her corsage as with luminous down. 'Please leave the blind alone,' she cried, 'I love the sun. I feel as though I were in a warm bath.'

Then she raised herself in her chair and glanced into the garden. But when she saw the gardener still kneeling there, with the back of his blue blouse turned towards them, she reverted to her reclining attitude again, smiling, and easy once more. Rougon, who had followed her glance, left the blind as it was, and the girl began to banter him. He was just like an owl, she said, to be so fond of darkness. However, he showed no resentment, but began to pace the room, swaying about like a bear contemplating some wily act of treachery.

'Oh, come and look here,' he said at last, pointing to a large photograph; 'you haven't seen my last portrait, have you?'

But she merely smiled, and replied: 'Oh! I can see it very well from here; and, besides, you've shown it to me before.'

Rougon was not yet discouraged. He drew down the blind of the other window, and invented several reasons to induce the girl to go into the shady corner which he had made by doing so. She would be much more comfortable there, he told her. But Clorinde, despising this obvious snare, merely shook her head. Then Rougon came and stood in front of her; and, dropping all attempts at stratagem, said straightforwardly: 'Oh, by the way, I want to show you my new horse, Monarque. You know that I have been making an exchange. You are fond of horses, and you shall tell me what you think of him.'

But the girl still refused to move. Then Rougon began to press her. The stable was only a few yards away. It wouldn't take her more than five minutes at the most. She continued to refuse, however, and thereupon Rougon murmured with a touch of scorn in his voice: 'What! are you afraid?'

At this she started up, as though lashed with a whip. She looked very grave and somewhat pale.

'Let us go and look at Monarque,' she said quietly.

As she gathered up the train of her riding-habit she fixed her eyes upon Rougon's, and for a moment they remained gazing at each other as if to read each other's thoughts. It was a challenge given and accepted, without any pretence of concealment. Then she led the way down the steps while Rougon, by force of habit, buttoned the house-coat which he was wearing. But the girl had only taken a step or two along the garden-walk when she stopped short. 'Wait a moment,' she said.

She went back into the room, and when she returned, she was toying with her riding-whip, which she had left behind the cushion of the couch. Rougon glanced at the whip, and then slowly raised his eyes to Clorinde. She was smiling again, and once more she walked on in front of him.

The stable was at the end of the garden, on the right. When they passed the gardener, the man was gathering up his tools and preparing to go away. Rougon, bareheaded in the blazing sun, followed Clorinde, who went quietly onward, tapping the shrubs with her riding-whip as she passed them. Neither spoke a word. Clorinde did not even turn her head. On reaching the stable, she waited while Rougon opened the door, and then went inside, in front of him. The door, which Rougon swung back, closed noisily, and Clorinde still smiled, her face wearing an open expression, in which pride and confidence were clearly to be read.

The stable was a small and commonplace one, with four oak stalls. Although the slabs had been washed that morning, and the racks and mangers and other wood-work were kept scrupulously clean, there was a strong scent about the place, and the atmosphere was warm and damp, like that of a Turkish bath. From each of the two round dormer-windows there fell but a pale glimmer of light, and the corners remained wrapt in gloom. Clorinde, having just left the bright sunshine of the garden, could at first distinguish nothing; but she kept still, and did not open the door again for fear lest Rougon should think she was alarmed. Only two of the stalls were occupied. The horses snorted and turned their heads.

'This is the one, isn't it?' asked Clorinde, when her eyes had grown accustomed to the gloom. 'He looks a very nice animal.'

She patted the horse gently, and then slipped inside the stall, stroking the animal as she went without showing the least sign of fear. She wanted to see his head, she said; and when she had made her way to the far end of the stall, Rougon could hear her kissing the horse's nose. The sound of those kisses exasperated him.

'Come back, I beg you!' he cried. 'If he were to step on one side, you might be crushed to death!'

But the girl only laughed, kissed the horse more affectionately than before, and spoke to him caressingly, while he, at this unexpected fondling, fairly quivered with pleasure. At last she came out of the stall again. She was very fond of horses, she said, they always knew her, and never tried to hurt her, even when she teased them. She knew how to manage them. Some were very skittish, but this one seemed very steady. Then she stooped down behind the horse, and lifted one of its hoofs with both hands as if to examine it. The animal remained quite still.

Rougon gazed at her while she thus stooped before him; but all at once she felt a slight touch under her arm-pits. She did not even start, however; she went on examining the horse's hoof, till the touch became more pronounced, and then letting the hoof drop, she stood up and inquired: 'What is the matter with you? What has come over you?'

Then, as Rougon suddenly tried to clasp her round the waist, she rapped his knuckles smartly, and, stationing herself against the wall in front of the stalls, raised the train of her riding-habit, which was thrown over her left arm, as a shield, while in her right hand she held her whip uplifted. Rougon's lips were trembling, but he did not say a

word; Clorinde, however, seeming quite at ease, went on talking free-
ly: 'You can't touch me, you'll see,' she said. 'When I was younger,
I used to take fencing-lessons. I'm sorry I did not go on with them.
Come, look out for your fingers! There! what did I tell you?'

She seemed to be only in fun. She did not strike Rougon severely,
but just playfully lashed at him whenever his hands came too near.
She was so quick in her defence that he could not even touch her
dress. A perfect hail came clattering down upon him on every side.
Before long he was tingling all over, and stepped back panting, with
his face very red, and drops of perspiration trickling down his brow.
Then, however, his manner changed, and still without a word he advanced menacingly; but Clorinde, though smiling and talking as before, at once struck him several smart blows of increasing severity.
She looked very beautiful as she stood there with her skirts drawn
tightly, and her corsage yielding to every movement of her lissom
figure. She was like a sinuous, bluish-black serpent, and whenever
she raised her arm to strike, at the same time slightly throwing her
head back, her throat and bosom formed a charming curve.

'Well, now,' she exclaimed, with a laugh, 'have you had enough?
You'll be the first to tire, I think, my friend.'

But in her turn she suddenly stopped talking. Rougon's eyes
were glaring fiercely now, and his face was quite crimson. Then
a bright light also appeared in Clorinde's eyes, and she seemed
to revel in the whipping she was administering to him. Again and
again did she wheel and slash about her. And at last, as he, goaded
to fury, made a yet more desperate onslaught, she put forth all her
strength and cut him clean across the face from ear to ear.

'Hussy!' he cried, and broke into a torrent of coarse language,
abominable charges, swearing and sputtering, half-choked by his
excitement.

She did not deign to reply. For a moment she stood there motionless and haughtily calm like a statue, with her face very pale.

But he burst into a strain of passionate pleading; and thereupon
she looked at him and answered: 'Well, then, marry me!'

At this, however, Rougon, as if recovering his self-possession,
forced a laugh, a sneering, insulting laugh, and shook his head.

Her retort, the only one that womanly pride could dictate, came
swift and forcible. Then neither spoke again.

The horses in the stalls had turned their heads and were snorting, disturbed by the contest which they had heard. The sun had just

risen high enough to shine through the dormer-windows, and two golden beams sent sparkles dancing through the gloom of the stable. Clorinde, now perfectly calm again, slipped up to Monarque's head, with her whip under her arm. She gave the horse two kisses on the muzzle and exclaimed: 'Good-bye, old fellow. You, at any rate, know how to behave yourself.'

Rougon, quite crushed and ashamed, was also now perfectly calm. With his hands still quivering he straightened his cravat, and felt his coat to ascertain if it was properly buttoned. Then they walked quietly back through the garden. Rougon's left cheek was stinging him, and he dabbed it with his handkerchief. When they reached his study, Clorinde's first glance was for the timepiece. 'That makes thirty-two tickets,' she said with a smile.

As Rougon looked at her in surprise, she once more broke into a laugh, and continued: 'You had better send me off at once. The hand is moving forward. The thirty-third minute has begun. See, I'm putting the tickets on your desk.'

Rougon gave her three hundred and twenty francs without a moment's hesitation. Scarcely did his fingers tremble as he counted out the gold. It was a fine which he had inflicted upon himself. Then Clorinde, carried away by the manner in which he put down such a sum of money, stepped up to him with an adorable expression, offering him her cheek. And when he had kissed it in a fatherly fashion, she went off, looking quite delighted, and saying: 'Thank you for the poor girls. I have only seven tickets left now. My godfather will take those.'

As soon as Rougon was alone again, he sat down at his desk by sheer force of habit. He resumed his work, and for some minutes wrote and consulted the papers that were lying in front of him. Then he held up his pen, and a grave expression came over his face as he gazed blankly through the open window into the garden. He again saw Clorinde's lithe form swaying before him like some bluish serpent. She glided on and entered the room, and sprang up on the living tail which her habit seemed to form. He saw her quivering as her arms uncoiled towards him; and gradually the room seemed full of her presence. Silently, passionately, it pervaded everything: the carpet, the chairs, the curtains, diffusing over all a penetrating perfume.

Then Rougon violently threw his pen down and rose in anger. Was that girl now going to prevent him from working? Was he going mad that he should see things which had no existence? he whose brain was so strong! He recalled to his mind a woman, nigh whom he had many a time written the whole night long, when he was a student, without even noticing her gentle breathing. Then he drew up the blind, and to establish a draught opened the other window and a door on the opposite side of the room, as though he were stifling. And with angry gestures similar to those with which he would have driven away some dangerous wasp, he tried to drive away the scent of Clorinde by flapping his handkerchief in the air. When he no longer noticed it, he drew a deep breath and again dabbed his face with his handkerchief to assuage the burning heat which Clorinde had brought there.

He could not, however, go on with the work he had commenced, but still slowly paced the room, from one end to the other. As he caught sight of himself in a mirror, he noticed a red mark on his left cheek. Clorinde's whip had only left a slight scratch behind it, and he could easily ascribe that to some trifling accident. However, although his skin revealed but a slight red line, his flesh still smarted with the slashing, galling cut. So he hastened to a little lavatory, curtained off from the rest of the room, and plunged his head into a basin of water. That afforded him considerable relief. He dreaded lest the whipping he had received from Clorinde should only sharpen his passion. He felt afraid to think about her till the scratch on his cheek should be quite healed; the smarting which he felt seemed to descend and thrill his whole body.

'No! never! I won't!' he said aloud, as he came back into his room. 'It would be madness!'

He threw himself on the couch and clenched his fists. Then a servant came in and told him that his *déjeuner* was getting cold, but he still sat there, struggling with himself. His stern, set face distended with the contest that was raging within him; his bull-like neck grew swollen and his muscles strained, as though silently, within his vitals, he were striving to suffocate some animal bent on devouring him. The battle went on for ten long minutes. He could not remember having ever exerted himself like this before; and, when he got up, he was quite pallid and his neck was moist with perspiration.

On the next two days Rougon admitted no one to see him. He shut himself up with a pile of work. He sat up one whole night. Three times again, when his servant came into the room, he found him lying on the couch, exhausted and with an alarming look on his face. On the evening of the second day, however, he dressed to go to Delestang's, where he was engaged to dine. But, instead of at once crossing the Champs Elysées, he turned up the avenue and entered the Balbis' house. It was only six o'clock.

'Mademoiselle isn't at home,' said the little servant Antonia, laughing like a black goat, as she stopped him on the staircase.

Rougon raised his voice on the chance of making himself heard, and was hesitating whether he should go down again, when Clorinde appeared up above, leaning over the balusters. 'Come up!' she called. 'What an idiot that girl is! She never understands anything that is told her.'

When Rougon reached the first floor, Clorinde took him into a small room adjoining her bed-chamber. It was a dressing-room, with light blue wall-paper of a flowery pattern, but she had furnished it with a big dingy mahogany desk, an arm-chair upholstered in leather, and a nest of pasteboard boxes. Papers were lying about, thickly covered with dust. The place looked like the office of some disreputable process server. To accommodate Rougon the girl was obliged to fetch a chair from her bedroom. 'I was expecting you,' she called out as she went there.

When she came back with the chair, she explained to him that she was busy with her correspondence. She showed him on her desk some big sheets of yellowish paper, covered with large round hand-writing. Then, as he sat down, she noticed that he was in evening dress.

'Have you come to ask for my hand?' she said in a playful way.

'Exactly,' he replied. Then he added with a smile: 'Not for myself, but for one of my friends.'

Clorinde gazed at him doubtfully, unable to tell whether he was joking or not. She was dirty and untidy, and was wearing an ill-fitting dressing-gown; but, nevertheless she looked very beautiful, like some antique statue which is soiled by the dust of a broker's shop, but whose beauty is beyond the power of dirt to conceal. And while she sucked one of her fingers which she had just smeared with ink, her eyes fell upon the slight scar which was still visible on Rougon's left cheek. Presently she said, in a low voice and with an air of absent-mindedness: 'I was sure you would come, but I expected you sooner.' Then, seeming to wake up, she continued in a louder tone: 'So it is for one of your friends; your dearest friend, no doubt.'

She laughed sonorously. She now felt sure that Rougon bad meant himself. She had a strong desire to touch his scar in order to satisfy herself that she had really put her mark upon him and that henceforth he belonged to her. But he took hold of her wrists and made her sit down in the leather-covered arm-chair.

'Let us have a little talk,' he said. 'We are good friends, aren't we? I have been thinking a good deal since the day before yesterday. You have been in my mind the whole time. I fancied that we had got married, and that we had been living together for three months. You'll never guess in what occupation I saw us engaged.'

Clorinde said nothing; she felt a little embarrassed, in spite of all her self-assurance.

'Well, I saw us standing by the fire-place,' he continued. 'You had taken up the shovel and I had seized the tongs, and we were belabouring each other.'

This idea struck Clorinde as so comical that she threw herself back in her chair and burst into ringing laughter.

'No, don't laugh,' said Rougon; 'I'm quite serious. It isn't worth while uniting our lives just to beat each other. I swear to you that is what would happen. First there would be blows, and then a separation. Be quite sure of this, that it is useless trying to assimilate two strong wills like ours.'—'And so?' she asked, becoming very grave.—'And so I think that the most sensible thing we can do is to shake hands and make up our minds to be nothing but good friends in the future.'

Clorinde made no reply, but fixed her eyes searchingly and blackly upon Rougon's. A terrible frown like that of an offended goddess appeared on her olympian brow. And her lips quivered slightly with a silent expression of scorn.

'Will you excuse me?' she said. Then, drawing her chair to her desk, she began to fold her letters. She used large yellow envelopes, such as are employed in French government offices, and fastened them with sealing-wax. She had lighted a taper and was watching the wax blaze. Rougon quietly waited till she had finished.

'And you came here to tell me that?' she resumed at last, without desisting from her work.

Rougon in his turn made no immediate reply. He wanted to get a glimpse of the girl's face. When she at last turned her chair round again, he smiled at her and tried to catch her eye. Then he kissed her hand, as though anxious to soften her; but she still remained cold and haughty.

'I told you,' he said, 'that I have come to ask you in marriage on behalf of one of my friends.'

Then he spoke at length. He loved her, he told her, much more than she imagined. He loved her particularly because she was intelligent and able. It cost him a great deal to give her up, but he was sacrificing his passion for their mutual advantage. He would like to see her ruling her own house. He pictured her married to a wealthy man whom she would mould to her own will. She would rule instead of having to surrender herself. That would be much better—would it not?—than for them to paralyse one another. He and she could speak out openly to each other. He ended by calling her his child. She was his perverse daughter, he said; her diplomatic bent of mind delighted him, and it would distress him very much to see her career end unsatisfactorily.

'Is that all?' she said, when he finished. She had listened to him with the greatest attention. And, raising her eyes to his face, she continued: 'If you want to get me married in the expectation of anything, I warn you that you are mistaken. Never! I told you.'

'What an idea!' he exclaimed, slightly blushing. Then he coughed, and took a paper-knife off the desk and began to examine its handle in order to conceal the trouble he was feeling. But the girl was deep in thought again, paying no attention to him.

'And who is the husband?' she eventually asked.

'Can't you guess?'

Then a faint smile came to her face once more, and she shrugged her shoulders, and began to drum on the desk with her finger tips. She knew very well who it was. 'He is so stupid,' she said, in a low voice.

But Rougon began to defend Delestang. He was a very well-bred man, and she would be able to do what she liked with him. And he gave her particulars as to his health and fortune and habits. Moreover, he promised that he would use all his influence in their favour should he ever return to power. Delestang was, perhaps, scarcely a man of lofty intelligence, but he would not be out of place in any position.

'Oh, yes, he'd scrape on well enough; I'm willing to allow that,' she said, with a frank laugh. And she continued, after a pause: 'Well, I don't say no; perhaps you are right. Monsieur Delestang is not distasteful to me.'

She looked at Rougon as she spoke those last words. She fancied she had noticed upon several occasions that he was jealous of Delestang. But so far as she could see not a muscle of his face now moved. He had found strength enough to destroy his passion in two days. And he seemed quite delighted with the success of his scheme, and again began to expatiate upon the advantages of such a marriage, as though he were some shrewd attorney negotiating an affair from which she would derive especial profit. He took her hands in his own and patted them affectionately, as he went on: 'It was last night that the idea struck me, and I said to myself, "It's the very thing!" I shouldn't like you to remain unmarried. You are the only woman who seems to me to be really deserving of a husband. Delestang settles everything. With him one has elbow-room.' Then he added gaily: 'I feel convinced that you will reward me by letting me see some very wonderful things.'

'Is Monsieur Delestang aware of your plans?' Clorinde now inquired.

Rougon looked at her in surprise for a moment, as though she had said something which he had not expected from her. Then he calmly replied: 'No; it was no use saying anything to him. I will tell him all about it later on.'

The girl had just resumed the sealing of her letters. After pressing a large blank seal upon the wax she turned the envelopes over and slowly addressed them in big handwriting. And as she tossed the letters to her right, Rougon tried to read the addresses. The names were mostly those of well-known Italian politicians. She must have noticed what he was doing, however, for, as she rose and collected her letters to send them to the post, she remarked: 'When my mother has one of her headaches, I have to do the letter-writing.'

When Rougon was left to himself, he began to walk about the little room. The pasteboard boxes in the stand were all labelled '*Receipts,*' '*Letters,*' and so on, like those of some man of business. He smiled, however, when among the litter of papers on the desk, he caught sight of a pair of old split stays. There was a piece of soap, too, in the inkstand, and some scraps of blue satin on the floor, clippings which had fallen during the mending of a skirt, and had not been swept away. The door leading to Clorinde's bedroom was ajar, and Rougon had the curiosity to peep inside; but the shutters were closed and the room was so dark that he could only see the shadowy folds of the bed-curtains. Just then, too, Clorinde came back.

'I must be off,' Rougon said to her. 'I am going to dine with your man this evening. Do you give me full permission to act?'

The girl made no reply. She had turned quite gloomy again, as though she had been reconsidering the matter on the staircase. Rougon had already got his hand upon the balusters, but she brought him back into the room and closed the door. Her dream was being dispelled, the hope of which she had felt so sure that only an hour previously she had regarded it as a certainty. The burning flush that comes from a deadly insult rose to her cheeks. She felt as though she had received a blow.

'Then you mean it seriously?' she said, turning her back to the light, so that Rougon might not see how flushed her face was.

When he had repeated his arguments for the third time, she remained silent. She was afraid that if she began to speak on the subject she would be carried away by an impulse of wild anger, which she could feel surging within her, and she feared she might strike Rougon in revenge for this crumbling away of the future which she had planned for herself. But it was only a momentary impulse. She was soon calm again, and then slowly asked, 'You wish this marriage to take place?'

Rougon did not hesitate, but answered in a full clear tone 'Yes.'

'Very well; let it be then.'

With slow steps, they returned to the door and went out on to the landing, both looking extremely calm. The only signs of Rougon's last victory over himself were a few drops of perspiration on his brow. Clorinde held herself erect, certain of her power. They stood looking at each other in silence for a moment, having nothing further to say, and yet unable to part. At last, as Rougon took the girl's hand to say goodbye, she detained him for an instant, and said without trace of anger: 'You think yourself much cleverer than I am, but you are mistaken. You will perhaps be sorry some day.'

Her threats went no further. She leant over the balusters and watched him go down the stairs. When he got to the bottom, he raised his head and they smiled at one another. She had no thought of taking any puerile vengeance upon him; she was already dreaming of punishing him by some splendid future triumph of her own. And as she went back to the dressing-room, she caught herself murmuring, 'Ah, well! all roads lead to Rome.'

That very evening Rougon began to lay siege to Delestang's heart. He told him of some very flattering imaginary remarks which Mademoiselle Balbi had made of him at the banquet at the Hôtel de Ville; and afterwards he never wearied of discoursing to him about the young girl's extraordinary beauty. He, who had formerly warned him so strongly to be on his guard against women, now did his best to deliver him over to Clorinde bound hand and foot. One day he would dwell upon the rare beauty of her hands; on another, he would glorify her figure, describing it in the most alluring language. Delestang, whose inflammable heart was already full of Clorinde's image, was soon stirred by hot passion. When Rougon told him that he himself had never thought about her, he confessed that he had been in love with her for the last six months, but had kept silent on the subject from fear of being too late. He now began to go to the Rue Marbeuf every evening to talk about her. There seemed to be a general conspiracy against him. He never spoke to anyone without hearing enthusiastic praises of the girl he loved. Even the Charbonnels stopped him one morning on the Place de la Concorde to express their admiration of the 'beautiful young lady whom they saw about with him everywhere.'

Clorinde, on her side, wore a smiling face. She had planned out her life afresh, and in a few days had grown accustomed to the new part she was to play. She did not attempt to win Delestang by the same bold tactics with which she had tried to subjugate Rougon. She quite changed her manner, affected soft languor, guileless innocence, and such a nervous disposition, that too tender a squeeze of the hand would upset her. When Delestang told Rougon that she had fainted in his arms just because he had kissed her wrist, the latter pretended to consider this as a convincing proof of her purity of mind. So at last Delestang began to think seriously about marrying her, and went to consult Rougon on the subject. But when the latter found his plans so near realisation he, just for a moment, felt so hurt and angry that he almost told Delestang then and there of all that had passed between himself and Clorinde. However, he refrained, and proceeded very cleverly to work upon the other's feelings. He did not actually advise him to marry Clorinde, but led him on to this determination by remarks that seemed almost irrelevant to the subject. He had been much surprised, he said, to hear the unpleasant stories which had been circulated about Mademoiselle Balbi, but he did not believe them, for he had made searching inquiries without discovering anything to her disadvantage. Moreover, a man ought not to doubt the woman he loved. Those were his last words.

Six weeks later, as Rougon came out of the Madeleine, where the marriage had just been celebrated with great magnificence, he said to a deputy who was expressing his astonishment at Delestang's choice: 'Well, what could you expect of him? I warned him a hundred times. But he was sure to be taken in by a woman some day.'

Towards the end of the winter, when Delestang and his wife returned from travelling in Italy, they learnt that Rougon was on the point of marrying Mademoiselle Beulin-d'Orchère. When they went to see him, Clorinde congratulated him very gracefully. He pretended that he was really taking the step to please his friends. For the last three months, he said, they had let him have no peace, but had constantly repeated that a man in his position ought to be married. He added with a laugh that when his friends came to see him in the evenings, there wasn't even a woman in the house to pour out the tea.

'Oh! so it's a sudden decision of yours; you never thought of it before, I suppose,' remarked Clorinde with a smile. 'You ought to have got married at the same time as we did, so that we could all have gone to Italy together.'

Then she began to question him playfully. No doubt it was his friend, Du Poizat, who had suggested this pretty idea. But this was denied by Rougon, who asserted that Du Poizat was strongly opposed to the marriage, as he personally abominated M. Beulin-d'Orchère. All the rest, however, M. Kahn, M. Béjuin, Madame Correur, and even the Charbonnels, had never wearied of singing the praises of Mademoiselle Véronique. According to them, she would bring every imaginable virtue, prosperity and charm into his home. Then he concluded jocosely: 'She seems to have been made on purpose for me, and so I really couldn't refuse to take her.' And he added with a subtle smile: 'Besides, if we are going to have war in the autumn, it is necessary to think about making alliances.'

Clorinde expressed her perfect approval; and she, too, began to sing Mademoiselle Beulin-d'Orchère's praises, though she had only seen her once. Delestang, who had hitherto confined himself to nodding, without ever taking his eyes off his wife, now commenced an enthusiastic disquisition upon the advantages of marriage. And he was starting on a detailed account of his own happiness, when his wife rose and said they had another visit to make. As Rougon escorted them to the door, she held him back for a moment, letting her husband go on in front.

'Didn't I tell you that you would be married within the twelve-month?' she whispered softly in his ear.

VI

IN RETIREMENT

SUMMER came round. Rougon was leading a life of perfect quietude. In three months' time Madame Rougon had replaced the somewhat equivocal tone of the house in the Rue Marbeuf by one of solemn respectability. An atmosphere of propriety pervaded the rather chilly rooms, where all was spick and span. The furniture, always in place, the closely drawn curtains, allowing but little light to enter, and the thick carpets muffling every sound, imparted an air of almost conventual austerity to the house. Moreover, everything seemed to have acquired an appearance of age; it was as if one had entered some ancient musty patriarchal abode. That tall plain woman exercised an ever-watchful surveillance over everything, gliding through the subdued stillness of the house with noiseless steps; and she managed matters in such a discreet ready way that it seemed as if she had spent twenty years in the place instead of a few months.

Rougon smiled when people congratulated him. He still asserted that he had got married on the advice of his friends, and that his bride was their choice. She made him very happy. He had long desired to have a quiet decorous home, which might stand forth as a material proof of his respectability. It freed him from all his doubtful past and placed him amongst honest men. There was still a deal of provincialism in his nature, and certain substantially furnished drawing-rooms that he remembered at Plassans, where the chairs and couches were kept swathed in white coverings the whole year round, still formed his ideals. When he called at Delestang's, where Clorinde made an extravagant display of luxury, he showed his contempt by shrugging his shoulders. Nothing seemed to him so ridiculous as throwing money, as it were, out of the window; not that he was miserly, but he said that he could find enjoyments far preferable to those that were to be purchased with money. He had committed to his wife the care of their fortune. Previously he had lived without calculating his expenses, but now Madame Rougon attended to money matters with the same zealous care as she showed in managing the house.

For the first few months after his marriage, Rougon lived a life of seclusion, preparing for the contest which he dreamt of. He loved power for its own sake, without any hankering for riches and honours. Very ignorant, and of little skill in things which were not connected with the management of men, it was only his keen craving for power that elevated him to a position of superiority. The ambition of raising himself above the crowd, which seemed to him to be compounded of fools and knaves, and of leading and driving men by sheer force, developed most energetic skill and cunning in his heavy nature. He believed only in himself, took his convictions for reasons, and held everything subordinate to the increase of his personal influence. Addicted to no vice, he yet revelled as at some secret orgy in the idea of wielding supreme power. Though he had inherited his father's massive shoulders and heavy face, he had derived from his mother, the redoubtable Félicité who governed Plassans, a strong fiery will and passion for force which made him disdainful of petty means and commonplace gratifications. He was certainly the greatest of the Rougons.

When he found himself solitary and unoccupied after years of active life, his first feeling was one of delightful drowsiness. It was as though he had had no sleep since the exciting days of 1851, and he accepted his dismissal as a well-deserved holiday earned by long service. He proposed to hold himself aloof for six months, which would give him time to choose a better battle-ground, and then at his own discretion he could join in the great fight again. But in a few weeks' time he was already weary of resting. He had never before been so clearly conscious of his own strength; and his head and limbs became a source of embarrassment to him now that he was no longer actively employing them. He spent whole days in pacing his little garden and yawning wearily, like one of those caged lions whom one sees restlessly stretching their stiffened limbs. And now he began to know a most distasteful existence, the overwhelming weariness of which he carefully strove to conceal. To his friends he professed himself perfectly happy, and declared that he was well pleased to be 'out of the muddle,' but his heavy eyelids would rise occasionally in order that he might watch the course of events, and then again drop over his glistening eyes as soon as he saw anyone looking at him. What helped more than anything else to keep him erect was the unpopularity which he realised he had incurred. His fall seemed to have caused much satisfaction. Not a day passed without some newspaper attacking him; he was spoken of as the personification of the *coup d'état,* the proscriptions, and of all the other violent measures to which people referred in veiled language; and some writers even went so far as to congratulate the Emperor upon having severed his connection with a servant who had done his best to compromise him.

At the Tuileries the feeling of hostility against Rougon was even more marked. Marsy, now triumphant, assailed him with witticisms which ladies retailed through the drawing-rooms of Paris. This bitterness, however, actually comforted Rougon and confirmed him in his contempt for the human flock of sheep. They had not forgotten him; they detested him; and that seemed very sweet. Himself against the world! It was a thought which had a peculiar charm for him; and he saw himself standing alone, whip in hand, and forcing the yelping pack to keep their distance. He revelled in the insults which were offered to him, and held his head higher than ever in his haughty seclusion.

His brawny body, however, was suffering terribly from his enforced inactivity. If he had dared, he would have seized a spade and dug up his garden. However, he preferred to commence a long piece of writing in which he would carefully compare the English constitution with the Imperial constitution of 1852, with the idea of proving—all allowance made for the history and political customs of the two nations—that the French had as much liberty as the English. However, when he had consulted all the necessary authorities and collected sufficient notes, he had to force himself into taking up the pen. He could easily have made a long speech on the subject before the Chamber, but to write a treatise in which each sentence must be carefully thought out appeared to him a task of immense difficulty; and one, too, of no immediate usefulness. To express himself in good literary style had always embarrassed him, and it was for this reason that he pretended to hold style in contempt. He only got ten pages of his treatise written, still he left the manuscript on his desk, though he did not add twenty lines to it a week. On the other hand, whenever anybody asked him how he employed his time, he explained his project at great length, and dwelt on its great import. This was the excuse which he employed to conceal the hateful emptiness of his life.

Months went on, and he turned a yet more serene and smiling face to the world. Not a sign of the utter weariness he was suffering did he allow to appear. When his intimates sympathised with him, he assured them of his perfect felicity and gave them the most convincing reasons for it. Had he not everything to make him happy? he asked. He delighted in study, and now he could work as he listed, which was infinitely preferable to the feverish agitation of public life. As the Emperor had no need of his services, he did well to leave him in quietude in his little corner. He never spoke of the Emperor in other terms than those of profound devotion. Still, he frequently said that at a sign from his master he was perfectly willing to take up the burden of power again, adding, however, that he would not venture on a single step to provoke that sign. To all appearances, indeed, he was very anxious to keep aloof. Amidst the quietude of those early years of the Empire, amidst the nation's strange stupor born of mingled dread and weariness, he could hear faint sounds as of a coming awakening, and, as a supreme hope, he reckoned on some catastrophe which would suddenly make him necessary to the State. He was the man for critical situations, 'the man with the big paws,' as M. de Marsy had put it.

The Rougons received their friends at their house in the Rue Marbeuf on Sundays and Thursdays. They chatted in the big red drawing-room till half-past ten o'clock, at which time Rougon pitilessly turned them out of doors, for he held that late hours fogged the brain. Exactly at ten o'clock, Madame Rougon herself served tea. Two plates of little cakes accompanied the tea, but no one ever touched them.

On the Thursday in the July of that year which followed the general elections, the whole band was assembled in the drawing-room at eight o'clock. Madame Bouchard, Madame Charbonnel, and Madame Correur sat in a circle near an open window to inhale the occasional whiffs of fresh air which came in from the little garden, and in their midst M. d'Escorailles related the pranks he had played in his Plassans days, when he had often gone off to Monaco for twelve hours or so, on the pretext of taking part in a shooting expedition with a friend. Madame Rougon, who, dressed in black, sat half concealed behind a curtain, paid no attention to all this, but would now and again quietly rise and leave the room. She frequently disappeared for a quarter of an hour at a time. M. Charbonnel, however, was perched at the edge of an easy chair near the ladies, in amazement at hearing a young man of high rank confessing such adventures. At the other end of the room stood Clorinde, listening inattentively to a conversation on crops which her husband and M. Béjuin had started. She wore a creamy dress, freely trimmed with straw-coloured ribbons, and she gently tapped the palm of her left hand with her fan while gazing at the bright globe of the one lamp with which the drawing-room was lighted. Meantime, Colonel Jobelin and M. Bouchard were playing piquet at a card-table, while Rougon, like a fortune-teller, was consulting a pack of cards in a corner, setting them out on the green cloth in a grave and methodical manner. This was his favourite amusement on Thursdays and Sundays, affording occupation both for his fingers and his mind.

'Well, will it come off?' Clorinde asked with a smile as she approached him.

'It always comes off,' he replied quietly.

She remained standing on the other side of the table while he dealt the pack into eight small heaps.

When he had turned the cards over and picked them up in pairs—two aces, two kings, two queens, and so forth—she remarked, 'Yes, you have managed it all right. But what did you want the cards to tell you?'

Rougon slowly raised his eyes as though surprised at the question. 'What kind of weather we shall have to-morrow,' he said at length.

Then he began to deal the cards afresh. Delestang and M. Béjuin had now ceased talking, and the silence was only broken by pretty Madame Bouchard's rippling laugh. Clorinde stepped up to a window and stood there for a moment peering into the deepening twilight.

'Is there any news of poor Monsieur Kahn?' she asked, without turning her head.

'I've had a letter from him,' said Rougon. 'I am expecting him this evening.'

Then the conversation turned upon M. Kahn's ill-fortune. During the last session of the Corps Législatif, he had been imprudent enough to criticise a government bill rather sharply, as, by authorising a very dangerous competition in a neighbouring district, it threatened the Bressuire blast-furnaces with ruin. In this, M. Kahn had not for a moment imagined that he had exceeded the bounds of permissible opposition; but on going down to Deux-Sèvres, to prepare for his re-election, he had been informed by the prefect himself that he was no longer the official candidate. He had lost favour, and the minister had just nominated a Niort attorney, a man of most mediocre abilities. This, of course, was a crushing blow.

Rougon was giving particulars of the matter, when M. Kahn himself came into the room, followed by Du Poizat. They had both arrived by the seven o'clock train, and had only taken sufficient time to dine before coming on to Rougon's.

'Well, what do you think of it?' said M. Kahn, standing in the middle of the room, while everyone pressed round him. 'Fancy me being a revolutionist!'

Du Poizat had thrown himself into an easy chair with a weary air. 'A nice campaign!' he cried. 'A pretty muddle! It's enough to disgust all decent people!'

However, the company insisted upon M. Kahn telling them the story in detail. He related that on his arrival in Deux-Sèvres he had noticed a sort of embarrassment among even his best friends. The prefect of the department, M. de Langlade, was a man of dissolute character, whom he accused of paying attentions to the wife of the new deputy, the Niort attorney. However, this Langlade had told him of the disfavour into which he had fallen in a kind enough fashion while they were smoking their cigars after a breakfast at the prefecture. Then M. Kahn repeated the conversation which had passed between himself and M. de Langlade. The worst of the matter, said he, was that his addresses and other bills were already being printed. He had felt so indignant at first that he had been in-clined to stand all the same.

'Ah! if you hadn't written to us,' interposed Du Poizat, turning to Rougon, 'we should have taught the government a pretty lesson!'

Rougon shrugged his shoulders. 'You would have failed, and have compromised yourselves for ever,' said he, as he shuffled his cards. 'That would have been a fine feat!'

'I don't know what you're made of!' retorted Du Poizat, jumping up with a gesture of indignation. 'For my part, that fellow Marsy is getting past all bearing. It was you that he was aiming at when he struck our friend Kahn. Have you seen his circulars to the prefects? A pretty business his elections have been! He settled them all with bits of rhetoric! Don't smile! If you had been Minister of the Inte-rior, you would have managed matters in a very different fashion.'

Then, seeing that Rougon still smiled as he looked at him, he added yet more violently: 'We were on the spot and saw the whole business. One unlucky fellow, an old comrade of mine, had the te-merity to come forward as a Republican candidate. You can't imag-ine the abominable way in which he was treated. The prefect, the mayors, the gendarmes, the whole clique, fell foul of him. They defaced and tore his bills and threw his bulletins into the ditches; they arrested the few poor devils who distributed his circulars; and they couldn't even leave his poor aunt alone, a most estimable woman, who was obliged to beg him not to come to her house any more, as he only compromised her. And as for the newspapers, they spoke of him as though he were a cut-throat, and now, whenever he passes through a village, all the women cross themselves.'

Du Poizat noisily drew breath, then flung himself into his chair again and continued: 'Well, although Marsy has got a majority in all the departments, Paris at any rate has returned five opposition deputies. That's the awakening. If the Emperor goes on leaving power in the hands of that big coxcomb of a minister and those wanton prefects, who send husbands off to the Chamber so that they may make love to their wives, why, in five years from now the Empire will be on the verge of ruin. For my part, I'm delighted with the elections in Paris. They have avenged us, I think.'

'So, if you had been a prefect—' began Rougon quietly, with such a slight touch of irony that his thick lips barely curled.

Du Poizat showed his irregular white teeth, and grasped the arms of his chair with his frail, delicate hands as though he wished to twist them. 'Oh!' said he, 'if I had been prefect—' But he did not finish. He again fell back in his chair, and exclaimed: 'It's getting quite sickening. Besides, in reality, I have always been a Republican.'

The ladies by the window had now turned their heads towards the others, and were listening to what was being said. M. d'Escorailles held a large fan, with which he was fanning pretty Madame Bouchard, who looked quite overcome by the heat. The colonel and M. Bouchard, who had just commenced a fresh game, ceased playing every now and then to express their approval or disapproval of what was being said by nodding or shaking their heads. A wide circle of chairs had been drawn up around Rougon. Clorinde, listening attentively with her chin resting upon her hand, did not venture even on a gesture. Delestang, dwelling upon some tender recollection, sat smiling at his wife; while M. Béjuin, with his hands clasped on his knees, looked at the ladies and gentlemen in succession with a scared face. The sudden arrival of Du Poizat and M. Kahn had stirred up a perfect storm in the quiet drawing-room. They seemed to have brought with them an odour of opposition.

'Well, in the end I followed your advice and retired,' resumed M. Kahn. 'I was warned that if I persisted I should receive even worse treatment than the Republican candidate—I who have served the Empire with such devotion! You must admit that such ingratitude is enough to damp the enthusiasm of the firmest supporters.'

Then he bitterly complained of a whole string of annoyances and vexations. He had been anxious to start a newspaper which should support his scheme of a railway line from Niort to Angers, and which later on would have become a very useful financial weapon in his hands; but he had been refused the necessary authorisation. M. de Marsy had suspected that Rougon was behind him, and that the proposed journal would be used for attacking his administration.

'They are afraid lest some one should at last write the truth about them,' said Du Poizat. 'Ah! I would have furnished you with some sweet articles! It is disgraceful to have such a press as we have, gagged and threatened with suppression at the first word of complaint it dares to print. A friend of mine, who is bringing out a novel serially, was recently summoned to the Ministry, where a head clerk requested him to change the colour of his hero's waistcoat, as the colour he had assigned to it was distasteful to the minister. Oh! it's perfectly true. It's no invention.'

He cited other facts, and told them of terrible stories which circulated among the people; of the suicides of a young actress and a relation of the Emperor's, and of an alleged duel between two generals, one of whom had killed the other, in one of the corridors of the Tuileries, as the outcome of some story of robbery.[1] 'Would such stories ever have found any credence if the press had been allowed to speak freely?' asked Du Poizat; and he added: 'I am a Republican, decidedly I am.'

'You are very fortunate,' remarked M. Kahn; 'I no longer know what I am.'

Rougon, bending his broad shoulders, had just then commenced a very elaborate *réussite*. His aim, after dealing his thirty-two cards three times, first into seven heaps, then into five, and finally into

---

[1] This was the duel between St. Arnaud and Cornemuse, in which the latter was killed. Both had been accused of stealing 4,000£. in notes off the Emperor's table, but the real culprit was probably King Jérôme, Napoléon's uncle.—*Ed.*

three, was to bring the eight clubs together. He seemed completely absorbed in what he was doing, still he pricked up his ears at certain words.

'The parliamentary system afforded us reliable guarantees,' remarked the colonel. 'Ah! if we could only have the princes back!'

When his fits of opposition were on, Colonel Jobelin was an Orleanist. He often recounted the engagement of Mouzaïa, when he had fought by the side of the Duc d'Aumale, at that time a captain in the fourth regiment of the Line. 'We all got on very well under Louis Philippe,' he continued, noticing the silence with which his expression of regret was received. 'Don't you believe that, if we had a responsible cabinet, our friend here would be at the head of the government within six months?'

M. Bouchard, however, showed signs of impatience. He professed himself a Legitimist, probably because his grandfather had had some connection with the Court in former days. Thus, he and his cousin Jobelin often had heated discussions upon politics. 'Nonsense!' he exclaimed, 'your July monarchy only existed by dint of expedients. There is only one real principle, as you know very well.'

Thereupon they began to get rather warm. They made a clean sweep of the Empire, and each installed in its place the government of his particular choice. Would the Orléans family, cried Jobelin, have ever made the decoration of an old soldier a matter of bargain? Would the Legitimist kings, retorted Bouchard, ever have been guilty of such unjust favouritism as was now to be seen every day in the government offices? Thus they went on till they covertly alluded to one another as fools, when all at once the colonel, angrily picking up his cards, exclaimed: 'Make less noise, do you hear, Bouchard, and please attend to the game!'

Delestang, whom the dispute had awakened from his reverie, now felt bound to defend the Empire. Certainly, said he, it was not everything that he could wish. He would have liked a government of broader sympathies. And he attempted to explain his aspirations, which embraced a somewhat involved form of socialism, with such desiderata as the extinction of pauperism and the co-operation of the working classes, a system, in fact, much like that of his model farm of Chamade, but on a large scale. While her husband spoke, wagging his handsome head with an official air, Clorinde kept her eyes on him, and slightly pouted.

'Yes, certainly I'm a Bonapartist,' he repeated; 'a liberal Bonapartist, if you like.'

'And you, Béjuin?' M. Kahn suddenly inquired.

'Oh, I am one too,' replied M. Béjuin; 'there are shades and distinctions of course, but I am certainly a Bonapartist.'

Du Poizat burst into a shrill laugh. 'Of course, you are!' he exclaimed. And as they pressed him to explain himself, he continued: 'Oh! you amuse me. You haven't been turned out, you see. Delestang is still a member of the Council of State, and Béjuin has just been re-elected.'

'That was a matter of course,' said Béjuin; 'the prefect of the Cher—'

'Oh, you are not responsible, I don't accuse you. We all know how these matters are worked. Combelot, too, is re-elected, and La Rouquette also. So, of course, the Empire is a magnificent institution!'

M. d'Escorailles, who was still fanning pretty Madame Bouchard, now felt constrained to put in a word. He defended the Empire from another point of view. He had adhered to it, he said, because it seemed to him that the Emperor had a grand mission to fulfil. 'The salvation of France before everything else!'

'You have retained your berth as auditor, haven't you?' asked Du Poizat, raising his voice. 'Well, then, there's no difficulty in guessing your opinions. You all seem terribly scandalised by what I'm saying; but it is a very simple matter. Kahn and I, you see, are no longer paid to keep our eyes shut.'

At this the others began to show a little temper. It was disgraceful to take such a view of politics, they said. There were other things besides personal interests to be considered. Even the colonel and M. Bouchard, although they were not Bonapartists themselves, admitted that a man might be a Bonapartist in all good faith; and they waxed hot in support of their own principles, as though an attempt was being made to wrench them from them. As for Delestang, he seemed much offended. He complained that he had been quite misunderstood, and went on to point out how he differed from the blind partisans of the Empire. This led him into fresh explanations of the democratic developments which he thought compatible with the Emperor's government. Then both M. Béjuin and M. d'Escorailles objected to be looked upon as Bonapartists pure and simple. They spoke of many different shades of opinion, each clinging to his own particular, but somewhat vaguely defined, views. And thus in ten minutes or so the whole company had gone over to the opposition. Voices rang out in dispute, and such terms as 'Legitimist,' 'Orleanist,' and 'Republican,' were bandied about amidst repeated declarations of political faith. Madame Rougon looked in at one of the doors for a moment, as if somewhat uneasy, and then quietly disappeared again.

Rougon, however, had now just succeeded in getting his clubs into proper sequence, whereupon Clorinde stooped and asked him amidst the general uproar: 'Well, have you managed it?'

'Certainly,' he replied, with his quiet smile. Then, as if he had only just become aware of the war of words that was going on, he shook his hand, remarking: 'You are making a lot of noise.'

Thinking that he wanted to say something, the others then ceased talking, and perfect silence ensued. However, while they waited, Rougon simply spread thirteen cards upon the table, reckoned them over, and finally, amidst general attention, exclaimed: 'Three queens, the sign of a quarrel. A dark woman, who is not to be trusted—'

But Du Poizat impatiently interrupted him. 'Well, Rougon, and what is your opinion?'

The great man thereupon threw himself back in his chair and stretched his legs, while raising his hand to his mouth to conceal a slight yawn. And he raised his chin as though his neck were paining him.

'Oh, I,' he said, with his eyes turned to the ceiling,' I believe in the principle of authority. It is a necessity with me. It was born with me. It is very foolish of you to wrangle. In France, whenever one gets five men together, it is certain that five different kinds of government are represented. But that doesn't prevent a man from loyally serving the established government. That is so, is it not? You're talking just for the sake of talking.'

Then he let his chin drop and glanced slowly round the room, as he resumed: 'Marsy has managed the elections very well. You did wrong to blame his circulars. The last one was an extremely good one. And as for the press, I think that it has too much liberty already. What kind of state should we be in, if any one could write everything he liked? I should have taken the same course as Marsy in refusing to grant Kahn permission to start a newspaper. It is always unwise to provide your opponents with weapons. Soft-hearted

Empires invariably come to grief. France requires an iron hand, and is none the worse for being grasped a little tightly.' Delestang felt bound to protest against this. 'But, at any rate, there are certain necessary liberties—' he commenced.

Clorinde, however, made him stop. She had expressed her approval of all Rougon had said by ostentatious nods. She had even brought herself forward so that he might see her better, submissive and convinced before him. And it was at her that he cast a quick glance as he exclaimed: 'Oh, yes! the necessary liberties! I was expecting that they would be dragged in! Well, if the Emperor took my advice, he would never grant a single liberty.'

Then as Delestang again showed an inclination to protest, his wife reduced him to silence by a threatening frown of her beautiful brow.

'*Never!*' repeated Rougon energetically. And he sprang from his chair and looked so formidable that no one ventured to speak a word. Then, however, he dropped down again, and his limbs seemed to grow limp as he muttered: 'You've made me shout as well.—However, I'm only a simple private citizen now, and have no occasion to mix myself up in it all, thank goodness. Heaven grant that the Emperor may have no further occasion for my services!'

Just at that moment the door of the drawing-room was opened, and Rougon, raising his finger to his mouth, added in a whisper: 'Hush!'

It was M. La Rouquette who entered. Rougon suspected that he came to the Rue Marbeuf at the instigation of his sister, Madame de Llorentz, to spy upon what went on there. M. de Marsy, although he had only been married six months, had just renewed his intimacy with this lady, whose name had been associated with his own for nearly two years. And so as soon as the young deputy made his appearance, politics were set aside and the drawing-room resumed its decorous quietude. Rougon himself went to fetch a large shade which he placed over the lamp, and then one saw only the withered hands of the colonel and M. Bouchard throwing down their cards in the circle of yellow light. At the window Madame Charbonnel was now telling her troubles in a low voice to Madame Correur, while M. Charbonnel punctuated each detail with a deep sigh. They would soon have been two years in Paris, the lady was saying sadly, and their wretched lawsuit seemed as though it would never end. On the day before she had been obliged to buy herself six new chemises and her husband six new shirts, having learnt that the matter had been again adjourned. Somewhat in the rear of this group, near a curtain, was Madame Bouchard, who had apparently dropped asleep, rendered drowsy by the heat. M. d'Escorailles approached her again, and then, as no one was looking, he had the calm impudence to print a kiss upon her half-closed lips. At this, she opened her eyes, looking very solemn, but she kept quite still.

'On dear, no!' M. La Rouquette was saying just at that moment; 'I haven't been to the Variétés. I saw the full-dress rehearsal of the piece. It's a tremendous success; the music is wonderfully gay. It will draw all Paris. But to-day I had some work to finish, something I am preparing.'

He had shaken hands with the men, and had gallantly kissed Clorinde's wrist above her glove. And he remained standing, smiling and leaning against the back of an armchair. He was irreproachably dressed, and there was an assumption of solemn gravity in the way in which his frock-coat was buttoned up.

'By-the-bye,' he said, addressing himself to the master of the house, '*apropos* of your great work, I should like to call your attention to a most interesting paper on the English constitution which has just appeared in a Vienna review. Are you making progress?'

'Oh, I'm getting on very slowly,' Rougon replied. 'I have got to a chapter which gives me a great deal of trouble.'

As a rule he delighted to make the young deputy talk, for through him he learnt all that went on at the Tuileries. He felt sure that La Rouquette had been sent to his house that evening to find out what he thought about the success of the official candidates, and he succeeded in worming a large amount of information out of him, though he himself did not make a remark that was worth repeating. He began by congratulating the young man upon his own election, and then kept up the conversation by occasional nods. La Rouquette, who was fond of talking, rattled on without a pause. The Court was delighted, he said. The Emperor had learnt the result of the elections, at Plombières, and it was said that on the arrival of the telegram he had been obliged to sit down, as his legs gave way with emotion. But there was one great source of uneasiness amidst the victory. Paris had shown monstrous ingratitude.

'Pooh! Paris can be muzzled!' said Rougon, stifling another yawn, as though bored at finding nothing of interest in all M. La Rouquette's chatter.

Ten o'clock struck, and Madame Rougon, having placed a small round table in the centre of the room, began to serve the tea. The company scattered in little groups about the room. M. Kahn was standing cup in hand in front of Delestang, who never took tea because it affected his nerves, and was giving him some additional particulars of his journey to La Vendée. His great scheme for a railway from Niort to Angers was no further advanced, he said. However, that scamp of a Langlade, the prefect of Deux-Sèvres, had audaciously availed himself of it to influence the constituency in favour of the new official candidate.

Meantime, M. La Rouquette, who had slipped behind the ladies, was whispering remarks which made them smile; while Madame Correur, screened by a rampart of chairs, talked somewhat excitedly to Du Poizat. She asked him about her brother Martineau, the notary at Coulonges, and the other told her that he had seen him for a moment in front of the church, looking just the same as ever, with his hard face and solemn air. Then, as she started on her usual recriminations, he mischievously advised her never to go home again, as Madame Martineau had sworn she would fling her out of doors. Madame Correur finished her tea, feeling quite choked.

'Come, my children, it's time to go to bed,' said Rougon paternally.

It was now twenty-five minutes past ten, and he gave them five minutes longer. Some of the company, however, withdrew at once. Rougon went to the door with M. Kahn and M. Béjuin, whom Madame Rougon invariably charged with compliments for their wives, though she saw the ladies twice a year at the utmost. Then Rougon gently pushed the Charbonnels towards the door. They were always greatly embarrassed about taking their leave. And afterwards, as pretty Madame Bouchard was going off between M. d'Escorailles and M. La Rouquette, he turned to the card-table and exclaimed: 'Come, Monsieur Bouchard, they are carrying off your wife!'

But the chief-clerk, without appearing to hear, went on calling out his points: 'A major quint in clubs! That's good, eh? Three kings; they are good too.'

However, Rougon gathered up the cards. 'Come, you've had enough!' said he. 'Get away home with you. You ought to be ashamed of yourselves for getting so excited over it. Come, colonel, come.'

It was just the same every Thursday and Sunday. He had to stop them in the middle of a game, and sometimes even turn the lamp out before they would give up their play. And they went off, disputing with each other.

Delestang and Clorinde were the last to go, and while her husband was hunting about the room for her fan, the young woman said to Rougon in an undertone: 'It is foolish of you not to take a little exercise; you will make yourself ill.'

However he made a gesture of indifference and resignation: Madame Rougon was already gathering together the cups and teaspoons. Then as Delestang shook hands with him, the great man frankly yawned in his face. In order, however, that they might not think his evening had bored him, he excused himself by saying: 'Ah! dash it, I shall sleep well to-night.'

The evenings always passed away in this manner. There was a sombre atmosphere about the room, and Du Poizat even said that 'it smelt too much of cant.' Clorinde called very frequently. She often came by herself in the afternoon to fulfil some commission with which she had charged herself. She would playfully tell Madame Rougon that she had come to make love to her husband, and the wife, with a smile on her pale lips, would leave them together for hours at a time. They conversed familiarly, without appearing to recollect the past, exchanging friendly grasps of the hand in the very room where but a year before Rougon had paced up and down, so restless with passion. But they seemed to have forgotten all that, and gave themselves up to quiet friendship. Rougon would push back the young woman's straying hair, which always seemed to be blowing loose, or help her with the train of her dress, which was invariably very long and apt to become entangled among the chairs. One day, as they went through the garden, she had the curiosity to push the stable-door open. She even entered, giving a glance at Rougon and laughing lightly. But he merely remarked with a smile, as he stood with his hands in his pockets: 'How foolish people can be sometimes!'

Whenever she came to see him, he always gave her good advice. He spoke much in favour of Delestang, who, on the whole, made a very good husband. Clorinde said that she had great esteem for him, and he did not appear to have any cause of complaint against her. She said that she never flirted, and this was quite true. Her slightest remarks seemed tinged with indifference, almost with contempt, for men. When any one spoke of a woman with more lovers than could be counted, an expression of surprise would come into her big childlike eyes, and she would ask what pleasure any one could find in such conduct. For weeks together she seemed unconscious of her beauty, and only recollected it in some emergency, when she availed herself of it as a weapon. One day when Rougon, who harped upon the subject with singular pertinacity, was advising her to keep faithful to Delestang, she ended by getting angry and exclaiming: 'Oh, leave me alone. I'm quite aware of all you're saying. Really, you are becoming offensive.' And on another day she added bluntly: 'After all, it is no concern of yours.'

Rougon blushed, and for some time afterwards said nothing more on the subject of her duties and the proprieties. A persistent thrill of jealousy was all that now remained to him of his old passion. He watched her in the drawing-rooms which she frequented; and, if he had scented any intrigue, he would probably have warned her husband. As a matter of fact, when he was alone with the latter, he did try to put him on his guard, by speaking of his wife's extraordinary beauty. But Delestang always laughed with an air of fatuous confidence, and it was Rougon who really endured all the jealous torments of a betrayed husband.

His other counsels, practical ones, testified to his great affection for Clorinde. It was he who by degrees persuaded her to send her mother back to Italy. Countess Balbi, left alone in her little house in the Champs Elysées, had begun to lead a careless life which gave rise to much talk. Rougon took upon himself to settle the delicate question of an allowance. The house was next sold, and thus the young woman's past was wiped out. Then Rougon tried to cure her of her eccentricities, but in this matter he found himself confronted by utter *naïveté* and resolute feminine obstinacy. Clorinde, now that she was married and wealthy, squandered money lavishly, though she was subject to sudden impulses of sordid avarice. She had kept her little maid, the dusky Antonia, who sucked oranges from morning till night; and between them they made an abominable mess of Clorinde's rooms in the big house in the Rue du Colisée. When Rougon went to see the young woman, he would find dirty plates on the chairs, and bottles of syrup strewn along the floor beside the wall. Beneath the furniture too he could espy an untidy accumulation of things which had been hastily thrust out of sight when he was announced.

And amidst the greasy hangings and soiled, dusty woodwork, Clorinde still indulged in the most extraordinary caprices. She would often receive her friends wrapt round with a rug, and lying on a couch, while complaining of the strangest disorders—of a dog, for instance, which was gnawing at her foot, or of a pin which she had accidentally swallowed, and the point of which must be trying to force its way out through her leg. At other times she would close the shutters at three o'clock in the afternoon, light all the candles, and begin to dance with Antonia, the one facing the other, and indulging in such paroxysms of laughter that when Rougon arrived the maid had to stand panting by the door for five minutes before she could leave the room. One day too Clorinde determined to remain invisible; she sewed her bed curtains together from top to bottom, and sat up on the bolster inside the cage she had thus formed, talking to Rougon for more than an hour, as calmly as though they had been sitting on either side of the fire. These extravagancies seemed quite natural to her. When Rougon chided her for them, she appeared quite surprised, and declared that she was doing nothing improper. It was in vain that he preached propriety to her, and promised to make her the most fascinating woman in Paris in a month's time, if she would let herself be guided by him; she only grew angry, and exclaimed: 'It's my nature to be like this; I always go on like this. What harm does it do anybody?' And sometimes she would smile and say: 'Oh, well, people love me all the same! Don't preach!'

Delestang, indeed, worshipped her. To him she was quite unlike a wife, but for that very reason exercised the more influence. He shut his eyes to her caprices, smitten with a terrible fear lest she should leave him, as she had one day threatened to do. Beneath his meek submission there was probably a feeling that she was his superior, well able to do whatever she liked with him. In society he treated her almost like a child, and spoke to her with the complacency of a serious man. But when they were by themselves, this handsome fellow, with the haughty head, would burst into tears if she would not let him kiss her. The only check he put upon her was to take possession of the keys of the first floor rooms, in order that the reception apartments might be kept free from grease and dirt.

Rougon, though he failed in some things, managed to induce Clorinde to dress a little more like other people. With all her failings she was very shrewd, with the shrewdness of those lunatics who in lucid intervals manage to appear perfectly rational before strangers. He met her at certain houses, looking very demure and reserved, allowing her husband to do all the talking, and remaining quite decorous amidst the admiration excited by her beauty. At her own house, Rougon frequently found M. de Plouguern, and Clorinde would sit between them making playful remarks, while they poured forth moral disquisitions for her benefit. Sometimes the old senator would familiarly pat the girl's cheeks, much to Rougon's annoyance, though he never ventured to express what he thought on the subject. He was more courageous with regard to Luigi Pozzo, Chevalier Rusconi's secretary, whom he had frequently noticed leaving the house at unusual hours. When he hinted to the young woman that this might compromise her very seriously, she raised her eyes with a pretty look of surprise, and burst out laughing. She didn't care for what people thought, she cried. Besides, Luigi counted for nothing. He was her cousin, and he brought her little Milanese cakes, which he purchased for her in the Passage Colbert.

It was with politics, however, that Clorinde's mind was chiefly occupied. Since she had married Delestang, her brain had been busy with deep and intricate matters, of which no one knew the importance. She found in them, however, a means of satisfying her craving for intrigue, which had so long found scope in her attempts to ensnare those whom she thought to be coming men; and she seemed to be preparing herself in this way for some yet greater schemes which she had in contemplation. She kept up a regular correspondence with her mother, who was now settled at Turin; and went almost every day to the Sardinian legation, where Chevalier Rusconi took her apart, and talked to her in low tones. Then too she went on mysterious errands to all parts of Paris, making furtive visits to great personages, and keeping appointments in the most out-of-the-way places. All the Venetian refugees, the Brambillas, and the Staderinos, and the Viscardis, came to see her secretly, and gave her scraps of paper covered with memoranda. She had bought a large red morocco case, a genuine ministerial portfolio with a steel lock, and in it she stowed away a wonderful collection of documents. When she drove out, she kept it on her knees like a muff; and wherever she called she carried it about with her under her arm; and she might even be met early in the morning, on foot, clasping it against her breast with both her hands. The case soon began to look worn, and it split at the seams. Then she buckled straps round it. And ever laden as she was with this shapeless leather case bursting with papers, she looked like some money-grubbing solicitor running from one police-court to another in the hope of picking up a petty fee.

Rougon had made several attempts to discover what it was that so engrossed Clorinde's thoughts. One day when he was left alone for a few moments with her famous portfolio, he had not scrupled to pull out some letters which protruded through its gaps. But all that he could find out in one fashion or another seemed to him so incoherent and disconnected that he smiled at the young woman's pretensions to politics. One afternoon, however, she quietly began to expound to him a vast scheme. She was working to bring about an alliance between France and Italy, in view of a speedy campaign against Austria. Rougon, who for a moment was very much struck by this, ended by shrugging his shoulders at the heap of absurdities which found place in her plan. He had in no way modified his opinion about women. Clorinde, on her side, so far as he was concerned, seemed to accept the subordinate position of a disciple quite willingly. When she went to see him in the Rue Marbeuf, she assumed an air of submissive humility, and questioned him, and listened to him with the eagerness of a neophyte anxious for instruction. For his part, he frequently forgot to whom he was speaking, and unfolded his theory of government, and talked to her in the most unrestrained and confidential manner. In fact, their conversations gradually became a regular habit, and he made her his confidante, breaking the silence which he observed in the presence of his best friends, and treating her like a discreet pupil, whose respectful admiration had a great charm for him.

During the months of August and September, Clorinde increased the frequency of her visits. She would call on Rougon three or four times a week, and never had she shown herself so gentle and affectionate. She paid him the most flattering compliments, eulogised his genius, and spoke regretfully of the great things which he would have accomplished if he had not retired. One day, as an idea flashed through his mind, he said to her with a laugh: 'There's something you want me to do for you?'

'Yes,' she replied candidly.

But she quickly reassumed her expression of admiring wonder. Politics were much more interesting than novels, she declared. However, whenever Rougon turned his back for a moment, she would open her eyes quite widely, and a momentary gleam would flash from them, suggesting some old feeling of bitterness which still lived on. She often let her hands linger in his, as though she still felt too weak for what she was contemplating, and was waiting till she had drained away sufficient of his strength to be able to throttle him.

However, his increasing lassitude at this juncture was really a source of much uneasiness to her. He seemed to be falling fast asleep amidst his boredom. She had made, at first, full allowance for all possible pretence which there might be in his demeanour, but was at length forced to believe that he really did feel discouraged. His movements had grown sluggish, and his voice languid; and sometimes he seemed so listless and indifferent that the young woman felt quite alarmed, and seriously wondered if he were not going to abide by his relegation to the Senate as a played-out politician.

Towards the end of September, however, Rougon seemed very thoughtful. At last, in one of his customary conversations with Clorinde, he told her that he was maturing a great scheme. He was growing weary of Paris, and needed fresh air. Then all at once he spoke out. It was a great scheme of an altogether fresh life: a voluntary exile to the Landes of Gascony, the clearing of several square leagues of ground, and the founding of a new town amidst the conquered territory. Clorinde turned quite pale as she listened to him.

'But your position here!' she cried; 'your prospects!'

'Bah! castles in the air!' he said disdainfully. 'I have come to the conclusion that I am not cut out for politics.'

Then he reverted to his pet idea of being a great landowner, with herds of cattle which he would rule in all sovereignty. But his ambition was now greater. In the Landes of Gascony he would be like the conquering king of a new territory. He would have a people under him. He gave Clorinde all kinds of particulars. For the last fortnight, without saying a word to anyone, he had been reading technical treatises. And in imagination he had been reclaiming marshes, clearing the soil of stones with the aid of powerful machines, checking the advance of the sandhills by plantations of pines, and dowering France with a tract of wondrously fertile country. All his dormant activity, all his latent giant's strength, awoke within him at the thought of this undertaking. He clenched his fists as though he were already face to face with rebellious rocks. In imagination he turned the whole soil over at a single stroke; carried houses completely built on his shoulders, and dropped them as his fancy listed on the banks of some river, whose bed he had hollowed out by a single kick of his foot. It all seemed so easy, and it would give him the work he so much desired. The Emperor, no doubt, still retained sufficient good-will towards him to let him reclaim those waste lands. And erect, bracing up his big form, and with his cheeks aglow, he burst into a proud laugh: 'It is a magnificent idea!' he cried. 'I shall give my name to the town, and I, too, shall found a little Empire!'

Clorinde imagined that it was all a mere caprice, a whim born of the boredom in which he was struggling. But when they subsequently met, Rougon again spoke of his scheme with even greater enthusiasm than before. Each time she came to see him, she found him amidst a litter of maps strewn over the desk, the chairs, and the carpet alike. One afternoon she was not able to see him, as he was conferring with two engineers. Thereupon she began to feel really alarmed. Could he really mean to give her the slip like that and go off and found this town of his in the wilderness? Wasn't it rather some new stratagem he was arranging? However, she relinquished her endeavours to ascertain the truth, and thought it best to give the alarm to the whole band.

There was great consternation. Du Poizat flew into a passion. For more than a year now he had been living by shifts, and on his last journey to La Vendee his father had hastily taken a pistol from a drawer on his venturing to ask him for ten thousand francs to float a magnificent speculation. So now the ex-sub-prefect was half-starving again just as in 1848. M. Kahn showed equal anger. His blast-furnaces at Bressuire were being threatened with speedy ruin, and he felt that he would be lost if he could not obtain the railway grant within the next six months. All the others, M. Béjuin, the colonel, the Bouchards, and the Charbonnels, were similarly upset. Things could not possibly be allowed to end like that, they cried. Really, such conduct on Rougon's part was not reasonable. They must talk to him about it.

A fortnight, however, went by. Clorinde, whose ideas were approved by the whole band, had come to the conclusion that it would be hazardous to make an open attack on the great man. They must wait for a fitting opportunity. This they did, and one Sunday evening, towards the middle of October, when they were all assembled in the drawing-room in the Rue Marbeuf, Rougon smilingly remarked to them: 'You'd never guess what I received to-day.'

Then he took a pink card from behind the timepiece and showed it to them. 'An invitation to Compiègne, from the Emperor,' he said.

At this moment his valet quietly opened the door, and told him that the gentleman he was expecting had arrived. Rougon excused himself and left the room. Clorinde had risen to her feet and stood there listening. Then, as silence fell, she exclaimed, energetically: 'He must go to Compiègne!'

The friends glanced round suspiciously; but they were quite alone. Madame Rougon had gone off some minutes previously. And so in low voices, and with their eyes fixed on the doors, they began to speak their minds. The ladies were gathered in a circle in front of the fire-place, where a huge log was smouldering. M. Bouchard and the colonel were busy with their everlasting piquet, while the other men had wheeled their chairs into a corner to isolate themselves. Clorinde alone remained standing in the middle of the room, her head bent as if deep in thought.

'He was expecting somebody, then?' began Du Poizat. 'Who can it be, I wonder?'

The others shrugged their shoulders, as if to say that they did not know.

'Something to do with this idiotic scheme of his, perhaps,' continued the ex-sub-prefect. 'One of these evenings, you'll see, I shall tell him plainly what I think of him.'

'Hush!' exclaimed M. Kahn, raising his finger to his lips.

Du Poizat had raised his voice in an alarming way. For a moment they all strained their ears to listen. Then M. Kahn himself said in a very low tone: 'There is no doubt but what he has pledged himself to us.'

'Say, rather, that he has contracted a debt,' interposed the colonel, laying down his cards.

'Yes, yes; a debt; that is the word,' declared M. Bouchard. 'We didn't mince matters that last day at the Council of State.'

All the others nodded assent. There was a general lamentation. Rougon had ruined them. M. Bouchard added, that if it had not been for his fidelity, he would have got his promotion long ago; and, to hear the colonel talk, anyone would have imagined that he had been offered a commander's cross, and a post for his son Auguste, on the part of M. de Marsy, and that he had simply refused them out of friendship for Rougon. M. d'Escorailles' parents, said pretty Madame Bouchard, were much disappointed at seeing their son remain a mere auditor when for the last six months they had been expecting his promotion to higher rank. Even those who said nothing, Delestang, M. Béjuin, Madame Correur, and the Charbonnels, bit their lips and raised their eyes to heaven with the expression of martyrs whose patience was at last beginning to fail them.

'Well, the long and the short of it is that we are being defrauded,' cried Du Poizat. 'But he shall not go away; I answer for that! Is there any sense in a man setting off and struggling with stones when there are such serious interests to keep him in Paris? Are you willing that I should speak to him?'

Clorinde now awoke from her reverie. She waved her hand to obtain silence; and after opening the door to see that there was no one outside, she repeated: 'I tell you that he must go to Compiègne!'

Then, as every face turned towards her, she checked all questions with another wave of her hand: 'Hush! not here!'

She told them, however, that she and her husband had also been invited to Compiègne, and she made some mention of M. de Marsy and Madame de Llorentz without consenting to enter into further details. However, they would push the great man into power in spite of himself, she said; they would compromise him, if he drove them to it. M. Beulin-d'Orchère and the whole judicial bench secretly supported him; and M. La Rouquette had confessed that the Emperor, amidst all the hatred expressed against Rougon by those who surrounded him, had kept absolute silence on the matter. Whenever the great man's name was mentioned in his presence, he became serious and lowered his eyes.

'It is not we alone who are concerned,' M. Kahn now declared. 'If we succeed, the whole country will owe us thanks.'

Then, raising their voices, they all began to sing the praises of the master of the house. A buzz of conversation in an adjoining room had just become audible. Du Poizat was so carried away by curiosity, that he pushed the door open as though he were going out, and then closed it again with sufficient deliberation to take a look at the man who was speaking with Rougon. It was Gilquin, wearing a heavy overcoat in good condition, and holding in his hand a stout cane with a knob of yellow metal. He was saying in his full voice, with exaggerated familiarity: 'Don't send any more, you understand, to the Rue Virginie at Grenelle. I'm at Batignolles now, Passage Guttin. Well, you can reckon upon me. Good-bye for the present.'

Then he shook hands with Rougon.

When the latter returned to the drawing-room he apologised for his absence, but gave Du Poizat a keen glance: 'A good fellow, whom you know, Du Poizat, don't you?' said he. 'He is going to enlist some colonists for my new world in the Landes. By the way, I mean to take you all with me; so you had better get your things together. Kahn shall be my Prime Minister. Delestang and his wife shall have the portfolio of Foreign Affairs. Béjuin shall be Postmaster. And I won't forget the ladies. Madame Bouchard shall be Queen of Beauty, and I'll give the keys of our store-rooms to Madame Charbonnel.'

In this wise he playfully rattled on, while his friends, very ill at ease, were wondering if he had perchance heard them through some chink or other. When he proceeded to say that he would decorate the colonel with all the orders in his gift, the latter almost lost his temper. Clorinde, however, was looking at the invitation to Compiègne which she had taken from off the mantel-piece.

'Do you mean to go?' she asked, with an appearance of unconcern.

'Oh, no doubt,' replied Rougon, surprised at the question. 'I mean to take advantage of the opportunity to get the Emperor to give me my department.'

Just then ten o'clock struck, and Madame Rougon returned to the room and served tea.

VII

AT COURT

Towards seven o'clock on the evening of her arrival at Compiègne, Clorinde was engaged in conversation with M. de Plouguern near one of the windows in the Gallery of the Maps. They were waiting for the Emperor and Empress before entering the dining-room. The second batch of the season's guests had scarcely been more than three hours at the château, and all of them had not yet come down from their rooms. Clorinde occupied herself by briefly criticising them as they entered the gallery, one by one. The ladies, in low dresses, and wearing flowers in their hair, put on smiles as soon as they reached the threshold; while the gentlemen, wearing white cravats, black knee-breeches, and silk stockings' preserved a solemn air.

'Ah; here comes the Chevalier!' muttered Clorinde. 'He looks very nice, doesn't he? But just look at M. Beulin-d'Orchère, godfather! Doesn't he look as though he were going to bark? And, good heavens, what legs!'

M. de Plouguern began to grin, much amused by this backbiting. Chevalier Rusconi came up and bowed to Clorinde, with the languid gallantry of a handsome Italian; then he made the round of the ladies, swaying to and fro with a series of gentle rhythmical reverences. A few yards away, Delestang, looking very serious, was examining the huge maps of the Forest of Compiègne, which covered the walls of the gallery.

'Whereabouts in the train were you?' Clorinde continued. 'I looked out for you at the station, so that we might travel together. Just fancy, I was squeezed up with a whole crowd of men.' Then she stopped, and stifled a laugh with her fingers. 'How demure Monsieur La Rouquette looks!' said she.

'Yes, indeed; he's like a simpering schoolgirl,' rejoined the senator sarcastically.

Just at that moment a loud rustling was heard by the door, which was thrown wide open to admit a lady wearing a dress which was so lavishly adorned with bows and flowers and lace, that she had to press it down with both hands in order to get through. It was Madame de Combelot, Clorinde's sister-in-law. The latter stared at her, and murmured: 'Good gracious!'

Then, as M. de Plouguern glanced at her own dress of simple tarlatan, worn over an ill-cut under-skirt of rose-silk, she continued, with an air of complete unconcern: 'Ah! I don't care about dress, godfather! People must take me, you know, as I am.'

Delestang, however, had quitted the maps, and after joining his sister, led her to his wife. The two women were not particularly fond of each other, and exchanged rather stiff greetings. Then Madame de Combelot walked off, dragging her satin train, which looked like a strip of flower garden, through the clusters of silent men, who stepped back out of the way of this flood of lace flounces. Clorinde, as soon as she was alone again with M. de Plouguern, referred playfully to the lady's great passion for the Emperor. And when the old senator had told her that there was no reciprocal feeling on the Emperor's part, she continued: 'Well, there's no great merit in that; she's so dreadfully lean. I have been told that some men consider her good-looking, but I don't know why. She has absolutely no figure at all.'

While talking in this strain, Clorinde none the less kept her eyes upon the door. 'Ah! this time it must surely be Monsieur Rougon,' she said as it opened again. But, almost immediately, she resumed with a flash in her eyes: 'Ah, no! it is Monsieur de Marsy.'

The minister, looking quite irreproachable in his black dress-coat and knee-breeches, stepped up to Madame de Combelot with a smile, and while he was paying compliments to her, he glanced round at the assembled guests, blinking his eyes as though he recognised no one. But, as they began to bow to him, he inclined his head with an expression of great amiability. Several men approached him, and he soon became the centre of a group. His pale face, with its subtle cunning air, towered over the shoulders clustering round him.

'By the way,' said Clorinde, pushing M. de Plouguern into a window-recess, 'I have been relying upon you for some information. What do you know about Madame de Llorentz's famous letters?'

'Only what all the world knows,' replied the old senator.

Then he began to speak of the famous three letters which had been written, it was said, by Count de Marsy to Madame de Llorentz nearly five years previously, a short time before the Emperor's marriage. Madame de Llorentz, who had just lost her husband, a general of Spanish origin, was then at Madrid, looking after her deceased husband's affairs. It was the heyday of her connection with Marsy, who, to amuse her, and yielding to his own sportive proclivities, had sent her some very piquant details concerning certain august personages with whom he was living on intimate terms. And it was asserted that Madame de Llorentz, who was an extremely jealous beauty, had carefully preserved these letters, and kept them hanging over M. de Marsy's head as an ever-ready means of vengeance, should he presume to wander in his affections.

'She allowed herself to be talked over,' continued M. de Plouguern, 'when Marsy had to marry the Wallachian princess; but, after consenting to their spending a month's honeymoon together, she gave him to understand that if he did not return to her feet, she would some day lay the three terrible letters on the Emperor's desk. So he has taken up his fetters again, and lavishes the most loving attention upon her in the hope that he may get her to give these letters up.'

Clorinde laughed heartily; the story amused her, and she began to ask all sorts of questions. If the Count should deceive Madame de Llorentz, would she really carry her threat into execution? Where did she keep those letters? Was it really in the bosom of her dress, stitched between two pieces of satin ribbon, as some people said? M. de Plouguern, however, could give no further information. No one but Madame de Llorentz herself had ever read the letters; but he knew a young man who had vainly made himself her humble slave for nearly six months in the hope of being able to get a copy of them.

'But look at Marsy,' he continued, 'he never takes his eyes off you. Ah! I had forgotten; you have made a conquest of him. Is it true that, at the last soiree at the ministry, he remained talking to you for nearly an hour?'

The young woman made no reply. Indeed she was not listening, but stood majestic and motionless under M. de Marsy's steady gaze. Then slowly raising her head and looking at him in her turn, she waited for him to bow to her. He thereupon stepped up, and she smiled upon him very sweetly. They did not, however, exchange a word. The Count went back to the group he had left, in which M. La Rouquette now was talking very loudly, perpetually speaking of him as 'His Excellency.'

The gallery had gradually filled. There were nearly a hundred persons present: high functionaries, generals, foreign diplomatists, five deputies, three prefects, two painters, a novelist, and a couple of academicians, to say nothing of the court officials, the chamberlains, and the aides-de-camp and equerries. A subdued murmur of voices arose amid the glare of the chandeliers. Those who were familiar with the château paced slowly up and down, while those who had been asked there for the first time remained where they stood, too timid to venture among the ladies. The want of ease which for the first hour or so prevailed among these guests, many of whom were unacquainted with one another, but who found themselves suddenly assembled in the ante-chamber of the Imperial dining-room, gave to their faces an expression of sullen reserve. Every now and then there were sudden intervals of silence, and heads turned anxiously round. The very furniture of the spacious apartment, the pier tables with straight legs, and the square chairs, all in the stiff First Empire style, seemed to impart additional solemnity to this spell of waiting.

'Here he comes at last!' murmured Clorinde.

Rougon had just entered and stood still for a moment, blinking. He had donned his expression of good-natured simplicity; his back was slightly bent, and his face had a sleepy look. He noticed at a glance the faint tremor of hostility which thrilled some of the guests at his appearance. However, in quiet fashion, shaking hands here and there, he steered his way so as to come face to face with M. de Marsy. They bowed to one another, and seemed delighted to meet; and they began to talk in very friendly fashion, though they kept their eyes on each other like foes who respected each other's strength. An empty space had been cleared around them. The ladies watched their slightest gestures with interest; while the men, affecting great discretion, pretended to look in another direction, though every now and then they cast furtive glances at them. Much whispering went on in different corners of the room. What secret plan had the Emperor got in his head? Why had he brought those two men together? M. La Rouquette felt sorely perplexed, but fancied he could scent some very grave business. So he went up to M. de Plouguern, and began to question him. But the old senator gave rein to his jocosity. 'Oh,' said he, 'perhaps Rougon is going to upset Marsy, so it is as well to treat him deferentially. On the other hand, perhaps the Emperor merely wanted to see them together, in the hope that something amusing might happen.'

However, the whispering ceased, and there was a general stir. Two officers of the household went from group to group saying something in low tones. Then the guests, who had suddenly become serious again, made their way towards the door on the left, where they formed themselves into a double line, the men on one side and the ladies on the other. M. de Marsy posted himself near the door, keeping Rougon by his side; and the rest of the company ranged themselves in the order of their rank. Then, keeping perfect silence, they continued waiting for another three minutes.

At last the folding-doors were thrown wide open. The Emperor, in full dress, and wearing the red ribbon of the Legion of Honour across his chest, came into the room first, followed by the chamberlain on duty, M. de Combelot. He smiled slightly as he stopped before M. de Marsy and Rougon, swaying slightly, and slowly twisting his long moustache, as, in an embarrassed tone, he said: 'You must tell Madame Rougon how extremely sorry we were to hear that she was ill. We should have much liked to see her here with you. We must hope that she will very soon be well again. There are a great many colds about just now.'

Then he passed on. After taking a few steps, however, he stopped to shake hands with a general, asking him after his son, whom he called 'my little friend Gaston.' Gaston was of the same age as the Prince Impérial, but was already much more vigorous. The guests bowed as the Emperor passed them. When he had got to the end of the line, M. de Combelot presented to him one of the two academicians, who had come to Court for the first time. The Emperor spoke of a recent work which this writer had issued, and declared that certain passages of it had afforded him the greatest pleasure.

By this time the Empress Eugénie had also entered the room, attended by Madame de Llorentz. She was dressed very simply in a blue silk gown with a tunic of white lace, and she advanced with slow steps, smiling towards the ladies and graciously inclining her bare neck, from which a diamond heart was suspended by a ribbon of blue velvet. The ladies curtsied to her with much rustling and spreading of their skirts, from which rose strong perfumes. Madame de Llorentz presented a young woman, who seemed deeply moved; whereas Madame de Combelot put on an air of affectionate familiarity.

When the sovereigns had reached the end of the double line, they retraced their steps; the Emperor now turning towards the ladies, and the Empress towards the men. There were some more presentations. No one spoke; respectful embarrassment kept all the guests face to face in silence. However, when the adjutant-general of the palace entered to announce that dinner was served, the lines broke up, remarks were exchanged *sotto voce,* and there came little bursts of cheery laughter.

'Ah! you don't want me any longer now!' said M. de Plouguern in Clorinde's ear.

She smiled at him. She had kept in front of M. de Marsy in order to compel him to offer her his arm, which he did with a gallant air. There was some little confusion. The Emperor and Empress went out first, followed by the guests who were to sit on their right and left. That day two foreign diplomatists, a young American lady, and a minister's wife had been selected for this honour. After these came the other guests in such order as they chose, each gentleman giving his arm to the lady he had been pleased to select. And thus the procession got slowly under way.

The entry into the dining-hall was very pompous. Five cut-glass chandeliers sparkled above the long table, illumining the silver centre-pieces, which represented such hunting scenes as the starting of the stag, the horns sounding the view-halloa, and the hounds seizing the quarry. Silver plates were disposed round the edge of the cloth like a border of glittering moons; and the silver warmers reflecting the blaze of the candles, the glass with its quivering coruscations, the fruit stands, and the bright pink flower vases, gave quite a splendour to the Imperial table, a sheeny brilliance which filled the whole huge room.

The procession slowly crossed the Hall of the Guards before entering the dining-room, whose folding doors stood wide open. The men bent down and said a word or two, and then drew erect again, feeling secretly vain of this triumphal march, while the ladies beamed radiantly, their bare shoulders steeped in the brilliant light. Their long trains, sweeping the carpets at regular intervals between each successive couple, lent additional majesty to the procession, the rustling of all the rich tissues sounding like a soft accompaniment. As the threshold of the dining-room was reached, and the superb array of the table came into sight, a military band, hidden from view in an adjoining gallery, greeted the company with a flourish, like a signal for some fairy gala, and, at the sound of it, the gentlemen, who felt somewhat ill at ease in their short breeches, involuntarily pressed their partners' arms.

However, the Empress passed down the room on the right, and remained standing by the centre of the table, while the Emperor, going to the left, took up position opposite to her. Then, when the selected guests had taken their places at the right and left of their Majesties, the others glanced round for a moment, and chose what places they liked. On that particular evening covers were laid for eighty-seven. Some three minutes elapsed before everyone had entered the room and chosen seats. The satiny sheen of the ladies' shoulders, the bright flowers in their dresses, and the diamonds sparkling in their piled-up hair, lent as it were living mirth to the full light of the crystal chandeliers. At last the footmen took the Court hats, which the gentlemen had hitherto carried in their hands; and then everyone sat down.

M. de Plouguern had followed Rougon. After the soup had been served, he nudged him and inquired—'Have you commissioned Clorinde to bring about a reconciliation between you and Marsy?'

Then, with a glance, he pointed out the young woman, who sat on the other side of the table beside the Count, to whom she was talking with an air of tender interest. Rougon seemed much annoyed, but he merely shrugged his shoulders, and pretended to look in another direction. In spite, however, of his attempt at indifference, his eyes strayed back to Clorinde, and he began to observe her slightest gestures, and even the movements of her lips, as though he were anxious to discover what she was saying.

Just then, however, he was spoken to.

'Monsieur Rougon,' said Madame de Combelot, who had got as near to the Emperor as she could, 'do you recollect that accident when you got a cab for me? One of the flounces of my dress was completely torn away.'

She was trying to make herself interesting by relating how her carriage had been nearly cut in halves by the landau of a Russian prince. Then Rougon was obliged to reply; and for a short time the incident became the subject of conversation among those placed near the middle of the table. All kinds of accidents were quoted, and, among others, one which had happened to a woman, a well-known dealer in perfumery, who had fallen from her horse during the previous week, and had broken her arm. The Empress on hearing this raised a slight exclamation of pity. The Emperor said nothing, but listened with a profound expression, while eating very slowly.

'Where's Delestang got to?' Rougon now asked of M. de Plouguern.

They looked about, and the senator at last caught sight of him at the end of the table. Seated next to M. de Combelot, among a row of men, he was listening to the broad conversation which was there being carried on under cover of the general talk. M. La Rouquette had been relating a somewhat free story about a laundress of his native place, and now Chevalier Rusconi was favouring the others with some personal criticisms of the women of Paris; while one of the two artists and the novelist, a little lower down the table, bluntly passed judgment on the ladies whose lean or over-fleshy arms excited their mockery. And Rougon angrily transferred his gaze from Clorinde, who was growing more and more amiable in her manner towards the Count, to her imbecile of a husband, who sat smiling, in a dignified way, at the rather strong anecdotes with which his ears were being regaled.

'Why didn't he come and sit with us?' muttered the great man.

'Oh! I don't pity him. They seem to be amusing themselves down there,' said M. de Plouguern. And he continued in a whisper: 'I fancy they are making merry at Madame de Llorentz's expense. Have you noticed how indecently she's dressed? Just look at her bodice, how low it is.'

However, as he turned to get a better view of Madame de Llorentz, who was on the same side of the table as himself, some five seats away, his face suddenly became very grave. The lady's countenance—she was a beautiful, plump blonde—had assumed a furious expression; she was white with suppressed rage, and her blue eyes seemed to be turning black as they glowered fiercely on M. de Marsy and Clorinde.

'There's going to be a row,' muttered the old senator between his teeth, in such wise that even Rougon could not tell what he was saying.

The band was still playing; the hidden, distant music sounding as though it proceeded from the ceiling. Every now and then, at some sudden blare of the brass instruments, the guests raised their heads, as though seeking to identify the strain which was being played; but the next moment they could hear nothing distinctly for the light notes of the clarionets mingled with the jingling of the silver plate, which the servants carried about in piles. The big dishes gave out a clanking sound, like so many cymbals. All round the table there was much silent hurrying to and fro. A whole army of servants flitted hither and thither without speaking a word; ushers in swallow-tails and bright blue breeches, with swords at their sides and cocked hats under their arms; and footmen with powdered hair, in full-dress livery of green cloth, laced with gold. The dishes were brought in and the wines circulated in proper order, while the heads of the different household services, the controllers, the chief carver, and the chief custodian of the plate, stood round, and superintended all the intricate manoeuvring which marked the seeming confusion, in which the roles of the most insignificant footmen had been carefully arranged beforehand. And behind the Emperor and Empress were their Majesties' own private valets, who waited upon them with an air of decorous dignity.

When the roasts arrived and the great wines of Burgundy were poured into the guests' glasses, the chatter of voices grew louder. Among the men at the end of the table, M. La Rouquette was now discoursing upon culinary matters, notably with regard to the

143

amount of cooking which the haunch of venison then being served
had received. The previous dishes had comprised Crecy soup, salmon *au bleu,* fillet of beef with shallot sauce, pullets *à la financière,*
partridges with cabbage, and oyster patties.

'I'll bet that we shall have stewed cardoons and vegetable-marrow with melted butter,' said the young deputy.

'I have seen some crayfish,' remarked Delestang politely.

However, as the cardoons and vegetable-marrow were just then
served, M. La Rouquette was loud in his expressions of triumph.
He knew the Empress's tastes, he declared. But the novelist glanced
at the artist, and said, with a cluck of the tongue: 'The cooking's
rather poor.'

The artist pouted his assent. Then, when he had taken a sip from
his glass, he said: 'The wines are exquisite.'

Just at that moment, however, a sudden laugh from the Empress
rang so loudly through the room that everyone became silent, and
craned forward to discover what had given rise to it. The Empress
was talking to the Prussian Ambassador, who sat on her right. She
was still laughing and uttering broken words which the guests could
not catch. But amidst the silence caused by the general curiosity,
a cornet-à-piston, softly accompanied by some bassoons, began to
play a pretty, sentimental air. Then the general murmur of conversation arose once more. Chairs were turned half-round and elbows
rested on the table as sections of the guests began to chat together,
as if they were at some luxurious *table-d'hôte.*

'Will you have a rout cake?' asked M. de Plouguern.

Rougon shook his head in refusal. For a moment he had been
eating nothing. The servants had replaced the silver plate by Sèvres
porcelain, beautifully decorated in blue and pink. Then the whole
dessert went in procession past Rougon, but he would only accept a
small piece of Camembert. He had ceased to exercise any restraint
over himself, and gazed openly at M. de Marsy and Clorinde, in
the hope, probably, of being able to intimidate the young woman.
But she affected such familiarity with Marsy that she seemed to
have forgotten where she was, and to fancy herself in some private
room where a light supper had been served for two. Her beautiful
face sparkled with tenderness; and as she munched the sweetmeats
which the Count handed to her, she tranquilly prosecuted her conquest with never-failing smile and superb assurance. The people
near them had begun to whisper.

However, the general conversation turned upon the subject of fashion, and M. de Plouguern mischievously asked Clorinde about the new shape of bonnets. Then, as she pretended not to hear him, he turned round in order to address the same question to Madame de Llorenz. But when he saw her angry, threatening face, with its clenched teeth and tragic expression of furious jealousy, he did not dare to carry out his intention. Clorinde, as it happened, had just surrendered her hand to M. de Marsy on the pretext of letting him look at an antique cameo which she wore on a finger-ring. And she let the Count hold her hand while he took off the ring and then put it back again. This seemed to be going too far. Madame de Llorentz, who was nervously playing with a spoon, upset a wine-glass and broke it. One of the servants immediately removed the fragments.

'They will be tearing each other's hair by-and-bye,' the senator whispered to Rougon. 'Have you watched them? But, the deuce take me if I can understand Clorinde's game! What's she up to, eh?'

Then, as he raised his eyes to his neighbour, he was quite taken aback by the strange change which he noticed in Rougon's face. 'What's the matter with you? Aren't you well?' he asked.

'Oh, yes,' Rougon replied, 'but it's so close here; these dinners last so long. And then there's such a strong scent of musk.'

The dinner, however, was now at an end, though a few ladies were still nibbling biscuits as they leant back in their chairs. No one moved; but the Emperor, who had hitherto preserved silence, suddenly raised his voice, and the guests at either end of the table, who had completely forgotten his Majesty's presence, suddenly strained their ears to catch his remarks. He was replying to a dissertation from M. Beulin-d'Orchère against the practice of divorcing married people, which at that time did not prevail in France. And after pausing and glancing at the very low bodice of the young American lady who sat on his right hand, his Majesty said in a drawling voice: 'In America I never knew of any but plain wives being divorced.'

At this a laugh ran through the guests. The remark seemed one of such fine and delicate wit that M. La Rouquette pondered over it in the hope of being able to discover some hidden meaning. The young American lady, however, appeared to think it a compliment, for she bowed to the Emperor in pleased confusion. Their Majesties now rose from their seats. There was a loud rustling and tramping round the table; and the ushers and footmen, standing gravely in line against the wall, alone preserved an attitude of decorum amidst the scramble of all these people who had dined so well. However, the procession was formed anew; their Majesties at the head, followed by the guests in double file, with the various couples parted by the ladies' spreading trains. They passed through the Guard Boom with somewhat panting dignity, while behind them, in the full light of the crystal chandeliers, over the litter of the disordered table, there resounded the big drum of the military band, which was finishing the last figure of a quadrille.

Coffee was served that evening in the Gallery of the Maps. One of the prefects of the palace presented the Emperor's cup on a silver-gilt salver. Several of the guests, however, had already gone off to the smoking-room, while the Empress had retired with a few ladies to her private drawing-room on the left of the gallery. It was whispered that she had expressed much displeasure at the peculiar manner in which Clorinde had behaved during dinner. During the yearly visits to Compiègne she tried to introduce something like homely decorum into the habits of the Court, with a taste for innocent amusements and rural pleasure; and she displayed a strong personal antipathy to certain eccentricities.

M. de Plouguern had taken Clorinde aside to preach her a little sermon, in the hope of worming a confession out of her. But the young woman affected great surprise. How had she compromised herself with Count de Marsy? They had only joked together, nothing more.

'Well, look there, then,' said the old senator. And forthwith he pushed back a door which already stood ajar, and showed her Madame de Llorentz storming away at M. de Marsy in a little adjacent *salon,* which he had previously seen them enter. Wild with rage, the beautiful blonde was assailing Marsy in the most unmeasured language, quite regardless of the fact that the loud voice in which she was speaking might bring about a terrible scandal. The Count, although a little pale, was smiling and trying to appease her, talking to her rapidly in low soft tones. Sounds of the quarrel had, however, reached the gallery, and the guests who heard them prudently retired from the neighbourhood of the little room.

'Do you want her to publish those famous letters all over the château?' asked M. de Plouguern, who had begun to pace up and down again, after giving his arm to Clorinde.

'It would be fine fun!' she exclaimed with a loud laugh.

Then the old senator, squeezing her arm like some young gallant, began to scold her again. She must leave all eccentric behaviour to Madame de Combelot, he told her. And he went on to say that her Majesty appeared very much annoyed with her. At this Clorinde, who cherished a sincere devotion for the Empress, seemed quite astonished. What had she done that could have displeased her?

Then, as they reached the entrance of her Majesty's private drawing-room, they stopped for a moment and peeped through the doorway, which had been left open. A circle of ladies had gathered round a large table, and the Empress was patiently teaching them ring-puzzles, while a few gentlemen stood behind the chairs and gravely followed the lesson.

In the meantime Rougon had been disputing with Delestang at the end of the gallery. He had not ventured to speak to him about his wife, but was reproaching him for the indifference with which he had allowed himself to be stowed away in a room which overlooked the courtyard of the château, and he tried to induce him to claim one with a view over the park. However, Clorinde came towards them leaning on M. de Plouguern's arm.

'Oh, don't bother me any more about your Marsy!' she said loudly enough to be heard. 'I won't speak to him again this evening. There! will that satisfy you?'

This remark quieted everybody. Just at that moment M. de Marsy came out of the little room looking quite gay. He stopped to joke for a moment with Chevalier Rusconi, and then entered the private drawing-room, where soon afterwards the Empress and the ladies could be heard laughing at some story he was telling them. Ten minutes later, Madame de Llorentz also reappeared. She looked weary and her hands were trembling. Observing, however, the curious glances which took note of her slightest gestures, she boldly remained in the gallery conversing with the various guests.

There was a growing feeling of weariness among the company, who began to yawn slightly behind their handkerchiefs. The evening was the most trying time. The newly-invited guests, not knowing how to amuse themselves, went up to the windows and gazed into the darkness. M. Beulin-d'Orchère continued his dissertation against divorce laws in a corner of the room; while the novelist, who felt greatly bored, asked one of the academicians in a whisper if it was permissible to go to bed. Every now and then, however, the Emperor made his appearance and lounged through the gallery with a cigarette between his lips.

'It was impossible to arrange anything for this evening,' M. de Combelot explained to the little group in which Rougon and his friends were gathered. 'To-morrow, after the stag-hunt, the offal will be given to the hounds by torchlight. Then on the day after to-morrow the artistes of the Comédie Française are coming to play *Les Plaideurs*. There is a talk, too, of some *tableaux vivants* and a charade, which will be performed towards the end of the week.'

Then he gave them details. His wife was going to take a part, and the rehearsals would soon begin. He also spoke at length about an excursion which the Court had made two days previously to a druidical monolith, in the neighbourhood of which some excavations were being carried on. The Empress had insisted upon getting down into the pit which had been dug.

'And do you know,' continued the chamberlain, in tones of emotion, 'the workmen were lucky enough to turn up two skulls in her Majesty's presence. No one was expecting such a thing, and it caused great satisfaction.'

So saying, he stroked that black beard of his which had been the source of so much of his success among the ladies. There was a somewhat sawny look about his handsome face, of which he was evidently vain, and he lisped as he spoke.

'But I was told,' said Clorinde, 'that the actors of the Vaudeville were coming down to perform their new piece. The women wear the most wonderful dresses, and it's excruciatingly funny, I hear.'

M. de Combelot assumed a prudish expression. 'Yes,' he said, 'it was talked of for a moment.'

'Well?'

'The idea has been abandoned. The Empress doesn't like that kind of piece.'

At this moment there was a general stir in the gallery. All the men had come down from the smoking room again, and the Emperor was going to play his game at table quoits. Madame de Combelot, who prided herself upon being a very skilful player, had just asked him to give her her revenge, for she recollected having been beaten by him during the previous season. As she spoke to him she assumed an air of such humble tenderness and such a meaning smile, that his Majesty, ill at ease and rather alarmed, was obliged to turn his eyes away from her.

The game began. A large number of guests gathered round and admiringly criticised the play. Standing at the end of the long table, which was covered with a green cloth, the young woman threw her first quoit, which alighted near the white point representing the pin. Then the Emperor, showing even greater skill, dislodged it with his own quoit, which slipped into its place. The spectators softly applauded. However, it was Madame de Combelot who won in the end.

'What have we been playing for, sire?' she boldly inquired.

The Emperor smiled, but made no reply. Then he turned round and said: 'Monsieur Rougon, will you have a game with me?'

Rougon bowed and took up the quoits, while apologising for his unskilfulness at the game.

A thrill of excitement ran through the spectators, who stood on either side of the table. Was Rougon really coming into favour again? The latent hostility which had encompassed him ever since his arrival now melted, and the guests bent forward and watched his quoits with an air of sympathy. M. La Rouquette, feeling still more perplexed than he had been before dinner, drew his sister aside to ask her what was the true state of affairs, but she was apparently unable to give him any satisfactory information, for he returned to the table making a gesture of perplexity.

'Ah, very good!' murmured Clorinde, as Rougon made a skilful cast.

She darted meaning glances at those friends of the great man who were present. The opportunity seemed a favourable one for helping him back into the Emperor's good graces. She commenced the onset herself, and for a moment or two there was a burst of laudatory remarks.

'The deuce!' exclaimed Delestang, who could think of nothing else to say, though he was anxious to obey the mute command of his wife's eyes.

'And you pretended that you were a very poor player,' said Chevalier Rusconi delightedly. 'Ah, sire, pray don't play for France with him.'

'But Monsieur Rougon would treat France very well, I'm sure,' interposed M. Beulin-d'Orchère, with a meaning expression on his dog-like face.

It was a direct hint. The Emperor deigned to smile; and he even laughed good-naturedly when Rougon, quite embarrassed by the compliments, modestly explained: 'Well, I used to play at pitch and toss when I was a boy.'

On hearing his Majesty laugh, all the company did likewise; and for a moment the gallery rang with merriment. Clorinde, with her sharp wits, had realised that by admiring Rougon, who was in fact a very poor player, one really flattered the Emperor, who was incontestably his superior. M. de Plouguern, however, had not yet come forward, feeling a touch of jealousy at Rougon's success. So Clorinde went up to him and nudged his elbow as if by accident. He understood her meaning, and warmly praised his colleague's next throw. Then M. La Rouquette made up his mind to risk everything, and exclaimed: 'Yes, that was beautiful, a delightfully soft throw!'

As the Emperor won the game, Rougon asked for his revenge, and the quoits were again gliding over the green cloth with a faint rustling sound like that of dry leaves, when a lady-attendant appeared at the door of the drawing-room, holding the Prince Impérial in her arms. The child who was then some twenty months old, was dressed in a plain white robe. His hair was in disorder and his eyes were heavy with sleep. When he awoke of an evening in this way he was generally brought to the Empress for a moment so that she might kiss him. He looked at the light with the serious expression characteristic of little children.

However, an old man, a great dignitary of the Empire, came forward, dragging his gouty legs. And bending down, with a senile tremor of his head, he took hold of the baby-prince's soft little hand and kissed it, saying in quavering accents as he did so: 'Monseigneur, monseigneur—'

But the child, alarmed by the other's parchment-like visage, hastily recoiled, clinging to the lady who carried him, and venting cries of fear. Still the old man did not let go his hold; he continued to protest his devotion, and it was necessary to release the little hand, which he held tightly to his lips, from his adoring grasp.

'Go away, take him off!' cried the Emperor impatiently, to the lady-attendant.

His Majesty had just lost the second game, and the deciding one began. Rougon, taking the praises which he received in serious earnest, exerted all his skill. Clorinde was now of opinion that he played too well, and, just as he was going to pick up his quoits, she whispered in his ear: 'I hope you do not mean to win.'

Rougon smiled. But all at once a loud bark was heard. It came from Nero, the Emperor's favourite pointer, which, taking advantage of an open door, had just bounded into the gallery. His Majesty ordered the dog to be taken away, and a servant had already caught hold of its collar when the aged dignitary again sprang forward and exclaimed: 'My beautiful Nero! my beautiful Nero!'

He almost knelt upon the carpet in order to take the dog in his tremulous arms. He pressed its head to his breast and kissed it as he said: 'I beg of you, sire, do not send him away. How handsome he is!'

The Emperor consented that the dog should remain, and the old man went on with his caresses. Unlike the little prince, Nero showed no sign of fear, but licked the withered hands that fondled him.

Rougon, meantime, was blundering in his play. He had just thrown a quoit so clumsily that the leaden disc, faced with cloth, flew into the corsage of a lady who, with a deal of blushing, drew it from amidst her lace. The Emperor won the game, and the company delicately gave him to understand that he had gained a real victory. His Majesty seemed quite affected by it, and went off with Rougon, chatting to him as though he wanted to console him for his defeat. They strolled to the end of the gallery, leaving the body of the room free for a little dance which was just then being arranged.

The Empress, who had left the private drawing-room, was trying to relieve the increasing boredom of her guests. She had proposed a game of 'Consequences,' but it was getting late, and the company seemed to prefer a dance. All the ladies were now assembled in the Gallery of the Maps, and a messenger was sent to the smoking-room to summon such gentlemen as were still hiding there. As the dancers took up their positions for a quadrille, M. de Combelot obligingly seated himself at the piano-organ, the handle of which he gravely began to turn.[1]

'Monsieur Rougon,' said the Emperor, 'I have heard some talk of a work you are engaged upon; a comparison of the English constitution with our own. I might be able to supply you with some useful documents.'

---

[1] There was a similar instrument—like a cottage piano in shape but with a handle at the side—in the Empress's private rooms at the Tuileries; and at her Majesty's Monday receptions, Prince Richard Metternich, the Austrian Ambassador, would 'grind' it by the hour just like some professional of the streets. Mérimée fell out for a time with Chevalier Nigra, Victor Emmanuel's representative, because he suggested one afternoon that the latter should relieve the Prince, maliciously adding that organ grinding was essentially an Italian art.—*Ed.*

'Your Majesty is very kind. But I am contemplating another design; a very great one indeed.'

Rougon, finding his sovereign so kindly disposed, was desirous of profiting by it, and he thereupon unfolded his plan, his dream of reclaiming and cultivating the Landes, of clearing several square leagues of soil, founding a town, and conquering, as it were, a new country. As he spoke, the Emperor looked at him, and in his eyes, usually so expressionless, there now shone a glistening light. For a time, however, he said nothing, merely nodding every now and then. But when Rougon at last finished, he rejoined: 'Yes, perhaps—it is to be thought over.' Then, turning towards Clorinde, her husband, and M. de Plouguern, who stood in a group near at hand, he said: 'Monsieur Delestang, come and give us your opinion. I have retained the most pleasant recollection of my visit to your model farm of La Chamade.'

Delestang stepped forward; however, the little group which was clustering round the Emperor now had to retreat into one of the window-recesses. A waltz was being danced, and as Madame de Combelot passed by, reclining in M. La Rouquette's arms, she had just swept her long train round his Majesty's silk stockings. At the piano M. de Combelot seemed to be quite enjoying the music he was calling forth, for he turned the handle more rapidly than ever, swaying his handsome head, and every now and then glancing towards the body of the instrument, as though surprised at the deep notes which came from it at certain turns he gave.

'I have bred some magnificent calves this year, by a fresh crossing of strains,' said Delestang. 'Unfortunately, when your Majesty visited me, the stalls and folds were under repair.'

Thereupon the Emperor began to speak slowly and spasmodically of agriculture, cattle-breeding, and manures. He had entertained great esteem for Delestang ever since his visit to La Chamade; and was particularly pleased with the system which the latter had introduced whereby his farmhands lived in common, shared certain profits, and became entitled to old-age pensions. Napoléon and Clorinde's husband had ideas in common, certain humanitarian principles which enabled them to grasp each other's thoughts at a word.

'Has Monsieur Rougon spoken to you about his plan?' the Emperor asked.

'Oh, yes!' answered Delestang. 'It is a magnificent scheme, and affords a chance of experimenting on a very grand scale.'

He evinced genuine enthusiasm. He was greatly interested in pig-breeding, he said. The best breeds were dying out in France. Then he remarked that he was perfecting a new plan for the improvement of meadow-lands; but to make it fully successful, large tracts of country would be necessary. However, if Rougon should succeed, he would join him and put his system to trial. Then, all at once he stopped short, for he had just noticed that his wife's eyes were earnestly fixed upon him. Ever since he had begun to express his approval of Rougon's scheme, she had been biting her lips, looking pale and wrathful. 'Come, my dear,' she said to him, motioning towards the piano-organ.

M. de Combelot's fingers had now grown cramped, and he was opening and shutting his hands to remove the stiffness. Nevertheless, with the smile of a martyr he got ready to begin a polka when Delestang hastened forward and offered to take his place; an offer which he accepted politely, as though giving up a post of honour. Then Delestang turned the handle, and the polka began. But somehow the music now sounded differently; he lacked the chamberlain's flexible, supple wrist.

Rougon, however, was anxious to get some definite expression of opinion from the Emperor. His Majesty, who really seemed impressed, asked him if he contemplated establishing some large industrial colonies over yonder, and added that he should be glad to grant a strip of land, water supply, and tools to each family. Moreover, he promised to show Rougon some plans of his own, which he had noted down on paper, for the establishment of a place of the kind, where the houses would be of uniform construction, and every want would be provided for.

'Certainly, I quite enter into your Majesty's ideas,' said Rougon, though, truth to tell, Napoléon's vague socialism made him impatient. 'We can do nothing without your Majesty's assistance and authority. It will doubtless be necessary to expropriate certain villages, and it will have to be stated that this is done for the public good. I shall also have to launch a company to provide the requisite funds. A word from your Majesty will be necessary—'

The Emperor's eyes grew dim; but he went on nodding.

Finally, in an indistinct voice, he said: 'We will see—we will talk about it.'

Then he walked away, passing with heavy steps through the quadrille party. Rougon put on a cheerful countenance, as though he felt sure of obtaining a favourable answer. Clorinde, however, was radiant. By degrees a report spread among the grave, staid men who did not dance that Rougon was going to leave Paris, and place himself at the head of a great undertaking in the south of France. Then they all came to congratulate him, and he was smiled upon from one end of the gallery to the other. Not a trace remained of the hostility which had been shown him when he first arrived. Now that he was voluntarily going into exile, they all felt that they could shake hands with him without risk of compromising themselves. This was genuine relief for many of the guests. M. La Rouquette, quitting the dancing party, discussed the matter with Chevalier Rusconi, with the delight of a man completely set at his ease. 'It's the right thing he's doing! He will make a great success down there!' said the young deputy. 'Rougon is an extremely able man, but in politics he is deficient in tact.'

Then he waxed quite emotional over the Emperor's kindness. His Majesty, he said, showed as much regard for his old servants as if they were old mistresses. He felt affection for them even after the most violent ruptures. It was some secret softening of the heart, no doubt, that had prompted him to invite Rougon to Compiègne. And La Rouquette cited other incidents which did honour to his Majesty's kindness of nature. He had given four hundred thousand francs to pay the debts of a general who had been ruined by a ballet girl; he had bestowed eight hundred thousand upon one of his old accomplices at Strasburg and Boulogne as a wedding present, and had laid out nearly a million for the benefit of the widow of a high functionary.

'His purse is at every one's disposal,' he said in conclusion. 'He only allowed himself to be chosen Emperor in order that he might be able to benefit his friends. It makes me shrug my shoulders when I hear Republicans reproaching him for his big civil list.[1] He would exhaust ten civil lists in doing good. All the money he gets comes back to France again.'

While chatting in an undertone after this fashion, La Rouquette and Chevalier Rusconi continued to watch the Emperor. He was just completing his round of the gallery. He adroitly threaded his way through the dancers, silently crossing the clear spaces which their

---

[1]One million sterling per annum for himself; 400,000 £. for the Empress Eugénie; and 200,000 £. for the Prince Impérial!—*Ed.*

respect opened out for him. Whenever he passed behind a lady who was sitting down, he slightly inclined his neck and cast an oblique glance at her bare shoulders.

'And he has such a mind, too!' said Chevalier Rusconi in a whisper. 'He is an extraordinary man!'

The Emperor was now quite close to them. For a moment he lingered where he stood, hesitating and gloomy. Then he seemed inclined to approach Clorinde, who was looking very merry and beautiful, but she suddenly fixed her eyes on him so boldly that he seemed frightened, for he went on again, holding his left arm behind his back, and twisting the ends of his waxed moustache with his right hand. At last, seeing M. Beulin-d'Orchère in front of him, he approached him sideways and said: 'You are not dancing.'

The judge confessed that he could not dance, that he had never danced in his life. Then the Emperor replied encouragingly: 'Oh, that doesn't matter! That needn't keep you from dancing now.'

Those were his last words for the evening. He quietly made his way to the door, and disappeared.

'Yes, indeed, he is an extraordinary man,' said M. La Rouquette, repeating Chevalier Rusconi's phrase. 'They think a great deal of him abroad, don't they?'

The Chevalier, with diplomatic reserve, nodded vaguely. He admitted, however, that the eyes of Europe were fixed upon the Emperor. A word spoken at the Tuileries made neighbouring thrones tremble.

'He is a prince who knows how to hold his tongue,' he added with a smile, the subtle irony of which escaped the young deputy.

Then they returned to the ladies and invited partners for the next quadrille. For the last quarter of an hour an aide-de-camp had been turning the handle of the piano-organ. Both Delestang and M. de Combelot now sprang forward and offered to take his place. The ladies, however, cried out: 'Monsieur de Combelot! Monsieur de Combelot! He does it much the best!'

The chamberlain thanked them for the compliment with a bow, and began to turn the handle with professional vigour. It was the last quadrille. Tea had just been served in the private drawing-room. Nero, having made his appearance from behind a couch, was glutted with sandwiches. The guests gathered in little groups and chatted familiarly. M. de Plouguern, who had carried a little cake to a side table, ate it and sipped his tea, while explaining to Delestang how it was that he, so well known to hold Legitimist opinions, had come to accept invitations to Compiègne. The reason was very simple, he said. He could not refuse his support to a government which rescued France from anarchy. Then he broke off to say: 'This cake is very nice. I didn't make a very good dinner this evening.'

His caustic tongue was always ready to wag when he found himself at Compiègne. He spoke of most of the ladies present with a bluntness which called blushes to Delestang's face. The only one for whom he showed respect was the Empress. She was a saint, he said, a woman of exemplary devotion. He asserted, too, that she was a Legitimist, and would have recalled Henry V. to the throne had she been free to do so. Then, for a moment, he dwelt upon the delights of religion. Just as he was sliding off into an indelicate story, the Empress retired to her own rooms, followed by Madame de Llorentz. On reaching the threshold of the salon, she made a low courtesy to the company, who bowed to her in silence.

The rooms now began to get empty. The remaining guests talked in louder tones, and exchanged parting shakes of the hand. When Delestang looked for his wife to go upstairs with her he could not find her. At last, Rougon, who helped him in his search, discovered Clorinde sitting with M. de Marsy in the little room where Madame de Llorentz had so violently upbraided the Count after dinner. The young woman was laughing loudly. When she saw her husband she rose up. 'Good-evening, Monsieur le Comte', she gaily said to Marsy; 'you will see to-morrow, at the hunt, if I don't win my bet.'

Rougon glanced after her as her husband led her away on his arm. He would have liked to accompany them to their door to ascertain what bet it was that she had spoken of, but M. de Marsy, evincing the greatest politeness, detained him, and he could not get away. When he was at last free, instead of going up to his room, he took advantage of an open door to slip into the park. It was a very dark October night, without a star or a puff of wind, a black, dead night. Lofty plantations arose far away like promontories of darkness. He could scarcely distinguish the paths in front of him. Holding his hat in his hand, he let the cool night air play on his brow for a moment. This freshened him like a bath. Then he lingered there looking at a brightly-lighted window on the left front of the château. The other windows gradually became black, and this was soon the only gleaming spot in the sleeping pile. The Emperor was sitting up. And Rougon fancied he could distinguish his shadow passing across the blind, a huge head beyond which projected the ends of a long moustache. It was followed by two other shadows; one very slight, and the other so big that it shut off all the light. In the latter Rougon clearly recognised the gigantic silhouette of an agent of the secret police, with whom his Majesty frequently closeted himself for hours. Then, as the slimmer shadow again passed before the window, Rougon thought it seemed like a woman's. However, nothing more appeared, the window glowed in all quietude, like some large bright eye gazing into the mysterious depths of the park. Perhaps, thought Rougon, the Emperor was now considering his scheme for clearing the Landes and founding an industrial centre, where the extinction of pauperism might be attempted on a large scale. He knew that Napoléon frequently came to important determinations at night-time. It was at night that he signed decrees, wrote manifestoes and dismissed his ministers. But presently Rougon began to smile. He had recalled a story of the Emperor wearing a blue apron, and hanging wall-paper at three francs a piece in a room at Trianon, where he intended to lodge a mistress; and he pictured him now, in the silence of his study, cutting out woodcuts and sticking them neatly in a scrap-book.

But all at once Rougon found himself raising his arms and involuntarily exclaiming aloud: 'Ah! *his* friends made him!'

Then he hurried back into the château. He was beginning to feel very cold, especially about the legs, which his knee-breeches left uncomfortably exposed.

A little before nine o'clock on the following morning Clorinde sent Antonia, whom she had brought with her, to ask Rougon if she and her husband might breakfast with him. He had already ordered a cup of chocolate, but did not touch it till they came. Antonia preceded them, carrying a large silver salver on which their coffee had been brought to their bedroom.

'Ah! this will be more cheerful!' exclaimed Clorinde as she entered. 'You have got the sun on your side. You are much better off than we are.'

Then she began to inspect the suite of rooms. It consisted of an ante-chamber, on the right of which there was a little room for a valet. Then there was the guest's bedroom, a spacious apartment hung with cream-coloured chintz having a pattern of big red flowers. There was a large square mahogany bedstead and an immense grate in which some huge logs were blazing.

'Of course! You ought to have complained!' said Rougon. 'I would not have put up with a room looking on to the courtyard. Ah! if people don't assert themselves—I was talking to Delestang about it only last night.'

The young woman shrugged her shoulders and replied: 'Oh! he would raise no objection if they wanted to lodge me in a garret!'

However, she now wished to examine the dressing-room, all the fittings of which were of Sèvres porcelain, white and gold, with the Imperial monogram. Then she went to look out of the window, and a faint cry of surprise and admiration came from her lips. For leagues in front of her, the lofty trees of the forest of Compiègne spread out like a rolling sea, their huge crests rising and falling in gentle billows, till they faded from sight in the distance. And in the pale sunlight of that October morning, the forest glowed alternately with gold and purple, with the splendour of a gorgeously embroidered mantle spread out from horizon to horizon.

'Come, let us have breakfast!' said Clorinde.

They cleared a table on which were an inkstand and a blotting-pad, finding it rather amusing to wait upon themselves. The young woman, who was in a very merry mood, declared that on awaking that morning it had seemed to her as if she were in an inn, an inn kept by a prince, at which she had alighted after a long journey through dreamland. This haphazard kind of breakfast, served upon silver salvers, delighted her like some adventure in an unknown country.

Meantime, Delestang gazed in wonder at the quantity of wood which was burning in the grate. And at last, with his eyes still fixed upon the flames, he muttered thoughtfully: 'I have been told that they burn fifteen hundred francs' worth of wood every day at the château. Fifteen hundred francs' worth! Don't you think it's rather a high figure, Rougon?'

Rougon, who was slowly sipping his chocolate, just nodded his head by way of reply. He was disturbed by Clorinde's gay anima-tion. She seemed that morning all aglow with feverish beauty, her eyes glistening as with the fire of battle.

'What was the bet you were talking about last night?' Rougon asked abruptly.

She began to laugh, but as he pressed his question, she replied: 'You will see presently.'

Then, by degrees, Rougon grew angry, and spoke harshly to

the young woman. It was an outburst of real jealousy, and veiled allusions soon developed into direct accusations. She had made a perfect exhibition of herself on the previous evening, he said; she had let M. de Marsy hold her hand for more than two minutes. Delestang listened to all this, but, instead of showing any concern, quietly steeped some strips of toast in his coffee.

'Ah! if I were your husband!' Rougon cried at last.

Clorinde had just risen, and, standing behind Delestang, with her hands resting on his shoulders, she responded: 'Well, supposing you were my husband, what then?'

And stooping down, she stirred Delestang's hair with her warm breath, as she added: 'He would behave properly, wouldn't he, dear, just as you do?'

Delestang turned his head, and, by way of answer, kissed the hand that lay on his left shoulder. He looked at Rougon with an expression of emotion and embarrassment, blinking as though he wished him to understand that he was really going a little too far. Rougon nearly called him a fool. However, when Clorinde made a sign to him over her husband's head, he followed her to the open window, on the handrail of which she leant. For a moment she remained silent, her eyes fixed on the far-spreading prospect. Then she abruptly asked him: 'Why do you want to leave Paris? Don't you care for me any longer? Listen now; I will be quite steady, and follow your advice, if you will give up that plan of exiling yourself to that horrid, outlandish place.'

Rougon became very grave at this proposal. He began to dwell on the great motives which influenced him; besides, it was impossible now, he said, for him to withdraw. While he was speaking, Clorinde vainly tried to read the real truth in his face. He seemed quite determined to go.

'Very well, then; you don't care for me any longer,' resumed the young woman. 'So I am at liberty to follow my own inclinations. Well, you will see!'

Then she left the window, and once more began to laugh. Delestang, who still seemed to find the fire a source of great interest, was trying to calculate how many grates there might be in the château. Clorinde, however, broke in upon his meditations, saying that she had only just time to dress, unless she was to miss the hunt. Rougon accompanied her and her husband into the corridor, a long conventual passage with a thick green carpet. And as Clorinde went off she amused herself by reading the names of the guests, which were written on small cards in wooden frames which hung from the different doors. When she had got to the very end of the corridor, she turned, and, thinking that Rougon looked perplexed, as if he wished to call her back, she halted, and for a moment waited smiling. But he went back into his room, slamming the door behind him.

The second breakfast was served early that morning. There was much conversation concerning the weather, which was all that could be wished for the hunt. There was a good clear light, and the atmosphere was calm. The Court carriages set out shortly before noon; the meet being at the King's Well, a large open space where several roads met in the middle of the forest. The Imperial hunting-train had been waiting there for more than an hour; the mounted huntsmen in crimson breeches and great laced hats; the dog-keepers wearing black shoes with silver buckles to enable them to run with ease among the brushwood; while the carriages of the guests invited from the neighbouring châteaux were drawn up in a semi-circle in front of the hounds, and in the centre were groups of ladies and gentlemen all in Court hunting-dress, like figures out of some old picture of the time of Louis XV. The Emperor and the Empress did not follow the hunt that day, and as soon as the hounds had been slipped their Majesties' char-à-bancs turned down a bye-road and came back to the château. Many others followed this example. Rougon had at first tried to keep up with Clorinde, but she spurred on her horse so wildly that he was left behind, and, thereupon, in disgust, determined to return, infuriated at seeing the young woman galloping in the distance down a long avenue, with M. de Marsy by her side.

Towards half-past five o'clock, Rougon received an invitation to take tea in the private apartments of the Empress. This was a favour which was usually granted to men of interesting and witty conversation. He found M. Beulin-d'Orchère and M. de Plouguern already there. The latter was relating a somewhat improper story in carefully-chosen words, and his narrative achieved enormous success. Only a few of the hunting-party had as yet returned. Madame de Combelot came in, saying that she felt dreadfully tired, and when the company asked her how matters had gone off, she replied with an affectation of semi-technical jargon: 'Oh, the animal beat us off for more than four hours. For a time he unharboured in the open. But at last he turned to bay near the Red Pool, and the death was superb.'

Then Chevalier Rusconi mentioned another incident with some uneasiness. 'Madame Delestang's horse bolted,' he said. 'She disappeared in the direction of Pierrefonds, and nothing has since been seen or heard of her.'

He was at once overwhelmed with questions, and the Empress seemed much distressed. He said that Clorinde had kept up a tremendous pace all the time, and had excited the admiration of the most experienced riders. All at once, however, her horse had bolted down a side lane.

'She had been dreadfully whipping the poor animal,' interposed M. La Rouquette, who was burning to get a word in. 'Monsieur de Marsy galloped off to her assistance, and he, also, has not been seen since.'

At this, Madame de Llorentz, who sat behind her Majesty, rose from her seat. She fancied that some of the company were looking at her and smiling, and she became quite livid. The conversation had turned upon the dangers of hunting. One day, said one of the guests, the stag had run into a farmyard, and had then turned and charged the hounds so suddenly that a lady had her leg broken amidst the confusion. Then the company began to indulge in various suppositions. If M. de Marsy had succeeded in checking Madame Delestang's horse, they had, perhaps, both dismounted for a few minutes' rest; there were a large number of shelter places, huts and sheds and pavilions, in the forest. However, it seemed to Madame de Llorentz that this suggestion prompted more smiling, and that the others were stealthily eyeing her jealous anger. As for Rougon, he kept silent, but beat a feverish tattoo on his knees with his finger tips.

The Empress had given orders that Clorinde should be asked to come and have some tea as soon as she returned. And all at once there was a chorus of exclamations. The young woman appeared on the threshold, with a flushed, smiling, radiant face. She thanked her Majesty for the concern which she showed about her, and then calmly continued: 'I am so sorry. You really shouldn't have made yourselves uneasy. I made a bet with Monsieur de Marsy that I would be in at the death before he was. And so I should if it hadn't been for that provoking horse of mine.' Then she added gaily: 'Well, we neither of us lost, after all.' However, they made her tell them her adventure in detail, which she did, without the least sign of confusion. After a mad gallop of ten minutes or so, her horse had fallen, she said, but she herself had sustained no hurt. Then, as she was trembling a little from the excitement, M. de Marsy had taken her for a moment into a shed.

'Ah, we guessed that!' exclaimed M. La Rouquette. 'You said a shed, didn't you? I myself mentioned a pavilion.'

'It must have been a very uncomfortable place,' said M. de Plouguern mischievously.

Clorinde, without ceasing to smile, replied slowly: 'Oh, dear no, I assure you. There was some straw, and I sat down. It was a big shed full of spiders' webs. It was growing dark, too. Oh! it was very droll.' Then, looking in Madame de Llorentz's face, and speaking with still more deliberation, she added: 'Monsieur de Marsy was extremely kind to me.'

While Clorinde had been narrating this story, Madame de Llorentz had kept two fingers closely pressed to her lips, and on hearing the conclusion she shut her eyes as if dazed by anger. She remained thus for another minute; and then, feeling that she could contain herself no further, she left the room. M. de Plouguern, curious as to her intentions, slipped away after her. As for Clorinde, when she saw Madame de Llorentz disappear, an involuntary expression of victory appeared upon her face.

The conversation now turned upon other subjects. M. Beulind'Orchère began to speak of a scandalous lawsuit which was exciting a deal of public interest. It was a wife's application for a judicial separation from her husband; and he gave certain particulars of the affair in such delicately couched language that Madame de Combelot did not fully understand him, but asked for explanations. Chevalier Rusconi then afforded the company much pleasure by softly singing some popular Piedmontese love songs, which he afterwards translated into French. In the middle of one of these songs Delestang entered the room. He had just returned from the forest, which he had been scouring for the last two hours in search of his wife. His strange appearance excited a general smile. The Empress seemed to have taken a sudden friendship for Clorinde, for she had made her sit beside her and was talking to her about horses. Pyrame, the horse which the young woman had been riding, was a hard goer, said the Empress; and she promised that she should have Cesar on the following day.

On Clorinde's arrival, Rougon had gone to one of the windows, feigning great interest in some lights which were gleaming in the distance to the left of the park. As he stood there no one could detect the slight quivering of his features. He remained thus, looking out into the darkness, for a long time, only turning when M. de Plouguern came back into the room and stepped up to him.

Rougon remained quite impassive as the other whispered in his ear, in a voice feverish with satisfied curiosity: 'There has been a terrible scene! I followed her out of the room. She met Marsy at the end of the corridor. They both went into a room together, and I heard Marsy telling her roundly that she bored him to death. She rushed out again like a mad woman, and went off towards the Emperor's study. I feel sure that she went to lay those famous letters on his desk.'

Just at that moment Madame de Llorentz reappeared. She was very pale; some of her hair strayed over her brow, and she panted. However, she resumed her seat behind the Empress with the despairing calmness of one who has just performed on herself some terrible operation which may have a fatal result.

'I'm sure she has taken the letters,' said M. de Plouguern, examining her.

Then, as Rougon did not seem to understand him, he left him; and, stooping behind Clorinde, began to tell her his story. She listened to him with delight, her eyes sparkling.

It was not until the approach of the dinner-hour, when the company quitted the Empress's private room, that she appeared conscious of Rougon's presence. Then she took his arm and said to him, as Delestang followed on behind: 'Well now, you see—If you had been more amiable this morning, I shouldn't have nearly broken my legs.'

That evening the offal of the stag was distributed by torchlight to the hounds in the courtyard. As the guests left the dining-room, instead of immediately returning to the Gallery of the Maps, they dispersed through the reception rooms in the front part of the château, where the windows were all wide open. The Emperor took up position on the central balcony, which afforded accommodation for a score of other personages.

Down below, on either side of the courtyard, a row of footmen, in full livery and with hair powdered, was ranged from the steps to the gate. Each held a long staff surmounted by a blazing cresset, in which tow had been steeped in spirits of wine. The lofty greenish flames seemed to dance in the air, glaring through the darkness without illuminating it, brightening nothing except the scarlet waistcoats, to which they lent a purplish tinge. Behind the footmen, on both sides of the courtyard, there were numerous middle-class people of Compiègne, whose dim faces swarmed in the darkness, the flaring tow every now and then revealing some hideous verdurous countenance. In the centre, in front of the steps of the château, the offal of the stag lay in a heap. Over it was stretched the skin of the animal, the head and antlers lying in front. At the other end, near the gate, were the hounds in charge of the huntsmen; and some dog-keepers, in green livery and white cotton stockings, were waving torches. In the bright ruddy glow, broken by clouds of smoke which rolled away towards the town, the hounds could be seen crowding together, and panting heavily with distended mouths.

The Emperor remained standing. Every now and then a sudden flash of torchlight showed up his blank impenetrable face. Clorinde had watched his every movement during dinner without detecting anything more than a melancholy weariness, the moodiness of an invalid who suffers in silence. Only once had she fancied that she saw him casting a faint side-glance at M. de Marsy. And there on the balcony he still remained moody, stooping a little and twisting his moustache, while behind him the guests rose upon tip-toe in order to get a better view.

'Come, Firmin!' he said, almost impatiently. Then the huntsmen sounded the 'Royale.' The hounds threw tongue, straining their necks and rearing on their hind legs with uproarious efforts. And, as the keeper held up the stag's head in sight of the maddened pack, Firmin, the chief huntsman, who stood upon the steps, let his whip drop; the hounds, which had been waiting for this signal, bounded in three great leaps across the courtyard, quivering and panting with hungry excitement. Firmin, however, had picked up his whip again; and the hounds, suddenly checked within a few yards of the offal, squatted upon the pavement, while their backs shook with excitement and their throats seemed like to burst with barks of desire. But they were obliged to retreat—to return across the courtyard and assume their previous position by the gate.

'Oh, the poor animals!' said Madame de Combelot, with an air of languid compassion.

'Splendid!' cried M. La Rouquette.

Chevalier Rusconi applauded loudly. Several of the ladies were leaning forward in their excitement, while their lips quivered and their hearts throbbed with desire to see the hounds devour their prey. Would they not be allowed to have the bones at once? they asked.

'No, not just yet,' said several voices.

Firmin had again twice dropped and then raised his whip. The hounds were exasperated and foamed at the mouth. But the third time, Firmin did not raise his whip again. The valet rushed away, carrying off the stag's head and skin, while the dogs leapt forward and seized the offal. Their furious barking subsided into a low quivering growl of enjoyment. Bones could be heard cracking. Then general satisfaction was expressed upon the balcony and at the windows. The ladies smiled in chilly fashion and clenched their white teeth, and the men looked on with glistening eyes, while twisting the toothpicks they had brought from the dining-room. In the courtyard came sudden brilliance. The huntsmen sounded a flourish on their horns; the dog-keepers waved their torches, and a blaze of coloured lights arose, setting the night aflare and then raining sanguineously on the placid heads of the townsfolk on either hand.

The Emperor, however, turned his back upon the scene, and on noticing Rougon close to him, he seemed to awake from the moody reverie in which he had been absorbed since dinner. 'Monsieur Rougon,' he said, 'I have been thinking about that scheme of yours. There are difficulties in the way—many difficulties.' Then, after a momentary pause, he opened his lips to speak again, but closed them without saying anything. However, as he went away, he added: 'You must remain in Paris, Monsieur Rougon.'

Clorinde, who heard him, made a gesture of triumph. The Emperor's remark immediately spread through the company, and the guests once more became grave and anxious, as Rougon slowly made his way through their midst, towards the Gallery of the Maps.

Down below in the courtyard, the hounds were finishing their bones. They flung themselves wildly a-top of one another in order to reach the prey. With their writhing backs, white and black, all jumbled together, they were like a living wave, surging and struggling and roaring hungrily. Their jaws snapped, and they bolted mouthful after mouthful in their feverish eagerness to devour all. Quarrels, brief and sudden, ended in a loud howl. One large hound, a magnificent creature, finding himself too far away from the quarry, stepped back and then sprang into the very middle of the pack. He forced his way through the others, and soon gulped down a great strip of the stag's entrails.

VIII

RECALLED TO POWER

SOME weeks went by. Rougon had relapsed into his life of lassitude and ennui. He never referred to the Emperor's order that he should remain in Paris. He only spoke of his disappointment and of the alleged obstacles which stood in the way of his clearing some portion of the Landes. Upon this topic he talked continually. What obstacles could there possibly be? he asked. For his part, he could see none. He even went so far as to show some irritation against the Emperor, from whom it was impossible, he complained, to obtain any explanations. Perhaps, however, his Majesty felt afraid lest he should be obliged to come forward with a subvention for the proposed expedition.

As the days went by, Clorinde's visits to the Rue Marbeuf increased in frequency. She seemed every afternoon to expect some great news from Rougon, and she gazed at him in surprise on finding him so silent. Ever since her visit to Compiègne she had been living in the hope of a sudden triumph. She had pictured a series of dramatic scenes: furious anger on the part of the Emperor, M. de Marsy's utter fall and disgrace, and the great man's immediate restoration to power. She no doubt imagined that her feminine wiles would have this result; and so her astonishment was unbounded when, at the end of a month, she still saw the Count in office. She began to feel contempt for the Emperor, who seemed incapable of avenging himself. What could he be thinking about in the everlasting silence he preserved?

However, Clorinde had not yet abandoned all hope. She had an intuition that some unforeseen turn of the wheel of chance would bring round the triumph she desired, for M. de Marsy's influence was certainly shaken. Rougon now treated her with all the watchful attention of a jealous husband. Ever since his strange outbreaks at Compiègne, he had exercised a most fatherly surveillance over her, had plied her with moral dissertations, and expressed his desire to see her every day. The young woman smiled, feeling certain now that he would not leave Paris. Towards the middle of December, however, after weeks of drowsy listlessness, he again reverted to his great scheme. He had consulted some bankers, and had hopes of doing without the Emperor's assistance. And once more he buried himself in maps and plans and technical treatises. Gilquin, he said, had already enrolled more than five hundred workmen who were willing to go out with him. They would form the first instalment of his future people. At this Clorinde, feeling quite provoked, again set the whole coterie of friends in motion.

It was a tremendous undertaking. Each of them took some special *rôle*; and whispered councils were held in the corners of Rougon's own drawing-room on Sunday and Thursday evenings. They portioned out the various difficult matters, and every day they scattered through Paris, invincibly determined upon gaining some influence or other to their cause. No assistance was too insignificant for their acceptance; the most trifling help might be useful. They availed themselves of everything, they drew whatever advantage they could from the most trivial incidents, and worked and worked from the first thing in the morning until the last thing at night. They enlisted their friends as accomplices, and their friends enlisted others. All Paris seemed to share in the intrigue. In the most out-of-the-way districts people began to yearn for Rougon's triumph, without being able to say why. The little band, though it only comprised some ten or twelve persons, was influencing the whole city.

'We are the coming government,' said Du Poizat, in all seriousness; and, establishing a parallel between themselves and the men who had made the Second Empire, he added: 'I shall be Rougon's Marsy.'

A pretender by himself was a mere name. A band of supporters was needed to establish a government. Twenty stout fellows of ambition are stronger than a mere principle, and when they can combine a principle with their ambition they become invincible. Such were Du Poizat's views. He himself spent his time in perambulating Paris, often calling at newspaper offices, where he smoked his cigar and did what he could to undermine M. de Marsy's reputation. He always had some secret little story to relate about the minister, whom he accused of ingratitude and egotism. Then, when he had managed to bring in Rougon's name, he would drop vague hints and promises of the rewards and presents and subventions which the latter would shower down upon every one should he be in the position to do so. In this way Du Poizat contrived to supply numerous suggestions, anecdotes, and quotations to the newspapers, which continually brought the great man under the notice of the public.

Two journals published an account of a visit to the house in the Rue Marbeuf, and others spoke of Rougon's famous work on the English constitution and that of 1852. Thus, after a hostile silence of two years, a murmur of eulogy arose, and Rougon's popularity seemed to be reviving. Du Poizat, too, devoted himself to other intrigues, very secret ones, such as the purchase of certain persons' support by a kind of gambling on the prospects of Rougon's return to office.

'Let us only think of him,' he often said, with that frankness of his which was distasteful to the more affected members of the band. 'Later on, he will think of us.'

M. Beulin-d'Orchère was not a very subtle intriguer. When he unearthed a scandalous affair to the detriment of M. de Marsy it was immediately hushed up. He showed greater shrewdness in hinting that he might very well become Minister of Justice if ever his brother-in-law should return to power, an intimation which brought all his brother judges over to his side. M. Kahn meanwhile had put himself at the head of another company of auxiliaries, financiers, deputies, and functionaries, who helped to swell the army of malcontents. He had a docile lieutenant in M. Béjuin, and even availed himself of the services of M. de Combelot and M. La Rouquette, without those gentlemen having the faintest idea of the object for which he made them work. For his part, he acted in the official world, even its highest spheres, carrying his propaganda into the Tuileries, and covertly labouring for days at a time in order that some remark or other might be repeated from mouth to mouth till it reached the Emperor himself.

But it was the women who manifested the most passionate enthusiasm. There were some terribly strange underplots, some complicated intrigues among them, whose full scope was never known. Madame Correur began to call pretty Madame Bouchard 'her little pet,' and took her, she said, on a visit to the country; so that for a week M. Bouchard was left to lead a bachelor's life, and M. d'Escorailles had to spend his evenings at the minor theatres. Du Poizat, however, met the two ladies one day in the company of some gentlemen who wore decorations, but he said nothing about having done so. Madame Correur now rented two flats: one in the Rue Blanche, and the other in the Rue Mazarine. The latter was very elegantly furnished, and Madame Bouchard would go there of an afternoon, taking the key from the doorkeeper of the house. It was said that the young woman had made an effectual conquest of a very high functionary.

Then, too, the minor members of the band bestirred themselves, doing all they could. Colonel Jobelin betook himself regularly to a café on the boulevards to catch his old army friends, whom he catechised between their games of piquet; and when he had enlisted the sympathies of half a dozen, he rubbed his hands gleefully in the evening and declared that the whole army had joined the good cause. M. Bouchard devoted himself to a like task in the government offices, and gradually instilled a strong feeling of enmity against M. de Marsy into the clerks. He even won over the messengers, and made the whole staff sigh for the golden age of which he hinted the advent. M. d'Escorailles, on his side, devoted himself to the wealthy young men he knew, extolling Rougon's broad views, his tolerance of certain misdemeanours, and his love of daring. Even the Charbonnels, as they sat on the benches of the Luxembourg garden, whither they went each afternoon while awaiting the issue of their interminable lawsuit, found a means of enlisting the sympathy and support of the petty cits residing in the neighbourhood of the Odéon.

Clorinde was not content with being the guiding spirit of the band, but engaged in very elaborate operations of her own, of which she never spoke. She was to be seen more frequently than ever, hurrying through streets of questionable repute, carelessly dressed and tightly hugging her big official-looking portfolio, which was now so split at the seams that it was only kept together by means of string. She also gave her husband extraordinary commissions to perform, and he did her bidding with the docility of a sheep, never seeking to understand her even. Then, too, she sent Luigi Pozzo about carrying letters; asked M. de Plouguern to give her his escort, and then kept him waiting in the street for her by the hour. At one moment she even thought of getting the Italian government to interfere in Rougon's favour. Her correspondence with her mother, who was still living at Turin, had become extremely active. She had dreams of turning Europe topsy-turvy, and would go twice a day to Chevalier Rusconi's to meet his diplomatic acquaintances. In this strange campaign of hers, she also frequently remembered her beauty, and would go out on certain afternoons most superbly arrayed. And when her friends, quite surprised by the change, told her that she looked lovely, 'I have need to be,' she replied, with an air of resigned weariness.

On her return from Compiègne, Du Poizat, having heard of her adventure at the hunt, had tried to find out on what terms she was with M. de Marsy. He had some vague idea of betraying Rougon in favour of the Count were Clorinde likely to become the latter's all-powerful mistress. She, however, with considerable irritation, denied the truth of any such supposition. He must think her very silly to suspect her of such a connection, she said. She even gave him to understand that she should never see M. de Marsy again. In her earlier days she might possibly have thought of becoming his wife. Now, however, she had other schemes in her head.

'There are often many ways of getting at what you want,' she sometimes said, 'but there is never more than one of them that is pleasant. I myself have a craving to satisfy.'

When she said this she would keep her eyes fixed upon Rougon as though she dreamt of fattening him up for some future feast of her own. She still displayed a disciple-like submission, however, and kept herself in the background with cajoling humility. Rougon himself seemed quite unconscious of all that was going on about him. In his drawing-room, on Sundays and Thursdays, he still consulted playing cards like a fortune-teller, bending over them, and apparently hearing nothing of the talk that went on behind him. The members of the band discussed his affairs, made signs to each other over his head, and plotted by his fireside as though he were not in the room. He seemed so unconcerned with what they whispered that they at last began to chat in louder tones, smiling at his absent-mindedness. However, when they turned the conversation upon the subject of his return to power he flew into a tantrum, and swore that he would not move even if he knew that triumph awaited him at the end of the street; and indeed he shut himself up more than ever, and affected absolute ignorance of what went on in the world. The little house in the Rue Marbeuf, whence streamed such a flow of feverish propaganda, was itself a silent, drowsy home, on the threshold of which Rougon's friends cast glances at one another as a warning to leave outside the scent of battle which they carried in the folds of their garments.

Du Poizat, however, would exclaim: 'I tell you he's drawing us all out. He listens to all we say. Just look at his ears in the evening; you can see that they are on the strain.'

This was frequently the subject of their conversation when they went away together at half-past ten. It really was impossible, they said, that the great man should be unaware of their devotion. The ex-sub-prefect repeated that he was playing the part of a Hindoo idol, squatting in a state of self-satisfaction with his hands across his abdomen, and smiling unctuously amidst a crowd of believers who cut themselves to pieces in his worship. And the others allowed that this comparison seemed a very true one.

'But I will keep my eye on him, you may depend upon that,' Du Poizat said in conclusion.

However, it was useless to study Rougon's face. It remained blank and unruffled, almost child-like. Perhaps, after all, there was no deception about his appearance. Clorinde, for her part, much preferred that he should remain inactive. She was afraid that if they compelled him to open his eyes he might thwart their plans. They were working for his advancement, in spite of himself, as it were. By some means or other, forcibly if necessary, they meant to thrust him into a position of high authority. Then they would have a settlement.

Still matters seemed to advance very slowly, and the band began to grow impatient. Du Poizat's views gained the mastery. They did not openly reproach Rougon with all that they were doing for him, but they assailed him with allusions and hints. The colonel would sometimes come to the evening receptions with his boots white with dust. He had not had time to go home and change them, he said. He was quite knocked up with running about on foolish errands for which he should probably never get any thanks. On other evenings M. Kahn, with heavy eyes, complained of the late hours he had been compelled to keep for a month past. He was going a great deal into society, he said, not for pleasure, indeed, but because it enabled him to meet certain people upon certain business. Then Madame Correur would relate affecting stories; telling them, for instance, of some poor young woman, a widow of the highest character, whom she visited, but was now unable to assist. If she were the government, she said, she would take good care to prevent injustice. Then the whole coterie would vent its own sorrows; each would lament his or her present situation, and compare it with what it would have been had they not behaved in the foolish, soft-hearted way they had done. And all these endless complaints were accentuated by meaning glances at Rougon. To rouse him they even went so far as to praise M. de Marsy. At first Rougon preserved unruffled tranquillity. He still showed no signs of understanding. But after a few evenings, when the talk was of this kind, slight twitchings would pass over his face at certain remarks made in his presence. He expressed no annoyance, but pressed his lips together as though he were pricked by some invisible needle. And at last he became so restless and uneasy that he gave up his card-tricks. He could no longer accomplish them successfully, and preferred to pace about the room, talking, and suddenly hastening away when his friends began to launch veiled reproaches at him. Every now and then he would turn white with anger, and seem to be forcibly holding his hands behind his back to restrain himself from turning the whole crew out of doors.

'My children,' said the colonel one evening, 'I sha'n't come here again for a fortnight. It will be good for us to sulk for a while and see how he can manage to amuse himself without us.'

Then Rougon, who had been thinking of closing his doors, felt very much hurt at the way in which he was abandoned. The colonel kept his word, and some of the others followed his example. The drawing-room looked very empty; there were always five or six of the circle absent. When one of them reappeared after a prolonged absence, and the great man asked him if he had been unwell, the other merely answered in the negative with an air of surprise, and gave no explanation. One Thursday not a single person came. Rougon spent the whole evening alone, pacing up and down the big room with his hands behind him and his head bent. For the first time he felt the strength of the chain which linked him to his band. He shrugged his shoulders to express his contempt for the stupidity of the Charbonnels, the envious rage of Du Poizat, and the suspicious affection of Madame Correur. Nevertheless, he felt a craving, the jealous craving of a master secretly pained by their slightest infidelities, to see and rule these friends of his, whom he held in such light esteem. Indeed at the bottom of his heart he was touched by their foolish behaviour and loved their faults. They seemed to be part of his being, so that he felt diminished and incomplete when they held aloof from him. As they continued to absent themselves he ended by writing to them, and even called at their residences to make peace with them after serious tiffs. Life at the house in the Rue Marbeuf was now so much chronic quarrelling—a series of constantly recurring ruptures and reconciliations.

Towards the end of December there was a particularly serious defection. One evening, without anyone quite knowing why, one bitter remark led to another, and it all ended by a very angry scene. For nearly three weeks afterwards the meetings ceased. The truth is that the band was beginning to lose hope. Their most earnest efforts seemed to have no appreciable result. It was unlikely that the general situation would change for a long time, and a sudden catastrophe, such as might render Rougon necessary, could hardly be anticipated. They had anxiously awaited the opening of the Corps Législatif, but this had gone off without any other incident than the refusal of two republican deputies to take the oath of allegiance. M. Kahn, who was the shrewd man of the group, no longer hoped for any advantage from the course of general politics.

Rougon, in his weary irritation, was occupying himself more energetically than ever with his Landes scheme, as though to conceal the feverish twitchings of his face, which he could no longer keep placid and sleepy as formerly. 'I don't feel very well,' he sometimes said. 'My hands tremble. My doctor has ordered me to take exercise. I am out-of-doors all day.' He did, indeed, go out a great deal now, and was to be met in the streets with his hands swinging and his head in the air, absorbed in thought. When anyone stopped and questioned him he said he had been tramping about all day.

One morning when he returned home to *déjeuner,* after a walk in the direction of Chaillot, he found a gilt-edged visiting-card awaiting him, on which was written Gilquin's name. The card was very dirty, and bore the marks of greasy fingers. Rougon rang for his servant. 'Did the person who gave you this card leave any message?' he asked.

The servant, who was new to the house, smiled. 'It was a gentleman in a green overcoat,' he replied. 'He was very pleasant and offered me a cigar. He only said that he was a friend of yours.' However, just as the servant was leaving the room he turned and added: 'I think there's something written on the back of the card.' Rougon turned it over and read these words written in pencil: 'Can't wait. Will call again this evening. Very urgent; a strange business.' Then he threw down the card with a careless air. After *déjeuner,* however, the expression 'Very urgent; a strange business,' recurred to his mind and haunted him, till it at last rendered him quite impatient. What could this 'strange business' of Gilquin's be? Since Rougon had charged the ex-commercial traveller with sundry obscure and intricate commissions he had seen him regularly once a week in the evening. Never before had Gilquin called in the morning, so that the matter in hand must surely be something out of the common. Rougon, quite at a loss to guess its nature, found himself all aglow with impatience, and although he could not help feeling that it was ridiculous, he resolved to go out and try to discover Gilquin before the evening.

'Some tipsy story, I dare say,' he reflected as he went through the Champs Elysées. 'Well, at any rate I shall satisfy myself.'

He was on foot, as he wished to carry out the directions of his doctor. It was a lovely day; a bright, sunny January noontide. Gilquin appeared to have removed from the Passage Guttin, for his card bore the address Rue Guisarde, Faubourg Saint-Germain.

Rougon had an immense amount of trouble to find this filthy street, which is situated near Saint-Sulpice's. At the end of a dark passage he discovered a woman lying in bed, who called out to him in a voice which quavered with fever: 'Monsieur Gilquin! I don't know whether he's in. It's the door on the left on the fourth floor, right up at the top.'

When Rougon reached the fourth floor he saw Gilquin's name inscribed on the door amidst some arabesques representing flaming hearts transpierced by arrows. However, he knocked to no purpose; he could hear nothing but the tick-tack of a cuckoo-clock and the mewing of a cat. He had expected that he was coming on a vain errand, still he was glad that he had come. His walk had relieved him. So he went downstairs again, feeling more composed, and reflecting that he could very well wait till the evening. When he got outside he slackened his steps, crossed the Saint-Germain market, and then went down the Rue de Seine, with no definite goal in view, but thinking that he would walk home, although he already felt a little tired. Then, as he reached the Rue Jacob, he remembered the Charbonnels, who lived there. He had not seen them for ten days. They were sulking with him. However, he resolved to call on them for a few minutes and offer them his hand. The afternoon was so warm that he felt quite tender-hearted.

The Charbonnels' room at the Hôtel du Périgord overlooked the yard, a gloomy well of a place which smelt like a dirty sink. It was a large, dark room, with rickety mahogany furniture and curtains of faded red damask. When Rougon entered it Madame Charbonnel was folding up her dresses and laying them in a big trunk, while her husband perspired and strained his arms in cording another trunk, a smaller one.

'Halloa! are you off?' Rougon asked, with a smile.

'Yes, indeed,' answered Madame Charbonnel, drawing a deep sigh. 'This time we've quite made up our minds.'

However, they gave him a hearty welcome, apparently quite flattered at seeing him in their room. All the chairs were littered with clothes, bundles of linen, and baskets with splitting sides. So Rougon sat down on the edge of the bed. 'Oh, don't trouble yourselves!' he said, good-naturedly; 'I'm very comfortable here. Go on with what you're doing; I don't want to disturb you. Are you going by the eight o'clock train?'

'Yes, by the eight o'clock tram,' M. Charbonnel replied. 'That gives us just six more hours to spend in this beastly Paris. Ah! we sha'n't forget it in a hurry, Monsieur Rougon!'

Then he, who generally spoke so little, launched into a flow of bitter invective, and even shook his fist at the window while declaiming against the horrid city, where one actually couldn't see clearly in one's room at two o'clock in the afternoon. That dirty light which filtered in through that narrow well of a yard was Paris! But, thank Heaven, he was going to see the sun again in his garden at Plassans! Then he looked round to make sure that he was forgetting nothing. He had bought a railway time-table in the morning, and he pointed to a cold roast fowl wrapt in some greasy paper, which they meant to take with them to eat on their journey.

'Have you emptied everything out of the drawers, my dear?' he asked. 'My slippers were in the night-table. I think, too, that some papers fell behind the chest of drawers.'

Rougon felt pained as he watched the preparations of these disconsolate old folks, whose hands trembled as they made up their packages. Their emotion seemed to him like a silent reproach. It was he who had kept them in Paris, and their sojourn there was ending in complete failure, a veritable flight.

'You are making a mistake,' he said at last.

But Madame Charbonnel answered with a gesture of entreaty as if to beseech him to be silent. 'Don't make us any promises, Monsieur Rougon,' she said sharply. 'They could only bring all our unhappiness over again. When I think that we've been here for two years and a half! Two years and a half, good heavens, in this hole of a place! My left leg will never be free from pain again as long as I live. I have slept on the far side of the bed, and that wall behind you fairly streams with water at night. Oh, I couldn't tell you all we've

gone through! It would be too long a story. And we've spent a ru-
inous amount of money! Only yesterday I was obliged to buy this
big trunk to carry away the things we have worn out while we have
been in Paris; the wretchedly sewn clothes, which the shopkeepers
charged us most extortionately for, and the linen which came back
from the laundress's in rags. Ah! I sha'n't be sorry to have seen the
last of your laundresses! They ruin everything with their acids.'

Then she threw a bundle of things into the trunk, and exclaimed:
'No, this time we are certainly going, I think it would kill me to stay
here an hour longer.'

Rougon, however, insisted upon talking about their lawsuit.
Had they had any bad news? he asked. Then the Charbonnels told
him, almost crying as they did so, that the property of their cousin
Chevassu was certainly lost to them. The Council of State was on
the point of authorising the Sisters of the Holy Family to receive the
legacy of five hundred thousand francs. Their last remaining hope
had expired on hearing of the arrival of Monseigneur Rochart in
Paris, whither he had come, for the second time, to hurry the matter
forward.

And all at once M. Charbonnel ceased to struggle with the cords
of the smaller trunk and raised his arms convulsively, while crying
in a broken voice: 'Five hundred thousand francs! Five hundred
thousand francs!'

They both seemed overwhelmed. They sat down, the husband on
the trunk and the wife on a bundle of linen, amidst all the litter of
the room. And they began to pity themselves in a mournful strain;
as soon as one stopped the other began. They recalled their affection
for their cousin Chevassu. How fond they had been of him! As a
matter of fact, they had not seen him for more than seventeen years
before his death. But, just now, they wept over him in all good faith,
and really believed that they had shown him every kind attention
during his illness. Then they began to accuse the Sisters of the Holy
Family of disgraceful scheming. They had brought undue influence
to bear on cousin Chevassu, they had kept him from his friends, and
had exerted constant pressure on his mind, which illness had weakened. Madame Charbonnel, though she was really a very devout
woman, went so far as to relate a dreadful story, according to which
cousin Chevassu had died of fright after signing his will at the dicta-
tion of a priest, who had shown him the devil standing at the foot of
his bed. And as for the Bishop of Faverolles, she said, it was a dirty

part that he was playing, in despoiling a couple of honest people, who were esteemed throughout Plassans for the integrity they had shown in getting a little competency together in the oil trade.

'But perhaps the case isn't hopeless yet,' said Rougon, seeing that they were wavering. 'Monseigneur Rochart isn't the Divinity. I myself haven't been able to do anything for you lately; I've had so much else to occupy me. But let me find out exactly how matters stand. I don't mean to let them prey on us.'

The Charbonnels looked at each other and shrugged their shoulders. 'It's really no use troubling about it, Monsieur Rougon,' murmured the husband.

And as Rougon persisted, swearing that he would make every effort in their favour, and could not let them go off in this way, the wife in her turn said: 'It's really no use your troubling yourself about it. You would only give yourself a lot of bother for nothing. We spoke of you to our lawyer, but he only laughed at us, and said you had no power now against Monseigneur Rochart.'

'And if you've no power, what's the good of troubling yourself?' asked M. Charbonnel. 'We had much better give it up.'

Rougon had bent his head. These remarks cut him like lashes. Never before had his powerlessness brought him such cruel pain.

'No; we are going back to Plassans,' continued Madame Charbonnel. 'It is much the wisest thing to do. But we are not going away with any grudge against you, Monsieur Rougon! When we see Madame Félicité, your mother, we shall tell her that you would have cut yourself in pieces for us. And if anyone else questions us you may be sure that we sha'n't say a word against you. Nobody can be expected to do more than he's able, can he?'

This was the last stroke. Rougon pictured the Charbonnels reaching their distant home in the provinces. As soon as they had told their news the little town would be yelping at him. It would be a personal defeat, from which it would take him years to recover.

'But you must stay here!' he exclaimed. 'I will have you stay. We will see if Monseigneur Rochart can gobble me up at a mouthful!'

He broke into a threatening laugh which quite alarmed the Charbonnels. They continued to resist for some time, and then at last consented to remain in Paris for another week, but not a single day longer. And thereupon M. Charbonnel began to unknot the cords which he had fastened about the smaller trunk, and his wife lighted a candle, although it was scarcely three o'clock, in order that she might see to put the linen and clothes in the drawers again. When Rougon left them he pressed their hands affectionately and renewed his promises to do all he could.

Before he had gone ten yards down the street, however, he already began to repent of what he had done. Why had he persuaded the Charbonnels to stay when they were so anxious to be off? It would have been a first-rate opportunity to get rid of them. And now he was more committed than ever to bring about a successful issue of their suit. He was especially vexed with himself for the motives of vanity which, as he realised, had influenced him. They seemed unworthy of a man of strength. However, he had promised, and must do what he could. Thus thinking he went down the Rue Bonaparte, followed the quay, and then crossed the Saints-Pères bridge.

The weather was still mild, but a rather sharp breeze was blowing along the river. Rougon was half-way across and was buttoning his coat when he saw a stout lady in furs immediately in front of him. It was Madame Correur; he recognised her by her voice.

'Ah! is it you?' she said in a mournful tone. 'Well, as I've met you I'll shake hands with you; but you wouldn't have seen me at your house for another week. You haven't been acting like a friend.'

Then she began to reproach him for not having made an application which she had been asking of him for months past. It was still the case of that Mademoiselle Herminie Billecoq, a former pupil of Saint Denis, whom her seducer, an officer, was willing to marry, if some good soul would only give her the regulation dowry. Then, too, added Madame Correur, the other ladies gave her no peace. The widow Leturc was anxiously waiting for her tobacco shop, and the others, Madame Chardon, Madame Testanière, and Madame Jalaguier, called on her every day to relate their woes and remind her of the promises she had made them.

'I was counting upon you when I made them,' she said, in conclusion. 'Oh, you've left me in a nice hole! Well, I'm now on my way to ask the Minister of Public Instruction for a scholarship for little Jalaguier. You promised me that scholarship, you know.'

She heaved a deep sigh as she continued: 'We are obliged to go tramping about all over the place now that you refuse to do anything for us.'

Rougon, whom the wind was slightly inconveniencing, had bent his shoulders and begun to look at the Port Saint Nicholas below the bridge. As he listened to Madame Correur he watched some men unloading a barge laden with sugar-loaves, which they rolled down a gangway formed of a couple of planks. A crowd of three hundred people or so was viewing the operation from the quays.

'I am nobody now, and I can do nothing,' said the great man. 'It is wrong of you to feel a grudge against me.'

'Stuff and nonsense!' replied Madame Correur scoffingly; 'I know you well enough. Whenever you choose you can be what you like. Don't be a humbug, Eugène!'

Rougon could not help smiling. The familiarity shown by Madame Mélanie, as he had called her in former days, brought back recollections of the Hôtel Vanneau, when he had no boots even to his feet, but was conquering France. He forgot all the reproaches which he had addressed to himself on leaving the Charbonnels. 'Well, well,' he said, good-naturedly, 'what is it you have to tell me? But don't let us stand here. It's almost freezing. As you are going to the Rue de Grenelle I will walk with you to the end of the bridge.'

Then he turned and walked along beside Madame Correur, without, however, offering her his arm; and the lady began to tell him her troubles at great length. 'After all,' said she, 'I don't so much mind about the others. Those ladies can very well wait. I shouldn't bother you, I should be as merry as I used to be—you remember, don't you?—if I hadn't such big troubles of my own. One can't help getting bitter over them. I'm still dreadfully bothered about my brother. Poor Martineau! His wife has made him completely mad; he has no feelings left.'

Then she gave a minute account of a fresh attempt at reconciliation which she had made during the previous week. In order, said she, to find out exactly what her brother's disposition towards her might be, she had sent him as ambassador one of her friends, that very Herminie Billecoq, whose marriage she had been trying to effect for the last two years.

'Her travelling expenses cost me a hundred and seventeen francs,' she continued. 'But how do you think they received her? Why, Madame Martineau sprang between her and my brother, foaming at the mouth and crying out that I was sending a crew of street-walkers to them, and that she would have them arrested by the gendarmes. My poor Herminie was still in such a tremble when I met her on her return at the Montparnasse station that we were obliged to go into a café and drink something.'

They had now reached the end of the bridge. The passers-by were jostling them. Rougon tried to console Madame Correur, thinking of all the kind things that he could say. 'It's extremely annoying. But, you'll see, your brother will make it up with you by-and-bye. Time puts everything straight.'

Then, as she still detained him at the corner of the footway, amidst the uproar of the passing vehicles, he slowly walked up the bridge again, she following and saying: 'When Martineau dies, his wife is quite capable of burning any will he may leave behind him. The poor, dear fellow is nothing more than skin and bones. Herminie says that he looks dreadfully ill. I am terribly bothered about it all.'

'Well, you can do nothing now,' said Rougon, with a vague gesture; 'you must wait.'

However, she stopped him again when he was halfway across the bridge, and, lowering her voice, continued: 'Herminie told me a strange thing. It seems that Martineau has gone in for politics now. He is a Republican. At the last elections he threw the whole neighbourhood into excitement. That news gave me quite a shock. He might get into trouble, eh?'

There was a short pause, during which Madame Correur looked searchingly at Rougon. He had glanced at a passing carriage as though he wished to avoid her gaze. Then, with an innocent air, he responded: 'Oh, don't make yourself uneasy. You have friends, haven't you? Well, rely on them.'

'You are the only person I rely on, Eugène,' she replied in a low, tender voice.

At this Rougon seemed moved. He glanced at her, and was stirred by the sight of her plump neck and painted face, which she struggled to keep beautiful. She personified his youth. 'Yes, rely on me,' he said, pressing her hands. 'You know very well that I am always on your side.'

He again accompanied her as far as the Quai Voltaire. And when she had left him he at last made his way across the bridge, slackening his steps as he went in order to watch the landing of the sugar-loaves at the Port Saint-Nicholas. For a moment even he halted and let his elbows rest on the parapet. But the sugar-loaves rolling down the gangway, the greenish water flowing beneath the arches of the bridge, the crowd of idlers and the houses all soon grew hazy and disappeared, and he fell into a reverie. He became absorbed in dim, strange thoughts; it seemed to him as if he were descending with Madame Correur into some black abyss of human iniquity. However, he felt no regrets, no qualms; he dreamt of becoming very great and very powerful, so that he might satisfy the desires of those about him to an extent unnatural—even, as it were, impossible.

A shiver roused him from his quiescence. He was trembling with cold. The night was falling and the breeze from the river was stirring up cloudlets of white dust on the quays. He felt very tired as he made his way alongside the Tuileries, and suddenly lacked the courage to return home on foot. All the passing cabs were full, however, and he had almost relinquished the hope of securing one when he saw a driver pull up his horse just in front of him. A head was thrust out of the window of the vehicle. It was M. Kahn's. 'I was just going to your house. Get in. I will drive you home, and we can talk as we go.'

Rougon got into the cab, and was scarcely seated before the ex-deputy burst into tempestuous words amidst the jolting of the vehicle as its horse went on at a sleepy trot: 'Ah, my friend,' said M. Kahn, 'I have just had such a proposal made to me! You would never be able to guess it! I feel as though I were choking!' Then he lowered one of the windows, adding: 'You have no objection, have you?'

Rougon lay back in a corner of the cab, watching the grey wall of the Tuileries gardens; while M. Kahn, very red in the face, and gesticulating spasmodically, continued: 'I have been following your advice, you know. For the last two years I have been struggling persistently. I have seen the Emperor three times, and I have reached my fourth petition on the subject. If I haven't succeeded in getting the railway grant for myself, I have, at any rate, prevented Marsy from getting it for the Western Company. Briefly, I manoeuvred so as to keep matters at a standstill till we should be the stronger party again, as you advised me to do.'

He stopped for a moment, as his voice was drowned by the dreadful clatter made by a passing cart laden with iron. When the cab had got clear of this cart he continued: 'Well, just now, while I was sitting in my study, a man whom I don't know, but who is a big contractor, it appears, called on me and calmly proposed, in the name of Marsy and the directors of the Western Railway Company, that if I would make a million francs' worth of shares over to those gentlemen I should be granted the necessary authorisation for my line. What do you think of that?'

'The terms are a little high,' said Rougon, with a smile.

M. Kahn jerked his head and crossed his arms.

'Oh, you've no idea of the coolness of these people,' he continued. 'You ought to have heard the whole of my conversation with the contractor. In consideration of the million's worth of shares Marsy undertakes to support me, and to bring my claim to a successful issue within a month's time. When I began to speak of the Emperor the contractor only laughed, and told me plumply that if the Emperor was my support I might as well give the whole thing up at once.'

The cab was now turning into the Place de la Concorde, and Rougon emerged from his corner with a bright colour on his cheeks, as if suddenly warmed. 'And did you show this fine gentleman the door?' he asked.

The ex-deputy did not immediately answer, but looked at him with an expression of great surprise. M. Kahn's anger had abruptly subsided. For a while he lay back in his corner of the cab and yielded to the jolts. Then he muttered: 'Ah, no; one doesn't show people like that to the door without a little reflection. And, besides, I wanted to take your advice. For my own part, I confess I am inclined to accept the offer.'

'Never, Kahn!' cried Rougon hotly. 'Never!'

Then they began to discuss the matter. M. Kahn quoted figures. No doubt, said he, a commission of a million francs was an enormous one, but he showed that it might easily be balanced by following certain methods. Rougon, however, refused to listen, and waved his hand to silence him. He himself held money in little account; if he was unwilling that Marsy should pocket a million it was because the gift of that million would be a confession of his own powerlessness, an acknowledgment that he himself was beaten, and that the influence of his rival was so much greater than his own that it might really be priced at that exorbitant figure.

'Can't you see that Marsy is getting tired of the struggle?' said he. 'He's coming round. Wait a little longer and we shall get the grant for nothing.' Then, in almost threatening tones, he added: 'I warn you that we shall quarrel if you accept. I cannot allow a friend of mine to be fleeced in that manner.'

A pause followed. The cab was now ascending the Champs Elysées. Both men, wrapped in thought, looked as though they were counting the trees in the side avenues. M. Kahn was the first to break the silence. 'Listen to me now,' he said in a low tone. 'I ask nothing better than to keep on with you, but you must acknowledge that for the last two years—'

Then he stopped; and, instead of finishing the sentence he had begun, he gave another turn to his answer: 'Well, it isn't your fault. Just now your hands are tied. We had better give them the million; believe me, we had.'

'Never!' cried Rougon energetically. 'In a fortnight you shall have your grant; in a fortnight, do you hear me?'

The cab had just stopped in front of the little house in the Rue Marbeuf. Neither of them alighted, however. For some moments they continued talking inside the vehicle, as though comfortably ensconced in their own home. M. Bouchard and Colonel Jobelin were coming to dine that evening with Rougon, and he pressed M. Kahn to join them; but the other, to his great regret, he said, was obliged to decline the invitation, as he was engaged elsewhere. The great man was now enthusiastically determined upon obtaining the railway grant. When he at length alighted from the cab he closed the door in a friendly way and gave the ex-deputy a parting nod.

'Till next Thursday, then?' cried the latter, thrusting his head out of the window as the cab drove off.

Rougon was feeling slightly feverish on his return. He could not even read the evening papers. Although it was scarcely five o'clock, he went straight to the drawing-room and began to walk up and down while waiting for his guests. The first sunshine of the year, though it was only a pale January sunshine, had given him a touch of headache. His afternoon had left a very vivid impression upon him. All his friends rose before him: those whom he put up with, those of whom he felt afraid, and those for whom he had a genuine affection. They all seemed to be goading him on, forcing him to some decisive step. And this did not displease him; he felt that their impatience was reasonable, and he realised that an anger akin to their own was rising up within himself. It was as though the ground in front of him had gradually diminished, as if the time was near when he would be compelled to make a formidable leap.

Then he suddenly thought of Gilquin, whom he had entirely forgotten. He rang for his servant to ask if 'the gentleman in the green overcoat' had called again during his absence. But the servant had seen no one. Then Rougon told him that if Gilquin should call during the evening he was to be shown into his study. 'And you will let me know immediately,' he added, 'even if we are at table.'

His curiosity was again roused, and he went to look for Gilquin's card. He read the inscription, 'Very urgent; a strange business,' several times over, without managing to make anything of it. When M. Bouchard and the colonel arrived he slipped the card into his pocket, feeling disturbed, even irritated, by those words, which kept buzzing in his brain.

The dinner was a very plain one. M. Bouchard had been a bachelor for the last two days, his wife having had to go into the provinces on a visit to a sick aunt, of whom, strangely enough, she had never previously spoken. The colonel, for whom there was always a cover laid at Rougon's table, had that evening brought his son, whose holidays were on just then. Madame Rougon did the honours in her kindly silent fashion. Under her ever-vigilant eyes the repast was served, slowly, but most carefully, and without the slightest noise. The conversation turned upon the subjects of study in the public schools. The chief clerk quoted some lines from Horace, and spoke of the prizes he had gained in the examinations, about 1813. The colonel said he would have liked a more military form of discipline among the pupils; and then he went on to explain why Auguste had failed in his examination for a bachelor's degree in November. The youth had such a lively intelligence, he said, that he always went beyond the questions asked by the examiners, and this had annoyed them. While his father was thus explaining his failure, Auguste himself was eating some fowl, with a sly smile on his beaming dunce's face.

They were at dessert, when the sound of a bell in the hall caused Rougon the greatest emotion, and quite distracted his attention from his guests. He felt sure that the ring was Gilquin's, and sharply raised his eyes to the door, already mechanically folding up his napkin in the expectation of being summoned from the room. But when the door opened, it was Du Poizat who appeared. The ex-sub prefect dropped into a chair at a few feet from the table, as though he were quite at home. He often called like this early in the evening, immediately after his dinner, which he took at a little boarding-house in the Faubourg Saint Honoré.

'I'm quite done up,' he said, without giving any particulars of the intricate business which he had been transacting during the afternoon. 'I should have gone straight to bed, but I felt an inclination to come and glance over the papers. They are in your room, I suppose, Rougon, aren't they?'

He stayed where he was, however, and accepted a pear and half a glass of wine. The conversation then turned upon the high price of provisions, which had doubled, it was said, during the last twenty years; M. Bouchard mentioning that he could remember having seen pigeons sold at fifteen sous the couple when he was young. However, as soon as the liqueurs and coffee had been handed round, Madame Rougon quietly disappeared, and the men went into the drawing-room without her. They all seemed quite at home. The colonel and the chief-clerk carried the card-table in front of the fire, and began to shuffle the cards, already preparing some wonderful combinations. Auguste sat down at a side table and turned over some numbers of an illustrated newspaper. Du Poizat had disappeared.

'Just look at the hand I hold,' exclaimed the colonel abruptly. 'Isn't it a strange one?'

Rougon went up to the table and nodded. Then, when he had returned to his chair in silence, and was taking up the tongs to move some of the logs of the fire, the servant came in very quietly, and said in his ear: 'The gentleman who called this morning is here.'

Rougon started. He had not heard the bell. When he went into his study, he found Gilquin standing there with a rattan cane under his arm, whilst, with a professional blinking of the eyes, he examined a somewhat poor engraving of Napoléon at Saint Helena. Gilquin's long green overcoat was buttoned up to his chin, and he had not even doffed his black silk hat, which looked almost new, and was tilted very much on one side.

'Well?' asked Rougon hastily.

Gilquin, however, seemed in no hurry, but jogged his head while looking at the engraving, and saying: 'It's well expressed. How dreadfully bored he looks, doesn't he?'

The room was lighted by a single lamp, which stood on a corner of the writing-table. As Rougon entered, a slight noise, a gentle rustling of paper, had come from behind a high-backed arm-chair which stood in front of the mantelpiece, but then such perfect silence had fallen that the previous sound might have been thought the mere cracking of some half-extinguished piece of firewood. Gilquin declined to take a seat; so he and Rougon remained standing near the door, in a patch of shadow cast by a book-case.

'Well?' Rougon asked again; and then he mentioned that he had called in the Rue Guisarde during the afternoon.

At this Gilquin began to speak of his doorkeeper, an excellent woman, who was, unfortunately, dying of consumption, which she had contracted owing to the dampness of the ground floor of the house.

'But this important piece of business of yours? What is it?' asked the great man impatiently.

'Oh, wait a moment,' rejoined the other, 'I have come about that. I'll tell you about it directly. But did you go upstairs, and did you hear my cat? It's a cat that came in by way of the roof. One night, when my window was open, I found her lying by my side. She was licking my beard. It seemed very droll, and so I kept her.'

Then, at last, he made up his mind to speak of the particular business which had brought him there. It was a long story.[1] He commenced by relating his amours with an ironing girl, with whom he had fallen in love one evening, as he was coming out of the Ambigu Theatre. Poor Eulalie, he said, had been distrained upon by her landlord, when only five instalments of her rent were due. For the last ten days, therefore, she had been staying at a lodging-house in the Rue Montmartre, near her work, and it was there that he himself had been sleeping all the week, the room being on the second floor, a dark little place at the far end of a passage, which overlooked a yard.

All this did not interest Rougon, still he listened with patient resignation.

'Well, three days ago,' continued Gilquin, 'I brought a cake and a bottle of wine with me in the evening. We ate the cake and drank the wine in bed. A little before midnight, Eulalie got up to shake out the crumbs; and then she went soundly to sleep. She sleeps like a log. I, myself, was lying awake. I had blown out the candle, and was staring up into the darkness, when I heard a dispute in the next room. I ought to tell you that between the two rooms there's a door which has been fastened up. After a time the voices quieted down and peace seemed to have been made; but I still heard such singular sounds that at last I got out of bed and fixed my eye to a crack in the door. Well, you'll never guess what I saw then!'

[1] The narrative which follows above is virtually matter of history, only for Gilquin's name one should substitute that of a detective officer who carried his information to M. Claude, afterwards famous as the chief of the French detective police.—*Ed.*

He stopped for a moment, and gazed at Rougon, revelling in the effect which he thought he was producing.

'There were two men there: a young one of about five-and-twenty, who was fairly good looking; and another who must have turned fifty, short and thin, and of sickly appearance. Well, they were examining a collection of pistols and daggers and swords, all kinds of brand new weapons which glistened in the light. They were talking in a jargon I which did not recognise at first, but afterwards, by certain words I heard, I knew it was Italian. I've travelled in Italy, you know, in the macaroni trade. Well, I strained my ear to listen, and then I understood, my dear fellow. Those gentlemen have come to Paris to assassinate the Emperor! There, what do you think of that?'

Then he crossed his arms and pressed his cane to his breast as he kept on repeating: 'It's a funny business, isn't it?'

So this was Gilquin's strange affair! Rougon shrugged his shoulders. Twenty times before had various conspiracies been reported to him.

'You told me to come and tell you all the gossip of the neighbourhood,' resumed the ex-commercial traveller. 'Well, I want to render you all the service I can, and so I tell you all I hear. It is wrong of you to shake your head like that. Do you think if I had gone to the prefecture that they would have sent me away without a nice little gratuity? But I prefer benefiting my friends. I tell you that the matter is really serious. So go and tell it to the Emperor, and just see how he embraces you.'

For the last three days, Gilquin had been keeping a watch over those fine gentlemen as he called them. During the daytime, two others made their appearance, a young man, and another of mature years, with a pale, handsome face and long black hair, who seemed to be the chief.[1] They all looked tired out when they entered the room, and they talked together in brief, guarded phrases. However, on the previous night, Gilquin had seen them filling some little iron 'machines' which he believed were bombs. He had got Eulalie's key, and had taken off his boots and kept a careful watch in the room, listening to every sound. In the evening he so managed matters that Eulalie began to snore at about nine o'clock, which, he had thought, would prevent the others from feeling any suspicion;

---

[1] Felice Orsini.

besides, it was never prudent, he added, to let a woman have any share in political matters.

As Gilquin went on speaking, a grave expression came over Rougon's face. He was beginning to believe the story. Beneath the ex-bagman's vinous hilarity, amid the odd details mingled with the narrative, he felt that there was a basis of positive truth. And then all his irksome expectation during the day, all his anxious curiosity appeared to him in the light of a presentiment, and he again experienced that inward trembling which he had felt every now and then since the morning; the involuntary emotion, as it were, of a strong man when he realises that his fortune depends upon a single card. However, he affected utter indifference: 'A set of imbeciles who must have the whole detective force watching them,' he said.

Gilquin began to grin. 'The police had better lose no time, then,' he rejoined.

Then he became silent, but he still smiled and gently tapped his hat. The great man realised that he had not been told everything, and looked at Gilquin searchingly. However, the other opened the door to take his leave. 'Well, at any rate, I have given you warning,' he said. 'I'm going to dine now, my good fellow. I've had no dinner yet; I've been playing the spy on my men all the afternoon, and I'm tremendously hungry.'

At this Rougon stopped him, saying that he could let him have some cold meat; and forthwith he ordered a cover to be laid for him in the dining-room. Gilquin seemed quite touched by this attention. He once more closed the study door, and, lowering his voice so that the servant should not hear him, said to Rougon: 'You are a good fellow. Listen to me, now. I don't want to tell you any lies. If you had received me badly, I should have gone straight to the prefecture. But, now, I'll tell everything. That's honest, isn't it? I'm sure you won't forget the service I'm rendering you. Friends are friends, whatever people may say.' Then he leant forward and continued in a whisper: 'It is to come off to-morrow night. They are going to blow Badinguet[1] up in front of the Opera-house when he arrives there. The carriage and the aides-de-camp and the whole lot will be clean swept away.'

---

[1] A favourite nickname for Napoléon III.; properly the name of the workman whose clothes he donned when escaping from the fort of Ham --*Ed.*

While Gilquin sat down to his meal in the dining-room, Rougon remained standing in the middle of his study, perfectly still and with an ashy face. He was deep in thought, and seemed to be hesitating. At length he sat down at his writing-table and took up a sheet of paper, but he tossed it aside again almost immediately. For a moment it seemed as if he were going to rush to the door and give an order. Then he slowly came back and again became absorbed in thought, which cast a shrouding gloom over his face.

Just at that moment the high-backed arm-chair in front of the fire-place moved, and Du Poizat stood up, calmly folding a newspaper.

'What! were you there?' cried Rougon roughly.

'Of course; I have been reading the papers,' replied the ex-sub-prefect, with a smile which revealed his irregular white teeth. 'You knew very well I was there; you saw me when you came in.'

This audacious falsehood cut all explanation short. The two men looked at each other for some moments in silence. Then, as Rougon seemed to consult him with his eyes, and again went towards the writing-table, Du Poizat made a little gesture, which plainly signified: 'Wait a minute; there is no hurry. We must consider matters.' Not a word was exchanged between them, they both went back to the drawing-room.

Such an angry dispute had broken out that evening between the colonel and M. Bouchard, on the subject of the Orléans Princes and the Count de Chambord, that they had banged their cards down, and sworn that they would never play with each other again. And then with glowering eyes they had seated themselves on either side of the fire-place. However, when Rougon returned, they were once more making friends by loudly singing the great man's praises: that being the one subject on which they could agree.

'Oh, I feel no constraint about it; I say it before his face,' the colonel continued. 'There is no one to equal him at the present time.'

'We are speaking ill of you, you hear,' said M. Bouchard, with a cunning smile.

Then the conversation went on:

'A brain far above the average.'

'A man of action, who has the *coup d'œil* of born conquerors.'

'Ah! France wants his help sadly just now.'

'Yes, indeed. He could do something to get us out of the mess. He is the only man who can save the Empire.'

As Rougon heard this his shoulders bent, and he affected a surly air by way of modesty. Such incense was, however, extremely pleasant to him. His vanity was never so delightfully titillated as when the colonel and M. Bouchard bandied laudatory phrases like these about for a whole evening. They talked a great deal of obvious nonsense, and their faces wore gravely ridiculous expressions; but the more they grovelled in their language the more did Rougon enjoy hearing their monotonous voices as they sang his praises and lavished altogether inapplicable commendation upon him. He sometimes made fun of them when they were not there, but, for all that, his pride and craving for power found gratification in their eulogies. They formed, as it were, a dunghill of praise in which his huge frame could wallow at its ease.

'No, no; I am only a weak sort of man,' he said, shaking his head. 'If I were really all that you believe—'

He did not finish his sentence, but sat down at the card-table and began to consult the cards, a thing which he now seldom did. Meanwhile M. Bouchard and the colonel continued to belaud him. They declared that he was a great orator, a great administrator, a great financier, and a great politician. Du Poizat, who had remained standing, nodded his head assentingly; and presently, without looking at Rougon, and as though the latter had not been present, he remarked: '*Mon Dieu!* Only the least thing is needed to bring him into power again. The Emperor is most favourably disposed towards him. If some catastrophe were to happen to-morrow, and the Emperor should feel the need of an energetic hand, why by the day after to-morrow Rougon would be minister—that's the long and short of it.'

The great man slowly raised his eyes. Then he dropped back in his chair, leaving his combinations with the cards unfinished, while his face again clouded over. But the untiring flattery of M. Bouchard and the colonel still rang out amidst his reverie as if to spur him on to some resolution from which he yet recoiled. And at last a smile appeared upon his face as young Auguste, who had just completed the abandoned *réussite* with the cards, exclaimed: 'It has come out all right, Monsieur Rougon.'

'Of course! things always come all right,' said Du Poizat, repeating the great man's favourite phrase.

However, at that moment a servant entered and told Rougon that a gentleman and a lady wished to see him. And he handed him a card, at the sight of which Rougon uttered a slight cry. 'What! Are they in Paris?'

The visitors were the Marquis and Marchioness d'Escorailles. Rougon hastened to receive them in his study. They apologised for the lateness of their visit; and, in the course of conversation, gave him to understand that they had been in Paris for a couple of days past, but had feared lest a visit from them to one so closely connected with the Emperor might be misconstrued; hence they had preferred to make their call quite privately and at this somewhat unseemly hour. The explanation in no way offended Rougon. The presence of the Marquis and Marchioness under his roof was an unhoped-for honour. If the Emperor himself had knocked at his door, he would not have felt more gratification. Those old people coming to ask a favour of him typified all Plassans offering him its homage; that aristocratic, cold and haughty Plassans, which had ever seemed to him a sort of inaccessible Olympus. An old ambitious dream was at last being realised, and he felt that he was avenged for the scorn shown him by the little town when, as a briefless advocate, he had dragged his worn-down boots about its ill-paved streets.

'We did not find Jules at home,' said the Marchioness d'Escorailles. 'We were looking forward with pleasure to giving him a surprise. But he has been obliged to go to Orléans on business, it seems.'

Rougon was not aware of the young man's absence; however, he quite understood it on recalling the circumstance that the aunt whom Madame Bouchard had gone to see lived at Orléans. Nevertheless he justified Jules, saying that it was a serious matter, a question of abuse of power, which had necessitated his journey. Then he told them that their son was a very intelligent young man and had a great future before him.

'It is necessary for him to make his way,' said the Marquis, thus lightly alluding to the ruin of the family. 'It was a great trial to us to part with him.'

Then he and his wife in discreet fashion began to deplore the necessities of those degenerate times which prevented sons from growing up in the faith of their parents. They themselves had never set foot in Paris since the fall of Charles X.; and they would not have come there now if it had not been a question of Jules's future. Since their dear boy, with their secret consent, had taken service under the Empire, they had pretended to deny him before the world, but in reality they were continually striving for his advancement.

'We make no pretence with you, Monsieur Rougon,' said the Marquis, in a tone of charming familiarity. 'We love our boy; it is natural we should. You have done a great deal for him already, and we thank you heartily for it. But we want you to do more still. We are friends and fellow-townsmen, are we not?'

Rougon bowed, feeling much moved. The humble demeanour of those old people whom he had seen so majestic when they repaired on Sundays to the church of Saint Marc, seemed to enhance his own importance. He gave them formal promises of help.

As they were going off, after twenty minutes' friendly conversation, the Marchioness took Rougon's hand and held it for a moment within her own. 'Then we may rely upon you, dear Monsieur Rougon?' she said. 'We came from Plassans especially for this purpose. We were beginning to feel a little impatient. At our age you can't wonder at it. Now, however, we shall go back feeling very happy. People told us there that you could no longer do anything.'

Rougon smiled. And with an air of decision that seemed prompted by some secret thoughts of his own, he replied: 'Where there's a will there's a way; rely on me.'

When they had left him, however, a shadow of regret passed over his face. He was still tarrying in the ante-room, when he espied a neatly-dressed man, who, balancing a small round felt hat between his fingers, stood in a respectful attitude in a corner.

'What do you want?' Rougon curtly asked him.

The man, who was very tall and broad-shouldered, lowered his eyes and replied: 'Don't you recognise me, sir?' And as Rougon declared that he did not, the other continued, 'I'm Merle, your old usher at the Council of State.'

At this Rougon became somewhat softer: 'Oh, yes! But you are wearing a full beard now. Well, my man, what do you want me to do for you?'

Then Merle proceeded to explain matters in studiously polite language. He had met Madame Correur in the afternoon, and she had advised him to see Monsieur Rougon that very evening. If it had not been for that, he, Merle, would never have presumed to disturb him at such an hour. 'Madame Correur is extremely kind,' he repeated several times. Then he went on to say that he was out of employment. If he now wore a full beard it was because he had left the Council of State some six months previously. When Rougon inquired the reason of his dismissal, he would not allow that he had been discharged for bad conduct, but bit his lip and said: 'They all knew there how devoted I was to you, sir. After you went away, I had to put up with all sorts of unpleasantness, because I have never been able to conceal my real feelings. One day I almost struck a fellow-servant who was saying provoking things, and then they discharged me.'

Rougon looked at him searchingly. 'And so, my man, it's on my account that you are now out of place?'

Merle smiled slightly.

'And I owe you another berth, eh? You want me to find you a situation somewhere?'

'It would be very kind of you, sir.'

There was a short pause. Rougon tapped his hands together in a fidgety, mechanical way. But soon he began to smile, having made up his mind. He had too many debts; he must pay them and get rid of them.

'Well, I will look after you,' he said, 'and get you a place somewhere. You did right to come to me, my man.'

Then he dismissed him. He now hesitated no longer. He went straight into the dining room where Gilquin had just finished off a pot of jam, after eating a slice of *pâté,* the leg of a fowl, and some cold potatoes. Du Poizat, who had joined him, was sitting astride a chair and talking to him. They were discussing women in somewhat crude language. Gilquin had kept his hat on his head, and leant back, lounging in his chair and picking his teeth, under the impression that he was behaving in proper aristocratic style.

'Well, I must be off now,' he said, after gulping down the contents of his glass, which was full, and smacking his lips. 'I am going to the Rue Montmartre to see what has become of my birds.'

Rougon, who seemed in high spirits, began, however, to joke at him. Now that he had dined, did he still believe in that story of a plot? Du Poizat, too, affected complete incredulity. He made an appointment for the next morning with Gilquin, to whom, he said, he owed a breakfast. Gilquin, with his cane under his arm, asked as soon as he could get a word in: 'Then you are not going to warn—'

'Yes, I am, of course,' Rougon replied. 'But they'll merely laugh at me. In any case there's no hurry. There will be plenty of time to-morrow morning.'

The ex-commercial traveller had already got his hand upon the handle of the door. However, he stepped back with a grin on his

face. 'For all I care,' he said, 'they may blow Badinguet to smith-
ereens.'

'Oh!' replied the great man, with an air of almost religious conviction, 'the Emperor has no cause for fear, even if your story is correct. These plots never succeed. There is a watchful Providence.'

That was the last word spoken on the matter. Du Poizat went
off with Gilquin, chatting with him familiarly. An hour later, at
half-past ten, when Rougon shook hands with M. Bouchard and the
colonel as they took their leave, he stretched his arms and yawned,
saying, as was often his wont: 'I am quite tired out. I shall sleep
well to-night.'

On the following evening three bombs exploded beneath the
Emperor's carriage in front of the Opera-house. A wild panic seized
the serried crowd blocking up the Rue Le Peletier.[1] More than fifty
people were struck. A woman in a blue silk dress was killed on
the spot and stretched stark in the gutter. Two soldiers lay dying
on the road. An aide-de-camp, wounded in the neck, left drops of
blood behind him. But, under the crude glare of the gas, amidst the
wreathing smoke, the Emperor descended unhurt from his riddled
carriage, and saluted the throng. Only his hat was torn by a splinter
from one of the bombs.

Rougon had spent the day at home. In the morning he had
certainly felt a little restless, and had twice been on the point of
going out. However, just as he was finishing *déjeuner,* Clorinde
made her appearance; and then, in her society, in his study, where
they remained till evening, he forgot everything. She had come to
consult him on a matter of great intricacy, and appeared extremely
discouraged. She could succeed in nothing, she said. But Rougon
began to console her, seemingly much touched by her sadness. He
gave her to understand that there was great reason for hope, and
that things would altogether change. He was by no means ignorant
of the devotion of his friends, and of all that they had done for him,
and would make it his care to reward them, even the humblest of
them. When Clorinde left him, he kissed her on the forehead. Then
after dinner he had an irresistible longing for a walk. He left the
house and took the shortest way to the quays, feeling suffocated
and craving for the fresh breezes of the river. It was a mild winter evening, and the low, cloudy sky hung over the city in silent

---

[1] The Opera-house then stood there.—*Ed.*

blackness. In the distance the rumbling traffic of the main streets could be faintly heard. Rougon walked along the deserted footways with a regular step, brushing the stone parapet with his overcoat. The lights which spread out in the far distance, twinkling through the darkness like stars that marked the boundaries of some dead heaven, brought him a sensation of the spreading magnitude of all those squares and streets, whose houses were now quite invisible. As he walked along Paris seemed to grow bigger, to expand more in harmony with his own huge form, and to be capable of giving him all the air he needed to inflate his lungs. From the inky river, flecked here and there with shimmering gold, there rose a gentle yet mighty breathing, like that of a sleeping giant—fit accompaniment to his colossal dream. Then as he came in front of the Palais de Justice, a clock struck the hour of nine. There was a tremulous throbbing in the air, and he turned to listen. Over the housetops he fancied he could hear the sounds of a sudden panic, distant reports like those of explosions, and cries of terror. He suddenly pictured Paris in all the stupor born of some great crime. Then he called to mind that afternoon in June, that bright triumphant afternoon of the Baptism, when the bells had pealed out in the hot sunshine, and the quays had been filled with a serried multitude, when everything had told of the glory of the Empire at its apogee, that glory beneath which he had for a moment felt crushed and almost jealous of the Emperor. Now he seemed to be having his revenge. The sky was black and moon-less; the city was terror-stricken and dumb; the quays were deserted and swept by a shudder which seemed to scare the very gaslights, as though some weird evil lay in ambush, yonder, in the darkness of the night. Rougon drew in long breaths of air, and felt that he loved that cut-throat Paris, in whose terror-striking gloom he was regaining supreme power.

Ten days later, he became Minister of the Interior, in the place of M. de Marsy, who was called to the Presidency of the Corps Législatif.

IX

IN OFFICE

ONE morning in March, Rougon sat in his room at the Ministry of the Interior, drawing up a confidential circular which was to be received by the prefects on the following day.

He kept stopping, and puffing, and dashing his pen into the paper. 'Jules, give me a synonym for authority,' he said. 'This language of ours is horrid. I keep putting authority in every line.'

'Well, there's power, government, empire,' the young man answered with a smile.

M. Jules d'Escorailles, whom Rougon had appointed his secretary, was opening the ministerial correspondence at a corner of the writing-table. He carefully cut the envelopes with a penknife, glanced over the letters and then classified them. Meantime, the colonel, M. Kahn and M. Béjuin sat in front of the grate where a large fire was burning. They were all three reclining in their chairs and toasting their feet in silence. M. Kahn read a newspaper, but the two others placidly twiddled their thumbs and looked at the flames.

All at once Rougon rose from his chair, poured out a glassful of water at a side table, and gulped it down at a draught. 'I don't know what I can have eaten yesterday,' he said, 'but I feel as though I could drink the Seine dry this morning.'

He did not immediately resume his seat, but began to pace the room and stretch his burly frame. His heavy step shook the parqueterie underneath the thick carpet. He drew back the green velvet window curtains to let in more light, and then, coming back to the middle of the room, which displayed the gloomy, faded magnificence of some palace turned into a lodging-house, he remained there with his hands clasped behind his neck, revelling, as it were, in the official perfume, the odour of power which he inhaled there. He even broke into an involuntary laugh, which grew louder and louder as it pealed forth his sense of triumph. The colonel and the others turned upon hearing this outburst of gaiety, and questioned him with their eyes.

'Ah! it's very nice, all the same,' were the only words he would say.

However, as he sat down again at the huge rosewood writing-table, Merle came into the room. The usher was irreproachably dressed in black, with a white tie. Not a hair remained upon his dignified face. He was again cleanshaven.

'I beg your excellency's pardon,' he said, 'but the prefect of the Somme—'

'Tell him to go to the deuce! I'm busy,' Rougon answered roughly. 'It's quite preposterous that I am never to be allowed a moment to myself.'

Merle seemed in no way disconcerted, however. 'The prefect,' he resumed, 'says that your excellency is expecting him. There are also the prefects of the Nièvre, the Cher, and the Jura.'

'Well, let them wait! That's what they're made for,' rejoined Rougon loudly.

The usher left the room. M. d'Escorailles had broken into a smile; while the others who were warming themselves at the fire lolled back more freely than ever in their chairs, and seemed amused by the minister's reply. He was flattered by his success.

'It is true,' he said,' that I have been going through the prefects for the last month. It was necessary that I should have them all here. A nice lot they are, too; some rare stupids amongst them. However, they are very obedient. But I feel that I have had enough of them. And, besides, it's for their benefit that I'm working this morning.'

Then he turned to his circular again. The warm silence of the room was only broken by the scratching of his quill-pen and the slight rustling of the envelopes which M. d'Escorailles opened. M. Kahn had taken up another newspaper, and the colonel and M. Béjuin were half asleep.

Outside, France was hushed in fear. The Emperor, in summoning Rougon to power, had been desirous of making examples. He knew the great man's iron hand, and had said to him on the morning after the attempt on his life, with all the anger of one who has just escaped assassination, 'No moderation, mind! They must be made to fear you.' He had just armed him, too, with that terrible Law of General Safety, which authorised the confinement in Algeria or the expulsion from the empire of anyone who might be convicted of a political offence. Although no single Frenchman had taken part in the crime of the Rue Le Peletier, the Republicans were about to be hunted down and transported; there was to be a general sweeping away of the ten thousand 'suspects' who had been passed over at the time of the *coup d'état*. There were rumours of contemplated action by the revolutionary party. The authorities were said to have made a seizure of weapons and treasonable documents. Already in the middle of March, three hundred and eighty persons had been shipped at Toulon for Algeria, and now every week a fresh contingent was sent off. The whole country trembled in the terror which like a black storm cloud rolled forth from the room with the green velvet curtains where Rougon laughed aloud while stretching his arms.

The great man had never before tasted such complete contentment. He felt well and strong, and was putting on flesh. Health had come back to him with his return to power. When he walked about the room he dug his heels into the carpet, as though he wanted his heavy tread to resound throughout France. He would have liked to shake the country by merely putting his empty glass down on the side-table or casting aside his pen. It delighted him to be a source of fear, to forge thunderbolts amidst the smiling gratification of his friends, and to crush a whole nation with his swollen parvenu fists. In one of his circulars he had written: 'It is for the good to feel confidence, and for the wicked only to tremble.' He revelled in playing this part of a divinity, damning some, and saving others. He was filled with mighty pride; his idolatry of his own strength and intelligence was becoming a real religion with him.

Among the new men who had sprung up with the Second Empire, Rougon had long been known as a partisan of strong government. His name was a synonym for stern repression, the refusal of all liberties; despotic rule, in fact. All knew therefore what they had to expect when they saw him called to office. To his intimate friends, however, Rougon unbosomed himself. He did not, he said, so much hold opinions as feel a craving for power. Power had too much attraction for him, and was too essential to his appetite for him to refuse it, whatever the conditions on which it might be offered to him.

To rule, to set his foot on the neck of the crowd, was his first and immediate ambition; the rest was merely secondary matter to which he could easily accommodate himself. The one thing which he really wanted was to be chief. It so happened, however, that the circumstances under which he was now returning to power made his success very pleasant. The Emperor had given him complete liberty of action, and he was at last in a position to realise his old dream of driving the multitude with a whip like a herd of cattle. Nothing filled him with greater satisfaction than to know that he was feared and disliked. And sometimes when his friends told him that he was a tyrant, he smiled, and said with deep meaning: 'If I should become a liberal some day, people will say that I have changed.'

Rougon's very greatest joy was to stand triumphant amidst those friends of his. He forgot France and the obsequious functionaries and the crowd of petitioners who besieged his doors, to regale himself with the perpetual admiration of his ten or twelve intimate associates. His office was open to them at any hour, he allowed them to make it a home, to take possession of his chairs, and even of his desk itself; he told them that it was a pleasure to have them always about him like a pack of faithful dogs. It was not he alone, but the whole coterie, that was the minister. The bonds between them seemed to be drawn closer now that success had come, and Rougon began to love his followers with a jealous love, keeping them in constant communion with him, feeling as if his greatness were increased by their several ambitions. He forgot his secret contempt for them, and began to consider them very intelligent and able, similar to himself. He particularly desired, moreover, that he himself should be respected in their persons, and defended them passionately as he might have defended the fingers of his hands. He made their quarrels his own, and, smiling at the recollection of their long endeavours on his behalf, he even ended by believing that he was greatly indebted to them. Desiring nothing for himself, he lavished upon them all the fruits of office, indulging to repletion in the pleasure of enhancing the brilliancy of his fortune by thus scattering the gifts at his disposal.

However, the big warm room remained silent for some time. Then M. d'Escorailles, after glancing at the address on one of the envelopes before him, handed it to Rougon without opening it. 'Here is a letter from my father,' he said.

Writing in a strain of excessive humility, the Marquis thanked the minister for having appointed Jules to be his secretary. There were two pages of fine writing which Rougon carefully read. Then he folded the letter and slipped it into his pocket. And before turning to his work again he asked: 'Hasn't Du Poizat written?'

'Yes, sir,' answered the secretary, picking a letter out from among the others. 'He is beginning to find his way about in his prefecture. He says that Deux-Sèvres, and the town of Niort in particular, want guiding with a firm hand.'

Rougon glanced over the letter, and remarked: 'Certainly; he shall have all the authority he requires. There is no occasion to send him any reply. My circular will be sufficient.'

Then he took up his pen again, and cudgelled his brains for some suitable concluding sentences. Du Poizat had particularly wished to be prefect at Niort, in his own native district, and the minister, when taking any important decision, invariably thought of the department of Deux-Sèvres, and governed France in accordance with the opinions and necessities of his old comrade in poverty. Just as he was at last finishing his circular to the prefects, something seemed to irritate M. Kahn.

'It is abominable!' the latter exclaimed; and, rapping the newspaper he was reading, he turned to Rougon, and cried: 'Have you read this? There is a leading article here appealing to the basest passions. Just listen to this: "The hand that punishes should be impeccable, for, if justice miscarries, the very bonds which unite society loosen of their own accord." You understand the insinuation, eh? And, here again, among the miscellaneous paragraphs, there's a story about a Countess eloping with the son of a corn-factor. The papers ought not to be allowed to publish such things. It tends to destroy the people's respect for the upper classes.'

'But the serial story is still more odious,' interposed M. d'Escorailles. 'It's all about a wife, a woman of good breeding, who betrays her husband. And the author does not even make her feel any remorse.'

Rougon made an angry gesture. 'Yes,' he said, 'my attention has already been called to that number. You will see that I have marked certain passages with a red pencil. And it is one of our own papers, too! Every day I am obliged to go over it line by line. Ah! the best of them are bad; we ought to suppress them all!' Then, compressing his lips, he added, in a lower tone: 'I have sent for the editor, and am expecting him here presently.'

The colonel had taken the paper from M. Kahn. He also soon vented expressions of indignation, and then handed the print to M. Béjuin, who likewise showed his disgust. Rougon, in the meanwhile, was resting his elbows on his table and reflecting, with eyes half-closed.

'By the way,' he said, turning to his secretary, 'that poor Huguenin died yesterday. That leaves an inspectorship vacant. We shall have to appoint somebody to it.' Then, as the three friends sitting before the fire briskly raised their heads, he continued: 'Oh, it's a post of no importance. Six thousand francs a year. But it's true that there's absolutely nothing to do—'

However, he was interrupted by a person opening the door of an adjoining room.

'Oh, come in, Monsieur Bouchard, come in!' he cried, 'I was just going to call for you.'

Bouchard, who had been appointed head of department a week previously, had brought with him a memorandum about the mayors and prefects who had asked for the crosses of chevalier and officer in the Legion of Honour. Rougon had twenty-five crosses to dispose of among the most meritorious of the applicants. He took the memorandum, read over the names and consulted various papers, while M. Bouchard went up to the fire and shook hands with the three others. Then, with his back against the mantelpiece, and his coat-tails raised in order that he might warm his legs, the chief of department said: 'A miserably wet day, isn't it? We shall have a late spring.'

'It's awful,' replied the colonel, 'I feel one of my attacks coming on. I had shooting pains in my left foot all night.'

'And how is your wife?' asked M. Kahn after a short pause.

'Thank you, she is very well,' replied M. Bouchard. 'I am expecting to see her here this morning.'

Then there was another pause. Rougon was still examining the papers. As he came to a certain name, he stopped. 'Isidore Gaudibert—that isn't the man who writes verses, is it?'

'Yes, that is the man,' M. Bouchard answered. 'He has been Mayor of Barbeville since 1852. On every happy event, the Emperor's marriage, the Empress's confinement, and the Prince Impérial's baptism, he has sent charming verses to their Majesties.'

The minister pouted scornfully. The colonel, however, asserted that he had read the odes and thought them very fine. He referred to one in particular, in which the Emperor was compared to a piece of fireworks. Then without any transition the friends began to eulogise the Emperor. They were all enthusiastic Bonapartists now. The two cousins, the colonel and M. Bouchard, were completely reconciled, and, instead of throwing the Orléans Princes and the Count de Chambord at each other's head, rivalled in singing their sovereign's praise.

'Oh, no! not this one!' Rougon suddenly exclaimed. 'This Jusselin is a creature of Marsy's. There is no call for me to reward the friends of my predecessor.' Then with a stroke of his pen, that cut through the paper, he effaced the name. 'But we must find some one,' he resumed. 'It is an officer's cross.'

The friends sat perfectly still. M. d'Escorailles, notwithstanding his extreme youth, had received the chevalier's cross a week previously. M. Kahn and M. Bouchard were already officers, and the colonel had just been named commander.

'Well, let us see: an officer's cross,' said Rougon, beginning to refer to his papers again. But he stopped short as if struck by a sudden idea. 'Aren't you mayor of some place or other, Monsieur Béjuin?' he inquired.

M. Béjuin contented himself with nodding twice, but M. Kahn answered more fully for him. 'Yes,' said he; 'he is Mayor of Saint Florent, the little commune where his glass works are.'

'Well, then, that's settled!' said the minister, delighted to have an opportunity of advancing one of his friends. 'You never ask for anything for yourself, Monsieur Béjuin, so I must look after you.'

M. Béjuin smiled and expressed his thanks. It was quite true that he never asked for anything, but he was always there, silent and modest, on the look-out for such crumbs as might fall, and ready to pick them up.

'Léon Béjuin, isn't it?—in the place of Pierre François Jusselin,' continued Rougon, as he altered the names.

'Béjuin, Jusselin; they rhyme,' observed the Colonel.

This remark struck the company as being very witty, and caused a deal of laughter. At last M. Bouchard took the signed documents away, and Rougon rose. His legs were paining him a little, he said. The wet weather affected him.

However, the morning was wearing on; a hum of life came from the various offices; quick steps resounded in the neighbouring rooms; doors were opened and closed, and whispers half-stifled by the velvet hangings were wafted hither and thither. Several clerks came into the room to obtain the minister's signature to other documents. It was a continual coming and going, the administrative machine was in full work, throwing out an enormous number of documents which were carried from office to office. And amidst all this hurrying to and fro, a score of people were wearily waiting in the anteroom till his excellency should be graciously pleased to receive them. Rougon, meantime, began to display feverish activity and energy; giving orders in a whisper in one corner of his room, then suddenly storming at some official in another, allotting some task, or deciding a knotty question with a word, while he stood there, huge and domineering, his neck swollen, and his face a picture of strength.

However, Merle came into the room again with that quiet composure which no rebuffs could ruffle. 'The prefect of the Somme—' he began.

'Again!' interrupted Rougon violently.

The usher bowed and then resumed, 'The prefect of the Somme has begged me to ask your excellency if you can receive him this morning. If your excellency cannot, then he would be much obliged to your excellency if you would kindly fix a time for to-morrow.'

'I will see him this morning. Confound it all, let him have a little patience!'

Merle had left the door open, and the ante-room could be seen. It was a spacious apartment, with a large table in the centre and a line of arm-chairs, covered with red velvet, along the walls. All the chairs were occupied, and there were even two ladies standing by the table. Every face was turned towards the minister's room, with a wistful, supplicating expression, as if seeking permission to enter. Near the door, the prefect of the Somme, a pale little man, was talking with his colleagues from the Jura and the Cher. He was on the point of rising, in the expectation that he was at last about to be received in audience, when Rougon again spoke. 'In ten minutes,' he said to Merle. 'Just at present I cannot see anyone.'

While he was speaking, however, he caught sight of M. Beulin-d'Orchère crossing the ante-chamber, and thereupon he darted forward, and drew him by the hand into his private room.

'Come in, my friend, come in!' he exclaimed. 'You have just come, haven't you? You haven't been waiting? Well, what news have you brought?'

Then Merle closed the door, and the occupants of the ante-chamber were left in silence and consternation. Rougon and M. Beulin-d'Orchère talked together in whispers near one of the windows. The judge, who had recently been appointed first president of the Court of Paris, was ambitious of holding the Seals; but the Emperor, when sounded on the matter, had shown himself quite impenetrable.

'Very good, very good,' said Rougon, suddenly raising his voice. 'Your information is excellent. I will take steps, I promise you.'

He was just showing the judge out by way of his private room, when Merle appeared once more. 'Monsieur La Rouquette,' he announced this time.

'No, no! I am busy, and he bores me,' said Rougon, signing energetically to the usher to close the door.

M. La Rouquette distinctly heard what was said; still, this did not prevent him from entering the minister's room with a smiling face. 'How is your excellency?' he said, offering his hand. 'It's my sister who has sent me. You seemed a little tired at the Tuileries yesterday. You know that a proverb is to be acted in the Empress's apartments next Monday. My sister is taking a part in it. Combelot has designed the costumes. You will come, won't you?'

He stood there for a whole quarter of an hour prattling away in wheedling fashion, addressing Rougon sometimes as 'your excellency,' and sometimes as 'dear master.' He dragged in a few stories of the minor theatres, praised a ballet girl, and begged for a line to the director of the tobacco manufactory so that he might get some good cigars. And he concluded by saying some abominable things about M. de Marsy, though still continuing to jest.

'Well, he's not such a bad fellow, after all,' remarked Rougon, when the young deputy had taken himself off. 'I must go and dip my face in the basin. My cheeks feel as if they were burning.'

He disappeared for a moment behind a curtain, and then a great splashing of water, accompanied by snorting and blowing, was heard. Meantime, M. d'Escorailles, who had finished classifying his letters, took a little file with a tortoise-shell handle from his pocket, and began to trim his nails. M. Béjuin and the colonel were still gazing up at the ceiling, so buried in their easy-chairs that it seemed doubtful whether they would ever be able to get out of them again. M. Kahn, however, was going through a heap of newspapers on a table near him. He just turned them over, glanced at their titles, and then threw them aside. Then he got up.

'Are you going?' asked Rougon, who now reappeared, wiping his face with a towel.

'Yes,' replied M. Kahn, 'I've read the papers, so I'm off.'

Rougon, however, asked him to wait a moment. And then, taking him aside, he told him that he hoped to go down to Deux-Sèvres during the following week, to attend the inauguration of the operations for the new line from Niort to Angers. He had several reasons, he said, for wishing to visit the district. At this M. Kahn manifested great delight. He had succeeded in getting the grant early in March, and was now floating the scheme. And he was conscious of the additional importance which the minister's presence would lend to the initial ceremony, the details of which he was already arranging.

'Then I may reckon upon you to fire the first mine?' he said, as he took his leave.

Rougon had returned to his writing-table, where he was consulting a list of names. The crowd in the ante-room was now growing more and more impatient. 'I've barely got a quarter of an hour,' he said. 'Well, I'll see such as I can.'

Then he rang his bell, and, when Merle appeared, he said to him: 'Show in the prefect of the Somme.' But he immediately added, still keeping his eyes on the list of names: 'Wait a moment. Are Monsieur and Madame Charbonnel there? Show them in.'

The usher's voice could be heard calling out, 'Monsieur and Madame Charbonnel.' And thereupon the couple from Plassans appeared, followed by the astonished eyes of the other occupants of the ante-chamber. M. Charbonnel wore a dress-coat with square tails and a velvet collar, and Madame Charbonnel was dressed in puce silk, with a bonnet trimmed with yellow ribbons. They had been patiently waiting for two hours.

'You ought to have sent your card in to me,' said Rougon. 'Merle knows you.' Then, interrupting their stammering greeting, in which the words 'your excellency' again and again recurred, he gaily exclaimed: 'Victory! The Council of State has given judgment. We have beaten that terrible bishop!'

The old lady's emotion upon hearing this was so great that she was obliged to sit down, while her husband leant for support against an arm-chair.

'I learned this good news yesterday evening,' the minister continued. 'And as I was anxious to tell it to you, myself, I asked you to come here. It's a pretty little windfall, five hundred thousand francs, eh?'

He began to jest, feeling quite happy at the sight of the emotion on their faces. Some time elapsed before Madame Charbonnel, in a choking timorous voice, could ask: 'Is it really all over, then? Really? Can't they start the suit again?'

'No, no; be quite easy about it,' answered Rougon. 'The fortune is yours.'

Then he gave them certain particulars. The Council of State had refused to allow the Sisters of the Holy Family to take possession of the bequest upon the ground that natural heirs were living, and that the will did not present the necessary appearances of genuineness. Monseigneur Rochart was in a terrible rage, said Rougon; he had met the bishop the previous day at the Ministry of Public Instruction, and still laughed at the recollection of his angry looks. He seemed, indeed, quite delighted with his triumph over the prelate.

'His Grace hasn't been able to gobble me up, you see,' he continued; 'I am too big a mouthful for him. I don't think, though, that it's all over between us. I could see that by the look of his eyes. He is a man who never forgets anything, I should imagine. However, the rest will be my own business.'

The Charbonnels were profuse in their expressions of gratitude and respect. They should leave Paris that same evening, they said; for all at once great anxiety had come upon them. Their cousin Chevassu's house, at Faverolles, had been left in the charge of a bigoted old woman who was extremely devoted to the Sisters of the Holy Family, and on learning the issue of the trial she might perhaps strip the house of its contents and go off with them. The Sisters, said the Charbonnels, were capable of anything.

'Yes, get off this evening,' the minister advised. 'If anything should happen to bother you down there, just write and let me know about it.'

Then on opening the door to show them out, he noticed the marked astonishment of the occupants of the antechamber. The prefect of the Somme was exchanging a smile with his colleagues of the Jura and the Cher, while an expression of scorn wreathed the lips of the two ladies standing by the table. And thereupon Rougon raised his voice, saying: 'You will write to me, won't you? You know how devoted I am to you. When you get to Plassans tell my mother that I am in good health.'

Thus speaking, he crossed the ante-chamber with them, accompanying them to the outer door so as to exalt them before all the waiting people, feeling in no wise ashamed of them, but proud, rather, of having come himself from their little town, and of now being able to raise them as high as he pleased. And the favour-seekers and the functionaries bowed low, doing reverence, as it were, to the puce silk gown and square-tailed coat of the Charbonnels.

When Rougon returned to his own room, he found that the colonel had risen from his chair.

'Good-bye till this evening,' said Jobelin. 'It's getting rather too warm in here.'

Then he bent forward to whisper a few words concerning his son Auguste, whom he was about to remove from college, as he quite despaired of the young fellow ever passing his examination. Rougon had promised to take him into his office, although according to the regulations all the clerks ought to hold a bachelor's degree.

'Very well, bring him here,' said the minister. 'I will have the regulation relaxed; I will manage it somehow. And he shall have a salary at once, as you are anxious about it.'

Thereupon the colonel went off, and M. Béjuin remained alone in front of the fire. He wheeled his chair into a central position, and seemed quite unaware that the room was growing empty. He always remained in this fashion till every one else had gone, in the hope of being offered something which had been hitherto forgotten.

Merle now received orders to introduce the prefect of the Somme. Instead of going to the door, however, he stepped up to the writing-table. 'If your excellency will kindly permit me,' he said, with a pleasant smile, 'I will at once acquit myself of a little commission.'

Rougon rested his elbows on his blotting-pad and listened.

'It is about poor Madame Correur,' continued Merle. 'I went to see her this morning. She was in bed. She has got a nasty boil in a very awkward place; such a big one too; and although there is nothing dangerous about it, it gives her a great deal of pain.'

'Well?' said the minister.

'Well, the poor lady very much wanted to come and see your excellency to get the answers you had promised her. Just as I was coming away, she asked me if I would bring her them after my day's work. Would your excellency be so good as to let me do so?'

The minister quietly turned and said: 'Monsieur d'Escorailles, give me those papers there, in that cupboard.'

It was to a collection of documents concerning Madame Correur that he referred. They were tightly packed in a large case of stout grey paper. There were letters, and plans, and petitions, in all kinds of writing and spelling; requests for tobacco-agencies, for licenses to sell stamps, petitions for pecuniary assistance, grants and pensions. Each sheet bore a marginal note of five or six lines, followed by Madame Correur's big masculine-looking signature.

Rougon turned the papers over and glanced at some brief memoranda which he himself had written on them with a red pencil: 'Madame Jalaguier's pension is raised to eighteen hundred francs,' he said. 'A tobacco-agency is granted to Madame Leturc. Madame Chardon's tender is accepted. Nothing has yet been done in Madame Testanière's matter. Ah! you can say, too, that I have been successful in Mademoiselle Herminie Billecoq's case. I have mentioned it to some ladies who will provide the dowry necessary for her marriage with the officer who seduced her.'

'I thank your excellency a thousand times,' said Merle, with a low bow.

As he was going out, a charming blonde head, surmounted by a pink bonnet, peeped in at the door, and a fluty voice inquired: 'Can I come in?'

Then, without waiting for a reply, Madame Bouchard entered the room. She had not seen the usher in the antechamber, so she had come straight on. Rougon, who addressed her as 'my dear child,' asked her to sit down, after momentarily detaining her little gloved hands within his own. 'Have you come about anything important?' he asked.

'Yes, very important,' answered Madame Bouchard with a smile.

Rougon thereupon told Merle to admit nobody. M. d'Escorailles, who had just finished trimming his nails, had advanced to greet Madame Bouchard. She signed to him to stoop, and immediately whispered a few words to him. He nodded assent, and then, taking his hat, turned to Rougon, saying: 'I'm going to breakfast. There doesn't seem to be anything else of importance excepting that matter of the inspectorship. We shall have to give it to someone.'

The minister looked perplexed. 'Yes, certainly,' he said, 'we shall have to appoint somebody. A whole heap of men have already been suggested to me; but I don't care to appoint people whom I don't know.'

Then he glanced round the room as though trying to find somebody, and his eye fell upon M. Béjuin, still silently lounging before the fire, with an expression of complete unconcern upon his face.

'Monsieur Béjuin,' said Rougon.

M. Béjuin opened his eyes, but remained quite still.

'Would you like to be an inspector?' added the minister. 'I may tell you that it's a post worth six thousand francs a year. There is nothing to do, and the place is quite compatible with your position as a deputy.'

M. Béjuin nodded gently. Yes, yes, he would accept the post. And so the matter was settled. However, he still lingered before the fire for a few more minutes, when it probably struck him that there was no likelihood of his picking up any more crumbs that morning, for with a dragging step he took himself off in the rear of M. d'Escorailles.

'There! we are alone now! Come, my dear child, what's the matter?' said Rougon to pretty Madame Bouchard.

He wheeled up an easy-chair and sat down in front of her in the centre of the room. And then for the first time he noticed her dress. It was of very soft pale rose cashmere, and hung round her in close, clinging folds. There seemed, also, to be something very bewitching about her appearance that morning.

'Well, what's the matter?' repeated Rougon.

Madame Bouchard smiled without making any immediate answer. She sat back in her chair, with parted lips showing her pearly white teeth. Little curls peeped from under her pink bonnet, and there was a coaxing expression on her little face, an air of mingled supplication and submission.

'It is something I want to ask of you,' she murmured at last; and then, in an animated way, she added: 'Promise me that you'll do it.'

But Rougon would promise nothing. He wanted to know what it was first. He mistrusted ladies. And as she bent towards him, he said to her: 'Is it something very unusual, that you daren't tell me? Well, I must get it out of you by questions. Let us set about it methodically. Is it something for your husband?'

But Madame Bouchard shook her head, while still continuing to smile.

'No! Is it for Monsieur d'Escorailles, then? You were plotting something together in whispers a little while ago.'

But Madame Bouchard again shook her head; and pulled a pretty little face which clearly signified that it had been necessary for her to get rid of M. d'Escorailles. Then, as Rougon was wondering what it could be that she wanted, she drew her chair still nearer to him. 'You won't scold me, will you?' she said. 'You do like me a little, don't you? Well, it's for a young man. You don't know him, but I'll tell you his name directly, when you have promised to give him the post. Oh, it's quite an insignificant one that I want for him. You will only have to say a word and we shall be very, very grateful to you.'

'Is he a relation of yours?' Rougon inquired.

Madame Bouchard sighed deeply, glanced at him with languishing eyes, and then let her hands slip down so that Rougon might take them in his own. And finally in a very low voice, she replied: 'No, he's a friend of mine—a particular friend—Oh! I am very unhappy!'

Her eyes added all that she left unsaid.

'But this is very shocking!' exclaimed the minister, and then, as she still leant towards him, raising her little gloved hand to his

lips to silence him, he roughly repulsed her, compelling her to rise
to her feet. She remained before him with pale lips and downcast
eyes. 'Yes, it is disgraceful! abominable!' he continued. 'Monsieur
Bouchard is an excellent man. He worships you. He trusts you with
blind confidence. No, no, indeed! I will certainly not help you to
deceive him. I refuse, refuse absolutely, do you hear? It is of no use
mincing words with you, my pretty young woman!'

Then he checked himself, and, gradually becoming calmer, assumed an air of great dignity. Seeing that Madame Bouchard had
begun to tremble, he made her sit down again while he himself
remained erect, lecturing her severely. It was a real sermon that
he preached to her. He told her that she was offending against all
laws, both human and divine; that she was standing on the brink
of a precipice, and preparing for herself an old age full of remorse.
Then, fancying that he could detect a faint smile hovering round
the corners of her lips, he proceeded to draw a picture of the old
age he predicted, when her beauty would be in ruins, her heart for
ever empty, and her brow flushed with shame beneath her white
hair. And afterwards he discussed her conduct from a social point
of view, in this respect showing much severity, and he went on to
rail at modern licentiousness, at the disgraceful dissoluteness of
the times. Then he spoke of himself. He was the guardian of the
laws, he said, and could never abuse his power by lending himself
to the encouragement of vice. Without virtue it seemed to him that
government was impossible. Finally, he concluded by defying his
enemies to name a single act of nepotism in his administration, a
single favour granted by him that was due to intrigue.

Pretty Madame Bouchard listened with downcast bead, huddling
herself up in her chair and letting her delicate neck show from under
the ribbons of her pink bonnet. When Rougon had at last finished
speaking, she rose and made her way to the door, without saying
a word. But as she laid her fingers upon the handle, she raised her
head and began to smile again. 'He is named Georges Duchesne,'
she murmured. 'He is principal clerk in my husband's division, and
wants to be assistant—'

'No, no!' cried Rougon.

Then she slowly left the room, casting a long contemptuous
glance at the minister, who came back from the door with an expression of weariness on his face. He had beckoned to Merle to follow
him. The door remained ajar.

'The editor of the *Vœu National,* whom your excellency sent for, has just arrived,' said the usher in a low tone.

'Very good,' replied Rougon; 'but I'll see the officials who have been waiting so long first.'

Just at that moment, however, a valet appeared at the door which led to the minister's private apartments, and announced that *déjeuner* was ready, and that Madame Delestang was waiting for his excellency in the drawing-room.

At this Rougon stepped forward. 'Tell them to serve at once,' he replied briskly. 'So much the worse for the gentlemen; I will see them afterwards. I'm frightfully hungry.'

Then he just popped his head through the doorway and gave a glance round the ante-room, which was still full. Not a functionary or a petitioner had moved. The three prefects were still talking together in their corner. The two ladies by the table were leaning upon their finger-tips, as if a little weary. The same people sat motionless and silent in the red velvet chairs along the walls. Then Rougon left his room, giving Merle orders to detain the prefect of the Somme and the editor of the *Vœu National.*

Madame Rougon, who was not very well, had left on the previous evening for the South of France, where she was going to stay for a month. She had an uncle living in the neighbourhood of Pau. On the other hand, Delestang had been in Italy for the last six weeks, on an important mission connected with agriculture. And thus it came about that the minister had invited Clorinde, who wanted to have a long talk with him, to partake of *déjeuner* at his official residence.

Patiently waiting for him, she was beguiling the time by glancing through a law-treatise which she had found upon a table.

'You must be getting dreadfully hungry,' he said to her gaily as he entered the drawing-room. 'I've had a tremendous lot to do this morning.'

Then he gave her his arm and conducted her into the dining-room, an immense apartment where the little table, laid for two, near a window, seemed quite lost. A couple of tall footmen waited upon them. Rougon and Clorinde, who both preserved a very serious demeanour, ate rapidly. Their meal consisted of a few radishes, a slice of cold salmon, some cutlets with mashed potatoes, and a little cheese. They took no wine—Rougon drank nothing but water of a morning—and they scarcely exchanged a dozen words. Then, when the two footmen had cleared the table and brought in the coffee and liqueurs, Clorinde glanced at Rougon and gave a slight twitch of her eyebrows which he perfectly understood.

'That will do; you can go now,' he said to the footmen. 'I will ring if I require anything.'

The servants left the room, and Clorinde, rising from her chair, tapped her skirt to remove the crumbs which had fallen on it. She was wearing that day a black silk dress, somewhat too large for her and laden with flounces, a very elaborate dress which so enveloped her figure as to make her look like a mere bundle.

'What a tremendous place this is!' she remarked, going to the end of the room. 'It's the kind of place for a wedding feast, this dining-room of yours,' Then she came back and said: 'I should very much like to smoke a cigarette, do you know?'

'The deuce,' replied Rougon; 'there's no tobacco. I never smoke myself.'

But Clorinde winked and drew from her pocket a little tobacco pouch, of red silk, embroidered with gold, and scarcely larger than a purse. She rolled a cigarette with the tips of her tapering fingers, and then, as they did not wish to ring, they began to search the room for matches. At last they found three on a sideboard, and Clorinde carefully carried them off. With her cigarette between her lips, she sat back in her chair and began to sip her coffee, while gazing smilingly at Rougon.

'Well, I am entirely at your service now,' he remarked, with an answering smile. 'You want to talk to me; so let us talk.'

Clorinde made a gesture as though to express that what she had to say was of no consequence. 'Yes,' she rejoined; 'I have had a letter from my husband. He is feeling very bored at Turin. Of course, he is much pleased at having got this mission, thanks to you, but he doesn't want to be forgotten while he is away. However, we can talk of all that presently. There's no hurry about it.'

Then she again began to smoke and look at Rougon with her irritating smile. The minister had gradually accustomed himself to seeing her, without worrying about those questions which had formerly so disturbed him. Clorinde had now become a feature of his daily life, and he accepted her as though he understood her, as though her eccentricities no longer caused him the faintest surprise. As a matter of fact, however, he knew nothing certain about her even yet: she was as great a mystery to him as she had been in the first days of their acquaintance. She constantly varied, sometimes acting childishly, sometimes showing herself very deep and knowing; for although, as a rule, she seemed very foolish, she occasionally manifested singular shrewdness. And now, too, she was very gentle, and now extremely spiteful. When she surprised Rougon by some word or gesture which he could not understand, he shrugged his shoulders with an expression of superiority, opining that all women behaved in that fantastic way. He fancied that he thus manifested a supreme contempt for the sex, but his manner merely sharpened Clorinde's smile, a smile which had an expression of crafty cruelty about it, revealing as it did her eager teeth between her ruby lips.

'Why are you looking at me in that way?' Rougon asked her at length, feeling disturbed by the steady gaze of her large eyes. 'Is there anything about me which displeases you?'

Some hidden thought had just brought a gleam from the depths of Clorinde's eyes, and her lips had assumed a hard expression. But she quickly put on a charming smile again, and began to puff out little whiffs of smoke while saying: 'Oh, dear no, you're very nice, I was thinking about something, my dear fellow. Do you know that you have been very lucky?'

'How's that?'

'Why, yes. Here you are on the pinnacle which you were so anxious to reach. Everybody has helped to lift you to it, and events themselves have worked for you.'

Rougon was about to reply when there came a knock at the door. Clorinde instinctively hid her cigarette behind her skirts. It was a clerk with an urgent telegram for his excellency. Rougon read the despatch with an air of displeasure, and after telling the clerk what reply was to be made to it, hastily closed the door with a bang and took his seat again.

'Yes,' he said, 'I have certainly had some devoted friends, and am now trying to remember them. And you are right, too, in saying that I owe something to events. It often happens that men are powerless, unless they are helped by events.'

As he spoke these words in slow deliberate tones he glanced at Clorinde, lowering his heavy eyelids so as to conceal the fact that he was trying to penetrate her meaning. Why had she spoken of his luck? he wondered. What did she know of the favourable events to which she had referred? Had Du Poizat been saying anything to her? But when he saw the smiling, dreamy look of her face, which had suddenly softened, he felt sure that she knew nothing whatever upon the subject. He himself, too, was trying to forget certain things, and did not care to stir up the inner chambers of his memory. There was an hour of his life which now seemed hazy and confused to him, and he was beginning to believe that he really owed his high position solely to the devotion of his friends.

'I didn't want anything,' he continued; 'I was driven into it in spite of myself. Well, I suppose things have turned out for the best. If I succeed in doing any good, I shall be quite satisfied.'

Then he finished his cup of coffee, while Clorinde rolled another cigarette.

'Do you remember,' she inquired, 'my asking you, two years ago, when you were leaving the Council of State, your reason for your sudden whim? You were very reserved then, but surely you can speak out now. Come, between ourselves, tell me frankly if you had a definite plan in your mind.'

'One always has a plan,' he answered shrewdly. 'I felt that I was falling, and preferred to jump down of my own accord.'

'And has your plan been realised? Have events happened just as you anticipated?'

'Well, hardly that. Things never turn out exactly as one calculates. One must be satisfied if one attains one's end somehow.' Then he paused to offer Clorinde a glass of liqueur. 'Which will you have, curaçoa or chartreuse?' She chose chartreuse; and, as Rougon was pouring it out, there came another knock at the door. Clorinde again hid her cigarette with a gesture of impatience, whilst Rougon got up angrily, still holding the decanter. This time it was a letter bearing a large seal which was brought for his inspection. When he had glanced at it, he put it into his pocket.

'Very well,' he said. 'Don't let me be disturbed again.'

When he came back to Clorinde, the young woman was steeping her lips in the chartreuse, slowly sipping it, while glancing upward at him with glistening eyes. There was a tender look upon her face again.

Then, putting down her glass and leaning on the table, she said, in a low voice: 'No, my dear fellow, you will never know all that was done for you.'

Rougon drew his chair closer to hers and, in his turn, rested his elbows on the table. 'Ah, you will tell me all about that now, won't you?' he cried with animation. 'Don't let us have any more mysteries, eh? Tell me all that you yourself did.'

She shook her head, however, while pressing her cigarette between her lips.

'What, is it something dreadful?' Rougon asked. 'Are you afraid that I shouldn't be able to repay you? Wait a moment, now; I'm going to try to guess. You wrote to the Pope and you dropped a bit of consecrated wafer into my water jug without letting me know?'

Clorinde seemed vexed by this jesting, and threatened to leave him if he continued it. 'Don't scoff at religion,' she said. 'It will bring you misfortune.'

Then, waving away the smoke which she was puffing from her lips and which seemed to inconvenience Rougon, she continued in an expressive tone: 'I saw a great many people indeed, and I won you several friends.'

She experienced a strong, an evil, inclination to tell him everything, for she did not want him to remain ignorant of the fact that she had done much for his advantage. Her confession would be a first instalment towards the satisfaction of her patiently hoarded rancour. 'Yes, yes,' she continued significantly; 'I won over to your side several men who were strongly opposed to you. And I destroyed the influence of others.'

Rougon had turned very pale, for he understood her only too well. 'Ah!' was all he said, as if to avoid the subject; but Clorinde defiantly fixed her large black eyes upon him, and giving way he began to question her. 'Monsieur de Marsy, eh?'

Clorinde nodded assent and then blew a whiff of smoke over her shoulder.

'Chevalier Rusconi?'

Again she nodded.

'Monsieur Lebeau, Monsieur de Salneuve, Monsieur Guyot-Laplanche?'

She nodded at each name, and then finished her glass of chartreuse in little sips, with an expression of triumph on her face.

Rougon had risen from his seat. He walked to the end of the room as if pondering, and then came back and stood behind Clorinde. She could hear him panting. And all at once she turned sharply, fearing he was going to kiss her hair. 'I know your thoughts,' said she, 'but remember, I had no need to plead your cause with yourself.'

Then, as he looked at her, white with anger, she burst into a laugh. 'Oh! how simple you are!' she cried. 'If I just joke a little, you believe all I say. Really, you are very amusing.'

Rougon stood there for a moment quite nonplussed. The ironical fashion in which she contradicted herself made her more irritating and provoking. Her whole person, her rippling laugh and glistening eyes, confirmed her confessions and repeated them. However, just then there came a third knock at the door.

'Well, I don't care, I shall stick to my cigarette this time,' said Clorinde.

An usher came into the room, quite out of breath, and stammered that the Minister of Justice wanted to speak to his excellency. Then he cast a furtive glance at the lady he saw smoking.

'Say that I have gone out!' retorted Rougon. 'I am not at home to any one, do you hear!'

When the usher had bowed and retired backwards from the room, Rougon vented his anger and brought his fist down upon the table. He was scarcely allowed to breathe! he cried. Why, on the previous day they had pursued him even to his dressing-room where he had gone to shave.

Clorinde, however, rose from her chair and deliberately walked to the door. 'Wait a moment,' she said; 'they sha'n't disturb us again.' And then she quietly turned the key in the lock. 'There!' she resumed. 'They may knock as much as they like now.'

She began to roll a third cigarette as she stood near the window. Rougon stepped up to her and whispered close to her neck: 'Clorinde.'

She stood still, and he continued in deeper tones: 'Clorinde, don't you know that I love you?'

She remained perfectly unruffled. She shook her head, but so feebly that it seemed as if she wished to encourage him, and he ended by planting a rough kiss on the back of her neck, just beneath her hair. Then, however, she swung herself round, and with scorn in her eyes and her voice she cried: 'Ah! so you've got another attack, my friend? I thought you were cured of that. What a strange man you are! You kiss a woman after eighteen months' consideration!'

Rougon remained for a moment with downcast head, but then sprang towards her, caught hold one of her hands and began to cover it with kisses. She made no attempt to withdraw it, but continued to jeer at him.

'Please don't bite my fingers. As long as you don't do that, I don't mind. I should really never have believed it of you! You had become so serious and steady when I went to see you in the Rue

Marbeuf. And now you're turned quite crazy again! Truly, you're a nice kind of man! I can't keep up a passion as you do. It's all quite over with me. Remember that I offered to be your wife, but you refused me then and now it is too late.'

'Hear me,' he murmured, 'I will do anything, everything, you want.'

But the young woman shook her head, punishing him for his old contempt, and enjoying, in so doing, a first instalment of her vengeance. She had wanted to see him all-powerful in order that she might in her turn treat him with contempt.

Then Rougon fell ignominiously at her feet and began to kiss her skirts, grovelling there, humbling himself, he who could be so haughty with others. As he gradually grew bolder, however, she said to him in a quiet voice: 'Take care!' and as he disregarded her caution, she suddenly touched his forehead with the burning end of her cigarette. He recoiled with a faint cry, and she on her side darted away and caught hold of the bell-rope which hung against the wall beside the mantelpiece. 'I shall ring,' she said, 'and I shall say it was you who locked the door!'

At this Rougon swung himself round, holding his hands to his temples, and shaken by a violent tremor. Then for a moment he remained quite still, feeling as though his head were going to split. He stiffened himself in the hope of calming his feverishness. There was a ringing in his ears, and his eyes were blinded by ruddy fires.

'I am a brute,' he murmured at last. 'It is folly.'

Clorinde laughed triumphantly, and began to point a moral. He did wrong to despise women, said she. Later on, he would find that there were such things as very clever women. Then she relapsed into a good-natured playful tone. 'You are not vexed with me, are you? You must never try to make love to me again, you know. I don't want you to do it. I don't like to think of it.'

Rougon paced up and down, full of shame; while she let go of the bell-rope, sat down at the table again, and compounded herself a glass of sugar and water.

'Well, I got a letter from my husband yesterday,' she quietly resumed. 'I had so much to do this morning that I should probably have broken my promise to come and lunch with you if I hadn't wanted to show you that letter. See, here it is! It reminds you of your promises.'

Rougon took the letter and read it as he walked about the room.

217

Then he threw it on the table in front of Clorinde with a gesture expressive of weariness.

'Well?' she asked.

He made no immediate reply, but stretched himself and yawned. 'He is a simpleton,' he said at last.

Clorinde was greatly offended. For some time past she had not tolerated any doubt of her husband's capabilities. She bent her head for a moment and repressed the rebellious twitchings of her hands. She was gradually emerging from her disciple-like submissiveness, draining, as it were, from Rougon sufficient of his strength to enable her to confront him as a formidable foe.

'If we were to show this letter, it would be all over with him,' said the minister, impelled by Clorinde's disdain to avenge himself upon her husband. 'Ah! it isn't so easy as you suppose to find a place that he's fit for.'

'You are exaggerating, my friend,' replied Clorinde, after a short pause. 'You used to say that he had a great future before him. He possesses some sterling good qualities; and it isn't always the sharpest men who go furthest!'

Rougon, however, still paced the room, and shrugged his shoulders.

'It is to your interest that he should join the ministry,' continued Clorinde. 'You would have a supporter in him. If it is true, as is reported, that the Minister of Commerce and Agriculture is in bad health and wishes to retire, the opportunity is a splendid one. My husband is quite competent to perform the duties of the office, and his mission to Italy would make his selection quite natural. You know that the Emperor is very fond of him, and that they get on very well together. They have the same ideas on many subjects. A word from you would settle the matter.'

Rougon took two or three more turns before replying. Then, halting in front of Clorinde, he said: 'Well, after all, I am agreeable. He won't be the only simpleton in office. But I'm doing this solely for your sake, remember. I want to disarm you. I am afraid you haven't a good heart. You're too vindictive, aren't you?'

He spoke playfully, and Clorinde laughed as she replied: 'Oh, yes, indeed; I'm very vindictive. I remember things a long time.'

Then, as she was about to leave him, he detained her for a moment by the door, and twice squeezed her fingers, but did not say another word.

Directly Clorinde had gone, Rougon returned to his private office. The spacious room was empty. He sat down at the writing-table and rested his elbows on his blotting-pad, breathing heavily in the surrounding silence. His eyelids dropped, and a deep reverie lulled him to a state of drowsiness for the next ten minutes. Then he suddenly started, stretched himself, and rang the bell.

Merle made his appearance.

'The prefect of the Somme is still here, isn't he?' asked Rougon. 'Show him in.'

Bracing up his short figure, the prefect entered the room with a pale, smiling face. He greeted the minister with all due deference. Rougon, who felt little energy, waited till he had finished. Then he asked him to be seated.

'I must tell you why I have sent for you, Monsieur le préfet,' he began. 'There are certain instructions which must be given by word of mouth. You are not ignorant of the fact that the revolutionary party is raising its head. We have been within an ace of a frightful catastrophe. The country requires to be reassured, to feel that it can rely upon the energetic protection of the Government. His Majesty the Emperor, on his side, has come to the conclusion that some examples must be made, for hitherto his kindness has been strangely abused.'

Rougon spoke slowly, reclining in his arm-chair and playing the while with a large agate seal. The prefect expressed his approval of each sentence by a brisk nod.

'Your department,' continued the minister, 'is one of the worst. The republican ulcer—'

'I make every effort—' interposed the prefect.

'Don't interrupt me. It is necessary that strong repressive steps should be taken there; and it was to express my views to you on the subject that I wished to see you. We have been drawing up a list—'

Then he began to search among his papers, took up a bundle of documents, and turned them over one by one.

'It is a return for the whole of France of the number of arrests that are considered necessary. The number for each department is proportionate to the blow which it is intended to strike. I want you to understand our object thoroughly. In the Haute-Marne, for instance, where the Republicans are in a very small minority, there are to be only three arrests. In the Meuse, on the other hand, there will be fifteen. As for your department, the Somme—isn't it?—well, for the Somme, we think—'

He turned the papers over again, blinking his heavy eyelids; then raised his head and looked the prefect in the face. 'Monsieur le préfet, you have twelve arrests to make,' said he.

The pale little man bowed. 'Twelve arrests,' he repeated. 'I understand your excellency perfectly.'

He seemed perplexed, however, as though affected by some slight misgivings which he would have preferred to conceal. However, after a few minutes' general conversation, just as the minister rose to dismiss him, he made up his mind to ask: 'Could your excellency tell me the persons who are to be arrested?'

'Oh! arrest anybody you like!' Rougon replied. 'I can't trouble myself about the details. I should never get through the work if I did. Leave Paris this evening and begin your arrests to-morrow. I advise you, however, to strike high. Down in your department you have some lawyers and merchants and druggists who busy themselves with politics. Just lock all those fellows up. It will have a good effect.'

The prefect passed his hand across his brow in an anxious way. He was already searching his memory, trying to think of certain lawyers, merchants, and druggists. However, he still nodded his head approvingly. But Rougon was not altogether pleased with his hesitating demeanour. 'I won't conceal from you,' he said, 'that his Majesty is by no means satisfied just now with the administrative staff. There will probably soon be a great change amongst the prefects. We need very devoted men in the present grave circumstances.'

This affected the prefect like a cut from a whip.

'Your excellency may rely on me,' he exclaimed. 'I have already fixed upon my men. There is a druggist at Péronne, a cloth merchant and a paper maker at Doullens; and, as for the lawyers, there's no lack of them; there's a perfect plague of them. Oh, I assure your excellency that I shall have no difficulty in making up the dozen. I am an old servant of the Empire.'

For another moment he chattered on about devoting himself to the saving of the country, and then took his leave with a very low bow. When he had closed the door behind him, the minister swayed his heavy frame with an air of doubt.

He did not believe in little men. Then, without sitting down again, he drew a red line through La Somme upon his list. The names of more than two-thirds of the departments were already scored out in the same way.

When Rougon again rang for Merle, he was annoyed to see that the ante-room was as full as ever. He fancied he could recognise the two ladies still standing by the table. 'I told you to send everybody away!' he cried. 'I am going out, and cannot see anybody else.'

'The editor of the *Vœu National* is there,' murmured the usher.

Rougon had forgotten the editor. He clasped his hands behind his back, and ordered Merle to admit him. The journalist was a man of some forty years of age, with a heavy face, and was very carefully dressed.

'Ah! here you are, sir!' said the minister roughly. 'Things cannot go on like this, I warn you of it.'

Then he began to pace the room, inveighing hotly against the press. It was demoralising everything, bringing about general disorganisation, and inciting to disorder of every kind. The very robbers who stabbed wayfarers on the high-roads were preferable to journalists, said he. A man might recover from a knife-thrust, but pens were poisoned. Then he went on to make even more odious comparisons; and gradually worked himself into a state of excitement, gesticulating angrily, and thundering forth his words. The editor, who had remained standing, bent his head to the storm, while his face wore an expression of submissive consternation.

'If your excellency would condescend to explain to me,' he at last ventured to say; 'I don't quite understand—'

'What?' roared Rougon furiously. Then he sprang forward, spread out the newspaper on his table, and pointed to the columns that were marked with red pencil. 'There are not ten lines free from offence!' he exclaimed. 'In your leading article, you appear to cast a doubt upon the government's capacities in the matter of repressive measures. In this paragraph on the second page you appear to allude to me when you speak of the insolent triumph of parvenus. Among your miscellaneous items there are a lot of filthy stories, brainless attacks upon the upper classes.'

The editor clasped his hands in great alarm, and tried to get in a word. 'I assure your excellency—I am quite in despair that your excellency could suppose for a moment—I, too, who have such very warm admiration for your excellency—'

Rougon, however, paid no attention to this. 'And the worst of the matter is, sir,' he continued, 'that everyone is aware of your connection with the administration. How is it likely that the other newspapers will respect us, when those in our own pay do not? All my friends have been denouncing these abominations to me this morning.'

Then the editor joined Rougon in declaiming against the incriminated matter. He had read none of those articles and paragraphs, he said. But he would at once dismiss all his contributors. If his excellency wished it, he would send him a proof-copy of the paper every morning. Rougon, who had relieved his feelings, declined this offer. He had not the time to examine a proof-copy, he said. Just as he was dismissing the editor, however, a fresh thought seemed to strike him. 'Oh, I was forgetting,' he said. 'That well-bred woman who betrays her husband in the novel you are publishing serially supplies a detestable argument against good education. It ought not to be alleged that a woman of that kind could possibly commit such a sin.'

'The serial has had a great success,' murmured the editor, again feeling alarmed. 'I have read it, and have found it very interesting.'

'Ah! you've read it, have you? Well, now, does this wretched woman feel any remorse in the end?'

The editor carried his hand to his forehead, amazed, and trying to remember. 'Remorse? No, I think not,' he replied. Rougon had already opened the door, and as he closed it upon the journalist, he called after him: 'It is absolutely necessary that she should feel remorse! Insist upon the author filling her with remorse!'

X

A TRIP TO NIORT

ROUGON had written to Du Poizat and M. Kahn asking them to spare him the infliction of an official reception at the gates of Niort. He arrived there one Saturday evening a little before seven o'clock, and at once went to the prefecture, with the intention of resting till noon the following day, for he was feeling very tired. After dinner, however, several people called. Doubtless the news of the minister's arrival had already spread through the town. A small drawing-room near the dining-room was thrown open, and a kind of impromptu reception was organised. Rougon, as he stood between the two windows, was obliged to stifle his yawns and reply as pleasantly as he could to the greetings offered to him.

One of the deputies of the department, the very attorney who had usurped M. Kahn's position as official candidate, was the first to make his appearance. He arrived quite out of breath, half scared, wearing a frock-coat and coloured trousers, for which he apologised on the ground that he had only just returned on foot from one of his farms, and had been anxious to pay his respects to his excellency as soon as possible. Then a short fat man appeared, wearing a somewhat tight-fitting dress coat and white gloves. There was an air of ceremonious regret about him. He was the mayor's first assessor, and had just been informed by his servant of Rougon's arrival. The mayor, he said, would be greatly distressed. He was not expecting his excellency till the following day and was at present at his estate of Les Varades, some six miles off. After the assessor there came a procession of six gentlemen with big feet, big hands, and big heavy faces. The prefect presented them to Rougon as distinguished members of the Statistical Society. Then the head-master of the state college arrived, bringing with him his wife, a charming blonde of eight-and-twenty. She was a Parisienne, and her dresses were the wonder of Niort. She told Rougon somewhat bitterly of her great dislike for provincial life.

M. Kahn, who had dined with the minister and the prefect, was on his side hotly plied with questions respecting the next day's ceremony. It had been arranged that the party would repair to a spot some two or three miles from the town, in the district known as Les Moulins, where it was intended that the first tunnel on the new line from Niort to Angers should be pierced; and there the Minister of the Interior was to fire the first mine. Rougon, who had assumed a homely good-natured manner, said that he merely wanted to do what he could to honour an old friend's laborious enterprise. He moreover considered himself to be an adopted son of the department of Deux-Sèvres, which in former days had sent him to the Legislative Assembly. To tell the truth, however, the real object of his journey was in accordance with Du Poizat's strongly urged advice to display himself, in the plenitude of power, to his old constituents, so as to make sure of their support should it ever become necessary for him to enter the Corps Législatif.

From the windows of the little drawing-room the town could be seen black and slumberous. No further visitors called. The news of the minister's arrival had come too late in the day. This circumstance, however, gave an additional feeling of triumph to the few zealous ones who had put in an appearance at the prefect's. They gave no hint of retiring, but seemed quite elated with joy at being the first to meet his excellency in private conversation. The mayor's assessor repeated in a doleful voice, through which rang a note of jubilation: '*Mon Dieu!* how distressed the mayor will be! And the presiding judge, too, and the public prosecutor and all the other gentlemen!'

Towards nine o'clock, however, it might have been supposed that the whole town was in the ante-room, for a loud tramping of feet was heard there. Then a servant entered the drawing-room and announced that the chief commissary of police desired to pay his respects to his excellency. And it was Gilquin who made his appearance: Gilquin, looking quite gorgeous in evening dress and straw-coloured gloves and kid boots. Du Poizat had given him a place in his department. He bore himself very well, the only traces of his old manner being a somewhat swaggering motion of his shoulders and a marked disinclination to part with his hat, which he persisted in holding against his hip in imitation of a pose which he had studied on a tailor's fashion-plate. He bowed to Rougon and addressed him with exaggerated humility. 'I venture to recall myself to the kind recollection of your excellency, whom I had the honour of meeting several times in Paris,' said he.

Rougon smiled, and he and Gilquin chatted for a few moments. Then the latter made his way into the dining-room, where tea had just been served, and he there found M. Kahn, who was glancing over a list of the guests invited to the next day's ceremony. In the little drawing-room the conversation had now turned upon the grandeur of the Emperor's reign. Du Poizat, standing by Rougon's side, was extolling the Empire, and they bowed to one another as though they were mutually congratulating themselves upon some personal achievement, while the citizens of Niort clustered round, agape with respectful admiration.

'What clever fellows they are, eh?' said Gilquin, who was watching the scene through the open doorway.

Then, as he proceeded to pour some rum into his tea, he gave M. Kahn a nudge. Du Poizat, lean and enthusiastic, with his irregular white teeth and feverish, childish face all aglow with triumph, appeared to take Gilquin's fancy. 'Ah, you should have seen him when he first arrived in the department,' said the commissary in a low voice. 'I was with him. He stamped his feet angrily as he walked along. He no doubt felt a grudge against the people here: and since he's been prefect, he's been amusing himself by avenging all his youthful grievances. The townspeople who knew him when he was a poor miserable fellow don't feel inclined to smile now when they see him go past. He makes a strong prefect; he's quite cut out for the post. He's very different from that fellow Langlade, whom he superseded, a mere ladies' man, as fair as a girl. We came across photographs of ladies in very low dresses even amongst the official papers in his room.'

Then Gilquin paused. He fancied that the wife of the head-master had her eyes on him. And so, desirous of displaying the graces of his person, he bent forward again to speak to M. Kahn. 'Have you heard of Du Poizat's meeting with his father?' he asked. 'Oh, it was the most amusing thing in the world. The old man, you know, is a retired process-server, who has got a nice little pile together by lending petty sums by the week at high interest; and he now lives like a wolf in an old ruin of a house where he keeps loaded guns in the hall. Well, he had told his son a score of times that he would come to the gallows; and Du Poizat had long dreamt of having his revenge. That, indeed, was one of his reasons for wanting to be prefect here. So one morning he put on his finest uniform, and, under the pretext of making a round, he went and knocked at the old man's house. Then, after a good quarter of an hour's parley, the father opened the door, a pale little old man he was, and he gazed with a stupefied look at his son's gold-laced uniform. Well, now, guess what was the first thing he said, as soon as he discovered that his son had become the prefect! "Don't send for the taxes any more, Leopold!" Yes, those were his very words. He didn't show the slightest fatherly emotion. When Du Poizat came back, he was biting his lips, and his face was as white as a sheet. His father's unruffled tranquillity had quite exasperated him. Ah! he'll never manage to subdue the old man!'

M. Kahn nodded his head discreetly. He had slipped the list of guests into his pocket, and was now sipping a cup of tea while glancing occasionally into the adjoining room. 'Rougon is half asleep,' he said. 'Those idiots ought to have enough sense to leave him and let him go to bed. I want him to be in good form for to-morrow.'

'I hadn't seen him for some time,' said Gilquin. 'He has put on more flesh.' Then, lowering his voice, he continued: 'They managed it very cleverly, those two fine fellows! They worked some quiet trick or other out of that bomb affair at the Opera which I had warned them of. It came off, as you know; but Rougon pretends that he went to the prefecture and that no one there would believe him. Well, that's his business, and there's no occasion to say any more about it. On the day of the affair, Du Poizat stood me a ripping *déjeuner* at a café on the boulevards. Oh! what a time we had! We went to a theatre in the evening, I think, but I haven't any very distinct recollection of it, for I slept for two days afterwards.'

M. Kahn now appeared to find Gilquin's confidences somewhat alarming, for he got up and left the dining-room. Then the commissary felt quite convinced that the headmaster's wife was certainly gazing at him. So he also went back into the drawing-room and busied himself about her, and ended by bringing her some tea, biscuits and cake. He really carried himself very well; he looked like a gentleman who had been badly brought up, and this appeared to influence the beautiful blonde in his favour.

However, the deputy was now engaged in demonstrating the necessity of having a new church at Niort; the mayor's assessor asked for a bridge; and the head-master urged the desirability of extending the college buildings, while the six members of the Statistical Society silently nodded approval of everything.

'Well, we will see about these matters to-morrow, gentlemen,' said Rougon, whose eyelids were half-closed. 'I am here for the purpose of inquiring into your needs and doing what I can to satisfy them.'

Ten o'clock was just striking when a servant came into the room and said something to the prefect, who at once whispered a few words in the minister's ear. The latter then hastened out of the drawing room. He found Madame Correur waiting for him in an adjoining apartment. She was accompanied by a tall, slim girl with a colourless freckled face.

'So you are in Niort, are you?' Rougon exclaimed as he joined them.

'Only since this afternoon,' replied Madame Correur. 'We are staying just opposite, on the Place de la Préfecture, at the Hôtel de Paris.'

And then she explained that she had come from Coulonges, where she had been spending a couple of days. But suddenly she paused to direct the minister's attention to the tall girl beside her. 'This,' said she, 'is Mademoiselle Herminie Billecoq, who has been kind enough to accompany me.'

Herminie Billecoq made a ceremonious bow, and Madame Correur proceeded: 'I didn't say anything to you about this expedition
of mine, because I thought you might oppose it; but I really couldn't
help going. I was very anxious to see my brother. When I heard of
your coming to Niort, I hastened here. We looked out for you and
saw you enter the prefecture, but we thought it better to defer our
visit till later on. These little towns are much given to malicious
scandal!'

Rougon nodded assent. He was indeed thinking that plump Madame Correur with her painted face and bright yellow dress might,
to provincial eyes, very well appear to be a compromising person.

'Well, and did you see your brother?' he asked.

'Yes,' Madame Correur replied, clenching her teeth; 'yes, I saw
him. Madame Martineau didn't venture to turn me out of the house.
She was burning some sugar over the fire when I went in. Oh, my
poor brother! I knew that he was ill, but it gave me quite a shock to
see him so emaciated. He has promised that he won't disinherit me;
it would be contrary to his principles. He has made his will; and his
property will be divided between me and Madame Martineau. Isn't
that so, Herminie?'

'Yes, the property is to be divided,' declared the tall girl. 'He
told you so when you first got there, and repeated it when he saw
you away from the door. Oh! there's no doubt about it; I heard him
say so.'

Then Rougon tried to get rid of the two women by saying: 'Well,
I'm delighted to hear it. You will feel much easier now. These family quarrels always get made up. Come, goodnight; I'm going to
bed now.'

But Madame Correur detained him. She had taken her handkerchief out of her pocket and was dabbing her eyes with it, seemingly
affected with sudden grief. 'Oh, my poor Martineau!' said she, 'he
was so kind and good, and forgave me with such readiness! I wish
you knew how good he is, my dear friend. It is on his account that I
have hurried here, to petition you in his favour—'

Her tears prevented her from saying more, and she began to sob.
Rougon was at a loss to know what it meant, and looked at the two
women in astonishment. Then Mademoiselle Herminie Billecoq
also began to cry, but less demonstratively than Madame Correur.
She was a very sensitive young person, and was readily affected by
another's grief.

'Monsieur Martineau has compromised himself in politics,' she stammered amidst her tears.

Thereupon Madame Correur began to speak with great volubility. 'You will remember,' she said, 'that I hinted my fears to you one day. I had a presentiment of what would happen. Martineau was showing Republican proclivities. At the last election he behaved very wildly, and made the most desperate exertions in favour of the opposition candidate. I was aware of things which I don't want to mention. However, it was all bound to have a bad result. When I got to the Golden Lion at Coulonges, where we had engaged a room, I questioned the people there, and I learnt a good deal more from them. Martineau has been guilty of all kinds of follies. No one in the neighbourhood would be surprised if he were to be arrested. Every day they expect to see the gendarmes come and take him off. You can imagine what a shock this was to me! And so I thought of you, my dear friend—'

Her utterance was again choked by her sobs. Then Rougon tried to reassure her. He would mention the subject to Du Poizat, he said, and he would stop any proceedings that might have been instituted. 'I am the master,' he even added; 'come, go to bed and sleep quietly.'

But Madame Correur shook her head and twisted her pockethandkerchief. Her eyes were quite dry now. 'Ah! you don't know everything,' she said. 'It is a more serious matter than you suppose. He takes Madame Martineau to mass, but stays outside himself and proclaims that he never sets foot in a church; and this causes a dreadful scandal every Sunday. Then, too, he frequents a retired lawyer in the neighbourhood, one of the men of '48, and can be heard talking to him for hours in the most dreadful way. Suspicious-looking men, too, have often been seen to slip into his garden at night-time, with the intention, no doubt, of receiving directions from him.'

Rougon shrugged his shoulders at each fresh detail, but Mademoiselle Herminie Billecoq, as though shocked by such tolerance, added sharply: 'And he receives letters with red seals from all sorts of countries. The postman told us that. He didn't want to speak about it at first, he was quite pale. We had to give him twenty sous. And then, a month ago, Monsieur Martineau left home for a week, without anyone in the neighbourhood having the slightest idea where he went. The landlady of the Golden Lion told us that he hadn't even taken any luggage with him.'

'Herminie, I beg of you to be quiet!' said Madame Correur uneasily. 'Martineau has got quite sufficient against him as it is. There is no occasion for us to add any more.'

Rougon was now listening and glancing at the two women in turn. He had become very serious. 'Well, if he has compromised himself so much as that—' he began, pausing, however, as he fancied that he could detect a fiery gleam igniting in Madame Correur's troubled eyes. 'Well, I will do all I can,' he resumed; 'but I make no promises.'

'It is all up with him; it is all up with him!' exclaimed Madame Correur. 'I feel quite certain of it. We don't want to say anything; but if we told all—' Then in her turn she paused and began to bite her pocket handkerchief. 'And to think that I hadn't seen him for twenty years, and have only now just seen him to be parted from him for ever, perhaps! He was so kind, so very kind!'

Herminie, however, gently shrugged her shoulders and made signs to Rougon, as if to tell him that he must excuse a sister's despair, but that the old attorney was really a great rascal. 'If I were you,' she said to Madame Correur, 'I would tell everything. It will be much the best.'

Then the elder woman seemed to brace herself up for a great effort. 'You remember,' she said, lowering her voice, 'the "Te Deums," which were sung everywhere, when the Emperor so miraculously escaped being murdered in front of the Opera-house? Well, on the very day when they were singing the "Te Deum" at Coulonges, one of Martineau's neighbours asked him if he wasn't going to church, and the wretched man replied, "Why should I go to church, indeed? I don't care a fig for your Emperor!"'

'I don't care a fig for your Emperor!' repeated Mademoiselle Herminie Billecoq, with an air of consternation.

'You can understand my alarm now,' continued the retired boarding-house keeper. 'As I told you before, no one in the neighbourhood would be the least surprised to see him arrested.'

As she spoke these last words, she fixed her eyes searchingly on Rougon. He made no immediate reply. He seemed to be trying to read her flabby face, her pale eyes, which blinked beneath light and scanty brows. For a moment his gaze rested on her plump white neck. Then he threw out his arms and said: 'I can do nothing, I assure you. I am not the master.'

And he gave his reasons. He felt certain scruples, he said, about interfering in affairs of this kind. If the law had been invoked, matters would have to take their course. It would even have been better if he had not known Madame Correur, as his friendship for her would tie his hands, for he had sworn never to render certain services to his friends. However, he would inquire into the matter. And he tried to console her, as though her brother were already on his way to some penal settlement. She bent her head, and her sobs shook the big coil of light hair which lay on the nape of her neck. Presently she grew calmer, and as she took leave, she pushed Herminie in front of her, exclaiming: 'Mademoiselle Herminie Billecoq; but I fancy I have already introduced her to you. Please excuse me, my head is in such a state. She is the young lady for whom we succeeded in obtaining a dowry. The officer who seduced her has not yet been able to marry her on account of the interminable formalities which have to be gone through. Thank his excellency, my dear.'

The tall girl expressed her thanks, blushing, as she did so, like an innocent maiden in whose presence some indelicate remark has been made. Madame Correur let her leave the room before her; then she pressed Rougon's hand tightly, and, bending towards him, said: 'I rely upon you, Eugène!'

When the minister returned to the little drawing-room, he found it deserted. Du Poizat had succeeded in getting rid of the deputy, the mayor's assessor and the six members of the Statistical Society. M. Kahn had also taken his departure, after making an appointment for ten o'clock the next morning. In the dining-room there only remained the head-master's wife and Gilquin, who were eating little cakes, and chatting about Paris. Gilquin made soft eyes at the lady and talked to her about the races, the picture-shows, and a new piece at the Comédie Française, with the ease of a man to whom all kinds of life were familiar. The head-master, in the meantime, was speaking in a low tone to the prefect about the fourth form professor, who was suspected of Republican proclivities.

However, eleven o'clock struck. The remaining visitors rose and bowed to his excellency, and Gilquin was just about to retire with the head-master and his wife, to the latter of whom he had offered his arm, when Rougon detained him.

'Monsieur le Commissaire,' he said, 'a word with you, I beg.'

When they were alone together, he addressed himself to the commissary and prefect simultaneously: 'What is this business of Martineau's?' he asked. 'Has the man really compromised himself?'

Gilquin smiled, and Du Poizat proceeded to give a few particulars: 'I wasn't thinking of taking any steps in the affair,' he said. 'The man has certainly been denounced to me, and I have received letters about him. There is no doubt that he mixes himself up in politics. But there have already been four arrests in the department, and I should have preferred making up my five, which was the number you fixed, by locking up the master of the fourth form at the college here who reads revolutionary books to his pupils.'

'I have been told of some very serious things,' said Rougon sternly. 'His sister's tears must not be allowed to save this man Martineau, if he is really as dangerous as is alleged. The public safety is at stake.' Then he turned towards Gilquin. 'What is your opinion on the matter?' he asked.

'I will arrest him in the morning,' the commissary replied. 'I know all about the matter. I have seen Madame Correur at the Hôtel de Paris, where I generally dine.'

Du Poizat made no objection. He took a little memorandum-book from his pocket, struck out a name, and wrote another in its place, at the same time recommending the commissary of police to keep his eye upon the master of the fourth form. Rougon accompanied Gilquin to the door. 'This man Martineau is not very well, I believe,' he said. 'Go to Coulonges yourself, and treat him decently.'

Gilquin pulled himself up with an offended air, and setting aside all respect for his excellency, familiarly exclaimed: 'Do you take me for a mere common policeman? Ask Du Poizat to tell you about the druggist whom I arrested on the day before yesterday. There was a lady with him, but nobody knows it. I always act with the greatest discretion.'

Rougon slept soundly for nine hours. When he opened his eyes the next morning, at about half-past eight, he sent a message for Du Poizat to come to him. The prefect arrived with a cigar in his mouth, and seemed in high-spirits. They talked and joked together as they had done in former days, when they had lodged at Madame Correur's, and had roused each other with playful slaps. However, while the minister was washing, he questioned the prefect about the neighbourhood, asking for particulars of the different officials and their various desires and vanities. He wanted to have a pleasant remark ready for each of them.

'Oh, don't worry yourself,' replied Du Poizat, with a laugh; 'I will prompt you.'

Then he gave him some information about the different people with whom he would come into contact. Rougon occasionally made him repeat what he said in order to impress it upon his memory. At ten o'clock, M. Kahn made his appearance. They all three had *déjeuner* together, and finally arranged the details of the ceremony. The prefect would make a speech, as would also M. Kahn. Rougon would follow the latter; but they considered that a fourth speech would be desirable. For a moment they thought of the mayor, but Du Poizat declared that he was a stupid fellow, and advised the selection of the chief surveyor of bridges and highways, to whom the proceedings of the day naturally seemed to point, though M. Kahn was afraid of this official's spirit of criticism. As they got up from table, M. Kahn took the minister aside to tell him of the points which he hoped he would bring forward in his speech.

It had been arranged that the party should meet at the prefecture at half-past ten. The mayor and his assessor arrived together. The former stammered forth his unbounded regret that he had been absent from Niort on the previous evening, while the latter affectedly hoped that his excellency had slept well, and had quite recovered from his fatigue. Then the President of the Civil Tribunal, the public prosecutor and his two assessors, and the chief surveyor of bridges and highways made their appearance. They were quickly followed by the receiver-general, the comptroller of the direct taxes, and the registrar of the department. Several of these officials were accompanied by their wives. The wife of the head-master of the college, the beautiful blonde, wore a most effective sky-blue dress, and attracted great attention. She begged his excellency to excuse her husband, who had been prevented from coming by an attack of gout, which had seized him soon after his return home on the previous evening. However, other personages were arriving; the colonel of the seventy-eighth regiment of the Line, which was stationed at Niort; the President of the Tribunal of Commerce, the two justices of the peace, the conservator of rivers and forests, accompanied by his three daughters, with various municipal councillors and delegates from the consultative Chamber of Arts and Manufactures, the Statistical Society, and the Council of the Board of Arbitration between employers and employed.

The reception was held in the large drawing-room of the prefecture. Du Poizat made the presentations, and the minister received all the guests with smiling bows as though they were old friends. He exhibited wonderful knowledge about each of them. He spoke to the public prosecutor of a speech lately made by him in the course of a trial for adultery; he asked the comptroller of taxes, in sympathetic tones, after the health of his wife, who had been laid up for the last two months; he detained the colonel of the seventy-eighth for a moment to let him see that he was not unacquainted with the brilliant progress made by his son at Saint Cyr; he talked about boots to a municipal councillor, who owned a great boot-making establishment; while with the registrar, who was an enthusiastic archæologist, he discussed a druidical stone which had been discovered during the previous week. Whenever he hesitated, thinking of the right thing to say, Du Poizat came to his assistance and cleverly prompted him in a whisper.

As the President of the Tribunal of Commerce came into the room and bowed to him, Rougon exclaimed, in an affable voice: 'Ah! are you alone, Monsieur le Président? At all events I trust that we shall have the pleasure of seeing your wife at the banquet this evening—'

He stopped short, noticing the expression of embarrassment which came over the faces around him. Du Poizat, moreover, nudged his elbow. Then he recollected that the President of the Tribunal of Commerce was living apart from his wife in consequence of certain scandals. He had made a mistake. He had thought that he was addressing the other president, the chief judge of the Civil Tribunal. However, he was in no way disconcerted. He still smiled; and, making no reference to his unfortunate remark, continued, with a shrewd air: 'I have a pleasant piece of news for you, monsieur. I know that my colleague, the Minister of Justice, has put your name down for the cross of the Legion of Honour. Perhaps I ought not to have mentioned it, but you will keep my secret.'

The President of the Tribunal of Commerce turned quite scarlet. He almost choked with joy. His friends pressed round him to congratulate him, while Rougon made a mental note of this cross—which he had so opportunely thought of bestowing—so that he might not forget to mention the matter to his colleague. It was the betrayed husband that he was decorating. Du Poizat smiled with admiration.

There were now some fifty people in the drawing-room. They still waited on; but the faces of many of them were beginning to show signs of weariness.

'Time is flying; we might perhaps make a start,' said the minister.

But the prefect bent towards him, and explained that the deputy, M. Kahn's former opponent, had not yet arrived. Presently, however, this gentleman made his appearance, perspiring profusely. His watch had stopped, he said, and he had been quite put out of his reckoning. Then, wishing to let the company know of his visit on the previous evening, he went on to remark, in a loud voice: 'As I was saying to your excellency last night—' And afterwards he walked off alongside of Rougon and informed him that he intended to return to Paris on the following morning. The Easter recess had terminated on the previous Tuesday, and the Chamber was again sitting. He had considered it his duty, however, to remain for a few days longer at Niort in order to welcome his excellency to the department.

All the guests trooped into the courtyard of the prefecture, where ten carriages, drawn up on either side of the steps, were awaiting them. The minister, the deputy, the prefect and the mayor got into the first barouche. The others installed themselves as hierarchically as they could. There were two more barouches as well as three victorias, and some waggonettes with seats for six or eight persons. The procession formed up in the Rue de la Préfecture, and started off at a gentle trot. The ladies' ribbons streamed in the air, and here and there their skirts protruded out of the carriages, while the gentlemen's black hats shone brightly in the sun. The procession had to pass through a considerable section of the town; and, owing to the rough pavement of the narrow streets, the vehicles jolted dreadfully as they passed on with a crash like that of iron. And at every door and every window were townsfolk who bowed in silence while looking for his excellency, and experiencing much surprise when they saw his plain frock-coat beside the prefect's gold-laced uniform.

On leaving the town, the procession passed along a wide promenade planted with magnificent trees. It was a warm, pleasant, April day, with a clear sky full of sunlight. The road, which was straight and level, lay between gardens gay with blossoming lilacs and apricot trees. Presently, however, cultivated fields spread out, dotted here and there with copses.

'That's a spinning mill, isn't it?' asked Rougon, towards whom the prefect had just bent. 'A mill which belongs to you, I believe,' he continued, addressing the mayor, and calling his attention to a red brick building on the river bank. 'I have heard of your new system of wool carding. I will try to find time to go and inspect all those wonders.'

Then he began to ask some questions respecting the motive power of the river. In his opinion, said he, hydraulic power, under favourable conditions, possessed enormous advantages. He quite astonished the mayor by the amount of technical knowledge he displayed. Meantime the other carriages followed on in somewhat irregular fashion. Snatches of conversation, bristling with figures, could be heard amidst the jog-trot of the horses. Then a rippling laugh attracted everyone's attention. It came from the headmaster's wife, whose sun-shade had just flown away and fallen on to a heap of stones.

'You have a farm about here, haven't you?' said Rougon, turning to the deputy with a smile. 'That's it on the hill, if I'm not mistaken, What splendid meadows! I know that you interest yourself in cattle-breeding, and won several prizes at the last shows.'

Then they began to talk about cattle. Steeped in the sunshine, the meadows looked like soft green velvet. Wild flowers were springing up all over them. Athwart the curtains of tall poplar trees one had glimpses of charming bits of landscape. However, an old woman leading an ass came along and was obliged to stop at the roadside to let the procession pass. The ass, frightened by the sight of so many carriages with panels gleaming in the sunshine, began to bray; but the gaily dressed ladies and begloved gentlemen remained perfectly serious.

The procession now climbed a slight hill on the left, and then descended again. They had reached the scene of the ceremony. It was a sort of *cul-de-sac,* a hollow gap walled in by hills on three sides. Nothing broke upon the prospect save the gaping ruins of a couple of windmills. And in this hollow, in the centre of a patch of grass land, a tent of grey canvas, with a wide crimson border, had been set up; its four sides were decorated with trophies of flags. A thousand sightseers, middle-class folks and peasants whose curiosity had induced them to walk over, had taken up position in the shade on the right-hand side, where one of the hills rose up like an amphitheatre. A detachment of the seventy-eighth regiment was ranged in front of the tent, opposite the Niort firemen, whose fine bearing was much noticed; while a gang of navvies in new blouses, with engineers in frock-coats at their head, stood waiting at the edge of the patch of grass. As soon as the carriages appeared, the Niort Philharmonic Society, composed of amateur instrumentalists, began to play the overture to 'La Dame Blanche.'

'Long live his excellency! cried a few persons whose voices were drowned by the sound of the instruments.

Rougon alighted from his carriage, raised his eyes, and looked about the hollow in which he found himself, vexed to find the spot so small, so shut in, for this seemed to detract from the impressiveness of the ceremony. He stood for a moment on the grass, waiting for some one to receive him. At last M. Kahn hastened up. He had left the prefecture immediately after *déjeuner,* and had just been to examine the mine which his excellency was to fire, to see if all were right. It was he who conducted the minister into the tent; and then the guests followed. There was some little confusion for a moment; and Rougon began to ask for particulars. 'It is yonder, then, in that cutting, that the tunnel is to commence?'

'Exactly,' replied M. Kahn. 'The first mine has been laid in that reddish rock where your excellency sees a flag flying.'

The hill-side at the end of the hollow had been broken up by picks till its rocky base was disclosed to view. Several uprooted trees were lying about amongst the excavations, and the cutting was strewn with foliage. M. Kahn pointed out the course the line would take. It was marked by a double row of stakes stretching away amid grass and paths and thickets. It was a pretty piece of quiet country that they were going to rip up.

However, the guests and officials had by this time collected in the tent. Some curious sightseers in the rear were bending forward to glance through the openings, and the instrumentalists of the Philharmonic Society was just finishing the overture to 'La Dame Blanche.'

'Monsieur le ministre,' suddenly exclaimed a shrill voice which vibrated amidst the silence, 'it is my privilege to be the first to thank your excellency for having so kindly accepted the invitation which we ventured to address to you. The department of Deux-Sèvres will ever preserve a grateful recollection—'

It was Du Poizat who had begun to speak. He stood some three yards away from Rougon; and at the finish of certain sentences they slightly bowed to one another. The prefect went on speaking for a good quarter of an hour. He reminded the minister of the brilliant fashion in which he had represented the department in the Legislative Assembly. The town of Niort had then inscribed his name in its annals as that of a benefactor, and longed for any occasion upon which it might show its gratitude. Every now and then the prefect's voice was quite lost in the air, and only his gestures, an even, regular working of his right arm, could be seen; and then the crowd ranged on the hill-side gave their attention to the gold embroidery on his sleeve, which flashed brightly in the sunshine.

Afterwards, however, M. Kahn stepped into the middle of the tent. He had a very deep voice, and seemed to bark out some of his words. The hill-side gave an echo which repeated snatches of sentences upon which he lingered too complacently.

He spoke of all the long efforts, studies and toilsome steps which had devolved upon him during nearly four years in his struggle to obtain a new line for the district. Now, every kind of prosperity would rain down upon the department. The fields would be fertilised; the factories would double their output; and commerce would make its way into the humblest villages. To hear him talk, it might have been supposed that Deux-Sèvres was about to become a sort of fairy-land, with rivers of milk and enchanted groves, where tables laden with good things would await every passer-by. All at once, however, he affected an exaggerated modesty. They owed him, said he, no gratitude whatever. He himself could never have carried out such a vast scheme without the high patronage of which he was so proud. Then, turning towards Rougon, he called him 'the illustrious minister, the promoter and supporter of every useful and noble idea.' In conclusion, he dwelt upon the financial advantages of the scheme. At the Bourse, he said, people were fighting for the shares. Happy were those who had been able to invest their money in an enterprise with which his Excellency, the Minister of the Interior had been willing to connect his name!

'Hear! hear!' cried some of the guests.

The mayor and several of the officials grasped M. Kahn's hand. He affected to be greatly moved. Outside there were bursts of cheering, and the bandsmen of the Philharmonic Society considered it proper to strike up a quick march. Thereupon the mayor's assessor sprang forward and sent a fireman to silence them. In the meantime, the chief surveyor of bridges and highways was hesitating and repeating that he had prepared no speech for the occasion. However, as the prefect continued to press him, he gave way. At this M. Kahn seemed very uneasy, and murmured to Du Poizat: 'You've made a mistake. He's sure to say something nasty.'

The chief surveyor was a tall, lean man, who considered himself endowed with great powers of irony. He spoke slowly, and gave a twist to his mouth every time he delivered himself of one of his epigrammatic thrusts. He commenced his speech by overwhelming M. Kahn with praises. Then the unpleasant remarks began; and he briefly criticised the projected railway with all the contempt of a government engineer for the plans and designs of a private one. He referred to the opposition scheme of the Western Company, which had contemplated carrying the line past Thouars, and he laid stress, without seeming to do so maliciously, upon the fact that the loop in M. Kahn's plan would benefit the blast-furnaces at Bressuire. There was nothing obviously bitter in what he said, but amidst his pleasant sentences there was many a little stab which could be felt only by the initiated. He became, however, more cruel towards the end of his speech, when he seemed to regret that 'the illustrious minister' should have run the risk of compromising himself by countenanc-ing an undertaking whose financial prospects were a source of disquietude to all men of experience. Enormous sums of money would be wanted, he said, as well as the greatest integrity and most perfect disinterestedness. Then, in conclusion, he gave his mouth a twist and spoke in this fashion: 'That these fears, however, are quite chimerical we can have no doubt, when we see at the head of the undertaking a man whose wealth and high commercial probity are so well known throughout the department.'

A murmur of approval ran through the audience; though a few people glanced at M. Kahn, who with pale lips was endeavouring to smile. Rougon had listened with his eyes half closed, as though he were inconvenienced by the brightness of the light. When he opened them again they were black and stern. His original intention had been to make a very brief speech indeed; but he now felt that he had to defend one of his own band. With three steps he reached the edge of the tent, and there, with a sweeping gesture that seemed to call upon all France to listen to him, he began: 'Gentlemen, let me in imagination overleap these hills which surround us and embrace the whole empire at one glance, and thus exalt the ceremony which has brought us together by making it a festival of industrial and commercial labour. At this very moment, while I am now address-ing you, from the north to the south of the country canals are being excavated, railway lines are being laid down, mountains are being tunnelled, bridges are being built—'

Perfect silence had fallen all around. Not a sound broke upon the speaker's words save the rustling of the trees or the grating of some river-lock in the distance. The firemen striving to bear themselves as martially as the soldiers beneath the hot sun, cast side-long glances at the minister, without turning their necks. The spectators on the hill-side, however, were taking their ease. Ladies had spread their handkerchiefs on the ground and were sitting on them; and two gentlemen, whom the sun was reaching, had just opened their wives' parasols. And Rougon's voice gradually grew louder and louder. He seemed ill at ease in that little hollow. It was as if the narrow valley did not afford him sufficient space for his gesticulations. As he threw his hands energetically in front of him, it seemed as if he desired to sweep away all obstructions and open out a wider horizon. Twice he gazed into the air as if seeking space, but nothing met his eyes on the hill tops save the gutted ruins of the windmills which were splitting in the sun.

He had taken up M. Kahn's text and was enlarging upon it. It was not, he said, the department of Deux-Sèvres alone that was about to enter upon an era of wonderful prosperity, but the whole of France, thanks to the branch line from Niort to Angers. For ten minutes he recounted the innumerable advantages which would rain down upon the people. He even went so far as to allude to the hand of God. Then he began to reply to what had been said by the chief surveyor, though he in no way discussed it or even referred to it. He simply said the direct opposite of what the surveyor had said, dwelling for a long time upon M. Kahn's devotion, and praising his great modesty and disinterestedness and nobility of mind. The financial aspect of the matter, he said, caused him no uneasiness whatever; and he smiled and seemed to be sweeping up big piles of gold with a rapid movement of his hands.

An outburst of cheering quite drowned his voice.

'One word in conclusion, gentlemen,' he said, after wiping his lips with his handkerchief. That one word lasted for a quarter of an hour. He was growing excited, and went further than he had meant to do. Indeed, in his peroration, while speaking of the grandeur of the reign, and extolling the Emperor's great ability, he even hinted that his Majesty would bestow his patronage in a special manner upon the branch line from Niort to Angers. It was as if the undertaking had become a State affair.

However, three great bursts of cheers rang out. A flight of crows, skimming aloft across the cloudless sky, took fright with much noisy croaking. Immediately the minister's speech had finished, the Philharmonic Society had begun to play again, a signal being given from the tent; while all the ladies sprang up, anxious to miss nothing of the ceremony. The guests were smiling around Rougon with delighted faces.

The mayor, the public prosecutor, and the colonel of the seventy-eighth infantry were wagging their heads approvingly while listening to the deputy, who expressed his admiration of his excellency in tones which, although subdued, were yet loud enough to reach the minister's ears. However, it was the chief surveyor of bridges and highways who manifested the greatest enthusiasm. He displayed an extraordinary amount of obsequiousness, and seemed quite thunderstruck by the great man's magnificent language.

'Would your excellency do me the honour to follow me?' now asked M. Kahn, whose fat face was perspiring with pleasure.

The concluding part of the ceremony was at hand. His excellency was about to fire the first mine. Orders had just been given to the gang of navvies in new blouses. The men preceded the minister and M. Kahn into the cutting and drew themselves up in two lines at the far end. Then a foreman who held a piece of lighted rope presented it to Rougon. The officials, who had remained in the tent, craned their heads forward. Everyone waited anxiously. The Philharmonic Society was still playing.

'Will it make very much noise?' the head-master's wife inquired, with an uneasy smile, of one of the public prosecutor's assessors.

'That depends upon the nature of the rock,' hastily interposed the President of the Tribunal of Commerce, who at once entered upon various mineralogical explanations.

'I shall stuff up my ears,' murmured the eldest of the three daughters of the conservator of rivers and forests.

Rougon felt that he was looking very foolish, standing in the midst of all these people with the burning rope in his hand. Up above, on the hill crests, the ruined windmills were creaking louder than ever in the warm sunlight. Then he hastened to light the fuse, the end of which, lying between two stones, was pointed out to him by the foreman. One of the navvies immediately blew a long blast on a horn, and all the gang hurried off, while M. Kahn hastily pulled his excellency back into the tent, manifesting much anxious solicitude for his safety.

'Well, why doesn't it go off?' stammered the registrar, who was blinking nervously, and would very much have liked to close his ears, as the ladies were doing.

The explosion did not take place for a couple of minutes.

It had been considered prudent to have a very long fuse. The expectation of the company turned almost to anguish; every eye was fixed upon the red rock; some spectators fancied they could see it moving, and timid ones expressed a fear of being struck by the fragments. At last there was a low reverberation, and the rock split, while a number of fragments, twice the size of a man's fist, shot up into the air amidst the smoke. Then everybody went away; and on all sides one could hear the same question repeated, 'Don't you smell the powder?'

In the evening the prefect gave a dinner, which the officials and functionaries attended. For the ball which followed he had issued five hundred invitations. It was a splendid affair. The great drawing-room was decorated with evergreens; and in each corner a small chandelier had been fixed, making with the central one five chandeliers in all, whose tapers flooded the room with brilliant light. Niort could remember no such scene of magnificence. The light that streamed from the six windows quite illuminated the Place de la Préfecture, where more than two thousand inquisitive sightseers had gathered together, straining their eyes in their eagerness to catch a glimpse of the dancers. The orchestra also could be so distinctly heard that children got up galops on the footways. From nine o'clock the ladies were fanning themselves, refreshments were being carried round, and quadrilles were following upon waltzes and polkas. In ceremonious fashion Du Poizat stood by the door, smilingly receiving the late arrivals.

'Doesn't your excellency dance?' the head-master's wife boldly asked of Rougon. She had just arrived, and was wearing a dress of tarlatan, spangled with gold stars.

Rougon excused himself, with a smile. He was standing in front of one of the windows, surrounded by a group of guests, and, while joining in a conversation on the desirability of a new land survey, he kept on glancing outside. In the bright light which the candles cast upon the houses on the opposite side of the square, he had just caught sight of Madame Correur and Mademoiselle Herminie Billecoq at one of the windows of the Hôtel de Paris. They were standing there, leaning and watching the ball, as though they were in a box at a theatre. Their faces glistened, and every now and then their bare throats rippled with laughter as some amusing incident attracted their notice.

However, the head-master's wife had gone all round the drawing-room, looking somewhat disconsolate, and never heeding the admiration which her sweeping train excited among the younger men. She was evidently looking for some one, as she thus stepped smilingly and languidly along.

'Hasn't Monsieur le Commissaire central arrived?' she at last asked Du Poizat, who was inquiring after her husband's health. 'I promised him a waltz.'

'Oh, he's sure to come,' the prefect answered. 'I am surprised that he is not here already. He had to go away on official business to-day; but he told me that he would be back by six o'clock.'

After the *déjeuner* at the prefecture, about noon, Gilquin had set out from Niort on horseback to go and arrest notary Martineau. Coulonges was some twelve miles away. He calculated upon arriving there at two o'clock, and upon being able to get away by four, or perhaps a little later, which would leave him plenty of time to attend the banquet, to which he had been invited. Consequently, he did not hurry his horse, but jogged along, while reflecting that he would make the running at the ball in the evening with that pretty blonde, the head-master's wife, whose only fault in his eyes was that she was rather too slim. When he reached Coulonges, he dismounted at the Golden Lion, where a corporal and two gendarmes ought to have been waiting for him. By arranging matters in this way, he had anticipated that his arrival would not be noticed; and he could hire a carriage, he thought, and carry the notary off without any of the neighbours being any the wiser. The gendarmes, however, were not there. Gilquin waited for them till five o'clock, swearing, and drinking grog, and looking at his watch every quarter of an hour. He should never be able to get back to Niort in time for the banquet, he muttered. He was just having his horse saddled, when the corporal at last made his appearance, followed by his two men. There had been some misunderstanding.

'Well, well, don't waste time in apologising!' cried the commissary angrily. 'We've got no time for that! It's already a quarter-past five. Let us get hold of our man as quickly as possible. We must be on our way back in another ten minutes.'

Generally speaking, Gilquin was a good-natured individual. He prided himself upon the urbanity with which he discharged his official duties. That day he had even arranged an elaborate scheme, by which he hoped to spare Madame Correur's brother any violent emotion. It had been his intention to enter the house alone, while the gendarmes waited with the carriage near the garden-gate, in a little lane which looked on to the open country. But his three hours' waiting at the Golden Lion had so exasperated him that he forgot all these fine precautions. He walked through the village, and rang loudly at the street-door of the notary's house. One of the gendarmes was posted at this door, and the other was directed to go round and keep a watch on the garden-wall. The corporal went in with the commissary. Ten or a dozen scared villagers watched them from a distance.

The servant who opened the door was seized with childish terror at the sight of the uniforms, and rushed away, crying at the top of her voice: 'Madame! Madame! Madame!'

A short plump woman, whose face maintained an expression of perfect calm, came slowly down the staircase.

'Madame Martineau, I presume?' said Gilquin rapidly. 'I have a painful duty to perform, madame. I have come to arrest your husband.'

Madame Martineau clasped her short hands, while her pale lips began to quiver. But she uttered no cry. She remained standing on the bottom step, blocking the way with her skirts. Then she asked Gilquin to show her his warrant, and required explanations, doing all she could to cause a delay.

'Be careful! He'll slip through our fingers if we don't mind,' the corporal murmured in the commissary's ear.

Madame Martineau probably heard this remark, for she looked at the two men with her calm eyes, and said: 'Come upstairs, gentlemen.'

She went up in front of them and took them into a room, in the middle of which stood M. Martineau in his dressing gown. Upon hearing the servant's cries of alarm he had risen from the arm-chair in which he spent most of his time. He was very tall; his hands seemed quite dead; his face was as pale as wax; and only his eyes—dark, soft, and yet determined eyes—appeared to retain any life. Madame Martineau pointed to him in silence.

'I regret to say, sir,' began Gilquin, 'that I have a painful duty to perform.'

When he had explained his errand, the notary nodded but did not speak. A slight quiver, however, shook the dressing-gown which covered his attenuated limbs. At last, with great politeness, he replied: 'Very well, gentlemen, I will follow you.'

Then he began to walk about the room, putting in order several articles, which were lying on different pieces of furniture. For instance, he moved a parcel of books to another place. Then he asked his wife for a clean shirt. The trembling which was affecting him had now become more pronounced. Madame Martineau, seeing him totter, followed him with outstretched arms, ready to catch him should he fall, just as one follows a little child.

'Come, sir, make haste!' repeated Gilquin. The notary took another couple of turns round the room, and then suddenly snatched at the air with his hands, and let himself fall into an arm-chair, distorted and stiffened by a paralytic seizure. At this his wife shed big silent tears.

Gilquin took out his watch. 'Confound it all!' he cried. It was half-past five, and he felt that he must now relinquish all hope of being back at Niort in time for the dinner at the prefecture. It would take at least another half hour to get this man into a carriage. He tried to console himself with the thought that at any rate he would not miss the ball, and just then he recollected that the head-master's wife had promised him the first waltz.

'He's shamming,' the corporal now whispered to Gilquin. 'Shall I lift him on to his feet?' And without waiting for a reply, he stepped up to the notary and advised him not to attempt to deceive justice. Martineau, however, was as rigid as a corpse; his eyes were closed and his lips pinched. Thereupon the corporal lost his temper, and indulged in strong language, till at last he laid his heavy hand on the collar of the notary's dressing-gown. But at this Madame Martineau, who had hitherto remained passive, energetically pushed him aside, and planted herself in front of her husband, clenching her fists with an air of devoted resolution.

'He's shamming, I tell you!' the corporal repeated.

Gilquin shrugged his shoulders. He had made up his mind to carry the notary off whether he were dead or alive. 'Send one of your men to get the carriage from the Golden Lion,' he said to the corporal. 'I have spoken to the landlord about one.'

When the corporal had left the room, Gilquin stepped up to the window, and looked complacently at the apricot trees which were blossoming in the garden. He was growing quite absorbed in his thoughts, when he felt a touch upon his shoulder. Madame Martineau stood behind him. Her cheeks were quite dry now, and she spoke in a calm steady voice. 'You mean a carriage for yourself, don't you?' she asked. 'You surely can't think of dragging my husband to Niort, in his present state.'

'I have a painful duty to perform, madame'—Gilquin began for the third time.

'But it is a crime! You will kill him!' Madame Martineau interrupted. 'You have not been ordered to kill him, have you?'

'I am acting under orders,' Gilquin replied in a rougher tone, for he wished to curtail the entreaties which he thought were coming. But a gleam of desperate anger flashed across Madame Martineau's plump face, and her eyes glanced round the room, as though she were trying to discover some possible means of saving her husband. However, she calmed herself by an effort, and reverted to her previous demeanour, like a strong-minded woman who realises that tears can be of no service.

'God will punish you, sir,' she quietly said, after a short pause, during which she had kept her eyes fixed on Gilquin.

Then, without a tear or entreaty she turned to lean over the chair in which her husband lay dying. Gilquin had merely smiled.

Just at this moment the corporal, who had gone in person to the Golden Lion, came back to say that the landlord asserted he had not got a vehicle of any sort. The arrest of the notary, who was extremely popular in the neighbourhood, must have been noised abroad, and the landlord was doubtless concealing his conveyances; for two hours previously, when the commissary had questioned him on the subject, he had promised to let him have an old brougham which he let out for drives in the neighbourhood.

'Go and search the inn!' cried Gilquin, enraged by this fresh obstacle. 'Search every house in the village! Do they think they will have a game with us? And be quick, I have an engagement to keep, and have no time to spare. I give you a quarter of an hour.'

The corporal hurried off again, taking his men with him; and each went in a different direction. Three-quarters of an hour passed, however, and then another quarter, and then another. At the end of an hour and a half one of the gendarmes returned with a very long face. All his searching had been futile. Gilquin, who had grown feverishly excited, kept rushing about and looking out of the window into the twilight. The ball would certainly begin without him, he reflected, and the head-master's wife would consider him guilty of great discourtesy. Each time that he went past the notary's chair he almost choked with anger. Never had any criminal caused him so much trouble as that man who lay there perfectly motionless, becoming ever paler and colder.

It was past seven o'clock when the corporal returned with a beaming countenance. He had at last discovered the landlord's old brougham, concealed in a shed half a mile from the village. The horse was harnessed and between the shafts, and it was the animal's snorting which had enabled him to discover it. However, when the vehicle was at the door, it became necessary to dress M. Martineau, and this took a very long time. His wife very slowly and deliberately put him on some clean white stockings and a clean white shirt. Then she dressed him in black from head to foot; black trousers, frock-coat and waistcoat. She would not allow the gendarmes to render her the slightest assistance. The notary quietly yielded to her touch. A lamp had been lighted, and Gilquin stood tapping his hands together impatiently, while the corporal remained perfectly still, his three-cornered hat casting a huge shadow upon the ceiling.

'Come, come, haven't you done now?' Gilquin repeated. For the last five minutes Madame Martineau had been searching in a drawer. At last she produced a pair of black gloves which she put into her husband's pocket. 'I hope, sir,' she said, 'that you will allow me to come in the carriage. I should much like to go with my husband.' 'That is impossible,' replied Gilquin roughly. She restrained herself instead of pressing her request. 'At any rate,' she said, 'you will allow me to follow him?'

'The roads are free to every one,' answered the commissary, 'but you won't be able to get a vehicle, as there are none in the neighbourhood.'

At this Madame Martineau shrugged her shoulders slightly, and left the room to give an order. Ten minutes afterwards a gig drew up in front of the door, behind the brougham. It was now necessary to get the notary downstairs. The two gendarmes carried him, while his wife supported his head. Whenever the dying man uttered the slightest groan, Madame Martineau imperiously ordered the gendarmes to stop, which they did, notwithstanding the angry glances of the commissary. In this way they halted for a moment on each successive step. The notary looked like a corpse in their arms, and he was quite unconscious when they seated him in the carriage.

'Half-past eight!' exclaimed Gilquin angrily, looking at his watch for the last time. 'Confound it all! I shall never get there!'

There was no doubt about that. He would be fortunate if he arrived before the ball was half over. However, he sprang on his horse with an oath and ordered the coachman to drive as fast as he could. The brougham led the way, the gendarmes riding at each side of it; then, a few yards behind, followed the commissary, and the corporal, and last of all came the gig with Madame Martineau. The night air was very sharp. The little *cortège* passed over the long grey road through all the sleeping country, accompanied by a rumbling of wheels and the monotonous footfalls of the horses. Not a word was spoken during the journey. Gilquin was thinking of what he should say when he met the head-master's wife. Every now and then, however, Madame Martineau sprang to her feet in the gig, fancying that she heard a death-rattle, but she could scarcely distinguish the brougham as it rolled on before her through the black night.

It was half-past ten when they reached Niort. The commissary, to avoid passing through the town, directed the driver of the brougham to go round by the ramparts. When they reached the gaol, they had to ring loudly. As soon as the gatekeeper saw the white, stiffened prisoner they were bringing him, he went off to rouse the governor. The latter, who was not very well, soon made his appearance in his slippers. And when he saw Martineau, he became quite angry, and absolutely refused to receive a man in such a condition. Did they take the gaol for an hospital? he asked them.

'The man has been arrested, and what do you expect us to do with him?' cried Gilquin, losing his temper at this fresh impediment.

'Whatever you like, monsieur le Commissaire, except bring him here,' replied the governor. 'I again tell you that I refuse to receive him. I won't take such a responsibility upon myself.'

Madame Martineau had profited by this discussion to get into the brougham with her husband. And she now proposed that he should be taken to the hotel.

'Very well, to the hotel or the devil, or wherever you like!' cried Gilquin. 'I've had quite enough of him! Take him along!'

He conformed sufficiently to his duty, however, to accompany the notary to the Hôtel de Paris, which Madame Martineau herself fixed upon. The Place de la Préfecture was now becoming empty, and only some children were left playing on the footways, while the middle-class couples slowly disappeared into the darkness of the neighbouring streets. However, the bright glow from the six windows of the prefecture still made the square almost as light as day. The band's brass instruments were blaring, and the ladies' bare shoulders and curled chignons could be seen between the open curtains, circling round the room. As the notary was being carried to the first floor, Gilquin raised his head and caught sight of Madame Correur and Mademoiselle Billecoq, who were still gazing at the festivities. The elder lady, however, must have noticed her brother, for, leaning out so far as to risk a fall, she made an energetic sign to Gilquin to come upstairs. He did so.

Towards midnight the ball at the prefecture reached its zenith. The doors of the dining-room, where a cold supper had been laid, had just been thrown open. The ladies, with hot, flushed faces, fanned themselves as they stood up and ate, amidst a deal of gay laughter. Others were still dancing, unwilling to lose a single quadrille, and contenting themselves with glasses of syrup and water, which gentlemen brought to them. The room was full of a hazy glitter of women's hair and skirts and braceleted arms. There seemed to be too much gold, too much music, and too much heat; and Rougon, who felt half suffocated, was glad indeed to make his escape on being discreetly summoned by Du Poizat.

Madame Correur and Mademoiselle Herminie Billecoq were waiting for him in the small adjoining salon where he had seen them on the previous evening. They were both crying bitterly.

'My poor brother! my poor Martineau!' stammered Madame Correur, while wiping her tears away with her handkerchief. 'Ah! I felt sure that you could do nothing for him. Oh, why couldn't you have saved him?'

Rougon was going to say something, but she would not give him time.

'He has been arrested to-day,' she continued. 'I have just seen him. Oh dear! oh dear!'

'Don't distress yourself,' replied Rougon, at last. 'The matter shall be looked into, and I hope that we shall be able to obtain his release.'

Thereupon Madame Correur ceased dabbing her eyes with her handkerchief. She looked at Rougon and exclaimed in her natural voice: 'But he is dead!' Then again she relapsed into a disconsolate tone and buried her face in her handkerchief. 'Oh dear! Oh dear! my poor, poor Martineau!'

Dead! A sudden tremor passed through Rougon's body. He could not find a word to say. For the first time he became conscious of a pit before him, a dark gloomy pit into which he was being gradually driven. To think that the man was dead! He had never intended that anything of that kind should happen. Things had gone too far.

'Alas! yes, the poor dear man is dead,' said Mademoiselle Herminie Billecoq, with a deep, long-drawn sigh. 'It seems that they refused to receive him at the gaol. Then, when we saw him arriving at the hotel in such a pitiable condition, madame went down and insisted upon being admitted, saying that she was his sister. A sister may surely claim to receive her brother's last breath. That is what I said to that hussy of a Madame Martineau, who threatened to turn us out of the room. But we forced her to let us remain by the bedside. *Mon Dieu!* it was soon all over. The death agony only lasted an hour. The poor man was lying on the bed dressed all in black. Anyone would have thought that he was a notary, just going to a marriage. And he died out just like a candle-flame, with a little twist of his face. He couldn't have had much pain.'

'And then—would you believe it?—Madame Martineau actually tried to pick a quarrel with me,' cried Madame Correur. 'I don't know what she was driving at, but she spoke about my brother's property, and accused me of having given him the last stroke. I said to her, "If I had been there, madame, I would never have allowed him to be taken away, I would have let the gendarmes hew me in pieces sooner!" And they *should* have hewn me in pieces sooner! I told you so, didn't I, Herminie?'

'Yes, yes, indeed,' said the tall girl.

'Well, I know my tears won't bring him to life again,' continued Madame Correur; 'but I'm crying because I can't help it. Oh, my poor Martineau!'

Rougon felt very ill at ease. He drew back his hands which Madame Correur had grasped. Still he could not think of anything to say, shocked as he was by the story of this death which seemed so abominable to him.

'Look!' exclaimed Herminie, who was standing in front of the window, 'you can see the room from here in this bright light. It is the third window to the left, on the first floor. There is a light behind the curtains.'

However, Rougon dismissed them, while Madame Correur in return apologised for having troubled him, calling him her friend, and saying that her first impulse had been to come and tell him the fatal news.

'It is a very annoying business,' Rougon whispered to Du Poizat, when he returned to the ball-room, with his face still pale.

'It is all that idiot Gilquin's doing!' replied the prefect, shrugging his shoulders.

The ball was still going on merrily. In the dining-room, a part of which could be seen through the open door, the mayor's assessor was stuffing the three daughters of the conservator of rivers and forests with sweetmeats; while the colonel of the seventy-eighth was drinking punch and listening attentively to the cutting remarks of the chief surveyor of bridges and highways, who was munching sugared almonds. M. Kahn, near the door, was repeating to the President of the Civil Tribunal the speech which he had delivered in the afternoon on the advantages of the new railway line; and round them stood a group of grave-faced men, the comptroller of taxes, the two justices of the peace, and the delegates from the consultative Chamber of Agriculture and the Statistical Society, all with gaping mouths. Then around the ball-room, in the glow of the chandeliers, the dancers revolved to the music of a waltz, which the band blared forth. The son of the receiver-general was dancing with the mayor's sister; one of the public prosecutor's assessors was with a girl in blue; and the other with a girl in pink. But one couple excited particular admiration, that composed of the commissary of police and the head-master's wife, who slowly revolved in a close embrace. Gilquin had hurried off to array himself irreproachably in black dress-coat, patent-leather boots and white gloves, and the beautiful blonde, having forgiven him for his tardy arrival, was now nestling against his shoulder, with languishing eyes. Gilquin threw his chest forward, and brought the motion of his hips into strong prominence, a vulgarism, which seemed to delight the spectators as if it had been something very tasteful. And as the pair revolved round the room they all but came into collision with Rougon, who had to step back to the very wall to let them pass him in a whirling cloud of tarlatan, spangled with golden stars.

XI

IN COUNCIL AT ST. CLOUD

ROUGON had at last succeeded in obtaining the portfolio of Agriculture and Commerce for Delestang. One morning, early in May, he went to the Rue de Colisée to fetch his new colleague, for there was to be a ministerial council at Saint Cloud, where the Court had just gone to reside.

'What! are you coming with us?' Rougon exclaimed in surprise, as he saw Clorinde taking her place in the landau which was standing in front of the steps.

'Yes,' she answered, with a laugh; 'yes, I'm going to the council, too.' Then, when she had arranged the flounces of her long gown of pale cherry-coloured silk, she added, more seriously: 'I have an appointment with the Empress. I am treasurer of a society for assisting young work-girls in which she is interested.'

In their turn the two men took their places. Delestang sat down by his wife's side. He had with him a brown morocco portfolio, which he kept upon his knees. Rougon sat opposite Clorinde, and carried nothing. It was nearly half-past nine, and the council was fixed for ten, so the coachman was ordered to drive as quickly as he could. To make a short cut, therefore, he went along the Rue Marbeuf, and thence through the Chaillot district, which the demolishers were already ripping up. There were deserted streets fringed with gardens and wooden shanties, steep winding passages and little neglected squares, planted with sickly-looking trees. It was a strange patch of the great city, a medley of villas and cabins, basking on a hill-side in the bright morning sunshine.

'How hideous it is here!' said Clorinde, lying back in the landau.

Then, half-turning, she glanced at her husband, at first gravely, but afterwards, as though she could not help it, she began to smile. Delestang, with his frock-coat buttoned round him, was sitting primly erect. His handsome, thoughtful face, and premature baldness, which gave an appearance of great height to his brow, attracted the attention of the passers-by. Clorinde noticed that no one looked at Rougon, whose heavy face seemed to be asleep. Presently, in a sort of maternal manner, she pulled her husband's left wristband forward a little, as it had slipped back inside his sleeve.

'What were you doing last night?' she then asked of the great man, as she saw him yawning behind his fingers.

'I was working very late,' he said. 'There were a lot of tiresome things to see to.'

There was another pause, and Clorinde began to study Rougon. He yielded unresistingly to the slight jolting of the carriage. His frock-coat was strained out of shape by his broad shoulders, and his hat was badly brushed, and bore marks of old rain stains. He reminded Clorinde of a jobber from whom she had bought a horse a month previously, and a smile, with which was mingled a touch of contempt, appeared upon her lips.

'Well?' said Rougon, at last, feeling somewhat annoyed by Clorinde's prolonged scrutiny.

'Well,' she replied, 'I'm looking at you. It isn't forbidden to do so, is it? You're not afraid that I shall eat you, are you?'

She spoke these last words with a provoking air, showing her white teeth. Rougon, however, began to joke. 'I'm too big for that,' he said; 'you wouldn't be able to get me down.'

'Oh, I don't know that, if I were very hungry,' she gravely answered, after apparently considering her appetite.

The landau was now reaching the Porte de la Muette. Here, on emerging from the narrow streets of the Chaillot district, the horizon suddenly spread out over the light verdure of the Bois de Boulogne. It was a lovely morning, and the distant turf was steeped in golden light, while the young leaves on the trees rustled gently in the warm air. They left the deer-park on their right, and took the gravelled avenue leading to Saint Cloud. The landau now rolled on without a jolt, as lightly and softly as a sledge gliding through the snow.

'How nasty those streets were!' said Clorinde, as she lolled back. 'Well, we can breathe here, and talk. Have you any news of our friend Du Poizat?'

'Yes, he's very well,' Rougon replied.

'And does he still like his department?'

Rougon made a vague gesture, not wishing to give her any definite reply. She was aware, however, that the prefect of Deux-Sèvres was becoming a source of some trouble to him, on account of the severity of his administration. Without pressing the point she next began to talk of M. Kahn, and Madame Correur, and finally, with a touch of mischievous curiosity, she asked Rougon about his visit to Niort. Then she broke off to say: 'By the way, I met Colonel Jobelin and his cousin Monsieur Bouchard yesterday. We talked about you. Yes, we talked about you.'

Rougon still kept silent, with his shoulders bowed. To rouse him, Clorinde began to speak of the past. 'Do you remember our pleasant little evenings in the Rue Marbeuf?' she inquired. 'Now you are so busy that we can't get near you. Your friends complain about it. They say that you are forgetting them. I'm always quite frank, you know, and conceal nothing. Well, to tell the truth, they say that you are deserting them, my dear fellow.'

At this moment, the carriage, which had just passed between the two lakes, encountered a brougham on its way back to Paris, and through the window of the latter vehicle a glimpse was caught of a sulky-looking face, which hastily withdrew, as if to avoid the necessity of bowing.

'Why, it's your brother-in-law!' exclaimed Clorinde.

'Yes, he's not very well,' replied Rougon, with a smile. 'His doctor has ordered him to take morning drives.'

Then he suddenly threw off his reserve, and began to talk freely, while the landau sped along beneath the tall trees of the gently curving avenue.

'What would you have?' said he. 'I can't give them the moon, however much they may cry for it! Take Beulin-d'Orchère, for instance, his dream is to be Minister of Justice. I have tried to effect the impossible, and have sounded the Emperor on the subject; but I can't get any answer. I fancy, however, that the Emperor feels afraid of him. Well, that isn't my fault, is it? Beulin-d'Orchère is first President of the Appeal Court. That really ought to satisfy him for the present. And yet, you see, he actually avoids bowing to me. He's a fool!'

Clorinde had lowered her eyes, and her fingers were playing with the tassel of her sun-shade. She now made no attempt to speak, but let Rougon talk on freely.

'The others,' said he, 'are almost as unreasonable. If the colonel and Bouchard complain of me, they do wrong, for I have already done too much for them. I say that for all my friends. I've got a dozen millstones about my neck! Till they've got the very skin off my body they won't be satisfied!' He paused for a moment, and then resumed with a good-natured laugh: 'Well, well, if they really needed something more, I would give it to them. When a man has once opened his hands it is impossible for him to shut them again.

In spite of all the unkind things my friends say of me, I spend my time in asking favours of all sorts for them.'

Then he touched Clorinde's knee to force her to look at him.

'Well, now, about yourself!' he continued. 'I am going to talk to the Emperor this morning. Is there anything that I can ask for you?'

'No, thank you,' she answered drily. And as he still persisted in his offers, she grew a little vexed, and accused him of reproaching herself and her husband with the few services he had already rendered them. They would not trouble him in future, said she. 'I manage my affairs myself now,' she added. 'I'm big enough to get on by myself, am I not?'

Meantime the carriage had emerged from the Bois. It was now passing through Boulogne amid the clatter of several heavy carts, which were jolting along the high street. Delestang had been silent ever since the start, keeping his hands upon his morocco portfolio, and apparently absorbed in momentous thoughts. However, he now bent forward and called to Rougon amidst the uproar: 'Do you think that his Majesty will keep us to *déjeuner?*'

Rougon made a gesture expressive of doubt. Then he exclaimed: 'We do generally have *déjeuner* at the palace when the council is a long one.'

Delestang fell back into his corner, and once more appeared to be absorbed in a very serious reverie. Presently he bent forward again, to ask: 'Will there be much business before the council this morning?'

'Perhaps so,' answered Rougon. 'But one can never tell beforehand. Several of our colleagues, I fancy, are going to report on certain important matters. For my own part, at any rate, I intend to raise the question of that book about which I am in dispute with the Licensing Committee.'[1]

'What book is that?' asked Clorinde eagerly.

'Oh! an idiotic publication; one of those volumes which are got up for circulation amongst the peasantry. It is called "Friend Jacques's Evening Chats." It is a mixture of socialism, witchcraft,

---

[1] The 'Commission de Colportage,' by which at that period all books dealing with politics or social economy had to be licensed before being hawked about. The object of this regulation was to prevent the circulation of all literature in any way hostile to the Imperial policy or the organisation of the Empire.—*Ed.*

and agriculture; and there's even a chapter on the advantages of trades' unions. Briefly, it is a very dangerous book!'

The young woman, whose curiosity did not seem quite satisfied, turned to her husband as if to question him.

'You are over severe, Rougon,' said Delestang. 'I have looked at the book, and have found some good matter in it. The chapter on the advantages accruing from the association of labour is very good, I think. I shall be surprised if the Emperor condemns the ideas contained in it.'

Rougon was about to reply hotly, and opened his arms with a gesture of protest. But he suddenly restrained himself, as though he did not want to discuss the matter further. And instead of speaking, he glanced at the country through which they were passing. The landau was now half-way across the bridge of Saint Cloud. Down below, the pale blue river was flowing sleepily, shimmering in the sunshine; the rows of trees along the banks being vigorously reflected in the water. Above and below steam climbed the sky, so whitened by the limpidity of springtide that scarcely a touch of blue could be seen.

When the carriage stopped in the courtyard of the château Rougon alighted first and offered his hand to Clorinde. But the young woman would not avail herself of his proffered support; she sprang lightly to the ground, and as he remained there still holding out his arm for her acceptance, she gently tapped his fingers with her parasol, saying: 'Didn't I tell you that I was big enough to manage by myself, now?'

She seemed to have lost all her old respect for her master's huge hands which she had so often held with disciple-like submission so as to drain away a little of their strength. Doubtless she now fancied that she had weakened him sufficiently, for she no longer displayed as of yore any adorable cajolery. She, in her turn, had acquired influence, and was becoming a power. When Delestang had got out of the carriage, she allowed Rougon to go on before them, and whispered in her husband's ear: 'I hope you won't try to prevent him from getting into a tangle with his "Friend Jacques." It will give you a good opportunity of not always appearing to say the very same as he does.'

In the entrance-hall, before leaving Delestang, Clorinde gave him a careful glance, and was worried to see one of the buttons of his coat hanging a little loosely. Then, while an usher went to in-form the Empress of her arrival, she smilingly watched Rougon and her husband take themselves off.

The ministerial council was held in a room near the Emperor's private study. In the centre stood a large cloth-covered table surrounded by a dozen arm-chairs. The high windows admitted a bright light from the terrace of the château. When Rougon and Delestang entered the room, they found all their colleagues already assembled there, with the exception of the Minister for Public Works and the Naval and Colonial Minister, who were on leave of absence. The Emperor had not yet made his appearance, and for ten minutes or so the ministers chatted together, standing by the windows and about the table. Two of them had scowling faces, and so cordially detested each other that they never exchanged a word, but all the rest were talking amicably and easily, till serious matters should demand their attention. Paris was just then much interested in an embassy from the extreme east, the members of which wore fantastic costumes, and indulged in the most extraordinary modes of salutation. The Minister for Foreign Affairs related a visit which he had paid to the chief of this embassy on the previous evening; and while speaking with due regard for his position as head of the diplomatic service, he contrived to indulge in some light sarcasm at the envoy's expense. Then the conversation turned upon more frivolous matters, and the Minister of State[1] furnished some particulars respecting the condition of a ballet girl of the opera-house who had narrowly escaped breaking her leg. However, amidst all this apparent unrestraint the ministers remained alert and distrustful of one another, wording certain of their sentences with extreme care, recalling at times half-uttered words, keeping a watchful look-out even as they smiled, and

---

[1] The functions of the Minister of State—an office which no longer exists, and which might therefore puzzle even the reader acquainted with French affairs—comprised the following matters:—The intercourse of the Crown with the Senate, the Corps Législatif, and the Council of State; the Sovereign's official correspondence with the various ministries; the duty of countersigning all decrees, appointing ministers, senators, and state councillors. The supervision of the Imperial opera-house, the Théâtre Français, the Odéon theatre, the Institute, the Salon, the public libraries, &c., was also within the attributions of the Ministry of State until June, 1863, when a decree instituted the Ministry of Fine Arts as an adjunct to that of the Imperial Household. —*Ed.*

suddenly becoming serious as soon as they noticed that they were being observed.

'Then it was a mere sprain?' said Delestang, who took a great interest in the ladies of the ballet.

'Yes, a sprain,' replied the Minister of State. 'The poor girl will simply have to keep her room for a fortnight. However, she feels very much ashamed of herself for having fallen.'

A slight stir now caused the ministers to turn, and they all bowed. The Emperor had just entered the room. He stood for a moment leaning upon the back of his arm-chair. Then, in his low deliberate voice, he asked: 'Is she better?'

'Much better, sire,' replied the minister, bowing again. 'I heard about her this morning.'

At a sign from the Emperor, the members of the council took their seats round the table. There were nine of them. Some of them spread out papers, while the others sat back in their chairs and began to examine their nails. There was silence for a while. The Emperor seemed unwell; and with lifeless face he slowly twisted the waxed ends of his long moustache. Then, as no one spoke, he appeared to recollect something and remarked: 'Gentlemen, the session of the Corps Législatif is about to end—'

The budget, which the Chamber had just voted in five days, was the first subject which engaged the attention of the council. The Minister of Finance mentioned the desires which the reporter of the Chamber had expressed. For the first time, indeed, the Chamber had indulged in criticism, and its reporter had asked that the sinking fund regulations might be properly carried out, and that the government would in future content itself with the supplies as voted, without constantly applying for supplementary credits. Moreover, some members of the Chamber had complained of the little weight which was attached to their observations by the Council of State, and one of them had even gone so far as to claim for the Corps Législatif the right to prepare the budget.

'In my opinion,' said the Finance Minister, concluding his remarks, 'there is no ground whatever for such claims. The government always observes the greatest desire for economy in preparing its budgets, and so true is this that the Committee of the Chamber had no end of trouble to effect a paltry saving of a couple of millions of francs. Still, I think it would perhaps be advisable to postpone the application for three supplementary votes of credit which we contemplated making. A transfer of funds will provide us with the necessary money for the time being, and matters can be put straight later on.'[1]

The Emperor nodded assent. However, he hardly seemed to be listening to what was said. There was a blank, listless look about his eyes, as he sat gazing at the bright light which was streaming through the middle window in front of him. There came another interval of silence. All the ministers followed the Emperor in nodding their approval, and for a moment or two only a slight rustling could be heard. The Minister of Justice and Keeper of the Seals was turning over some leaves of manuscript. At last when he had consulted his colleagues with a glance, he began: 'Sire, I have brought with me a memorandum relating to the creation of a new nobility. As yet it consists merely of some rough notes, which I thought it would be advisable to put before the council before proceeding any further in the matter, in order that I may profit by any hint—'

'Yes, yes; read it,' interrupted the Emperor. 'You are quite right.'

Then he turned so as to look at the minister while the latter read the memorandum. He seemed more animated now; a yellow light had come into his grey eyes.

The Court was at that time extremely interested in this scheme for a new nobility. The government had begun by submitting to the Corps Législatif a bill which punished with fine and imprisonment anyone who might assume any title of nobility without being entitled to do so. It was a question of giving official sanction to the old titles, and of thus preparing the way for new ones. However, this bill had given rise to a heated discussion in the Chamber. Some deputies, though enthusiastically devoted to the empire, had protested that a nobility could not exist in a democratic state; and, when a division was taken, twenty-three votes had been given against the bill. The Emperor, however, still clung to his dream; and he himself had suggested some very comprehensive ideas to the Minister of Justice.

The memorandum commenced by some historical references. Then the projected scheme was detailed at length. Titles were to

---

[1] This was the favourite device of the Imperial Government. Even money voted for the army was diverted to other purposes, and France paid the penalty in 1870.—*Ed.*

be conferred for different kinds of public service, so as to make the new honours accessible to all deserving citizens, a democratic arrangement which seemed to fill the minister with great enthusiasm. Then a draft of the proposed decree was set out, and when the minister came to the second clause of it he raised his voice and read on very slowly: 'The title of Count shall be conferred upon the following persons after five years' service in their respective functions or dignities, or after we may have bestowed upon them the grand cross of the Legion of Honour: namely, our ministers and the members of our Privy Council, the cardinals, marshals, admirals, senators, and ambassadors, and such of the generals of division as shall have held a chief command in the field.'

The minister paused for a moment, and cast a questioning glance at the Emperor as if to ask whether he had omitted anyone. His Majesty reflected, with his head slightly inclined towards his left shoulder.

'I think we must include the Presidents of the Corps Législatif and the Council of State,' he said, after a pause.

The Minister of Justice nodded approbation, and hastily made a note on the margin of his manuscript. Just as he was about to resume his reading, he was interrupted by the Minister for Public Education and Worship, who wanted to call attention to an omission.

'The archbishops—' he began.

'Excuse me,' interrupted the Minister of Justice drily, 'the archbishops are to be merely barons. Let me read the whole of the decree.'

However, his papers had got mixed, and he spent some time in looking for the next leaf. Rougon, who sat there with his elbows spread out and his thick neck sinking between his broad peasant shoulders, was faintly smiling; and, as he turned round, he caught sight of his neighbour, the Minister of State, the last scion of an old Norman family, likewise indulging in a quiet smile of contempt. A significant glance passed between them. The parvenu and the nobleman were evidently of the same way of thinking.

'Ah, here it is!' exclaimed the Minister of Justice at last. 'Clause III. The title of baron shall be conferred, firstly, upon such members of the Corps Législatif as shall have been honoured three times with the confidence of their fellow-citizens; secondly, upon members of the Council of State of eight years' standing; thirdly, upon the first president and the public prosecutor of the Supreme Court, upon the first president and public prosecutor of the Exchequer Court, upon the generals of division and vice-admirals, upon the archbishops and ministers-plenipotentiary, after five years' service in their respective offices, or if they have attained the rank of commander in the Legion of Honour—'

And so the minister read on. The first presidents and public prosecutors of the appeal courts, the generals of brigade and rear-admirals, the bishops, and even the mayors of the chief cities of first-class prefectures, were in their turn all to be made barons, but on condition that they had served in their respective offices for ten years.

'Then everybody will be a baron,' murmured Rougon.

At this some of his colleagues, who affected to consider him a very ill-bred man, assumed grave expressions, so as to make him understand that they thought his remark in very bad taste. The Emperor, however, did not seem to have heard.

'Well, gentlemen, what do you think of the scheme?' his Majesty asked, when the keeper of the seals had finished his perusal.

They all hesitated, waiting as it were for a more direct question.

'Monsieur Rougon,' resumed the Emperor, 'what is your opinion?'

'Well, sire,' replied the Minister of the Interior, with his quiet smile, 'I cannot say that I think very favourably of it. It is exposed to the greatest of all dangers, that is to say, to ridicule. I am afraid that all those barons will merely raise a laugh. I say nothing about more serious matters, such as the sentiment of equality which is so much in the ascendant at the present time, or the vanity which such a system would tend to develop—'

But when he had got thus far he was interrupted by the Minister of Justice, who seemed greatly put out, and began to defend himself as though a personal attack had been made upon him. He said that he was a middle-class man himself, and the son of a middle-class father, and was quite incapable of attempting anything to impair the principles of equality held by modern society. The new nobility was going to be a 'democratic nobility,' and this expression 'democratic nobility 'seemed to convey his idea so perfectly that he repeated it several times over. Then Rougon briefly replied, still smiling and unruffled. But the Minister of Justice, a little lean, dark man, at last began to indulge in somewhat offensive personalities. The Emperor meantime held himself aloof from the dispute, and with a slight swaying of the shoulders, again gazed at the sunlight streaming through the window in front of him. However, when the voices of the others finally grew so loud as to interfere with his sense of dignity, he murmured: 'Gentlemen, gentlemen.' And after a pause, he added: 'Monsieur Rougon is perhaps right. The scheme is not quite ripe yet. We shall have to consider if it cannot be put upon another basis. We can see to that later on.'

Then the council took some minor matters in hand. The newspaper *Le Siècle* became the subject of a deal of talk, for it had just published an article which had given great offence at Court. A week never passed without those about the Emperor entreating him to suppress this journal, which was the only Republican organ still in existence. His Majesty, however, was personally inclined to be indulgent towards the press, and often amused himself, in the secrecy of his study, by writing long articles in reply to the attacks which were made upon his government. An unacknowledged dream of his was to have a newspaper of his own, in which he might publish manifestoes and engage in polemical discussions. However, he that day decided that a warning should be addressed to the *Siècle*.

Their excellencies now thought that the council was over, as was evident from the manner in which they sat on the very edges of their chairs. Indeed, the Minister for War, a general who looked very much bored, and who had not spoken a word during the whole sitting, had already taken his gloves from his pocket, when Rougon leant heavily on the table.

'Sire,' he said, 'I desire to speak to the council of a conflict which has arisen between the licensing committee and myself with respect to a book which has been presented for authorisation.'

The other ministers thereupon ensconced themselves in their chairs again. The Emperor turned towards Rougon and with a nod authorised him to continue.

Rougon then entered into details. He no longer smiled, his good-natured expression had quite vanished. He leant over the table, and, sweeping the cloth as it were with a regular mechanical movement of his right hand, he stated that he had determined to preside at one of the recent meetings of the committee in order to stimulate the zeal of its members. 'I pointed out to them,' said he, 'the views of the government as to the improvements it was desirable for them to effect in the important branch of the public service with which they are entrusted. The *colportage* system,[1] I told them, would be a

---

[1] That of retailing books and pamphlets by peddlers.

source of grave danger if it were allowed to become a weapon in the hands of the revolutionists, and should prove a means of reviving political discussions and ill-will. So it is the duty of the committee, I said, to reject all publications which might foment afresh such passions as are unsuited to the present time. It ought, on the other hand, to encourage those healthy works which teach the worship of God, the love of one's country, and gratitude to one's Sovereign.'

The other ministers, although very cross at being thus detained in council, felt constrained to bow approvingly on hearing these last words.

'The number of pernicious books increases every day,' continued Rougon. 'They form a rising flood against which we cannot take sufficiently energetic steps for protecting our country. Out of every dozen books that are published, eleven and a half are only fit to be thrown into the fire. That is the average. Never before have wicked sentiments, subversive theories, and anti-social monstrosities of all kinds, found so many exponents. I am occasionally compelled to read certain publications; well, I tell you—'

At this moment the Minister for Public Education ventured on an interruption. 'Novels,' he began.

'I never read novels,' retorted Rougon drily.

His colleague made a gesture of virtuous protest, and rolled his eyes in a shocked sort of way, as though he also repudiated all reading of novels. Then he explained himself, saying: 'I merely wanted to remark that novels are an especially poisonous food offered to the unhealthy curiosity of the people.'

'Doubtless,' replied the Minister of the Interior; 'but there are other works quite as dangerous. I am speaking of those cheap treatises which disseminate among the peasantry and the working-classes a heap of false social and economic science, the most evident effect of which is to seriously disturb weak brains. A work of the kind to which I am alluding, "Friend Jacques's Evening Chats," has just been submitted to the committee for consideration. It is the story of a sergeant who comes back to his native village and holds discussions with the school-master every Sunday evening in the presence of a score of labourers. Each discussion is upon a different subject, such as new systems of cultivation, trades unions, and the great part which the producer plays in society. I have read this book, to which one of the clerks called my attention, and it seems to me to be all the more dangerous since it veils its baleful theories beneath a pretended admiration for the imperial institutions. No one can be deceived by it, however; it is clearly the production of a demagogue. And so I was extremely surprised when I heard some members of the committee speak of it in eulogistic terms. I have discussed certain passages of it with them, but apparently without convincing them. The author, they have assured me, has even offered a copy of the book for your Majesty's acceptance. On that account, sire, I thought it right, before taking any active steps, to ask for your opinion and that of the council.'

So saying Rougon fixed his glance on the Emperor, whose shifty eyes at last settled on a paper-knife which was lying on the table in front of him. His Majesty took up the knife and began to turn and twist it while murmuring: 'Yes, yes, "Friend Jacques's Evening Chats—"'

Then, without committing himself any further, he glanced to the right and left of the table. 'You have perhaps seen the book, gentlemen. I should be very glad to know—'

Then he stopped again. The ministers glanced furtively at one another, each hoping that his neighbour would speak and express an opinion. The silence, however, continued unbroken, and the feeling of constraint increased. It seemed clear that none of them had even known of the existence of the book. At last the Minister for War took it upon himself to express by a gesture the general ignorance which prevailed of the publication in question.

The Emperor twisted his moustaches, showing no sign of haste. 'Well, Monsieur Delestang, have you anything to say?' he eventually inquired.

Delestang was restlessly moving on his chair, as though a prey to some inward struggle. This direct question seemed to decide him; however, before speaking, he glanced involuntarily towards Rougon. 'I have had the book in my hands, sire,' he said.

He checked himself, feeling that Rougon's big grey eyes were fixed upon him; but then, observing the Emperor's satisfaction, he began to speak again, though his lips could be seen quivering slightly. 'I regret that I find myself in disagreement with my friend and colleague the Minister of the Interior. Certainly the publication in question might be less sweeping in some parts and insist more than it does upon that prudent deliberation with which all really useful progress must be accomplished. Still, "Friend Jacques's Evening Chats" seems to me to have been conceived with most excellent intentions. The hopes which are expressed in it for the future evince no hostility to imperial institutions. On the contrary, indeed, they are what the legitimate expansion of our institutions may lead us to expect.'

He paused again. Notwithstanding the care which he had taken to turn towards the Emperor, he could not shake off the consciousness that Rougon was sitting on the other side of the table, leaning on his elbows and looking at him, pale with surprise. Generally speaking, Delestang's views were identical with those of the great man. And so the latter had a momentary hope that a word from him might bring back his erring disciple.

'Well, now,' he exclaimed with a frown, 'I'll just give you an example. I'm sorry I haven't brought the book with me, but I can give you the substance of a chapter which I remember very well. Jacques is speaking of two beggars who go through the village soliciting alms from door to door, and, in reply to a question from the school-master, he asserts that he will show the peasants a way by which they will never have a single poor person among them. Then follows a very elaborate system for the extinction of pauperism. It contains the whole communistic theory. Surely the Minister for Agriculture and Commerce cannot approve of that chapter.'

Delestang summoned up all his courage and looked Rougon boldly in the face. 'You are going too far in saying the whole communistic theory,' he replied. 'It merely struck me as being an ingenious exposition of the principles of combination.' He had been searching in his portfolio as he spoke. 'I have got the book here,' he added.

Then he began to read the chapter under discussion. He read it in a low monotonous voice, and his wise-looking face assumed an expression of extraordinary gravity at certain passages. The Emperor listened with an air of deep attention. He seemed to particularly appreciate the more touching portions, in which the author made his peasants speak in a strain of childish stupidity. Meanwhile the ministers were quite delighted. What an amusing affair! There now was Rougon abandoned by Delestang, whom he had brought into the ministry solely that he might have some one to rely upon amidst the unexpressed hostility of his other colleagues. The latter were often indignant with him for his constant arrogation of power, that craving for authority which impelled him to treat them as though they were mere clerks, while he himself assumed the position of his

Majesty's private adviser and right-hand man. And now he was on the point of finding himself completely isolated! This fellow, Delestang, thought the others, was a man to be well received.

'There are perhaps one or two words—' muttered the Emperor, when Delestang had finished his perusal; 'but, really, taking it altogether, I don't see anything—eh, gentlemen?'

'It is quite innocent,' chorused the ministers.

Rougon made no reply to his Majesty, but seemed to bend his shoulders. When he returned to the charge, he singled out Delestang for his attack. For several minutes a contest went on between them in short sentences. Handsome Delestang grew warlike, and indulged in cutting remarks, while Rougon's anger also gradually rose. He for the first time felt his authority giving way beneath him. And springing all at once to his feet, he addressed himself to the Emperor with vehement gestures.

'Sire,' he said, 'it is a petty matter, and the book will be authorised, since your Majesty in your wisdom declares there is no danger in it. But I must warn you, sire, that it would be perilous to confer on France one half of the liberties which are claimed by this "Friend Jacques". You summoned me to power under terrible circumstances. You told me that I was not to attempt, by any untimely moderation, to reassure those who were quaking with alarm. In accordance with your commands, sire, I have made myself feared. I believe that I have obeyed your slightest instructions and have rendered you the services you expected of me. If any one should accuse me of excessive severity or of abusing the power with which your Majesty has entrusted me, such an accusation could only come from an adversary of your Majesty's policy. Believe me when I tell you that society is as deeply disturbed as ever it was. In the few weeks that I have been in office, it has unfortunately been impossible for me to heal the diseases which are preying upon it. Anarchical passions are still fermenting among the lower strata of the people.

'I do not wish to lay this festering wound bare to you, or to exaggerate its horror, but it is my duty to remind you of its existence, so that I may put your Majesty on your guard against the generous impulses of your own heart. For a moment it was possible to hope that the energy of the sovereign and the solemnly expressed will of the nation had swept all abominable periods of public baseness away without possibility of revival. Events, however, have shown what a mournful error this was. In the name of the country, sire, I beseech you not to draw back your powerful hand. The danger does not lie in the possession of excessive authority, but in the absence of repressive laws. If you should draw back your hand, sire, you would see the scum of the people bubbling up, you would at once find yourself overwhelmed by revolutionary demands, and your most energetic servants would soon be at a loss how to defend you. I venture to press this upon you strongly, for the dangers of the morrow would be terrible.

'Liberty without restraint is impossible in a country where there exists a faction which is obstinately bent upon denying the fundamental basis of the government. Many long years must elapse before your Majesty's absolute power is accepted by all, before it effaces from men's memories the recollection of old struggles, and passes so far beyond the pale of discussion that it may be discussed without danger. And outside the principle of despotic power, vigorously exercised, there is no safety for France. On the day when your Majesty may consider it your duty to restore to the nation the most harmless of its liberties, on that day your Majesty will be committed to everything. One liberty cannot be granted without a second; and then comes a third one, and everything is swept away, both institutions and dynasties! It is like an implacable, devouring piece of machinery. First, the tip of the finger is caught, then the hand is drawn in, then the arm, and finally the whole body is ground to pieces.

'And, sire, since I have ventured to express myself so freely on this matter, I will make this further remark. Parliamentary rule once destroyed a French monarchy; do not let us allow it to destroy an empire. The Corps Législatif ventures to interfere too much as it is. Do not allow it any share in directing the sovereign's policy. To do so would only give rise to the most vehement and deplorable discussions. The last general elections have once again testified to the country's gratitude, but none the less, no fewer than five candidates were elected whose disgraceful success ought to serve as a warning. To-day the all-important question is to prevent the formation of an opposition minority; and, what is still more important, is to take care not to provide it—if by chance it should come into existence—with weapons which might enable it to contend against the constituted authority with yet greater impudence than now. A parliament which holds its tongue is a parliament which does some work.

'As for the press, sire, it is turning liberty into license. Since I entered the ministry I have read the reports carefully, and every morning I am filled with fresh disgust. The press is the receptacle of nauseous leaven of every kind. It foments revolutions, it is an ever-burning fire which serves to kindle great conflagrations. It will only become useful when we have brought it under our authority and can use its influence as an instrument of government. At present I say nothing of other forms of liberty, such as the liberty of combination, of public meeting, or of doing anything a man likes. These, however, are all respectfully asked for in "Friend Jacques's Evening Chats." Later on they will be demanded. That is what I am afraid of. I hope that your Majesty will fully understand me. It is necessary that France should for a long time yet feel the weight of a hand of iron.'

He went on in this strain for a long time, defending, with increasing energy, the way in which he had used his authority, sheltering himself beneath the principle of plenary power, wrapping himself round with it, covering himself with it, as it were, like a man who would avail himself of his armour to the fullest extent possible. And in spite of his apparent excitement, he retained sufficient coolness to keep a watch on his colleagues and to note the effect of his words on their pale, fixed faces. Then all at once he abruptly ceased speaking.

There was a rather long interval of silence. The Emperor had again begun to play with his paper-knife.

'His Excellency the Minister of the Interior takes too black a view of the situation,' at length said the Minister of State. 'In my opinion nothing threatens our institutions. Order is perfectly maintained. We can trust with confidence to his Majesty's great wisdom. Indeed, it is a lack of such confidence to show fear—'

'Certainly, certainly,' murmured several voices. 'I will add,' said the Minister for Foreign Affairs, 'that France has never been more respected by Europe than she is now. Everywhere abroad his Majesty's firm and dignified policy is regarded with admiration. The opinion of the chancelleries is that our country has entered for good upon an era of peace and greatness.'

However, none of the ministers cared to attack the political programme defended by Rougon. They all looked at Delestang, who understood what was expected of him. He began to speak, and compared the empire to an edifice.

'The principle of authority ought certainly not to be shaken,' said he, 'but there is no necessity for systematically shutting the door upon every public liberty. The empire is like some great place of refuge, some vast and magnificent edifice whose indestructible foundations have been laid by his Majesty with his own hands. He is still engaged in raising its walls; but the day will come when his task will be finished, and he will have to think of how he can crown his edifice, and it is then—'

'Never!' interrupted Rougon violently. 'The whole thing will topple down!'

The Emperor stretched out his hand to stop the discussion. He was smiling, and seemed to be awaking from a reverie. 'Well, well,' he said; 'we are getting away from current affairs. We will see about all this later on.' Then, having risen from his seat, he added: 'It is late, gentlemen; you must have *déjeuner* at the château.'

The council was now at an end. The ministers pushed back their chairs and stood up and bowed to the Emperor, who was slowly retiring. All at once, however, his Majesty turned and muttered: 'A word with you, Monsieur Rougon, I beg.'

Then as the Emperor took Rougon into the embrasure of one of the windows, the other ministers thronged round Delestang a the farther end of the room. They congratulated him in subdued tones, with nods and becks and wreathed smiles, quite a buzzing of murmured praise. The Minister of State, a man of very shrewd mind and great experience, was particularly flattering. He had an idea that it was lucky to have a shallow-pated fellow for a friend. Meantime, Delestang bowed with grave modesty to all the compliments lavished upon him.

'After all,' said the Emperor to Rougon, 'I won't speak to you here, come along with me,' and he thereupon took him into his own study, a rather small room, where the furniture was littered with books and newspapers. Then, having lighted a cigarette, he showed Rougon a small model of a new cannon lately invented by an officer. The little weapon looked like a child's toy. His Majesty affected a very kindly tone, and tried to convince the minister that he still possessed his favour. Rougon, however, divined that an explanation of some sort was coming, and he wanted to have the first word.

'Sire,' he began, 'I am well aware of the violence with which I am attacked by those who surround your Majesty.'

The Emperor smiled without saying anything. It was true, however, that the Court had again put itself in opposition to Rougon. He was now accused of abusing his power, and of compromising the empire by his harshness. The most extraordinary tales were circulated about him, and the corridors of the palace were full of complaints and stories, which echoed every morning in the Emperor's study.

'Be seated, Monsieur Rougon, be seated,' his Majesty at last said, in a good-natured way. And then, taking a seat himself, he continued: 'People are always dinning things into my ears. So it is, perhaps, best that I should quietly talk them over with you. What is this affair of a notary at Niort, who died after being arrested? A Monsieur Martineau, I think?'

Rougon quietly entered into particulars. This Martineau, he said, was a man who had very gravely compromised himself; a Republican whose influence in the department might have led to great danger. He had been arrested, and he had since died.

'Yes, that's just it,' replied the Emperor; 'that's the tiresome part of the matter. The opposition papers have got hold of the story, and relate it in a very mysterious fashion, and with a reticence which is calculated to have a most deplorable effect. I am much distressed about it, Monsieur Rougon.'

However, he said no more on that subject, but sat for a few moments puffing at his cigarette.

'You have been down to Deux-Sèvres lately, and you were present at some ceremony there, were you not?' he presently continued. 'Are you quite sure of Monsieur Kahn's financial stability?'

'Oh, quite so!' exclaimed Rougon. And he launched into a series of explanatory details. M. Kahn, said he, was supported by a very rich English company. The shares of the railway from Niort to Angers were at a premium at the Bourse. The undertaking had very fine prospects before it.

The Emperor, however, seemed incredulous. 'I have heard a certain amount of fear expressed,' he said. 'You can understand that it would be very unfortunate for your name to be mixed up with a catastrophe. However, since you tell me that there is no reason for fear—' Then he again broke off and passed to a third subject. 'Now, about the prefect of Deux-Sèvres. He is very unpopular, people tell me. He appears to have thrown everything into confusion down there. I hear, too, that he is the son of a retired process-server, whose strange vagaries are the talk of the whole department. This Monsieur du Poizat is a friend of yours, I believe?'

'One of my best friends, sire.'

As the Emperor now rose from his seat, Rougon also got up. The former went to a window, and then came back again, puffing out a little cloudlet of smoke.

'You have a good many friends, Monsieur Rougon,' he said, with a meaning look.

'Yes, sire; a great many,' the minister frankly replied.

Evidently enough, the Emperor had hitherto merely repeated the gossip of the château, the accusations made by those who surrounded him. He was doubtless acquainted, however, with other stories, matters which were unknown to the Court, but of which he had learnt from his private agents, and in which he took a yet livelier interest, for he revelled in the spy system, in the secret manoeuvring of the police. He looked at Rougon for a moment, while a vague smile played about his face. Then, in a confidential tone, and with a somewhat playful air, he said: 'Oh, I know a good many things; more, perhaps, than I care to know. Here is another little matter, now; you have taken in your offices a young man, a colonel's son, who has not obtained a bachelor's diploma. It is not a matter of any importance, I am aware of that; but if you only knew all the fuss that is made about such things! Little things like these put everybody's back up. It is really very bad policy on your part.'

Rougon made no reply. His Majesty had not finished. He opened his lips as though he were going to say something, but it was apparently something that he found rather difficult to express, for he hesitated for a moment or two. At last he stammered: 'I won't say anything to you about that usher, one of your protégé's named Merle, I think. But he gets drunk and behaves insolently; and both the public and the clerks complain of him. All this is very annoying, very annoying indeed.' Then he raised his voice, and concluded somewhat bluntly: 'You have too many friends, Monsieur Rougon. All these people do you harm. It would be rendering you a service to make you quarrel with them. Well, at any rate let me have the resignation of Monsieur du Poizat, and promise me that you will abandon all the others.'

Rougon had remained quite impassive. He now bowed, and replied in a deep, meaning voice: 'On the contrary, sire, I ask your Majesty for the ribbon of officer of the Legion of Honour for the prefect of Deux Sèvres. And I have several other favours to solicit.' Then he took a memorandum-book from his pocket, and continued: 'Monsieur Béjuin begs that your Majesty will be graciously pleased to visit his cut-glass works at Saint-Florent, when you go to Bourges. Colonel Jobelin desires an appointment in the Imperial Palaces. The usher Merle calls your Majesty's attention to the fact that he has gained the military medal, and desires a tobacco-agency for one of his sisters.'

'Is that all?' asked the Emperor, who had begun to smile again. 'You are a magnificent patron. Your friends ought to worship you.'

'No, they do not worship me, sire, they support me,' Rougon replied with his blunt frankness.

This retort seemed to make a deep impression upon the Emperor. Rougon had just revealed to him the whole secret of his fidelity. On the day when he might allow his credit to stagnate, on that day his credit would be killed; and in spite of scandal, in spite of the discontent and treason of his hand, it was his only possession and support, and he was obliged to keep it sound and healthful, if he himself wished to remain unshattered. The more he got for his friends—the greater and the less deserved the favours that he lavished on them—the stronger he became himself.

He added very respectfully, and in a very meaning tone: 'For the glory of your Majesty's reign, I hope from the bottom of my heart that your Majesty may long preserve about you the devoted servants who helped you to restore the empire.'

The Emperor no longer smiled. He took a few steps about the room, with downcast eyes and pensive air. He seemed also to have turned pale and to be trembling slightly. Presentiments occasionally affected his mystical nature with great force. And to obviate the necessity of any immediate determination, he decided to drop the subject. He again assumed a kindly demeanour; and, referring to the discussion which had taken place at the council, seemed even inclined to think that Rougon was right, now that he could speak freely without any danger of irrevocably committing himself. The country, said he, was certainly not yet ripe for liberty. For a long time to come an energetic hand would be necessary to guide matters with resolution and firmness. Then he concluded by once more assuring the minister of his entire confidence. He gave him full liberty of action, and confirmed all his previous instructions. Rougon, however, thought it necessary to add another word on the subject.

'Sire,' he said, 'I could never allow myself to be at the mercy of malevolent gossip. I stand in need of stability if I am to accomplish the great task for which I am now responsible.'

'Monsieur Rougon,' replied the Emperor, 'go on fearlessly; I am with you.'

Then, bringing the conversation to a close, he stepped towards the door, followed by the minister. They both went out and crossed several apartments on their way to the dining-room. Just as they were reaching it, the Emperor turned round and again took Rougon aside. 'You don't approve, then,' he asked, in an under-tone, 'of that scheme for a new nobility? I should have been very glad to see you support it. Study the matter.' Then, without waiting for a reply, he added with that quiet stubbornness which formed part of his character:[1] 'There's no hurry, however. I will wait; for ten years, if it be necessary.'

After *déjeuner,* which lasted scarcely half an hour, the ministers went into a small adjoining drawing-room where coffee was served. They remained there chatting for a little time, standing round the Emperor. However, Clorinde, whom the Empress had kept with her all this time, came to look for her husband, with the easy manner of a woman who mixed freely with politicians. She shook hands with several of the ministers. They all clustered round her, and the subject of conversation was changed. However, his Majesty began to pay the young woman such marked attention, and kept so close to her, that their excellencies thought it discreet to take themselves off by degrees. Opening one of the glass doors which led on to the terrace of the château, four of them went outside, and these were speedily followed by three others. Only two remained in the room to keep up an appearance of propriety. The Minister of State, with a pleasant, cheery expression upon his aristocratic face, had taken Delestang in tow, and was pointing out Paris from the terrace. Rougon, likewise standing in the sunshine, also became absorbed in the spectacle of the great city looming like a mass of bluish cloud on the horizon beyond the great green carpet of the Bois de Boulogne.

That morning Clorinde was looking very beautiful. Clumsily dressed, as usual, with her gown of pale cherry-coloured silk dragging over the floor, she appeared to have slipped into her things in all haste, as if goaded on by some strong desire. She laughed with the Emperor, and her whole demeanour was very free and unre-

---

[1] When Napoléon III. was a lad his mother, Queen Hortense, as her letters show, was wont to call him '*mon doux entêté,*' virtually 'my gentle but stubborn boy.'— *Ed.*

served. She had made a conquest of his Majesty at a ball given by the Naval Minister which she had attended in the character of the Queen of Hearts, wearing diamond hearts about her neck and her wrists and her knees; and ever since that evening she had remained on very friendly terms with Napoléon, jesting playfully whenever he condescended to compliment her upon her beauty.

'Look, Monsieur Delestang,' the Minister of State was saying to his colleague on the terrace, 'see yonder on the left, what a wonderfully soft blue hue there is about the dome of the Pantheon.'

Then, while Delestang gazed admiringly at the prospect, the Minister of State cast furtive glances into the little drawing-room through the open window. The Emperor was bending forward, and was speaking with his lips close to the young woman's face, while she threw herself back with tightly strained breast as though to escape him. Nothing could be seen of his Majesty from outside save an indistinct profile, the tip of an ear, a long red nose, and a heavy mouth half-buried beneath a quivering moustache. His cheek and eyes were glowing, whilst Clorinde, who looked irritatingly fascinating, gently swayed her head like a coy young shepherdess.

In spite of all the unpleasantness at the council, Rougon returned to Paris with Delestang and Clorinde. On the journey home the young woman appeared anxious to make her peace with him. She no longer manifested that nervous restlessness which in the morning had impelled her to choose disagreeable subjects of conversation, but even occasionally looked at Rougon with an air of smiling compassion. When the landau, passing through the Bois de Boulogne, now steeped in sunshine, rolled gently alongside the lakes, she murmured with a sigh of enjoyment: 'What a lovely day it is!' Then, after a moment's reverie, she said to her husband: 'Tell me, is your sister, Madame de Combelot, still in love with the Emperor?'

'Henriette is mad!' replied Delestang, shrugging his shoulders.

But Rougon intervened: 'Yes, indeed, she's still in love,' said he: 'people assert that she actually threw herself at his Majesty's feet one day. He raised her and advised her to be patient.'

'Ah, yes, indeed,' cried Clorinde gaily, *'She'll* have a long time to wait!'

XII

DEFECTION

CLORINDE was now revelling in a florescence of fantasy and power. In character she was still the big eccentric girl who had scoured Paris on a livery-stable hack in search of a husband; but the big girl had developed into a woman, who calmly performed the most extraordinary actions, having at length realised her long-cherished dream of becoming a power. Her everlasting prowlings in out-of-the-way neighbourhoods, her correspondence which inundated the four corners of France and Italy with letters, her continued contact with politicians, into whose intimacy she managed to insinuate herself, and all her erratic schemings, full of gaps and illogical as they were, had ended in the acquirement of real and indisputable influence. She still indulged in strange eccentricities, and propounded wild schemes and extravagant hopes, even when she was talking seriously. And when she went out, she still took her tattered portfolio with her, carrying it in her arms like a baby, and with such an air of earnestness that people in the streets smiled as she passed them in her dirty, draggling skirts. However, she was consulted now, and even feared. No one could have exactly told the origin of her power, which seemed to come from numerous distant and invisible sources, now difficult to trace. Folks knew nothing but a few scraps of gossip, anecdotes that were whispered from ear to ear. There was something to mystify one in the young woman's strangely compound character, in which wild imagination was linked to common sense which commanded attention and obedience, while apart from all mental attributes there was her magnificent person, in which, perhaps, lay the true secret of her power. It mattered little, however, upon what foundations Clorinde's throne was reared. It was sufficient that she did reign, though it were in a whimsical, erratic fashion, and that people bowed down before her.

This was a real period of power for the young woman. In her dressing-room, amidst a litter of dirty basins, she contrived to centralise the policy of all the courts of Europe. She received information, even detailed reports, in which the slightest pulsations of governmental life were carefully noted, before the embassies did, and without anyone knowing whence her news was derived. As a natural consequence she was surrounded by a court of bankers, and diplomatists, and friends, who came to her in the hope of obtaining information. The bankers showed her particular attention. She had enabled one of them to gain a hundred million francs in a single haul by merely telling him of an approaching change of ministry in a neighbouring state. Truth to tell, however, she disdained to employ her knowledge for purposes of gain, and she readily told all that she knew—the gossip of diplomatists, and the talk of the different capitals—for the mere pleasure of hearing herself speak, and of showing that she had her eyes upon Turin, Vienna, Madrid, and London, as well as on Berlin and St. Petersburg. She could supply endless information concerning the health of the different sovereigns, their amours and habits, the politicians of the various states, and all the scandals of even the smallest German duchies. She judged statesmen in a single phrase; jumped from north to south without the slightest transition; spoke as carelessly of the different countries of Europe as if they had been her own, as if, indeed, the whole wide world, with its cities and nations, had formed part of a box of playthings, whose little cardboard houses and wooden men she could set up, and move about as she pleased. And, when at last her tongue ceased wagging, and she was tired of chattering, she would snap her fingers, as though to say that this was quite as much as all these things were worth.

For the time being, amidst her many tangled schemes, there was one very serious matter which excited her warmest enthusiasm, and on which she tried her best to keep silent, though, occasionally, she could not deny herself the pleasure of alluding to it. She wanted Venice. Whenever she spoke of the great Italian minister, she referred to him familiarly as 'Cavour.' 'Cavour,' said she, 'did not want it, but I want it, and he has understood.' Morning and night she shut herself up at the embassy with Chevalier Rusconi. And tranquilly lounging, throwing back her narrow, but goddess-like brow, as if in a sort of somnambulism, she would utter scraps of disconnected sentences, shreds of revelations; a hint of a secret interview between the Emperor and some foreign statesman; a projected treaty of alliance, some clauses of which were still under discussion; a war which would take place in the coming spring. On other days she became excited and angry, kicked the chairs about her room and knocked the basins over at the risk of breaking them. On these occasions she looked like some angry queen who has been betrayed by imbecile ministers, and sees her kingdom going from bad to worse; and, with a tragic air, she would stretch her bare majestic arm in the direction of Italy and clench her fist, exclaiming: 'Ah! if I were over yonder there would be none of this folly!'

However, the worries of high politics did not prevent Clorinde from engaging in all sorts of other businesses, in which she seemed to get quite lost. She was often to be found sitting on her bed with the contents of her large portfolio spread over the counterpane, while she plunged her arms into the papers, distracted and crying with irritation. She would be unable to find anything amidst such a chaos of documents; or else, after long hunting for some lost batch of papers, she would at length discover it behind some piece of furniture or amongst her old boots or dirty linen. When she went out to conclude any particular piece of business, she generally contrived to involve herself in two or three fresh affairs on her way. She was for ever rushing about to all sorts of places, lived in a perfect whirl of ideas, a state of perpetual excitement; while beneath her lay the mazy depths of mysterious, unfathomable intrigues. When she came home again in the evening, after a day's scouring of Paris, tired out by climbing so many flights of stairs, and carrying in the folds of her skirts an odour of all the strange haunts which she had visited, no one would have guessed one half of the errands that she had been engaged upon. And if anyone happened to question her, she only laughed; she herself did not always remember what she had been doing.

It was about this time that she had the extraordinary whim of engaging a private room at one of the great restaurants on the boulevard. The house in the Rue du Colisée was so far away from everything, she said; she wanted a place in some central position; so she turned the private room at the restaurant into an office. For two months she received there all who wanted to see her, simply attended by the waiters, who had to usher in persons of the highest position. Great functionaries, ambassadors, and ministers presented themselves at the restaurant. Clorinde, entirely at her ease there, made them sit down on the couch, damaged by the supper parties of the Carnival, while she herself remained in front of the table, the cloth of which was always laid, strewn with bread-crumbs and littered with papers. She camped there like a general officer. One day, however, when she did not feel very well, she calmly went upstairs to the top of the house and lay down on the bed of the *maître d'hôtel* who usually waited upon her, and she could not be induced to go home till it was nearly midnight.

Delestang, in spite of everything, was a happy man. He appeared to be quite ignorant of his wife's eccentricities. She was now completely master of him, and treated him as she liked, while he never made the least complaint. His natural temperament predisposed him to this kind of servitude. He found far too much happiness in the secret surrender of his authority to attempt any revolt. In the privacy of their domestic life, it was he who rendered Clorinde all kinds of little services. He hunted about for her lost boots, or went through all the linen in the wardrobe to find a chemise that was not in holes. He was quite satisfied with preserving a serene appearance of superiority when he was at other people's houses. The unruffled air of loving protection with which he then spoke of his wife almost won him public respect.

Clorinde, having now become all-powerful at home, had decided to bring her mother back from Turin. She intended, she said, that Countess Balbi should henceforth spend six months of each year with her. She seemed to be suddenly overwhelmed by an outburst of filial affection. She threw a whole floor of the house into confusion so as so instal the old lady as near as possible to her own apartments. She even provided a door of communication between her dressing-room and her mother's bedchamber. In Rougon's presence especially she made an excessive parade of her affection, indulging in the most exaggerated Italian expressions of endearment. How had she ever been able, she wondered, to resign herself to such a long separation from her mother, she who, before her marriage, had never left her for an hour? She accused herself of want of heart. But it was not her fault, she protested; she had been forced to yield to other people's advice, to give way before pretended necessities, in which even now she could see no force. Rougon remained quite unmoved by this rebellion. He had altogether ceased to lecture her, and no longer attempted to make her one of the most distinguished women in Paris. In former times she had filled up a gap in his life, but now that he was in the forefront of the battle with fourteen hours' work to get through every day, he gave little thought to love and passion. Nevertheless, he continued to treat her with an air of affection, mingled with that kind of contempt which he usually manifested for women. He came to see her from time to time, and then his eyes would occasionally gleam as in the days of old. She was still his one weakness; the one woman who perturbed him.

Since Rougon had gone to live at the official residence of the Minister of the Interior where his friends complained that they could no longer see him in intimate fashion, Clorinde had thought of receiving the band at her own house, and it had gradually become a custom for the others to go there. To mark more plainly the fact that these receptions took the place of those in the Rue Marbeuf, she fixed the same evenings as Rougon had chosen, namely Sundays and Thursdays. There was this difference, however, that in the Rue du Colisée the guests remained till one o'clock in the morning. Clorinde received them in her boudoir, as Delestang still kept the keys of the big drawing-room for fear of it being damaged by grease-spots. And as the boudoir was a very small apartment, Clorinde left the doors of her dressing-room and bed-room open; so that, very frequently, the friends were to be found crowding together in the sleeping-chamber amid a litter of feminine finery.

On Thursdays and Sundays, Clorinde usually made a point of hastening home early so as to get through her dinner in time to receive her guests. But, in spite of all her efforts to remember these evening receptions, she twice forgot all about them, and was taken quite aback on finding a crowd of people in her bed-room when she returned home after midnight. One Thursday, towards the end of May, she got home at the unusually early hour of five. She had been out on foot and had preferred to walk all the way from the Place de la Concorde in a heavy fall of rain rather than pay thirty sous for a cab. She was quite soaked when she reached the house, and she went straight to her dressing-room where her maid, Antonia, whose mouth was smeared with jam, undressed her, laughing merrily the while at the stream of water which poured from her mistress's clothes on to the floor.

'There is a gentleman come to see you,' said the servant, presently, as she sat down on the floor to take off Clorinde's boots. 'He has been waiting for an hour.'

Clorinde asked her what he was like. The maid, with her greasy dress and unkempt hair, and her white teeth gleaming in her dusky face, remained sitting on the floor. The gentleman, she said, was fat and pale, and stern-looking.

'Oh, it must be Monsieur de Reuthlinguer, the banker,' cried Clorinde. 'I remember now, he was to come at four o'clock. Well, let him wait. You have the bath ready for me, haven't you?'

Then she quietly got into the bath which was concealed behind a curtain in a corner of the room, and while in it, she read the letters which had arrived during her absence. Half an hour went by when Antonia, after leaving the room for a few minutes, came back again and said to her mistress: 'The gentleman saw you come in and would very much like to speak to you, madame.'

'Oh, dear, I'd forgotten all about him!' cried Clorinde. 'Come and dress me, quickly.'

However, the young woman showed much capriciousness over her toilette that evening. In spite of the neglect with which she usually treated her person, she was occasionally seized with a sudden idolatry for it. At these times she would indulge in the most elaborate toilette; even having her limbs rubbed with ointments and balms and aromatic oils, of a nature known only to herself, which had been bought at Constantinople, so she said, from the perfumer to the Seraglio, by an Italian diplomatist, a friend of hers. While Antonia was rubbing her, she threw herself into statuesque attitudes. This anointing made her skin white and soft, and beautiful as marble. One of the oils, of which she herself carefully counted the drops as she let them fall on to a small piece of flannel, had the miraculous quality of at once effacing every wrinkle. And when this business was over, she would commence a minute examination of her hands and feet. She could have spent a whole day in adoring herself.

At the end of three quarters of an hour, however, when Antonia had slipped some wraps over her, she suddenly seemed to recollect her visitor. 'Oh, dear, the Baron!' she cried. 'Well, never mind, show him in here!'

M. de Reuthlinguer had been patiently sitting in Clorinde's boudoir, with his hands clasped over his knees for more than two hours. He was a pale frigid man of austere morals, the possessor of one of the largest fortunes in Europe, and for some time past he had been in the habit of thus dancing attendance upon Clorinde twice or thrice a week. He even invited her to his own house, that abode of rigid decorum and glacial strictness, where the young woman's startling eccentricities quite shocked the footmen.

'Good day, baron!' Clorinde exclaimed as he came in. 'I'm having my hair dressed, so don't look.'

An indulgent smile played round the baron's pale lips. After bowing with the most respectful courtesy, he remained standing quite close to her, without a quiver of his eyelids.

'You've come for news, haven't you?' she asked. 'Well, I've just heard something.'

Then she got up and dismissed Antonia, who went away leaving the comb stuck in her mistress's hair. Clorinde was doubtless afraid of being overheard, for laying her hand on the banker's shoulder and, standing on tiptoe, she whispered something in his ear. As he listened to her, he nodded his head briskly.

'There!' concluded the young woman, raising her voice. 'You can go now.'

But the banker took hold of her bare arm and brought her back towards him to ask for certain explanations. He could not have been more at his ease if he had been talking to one of his clerks, instead of to this beautiful woman in deshabille. When he left her, he invited her to dine at his house on the following day. His wife was very anxious to see her again, he said. She accompanied him to the door, but all at once crossed her arms over her bosom and turned very red as she exclaimed: 'Good gracious! I was actually about to go out with you like this!'

She now began to scold Antonia for being so slow. She would never get finished! she cried; and then she scarcely gave the girl time to dress her hair, saying that she hated being so long over her toilette. In spite of the time of the year, she insisted upon wearing a long robe of black velvet, a sort of loose blouse, drawn in at the waist with a red silk girdle. Twice already, a servant had come to tell her that dinner was served. However, as she passed through her bedroom, she found three gentlemen there, of whose presence no one had had the slightest idea. They were the three political refugees, Signori Brambilla, Staderina, and Viscardi. Clorinde, however, showed no surprise at meeting them.

'Have you been waiting for me long?' she asked. 'Yes, yes,' they replied, gently nodding their heads. They had arrived before the banker, but had remained extremely quiet, for political misfortunes had made them taciturn and reflective. They were seated side by side on the same couch, all three lolling in much the same position, with big extinguished cigars between their lips. But they now rose and clustered round Clorinde, and a rapid muttering in Italian ensued. The young woman seemed to be giving them instructions. One of the refugees took notes in cipher in a pocket-book, while the others, appearing much excited by what they heard, stifled slight cries with their gloved hands. Then they all three went off in single file, with quite impenetrable faces.

That Thursday evening it had been arranged that several of the

ministers should confer together on a very important financial matter. When Delestang went off after dinner, he told Clorinde that he
would bring Rougon back with him, at which his wife made a little
grimace which seemed to imply that she was not very anxious to
see her whilom master. There was as yet no positive break in their
friendship, but the young woman showed an increasing coldness
towards Rougon. Towards nine o'clock, M. Kahn and M. Béjuin
arrived together. They were the first of the band to put in an appearance, but were soon followed by Madame Correur. Clorinde
was found in her bedroom, stretched upon a couch there. She
complained of one of those extraordinary and unheard-of troubles
which suddenly came upon her every now and then. She must have
swallowed a fly, she said, while drinking, for she could feel it flying
about inside her stomach. Draped in her long black velvet robe, her
shoulders supported by three pillows, she none the less looked superbly beautiful with her pale face and bare arms, recalling indeed
one of those reclining, dreaming figures, which sculptors portray
on monuments. At her feet was Luigi Pozzo, gently twanging the
strings of a guitar. He had deserted painting for music.

'Sit down, won't you?' she said to the others. 'Please excuse me.
A wretched little insect has got inside me somehow.'

Pozzo went on twanging his guitar, and singing in a low voice,
with an ecstatic expression on his face, as if lost in a reverie. Madame Correur wheeled a chair up to Clorinde's side, and M. Kahn
and M. Béjuin, after a little searching, also succeeded in finding
seats. It was not an easy matter to do so, for the five or six chairs
were hidden beneath a litter of dresses and petticoats, so that when
Colonel Jobelin and his son Auguste arrived five minutes later, they
had to remain standing.

'Little one,' said Clorinde to Auguste, whom she still treated
quite familiarly in spite of his seventeen years, 'go and bring two
chairs out of my dressing-room.'

These were cane-seated chairs, with all the varnish worn away
by the damp linen which was constantly hung over their backs. The
bedroom was lighted by a single lamp with a shade of pink paper.
There was another in the dressing-room and a third in the boudoir,
which, seen through the doorways, seemed to be full of dusky
shadow, as though merely illuminated by a night-light. The bedroom itself, with hangings of a tender mauve that had now turned to
a pale grey, was full of a floating haze, in which one could scarcely

distinguish the rents in the coverings of the easy-chairs, the dust-marks on the furniture and the big ink-stain in the middle of the carpet where some inkstand had fallen with such force that even the wainscotting was splashed. The bed-curtains had been drawn, probably in order to conceal the untidiness of the bed. And amidst this hazy gloom, there rose a powerful scent as though all the bottles and flasks in the dressing-room had remained uncorked. Clorinde obstinately refused to have any of the windows open, even in warm weather.

'What a nice scent you've got here,' said Madame Correur, complimentarily.

'Oh, it's I who smell so nice,' the young woman naively replied.

Then she began to talk of the essences which she obtained direct from the perfumer to the Sultanas, and even held her arm under Madame Correur's nose. Her black velvet blouse had got a little disarranged, and her feet, in their little red slippers, showed below it. Pozzo, languid and intoxicated by the strong perfumes which she exhaled, was tapping his instrument gently with his thumb.

However, after a few minutes, the conversation turned of necessity on Rougon, as was invariably the case every Thursday and Sunday. The band seemed to come together for the sole purpose of discussing this one everlasting subject. Its members felt an ever-growing rancour against the great man, a craving to relieve themselves by ceaseless recrimination.

Clorinde no longer had any trouble to set them going. They always arrived with a fresh burden of grievances, ever discontented and jealous, actually embittered by what Rougon had done for them, and burning with a violent fever of ingratitude.

'Have you seen the fat man to-day?' the colonel asked. Rougon was no longer 'the great man.' 'No,' said Clorinde; 'but we may see him here this evening. My husband persists in bringing him to see me.'

'I was in a café this afternoon, where they were criticising him very severely,' the colonel continued, after a pause. 'They say that his position is very shaky, and that he won't last another two months.'

M. Kahn made a gesture of contempt. 'Well, for my part,' he said, 'I don't give him three weeks. Rougon, you see, is not cut out for governing. He is too fond of power, and gets intoxicated with it;

and then he strikes out right and left and treats people with revolting harshness. During these last five months he has been guilty of some most monstrous acts.'

'Yes, yes, indeed,' the colonel interrupted; 'all kinds of injustices and unfairnesses and absurdities. He abuses his power, most certainly he does.'

Madame Correur said nothing, but expressed, by a gesture, her opinion that Rougon's head was not particularly well balanced.

'Ah, yes, indeed,' said M. Kahn, noticing the gesture. 'He hasn't got a well-fixed head, has he?'

Then M. Béjuin observed that the others were looking at him, and felt called upon to say something. 'No! Rougon's not at all an able man,' he remarked; 'not at all.'

Clorinde lay back on her pillows, gazing at the luminous circle which the lamp east on the ceiling, and letting the others talk on. When they paused, she said, with the intention of starting them again: 'There is no doubt that he has abused his power, but he asserts that the things with which people reproach him were done for the sole purpose of obliging his friends. I was talking to him on the subject the other day. The services which he has rendered you—'

'Rendered us! rendered us!' they all cried furiously. And they went on talking all together, eager to protest against any such insinuation. However, M. Kahn shouted the others down.

'The services which he has rendered me! That's a fine joke! I had to wait two years for my railway grant, with the result that the prospects of the scheme, once very brilliant, have suffered considerably. If he is such a friend of mine, why doesn't he come to my assistance now? I asked him to obtain the Emperor's sanction to a bill authorising the amalgamation of my company with the Western Company, and he told me that I must wait. Rougon's services to me, indeed! Well, I should like to know what they are! He has never done anything for me, and he *can't* do anything now!'

'And I, and I, do you imagine that I am indebted to him for anything?' cried the colonel, breaking in before Madame Correur could speak. 'He surely doesn't take any credit to himself for that commander's cross, which had been promised to me for five years and more? He has taken Auguste into his office, it is true; but I bitterly regret now that I ever let the boy go there. If I had put him into business he would have been earning twice as much. That wretched Rougon told me only yesterday that he would not be able to increase Auguste's pay for another eighteen months. That is the way he ruins his credit for the sake of his friends!'

At last Madame Correur also was able to relieve her feelings. 'Did he mention my name?' she said, bending towards Clorinde. 'I never asked that much from him; and have yet to learn the nature of his services to me. He can't say as much with regard to my services to him; and if I liked to talk—. But no matter. I certainly asked him for a few favours on behalf of my friends. I don't deny that. I delight in being of use to anyone. But I must say that everything he has a hand in turns out badly, and that his favours seem to bring ill-luck. There's that poor Herminie Billecoq, an old pupil of Saint Denis, who was wronged by an officer, and for whom Rougon procured a dowry. Well, the poor girl came to me with a dreadful story this morning. There's no chance of her getting married after all, for the officer has absconded, taking the dowry with him. And you understand me. Anything that Rougon has done at my request has been done for others, and not for myself. When I came back from Coulonges, after the settlement of my brother's affairs, I went to tell him of the tricks that Madame Martineau had been playing with respect to the division of the property. I wanted the house in which I was born as part of my share, but the wretched woman contrived to keep it herself. Well, do you know what was the only answer I could get from Rougon? He told me three times over that he couldn't trouble himself any further about the miserable business!'

While Madame Correur was speaking, M. Béjuin, in his turn, had begun to show signs of excitement, and he now stammered: 'I am exactly in the same position as Madame. I have never asked Rougon for anything—never, never! Anything that he may have done has been done in spite of me, and without my knowing anything about it. He avails himself of one's silence to take every advantage of one, yes, every advantage.'

His words died away in a mutter; and then all four remained for a moment silently wagging their heads.

Presently M. Kahn resumed, in a solemn voice: 'The truth of the matter is this. Rougon is an ungrateful fellow. You all remember how we used to scour Paris, working to get him back into office. We devoted ourselves to his cause to such a point as to take our meals anywhere and anyhow. And he then contracted a debt towards us which in his whole lifetime he could not fairly discharge. Now, however, he finds gratitude too heavy a burden for him, and so he casts us adrift. Well, we might have expected as much!'

'Yes, yes, indeed,' cried the others. 'He owes everything to us, and he's repaying us in a pretty fashion.'

Then for a while they completely overwhelmed Rougon with an enumeration of all the things they had done for him; whenever one of them became silent another brought forward some still more crushing detail. The colonel, however, suddenly felt uneasy about Auguste, who had disappeared from the bedchamber. Just then a peculiar noise was heard in the dressing-room—a sort of gentle, continuous dabbling sound—and the colonel hurried off to see what it could be. He then found Auguste apparently much interested in the bath, which Antonia had forgotten to empty. Some slices of lemon, which Clorinde had used for her nails, were floating on the water, and these Auguste was inquisitively examining.

'The boy is quite a nuisance,' murmured Clorinde. 'He goes poking about everywhere.'

'Really, now,' said Madame Correur, who seemed to have been waiting for the colonel's absence, 'the thing in which Rougon is most deficient is tact. Between ourselves, I may say, now that the gallant colonel can't hear us, that it was a great mistake on Rougon's part to take that young man into his office in defiance of the regulations. That is not the kind of service a man ought to render to his friends. It only brings him into discredit.'

However, Clorinde interrupted her. 'Do go, my dear madam,' said she, 'and see what they're doing in the bathroom.'

M. Kahn had begun to smile, and, when Madame Correur left the room, he also lowered his voice and put in a word. 'How fine it is to hear her talk,' he said. 'The colonel has, no doubt, been well looked after by Rougon, but she herself has no reason to complain. Rougon absolutely compromised himself on her account in that troublesome Martineau business. He showed himself very deficient in morality in that matter. Nobody ought to kill a man for the mere sake of pleasing an old friend, ought he?'

Then M. Kahn got up and began to stroll about the room, and ultimately he went back to the ante-room to get his cigar-case, which he had left in his overcoat. At that moment the colonel and Madame Correur came back.

'Hallo! has Kahn gone?' exclaimed the colonel; and, without any transition, he went on: 'Well, we others may have a right to run down Rougon, but Kahn, in my opinion, ought to remain dumb. I don't like heartless people. Just now I kept from saying anything, but in a café where I was this afternoon it was openly said that Rougon was falling through having lent his name to that swindling railway line from Niort to Angers. A man ought not to make such a blunder as that! To think of that big fat imbecile firing mines and delivering speeches a mile long, and even trying to make the Emperor responsible for the success of the line! Ah! it's Kahn, my good friends, who's made a mess of it for all of us! Don't you agree with me, Béjuin?'

M. Béjuin briskly nodded his head. He had already agreed with Madame Correur and M. Kahn. Meanwhile, Clorinde, still reclining on the couch, was amusing herself with biting the tassel of her girdle, which she kept drawing over her face, as though she wanted to tickle herself. Her eyes were wide open and smiling at the ceiling.

'Hush!' she said, all at once.

M. Kahn was just coming back, biting off the end of a cigar between his teeth. He lighted it and blew out two or three big puffs of smoke, for smoking was allowed in Clorinde's bedroom. Then, resuming the previous conversation, he said: 'Well, if Rougon asserts that he has weakened his power by serving us, I can truthfully declare that we have been dreadfully compromised by his patronage. He has such a rough, brutal way of pushing one forward that it's no wonder if one breaks one's nose against a wall. However, as a result of all these violent ways of his, he's now tumbling down again. For my part, I feel no desire to help to pick him up any more. If a man can't preserve his own credit, there must be something wrong with him. I tell you that he is seriously compromising us. I have got heavy enough responsibilities as it is, and I give him up.'

While saying this, however, M. Kahn spoke hesitatingly, and his voice grew faint. Madame Correur and the colonel bent their heads to escape the necessity of declaring themselves in the same peremptory fashion. In spite of everything, Rougon was still in office, and before abandoning him they wanted to secure some other powerful patron.

'The fat man isn't everybody,' said Clorinde carelessly. At this they all looked at her, hoping that she was going to give them some formal promise. But she made a little gesture, as though to bid them have patience. This tacit hint of some new patronage which would shower benefits upon them was really the mainspring of their assiduous attendance at the young woman's Sundays and Thursdays. Among the strong odours of her room they scented a coming triumph; and, believing that they had exhausted Rougon in obtaining the satisfaction of their early desires, they looked forward to the advent of some new power that should realise their more recent dreams, which were far greater and more numerous than the others had been.

However, Clorinde at last raised herself up from her pillows, and, bending towards Pozzo, she blew into his neck, laughing loudly as she did so, as though thrilled with some wild impulse of merriment. When she felt pleased she often gave way to some such outburst of childish gaiety. Pozzo, whose hand seemed to have gone to sleep on his guitar, threw back his picturesque Italian head and showed his white teeth when he was thus roused, but Clorinde went on laughing and blowing with such force that at last he begged for mercy. Then, when she had scolded him in Italian, she turned towards Madame Correur. 'He must sing to us, mustn't he?' she said. 'If he will sing I won't blow any more. He has composed a very pretty song. You will like it.'

They all asked to hear the song, and Pozzo began to finger his guitar again. Then he sang, keeping his eyes fixed upon Clorinde all the time. The song was like a passionate murmur accompanied by short soft notes. The tremulous Italian words could not be distinguished; however, at the last couplet, which seemed to be expressive of the pains of love, Pozzo, while assuming a very mournful tone, began to smile with an expression of mingled joy and despair. When he finished, his audience enthusiastically applauded him. Why didn't he publish those charming songs of his? they asked. Surely his position in the diplomatic service could be no impediment.

'I once knew a captain who brought out a comic opera,' said Colonel Jobelin; 'and nobody in the regiment thought any the worse of him for it.'

'Ah, but in the diplomatic service—' murmured Madame Correur, shaking her head.

'Oh, I think you are wrong there,' remarked M. Kahn. 'Diplomatists are like other men, and many of them cultivate the social arts.'

However, Clorinde touched Pozzo lightly with her foot and whispered something to him, and thereupon the young man rose, laid his guitar on a heap of clothes, and left the room. When he returned, some five minutes afterwards, he was followed by Antonia, carrying a tray on which were a water-bottle and some glasses. Pozzo himself held a sugar-basin for which there was no room on the tray. Nothing stronger than sugared water was ever drunk at Clorinde's receptions, and her friends knew that she was well pleased if they simply took the water by itself.

'Hallo! what's that?' she suddenly exclaimed, turning towards the dressing-room, where a door could be heard creaking. Then, as though remembering, she added: 'Oh, it's my mother! She's been in bed.'

It was, indeed, Countess Balbi; who made her appearance in a black woollen dressing-grown, with a piece of lace tied round her head. Flaminio, the big footman with the long beard and brigand's face, was supporting her from behind, almost carrying her, in fact, in his arms. However, she did not appear to have aged, her pale face still smiled with the smile of one who had been a queen of beauty.

'Wait a moment, mother!' exclaimed Clorinde, 'I'll give you this couch. I'll lie down on the bed. I'm not feeling very well. I've got an insect inside me; and it's begun to bite me again.'

There was a general movement. Pozzo and Madame Correur assisted the young woman to her bed. They had to turn down the coverings, and flatten the pillows. Countess Balbi, meantime, lay down on the couch while Flaminio remained standing behind her, black and silent, though glaring ferociously at the visitors.

'You don't mind my lying down, do you?' said Clorinde to the others. 'I feel so much better when I'm lying down. I'm not going to send you away. You must stay where you are.'

She was stretched out at full length, her elbow resting on a pillow, while her spreading black blouse looked like a stream of ink upon the white counterpane. Nobody had had any idea of going away. Madame Correur was talking in a whisper to Pozzo about Clorinde's superb figure, while M. Kahn, M. Béjuin and the colonel paid their respects to the Countess, who nodded her head and smiled. Every now and then, without turning round, she would call in a soft voice: 'Flaminio!'

The tall footman knew what she meant, and at once raised a cushion or brought a stool, or took a scent bottle from his pocket, retaining, however, in all he did the ferocious air of a brigand in evening dress.

All at once Auguste happened to have an accident. After prowling through the three rooms, stopping to examine all the garments that were lying about, he had felt a little bored, and to amuse himself had begun to drink glassful after glassful of sugared water. Clorinde kept her eye upon him, watching the sugar-basin gradually empty, when suddenly the youth broke his glass, against the side of which he had been pressing his spoon too violently.

'It's all because he puts too much sugar in!' cried Clorinde.

'Dunderhead!' exclaimed the colonel. 'You can't even drink water rationally! One big glassful every morning and every evening, that's the way. There is nothing better. It keeps away all diseases.'

Fortunately there was a diversion, for M. Bouchard now made his appearance. It was past ten o'clock. He had dined in town, which had caused him to he a little late. He seemed surprised at not finding his wife there. 'Monsieur d'Escorailles said he would bring her,' he remarked, 'and I promised to call for her and take her home.' Half an hour later Madame Bouchard at length arrived, accompanied by M. d'Escorailles and M. La Rouquette. After a coolness which had lasted a year, the young Marquis had returned to his allegiance to the pretty blonde. He and she, it appeared, had met M. La Rouquette as they were driving in an open cab to the Delestangs', and thereupon they had all three gone on to the Bois together, laughing loudly and indulging in somewhat broad pleasantries; indeed, M. d'Escorailles had even fancied for a moment that the deputy's arm was behind Madame Bouchard's waist. The trio brought a whiff of gaiety into Clorinde's room, something of the fresh air of the dark avenues of the Bois along which they had just passed so merrily.

'Yes, we've been to the lake,' said M. La Rouquette. 'They insisted upon taking me off. I was quietly going home to work.'

Then he suddenly became serious. During the previous session he had made a speech upon a financial question after a whole month's special study of his subject, and since then he had affected a very steady-going air, as though he had buried all his youthful frivolities.

'By the way,' began Kahn, taking him to the end of the room, 'you who are on such good terms with Marsy—'

Then he continued in such a low tone that nothing further could be heard. Pretty Madame Bouchard, who had bowed to the Countess, was now sitting beside the bed, holding Clorinde's hand, and sympathising with her in a fluty voice. Meantime, M. Bouchard, who remained standing in a prim and dignified attitude, suddenly began to speak aloud amidst all the surrounding buzz of conversation, 'I have something to tell you,' he said, 'our fat man is a nice sort of fellow.'

Before explaining himself, however, he began to rail at Rougon as the others had done. It was now impossible, he said, to ask him for anything, for he could not even return a polite answer; and he, M. Bouchard, considered that politeness came before everything. Then as they continued to ask him what Rougon had done, he at last told them.

'I can't bear injustice,' said he. 'I spoke to him about one of the clerks in my division, Georges Duchesne; you know him, don't you? You've met him at my house. Well, he's a young fellow of sterling merit, and we treat him as though he were our own son. My wife is very fond of him, as he comes from the same part of the country as herself. Well, we had lately been scheming to get Duchesne appointed assistant head clerk. It was my idea, but you approved of it, didn't you, Adèle?'

Madame Bouchard looked embarrassed, and bent yet more closely to Clorinde to escape the eyes of M. d'Escorailles, which she felt were fixed on her.

'Well,' continued the head of department, 'how do you think the fat man received my request? He glared at me in his offensive way for a full minute, and then he bluntly refused to make the appointment. When I pressed the matter, he said to me with a smile: "Monsieur Bouchard, don't press your request; you distress me. There are very grave reasons why I cannot accede to it." I couldn't get him to say another word. He saw, however, that I was very much put out, and so he begged me to remember him kindly to my wife.'

That very evening, as it happened, Madame Bouchard had had a rather lively passage of arms with M. d'Escorailles on the subject of this same Georges Duchesne. 'Oh well!' she now deemed it advisable to say in a rather petulant voice, 'Monsieur Duchesne will have to wait. I don't know that we need trouble ourselves about him.'

But her husband seemed quite determined. 'No, no,' he returned; 'he deserves to be assistant head clerk, and he shall be! My credit is involved. Oh, I really can't stand injustice!'

He grew so excited that some of the others had to soothe him. Clorinde, who appeared somewhat absent-minded, was in reality trying to hear the conversation between M. Kahn and M. La Rouquette, who had ensconced themselves at the foot of her bed. The former was explaining the state of his affairs. His great undertaking of a railway line between Niort and Angers was in a very critical position. The shares had at first been sold on the Bourse at a premium of eighty francs, before a single stroke of work had been done. Relying upon his much-talked-of English company, M. Kahn had indulged in the most reckless speculation, and now the whole business was on the verge of bankruptcy, and must collapse unless he could at once obtain some powerful support.

'Some time ago,' he said, 'Marsy offered to bring about a sale of the concern to the Western Company. For myself I'm quite ready to enter into negotiations. We should only want to get an Act passed.'

Clorinde heard this, and thereupon quietly beckoned to the two men, who drew near and began a long conversation with her. Marsy, said the young woman, bore no spite. She would speak to him on the subject, and would offer him the million francs for which he had asked, the previous year, as his price for supporting the grant. His position as President of the Corps Législatif would make it an easy matter for him to get the necessary Act passed.

'Marsy's the only man who's of any good in matters of this kind,' she added with a smile. 'If you try to manage without him, you always have to call him in later on to patch up the broken pieces.'

However, all the other visitors were now speaking at once, and the room was full of noise. Madame Correur was telling Madame Bouchard of her latest desire, which was to go to Coulonges and die there in the family home. She grew quite pathetic as she spoke of the neighbourhood where she had been born, and she declared that she would compel Madame Martineau to give up the house which was full of the associations of her childhood. Meantime, as was fatal, the men were again harping on the subject of Rougon. M. d'Escorailles was describing the anger of his father and mother, who had written to him upon learning how Rougon was abusing his power, bidding him break with the minister and return to the Council of State. The colonel, on his side, related how the fat man had flatly refused to ask the Emperor for a post for him in the imperial palaces. Even M. Béjuin complained that his Majesty had never visited the cut-glass works at Saint Florent upon the occasion of his journey to Bourges, although Rougon had solemnly promised to obtain that favour. And amidst all this babel, Countess Balbi reclined smiling, on her couch, looking the while at her still plump hands.

'Flaminio!' she said, softly. Then the tall footman took a little tortoise-shell box full of mint lozenges out of his waistcoat pocket, and the Countess crunched these lozenges with an air of quiet enjoyment.

It was nearly midnight when Delestang returned home. When they saw him raise the hangings of the doorway leading to the boudoir, they all became silent and turned anxiously towards him. But he let the curtain fall again; there was no one with him. Then, after a further pause, the visitors broke into various exclamations:

'Are you by yourself?'

'You haven't brought him with you then?'

'Have you lost the fat man on the way?'

Truth to tell, there was a general feeling of relief. Delestang explained that Rougon had felt very tired and had left him at the corner of the Rue Marbeuf.

'And a good thing, too!' exclaimed Clorinde, stretching herself out on the bed; 'he's by no means entertaining.'

This was the signal for a fresh outburst of complaint and accusation. Delestang protested and tried to get a word in; for he usually made a pretence of defending Rougon. 'There is no doubt that he might have acted better than he has done towards certain of his friends,' he slowly said as soon as he was allowed to speak. 'But, in spite of everything, he's a wonderfully clever fellow. I myself shall be eternally grateful to him.'

'Grateful for what?' cried M. Kahn, snappishly.

'For all that he has done—'

But the others angrily interrupted him. Rougon had never done anything for him, they cried. What was it that he supposed Rougon had done for him?

'You quite surprise me!' said the colonel. 'It is ridiculous to carry modesty to that extent. You don't stand in need of anyone's help, my dear friend. You have succeeded through your own merits.'

Then they all began to sound Delestang's praises. His model farm at La Chamade was something unparalleled, they asserted; it had long ago proved that he possessed all the qualifications of an able administrator and statesman. He had a quick eye, a clear mind, and a hand that was energetic without being rough. And besides, had not the Emperor himself manifested the greatest appreciation of him all along? His Majesty and himself were in accord upon almost every point.

'Pooh!' M. Kahn ended by saying; 'it is you who keep Rougon up. If you weren't his friend and didn't support him in the council, he would have come to grief a fortnight ago!'

Delestang, however, went on with his protestations. He himself might indeed be of some service, but it was only right to give everyone his due. That very evening, at the Ministry of Justice, in discussing a very complicated financial question, Rougon had given proof of extraordinary lucidity of mind.

'Oh yes, I daresay,' said M. La Rouquette scornfully; 'the cunning of a smart attorney.'

Clorinde had not yet opened her lips. The visitors kept glancing at her as though they expected her to say something. But for some time she rolled her head on her pillow, as though she were trying to rub the nape of her neck.

'That's right; scold him,' she said at last, speaking of her husband, though not mentioning him by name. 'He will have to be beaten into taking his real place.'

'The position of Minister for Agriculture and Commerce is quite a secondary one,' remarked M. Kahn in order to precipitate matters.

This was touching a sore spot. Clorinde was annoyed at her husband being shelved to what she considered a minor post. And she now sharply sprang into a sitting posture, and let fall the words that everyone had been waiting for: 'He can go to the office of the Interior as soon as ever we wish it,' said she.

Delestang tried to speak, but all the company rushed towards him amid an outburst of delight. Then at last he seemed to give in, a rosy flush suffused his cheeks, his handsome face fairly beamed with pleasure. Madame Correur and Madame Bouchard whispered to each other that he was remarkably good looking, and the latter, with that perverted taste which makes some women admire baldness, cast loving glances at his bare skull. Then M. Kahn, the colonel and the others, expressed by winks, gestures and hasty words the high estimate which they set upon his ability. They prostrated themselves before the feeblest mind of the whole coterie, and admired one another in his person. He, at any rate, would be an easy and docile master, and would never compromise them. They could set him up as a god with impunity, free from all fear of his thunderbolts.

'You are quite fatiguing him,' at last exclaimed pretty Madame Bouchard in her tender voice.

Fatiguing him, were they? At this there was a general outburst of sympathy. In point of fact Delestang was looking rather pale again, and his eyes had a sleepy expression. But nothing tries a man like brain-work, the visitors remarked to each other with an air of commiseration, and the poor fellow had been working since five o'clock that morning! Then they gently insisted that he should go to bed. And he obeyed them with quiet docility, kissing his wife on the forehead and then quitting the room.

It was now one o'clock, and the guests began to speak of retiring, whereupon Clorinde assured them that she was by no means sleepy, and that they might stay on. However, no one sat down again. The lamp in the boudoir had just gone out, and there was a strong smell of oil in the room. It was with difficulty that they could find sundry small articles, such as Madame Correur's fan, the colonel's stick, and Madame Bouchard's bonnet. Clorinde, calmly stretched on her bed, stopped Madame Correur just as the latter was going to ring for Antonia. The maid, it appeared, always went to bed at eleven o'clock. Then just as they were all going away, the colonel suddenly bethought himself of Auguste, whom he had forgotten. He found him asleep on a sofa in the boudoir, with his head resting on a dress which he had rolled up to form a pillow; and the others scolded him for not having attended to the lamp. In the gloom of the staircase, where the gas was turned very low, Madame Bouchard gave a little scream. She had twisted her foot, she said. Finally, as the visitors carefully felt their way with the aid of the balusters, loud peals of laughter were heard upstairs, Pozzo having lingered after the others had gone.

Every Thursday and Sunday the friends met at Clorinde's in this way; and it was generally rumoured that Madame Delestang now held political receptions. It was said that extremely liberal proclivities were aired at them, and that Rougon's despotic administration was vigorously attacked. The whole band indeed had now begun to dream of a sort of democratic empire in which every public liberty would gradually expand. The colonel, in his leisure moments, drew up codes of rules for trades-unions. M. Béjuin spoke of building cheap workmen's houses round his cut-glass works at Saint Florent, and M. Kahn talked to Delestang for hours at a time, of the democratic part that the Bonapartes were destined to play in modern society. And every fresh act of Rougon's was hailed with indignant protests, with expressions of patriotic alarm lest France should be ruined by such a man. One day Delestang started the theory that the Emperor was the only genuine Republican of his time. The coterie put on the airs of a religious sect to which the only means of salvation had been exclusively entrusted, and its members soon openly plotted the fat man's overthrow for the good of the country.

Clorinde, however, showed no inclination for haste. They would find her lying at full length on one or other of the couches in her rooms, gazing into the air as if examining patches of the ceiling. And while the others prated and walked impatiently about the room, she remained silent and impenetrable, merely glancing at them every now and then as though to advise them to be more guarded in their language. She now went out less than she had done previously, and with Antonia's assistance often amused herself by dressing as a man, seemingly to while away her time. She manifested, too, a sudden affection for her husband, kissing him before company, talking caressingly to him, and showing a lively anxiety about his health, which was excellent. It might be that she adopted these tactics to conceal the absolute sway and ceaseless surveillance which she maintained over him. She directed his slightest actions, taught him his lesson every morning like a school-boy who could not be trusted. Delestang on his side evinced the most docile obedience. He bowed, smiled, or frowned, said black was white or white was black, just as she pulled the string. And whenever he felt that he wanted winding up again, he voluntarily came back to her and placed himself in her hands to be manipulated. But all the while he seemed to outsiders to be the head of the household.

Clorinde still waited. M. Beulin-d'Orchère, although he avoided coming to her evening receptions, frequently saw her during the day. He complained bitterly of his brother-in-law, whom he accused of making the fortunes of a crowd of strangers, while he seemed to think nothing of his own relatives. It was entirely Rougon's doing, he asserted, if the Emperor had not entrusted the seals to himself. Rougon was afraid of having anyone in the council with whom he might have to share his influence. Clorinde did all she could to whet the judge's anger, and she also dropped hints of her husband's approaching triumph, and held out a vague hope that the rejected one might be included in the new ministry. She was, however, really making use of Beulin-d'Orchère to find out what went on at Rougon's house. With feminine vindictiveness she would have liked to see the great man unhappy in his domestic relations, and accordingly she spurred the judge on to persuade his sister to take his side against her husband. He tried to do so, no doubt, and may even have voiced his regrets respecting a marriage from which he had derived no benefit. But probably his words had no effect upon Madame Rougon's quiet, placid nature. To Clorinde he would say that his brother-in-law had seemed very nervous for some time past, and he would even hint that the fitting time for his overthrow had come. Then with his eyes fixed on the young woman, but with the amiable way of one who in all innocence retails the gossip of society, he would recount a whole series of Rougon's characteristic actions. Why did she not act, if she were really mistress of the situation? he seemed to urge. But Clorinde only stretched herself out the more, and put on the air of one who is kept indoors by wet weather, and must patiently await a ray of sunshine.

However, at the Tuileries the young woman's influence was certainly increasing; and courtiers spoke in whispers of his Majesty's strong admiration for her. At the balls and official receptions, indeed, everywhere that the Emperor met her, he was always hanging about her, casting sidelong glances at her and whispering to her with a quiet smile. She on her side was playing her old part, the part she had played when she was looking for a husband, putting on the most enticing airs, behaving with a semblance of easy freedom, but always keeping on her guard and making her escape at the critical moment. She seemed, indeed, to be biding her time, waiting for the hour when the Emperor would be unable to refuse her any request that she might make of him. Doubtless she wished to secure the triumph of some long-planned scheme.

It was about this time that she suddenly began to manifest great affection for M. de Plouguern. For several months there had been a coolness between them. The old senator, who had been most constant in his attendance upon her, coming to see her almost every morning while she was dressing, was much annoyed one day at being refused admittance while she was engaged with her toilette. He thought this a great shame, for wasn't he her godfather, he asked, and hadn't he dandled her upon his knees when she was quite a little child? However, M. de Plouguern urged all this in vain. Matters ended in a rupture, and whenever M. Kahn or Colonel Jobelin happened to ask the young woman about the old senator, she would somewhat stiffly reply: 'I'm told that he is growing young again. But I never see him now.'

This lasted for a time. Then, all at once M. de Plouguern was to be constantly found at her house. He wandered about it at all hours of the day, doing Clorinde's bidding like a maid of all work:

'Godfather, go and get me my nail-file!' she would say, 'It is in the drawer, you know—Godfather, get me the sponge.'

She called him godfather in a caressing, affectionate manner. On his side he now frequently spoke of Count Balbi, and gave details of Clorinde's birth. He asserted that he had been introduced to her mother but a short time before that birth; which was distinctly false. However, the relative positions of the two were never clearly ascertained. Nor did people learn what business it was that had again brought Clorinde and the old senator together. In all probability he was just then necessary to her; she had some part for him to play in a drama of which she was constantly dreaming. She would indeed talk to him in obscure terms of some vague indefinite event which was very slowly approaching consummation. And on his side he seemed to be calculating combinations like a chess-player, though he generally ended by shaking his head as though he could come to no satisfactory conclusion.

On the few occasions when Rougon came to see Clorinde, she affected great weariness and spoke of going to Italy for three months. But then with lowered eyelids she would examine him with a sharp gleaming glance, while a smile of refined cruelty hardened her lips. She would have liked to strangle him then and there with her tapering fingers, but she was anxious that her attack should prove quite effective when it did come; and this long wait for the time when her nails would be fully grown was not without a spice of pleasure to her. Rougon, who was always very absent-minded, shook hands with her mechanically, never noticing the nervous fever of her flesh. He even fancied that she had given up her eccentricities, and complimented her upon rendering obedience to her husband. 'You are now nearly all that I wished you to be,' he said to her. 'You have taken the right course. Women ought to remain quietly at home.'

'Good heavens! what an idiot he is!' she exclaimed with a shrill laugh when he had gone away. 'And he thinks that it is the women who are the idiots!'

At last, one Sunday evening towards ten o'clock, when the whole band had assembled in Clorinde's bedroom, M. de Plouguern came in with a triumphant air: 'Well,' he exclaimed, trying to appear extremely indignant, 'have you heard of Rougon's last exploit? This time, surely, the measure is full!'

They all eagerly clustered round him. No one had heard of anything.

'Ah! It is abominable!' he added, excitedly waving his arm in the air. 'It is inconceivable that a minister could sink to such depths!'

Then he entered into particulars. When the Charbonnels had gone to Faverolles to take possession of their cousin Chevassu's property, they had made a great out-cry about the alleged disappearance of a large quantity of silver plate. They accused the woman who had been left in charge of the house, a very pious person, of having stolen it. They asserted that this miserable creature, upon learning the decision of the Council of State, had conspired with the Sisters of the Holy Family and carried to their convent all such valuables as could easily be concealed. Three days later the Charbonnels dropped the accusations against the housekeeper and charged the Sisters themselves with having ransacked the house. This caused a terrible scandal in the town. However, the commissary of police still refused to search the convent, when Rougon, after receiving a letter from the Charbonnels, telegraphed to the prefect directing him to order a strict perquisition at once.

'Yes, a strict perquisition, those were the words in the message,' M. de Plouguern said in conclusion, 'And then the commissary and two gendarmes were seen ransacking the convent. They were there for five hours. The gendarmes insisted upon poking into every corner. They even examined the Sisters' beds to see if the missing plate were under the mattresses.'

'Oh! how abominable!' cried Madame Bouchard, in disgust.

'He must be entirely destitute of the slightest idea of religion!' declared the colonel.

'Well, what can you expect?' asked Madame Correur. 'Rougon has never conformed with the requirements of faith. I often tried to reconcile him with God, but always failed in my efforts.'

M. Bouchard and M. Béjuin shook their heads in a hope sort of way, as though they had just heard of some frightful social catastrophe which made them despair of humanity; while M. Kahn, energetically rubbing his fringe of beard, inquired: 'Of course they discovered nothing in the convent?'

'Absolutely nothing!' replied M. de Plouguern. Then he continued hastily: 'A silver sauce-pan, I think, two cups, and a cruet-stand, mere trifles, presents which the esteemed deceased, an old man of extreme piety, had given to the Sisters in acknowledgment of their kind attention to him during his long illness.'

'Yes, yes, of course!' said the others.

The old senator dwelt no further on that subject; but in a very deliberate way, accentuating each sentence by bringing one hand down upon the other, he resumed: 'That, however, is not the important point. The question is one of the respect due to a convent, to one of those holy houses where the virtues, driven from our impious society, have sought refuge. How can we expect the masses to be religious when they see attacks made upon religion by men in such high positions? Rougon has been guilty of utter sacrilege in this matter, and he will be called to account for it. All the decent minded folks in Faverolles are bursting with indignation. Monseigneur Rochart, the well-known bishop, who has always manifested a particular affection for the Sisters, has come to Paris to demand justice. In the Senate, too, to-day a great deal of annoyance was shown, and there was some talk of raising a discussion on the strength of a few details which I was able to supply. And finally the Empress herself—'

Every head was now eagerly craned forward.

'Yes, the Empress has learnt this deplorable story from Madame de Llorentz, who heard it from our friend La Rouquette, to whom I myself told it. When she heard it her Majesty exclaimed: 'Monsieur Rougon is no longer worthy of speaking in the name of France!'

'Quite right!' said all the others.

All through that Thursday night and until one o'clock the next morning nothing else was talked of. Clorinde had not opened her mouth. At M. de Plouguern's first words she had lain back on her couch, looking a little pale and compressing her lips. Then, unnoticed, she quickly crossed herself three times, as though thanking heaven for having at last granted her a long-entreated favour. The narrative of the perquisition wrung from her various gestures expressive of outraged piety, and gradually she flushed quite red. Then, gazing up towards the dim ceiling she became absorbed in reverie.

And while the others were discussing the matter, M. de Plouguern glided to the young woman's side, and with his sceptical snigger softly whispered in her ear: 'He has insulted God Almighty! He is done for!'

XIII

CLORINDE'S REVENGE

DURING the ensuing week, Rougon heard a growing clamour rise
around him. Everything else might have been forgiven: his abuse
of power, the grasping greed of his band, and the choking grip in
which he held the whole country; but to have sent gendarmes to
poke about the cells of the Sisters was so monstrous a crime that
the ladies of the Court affected to shudder when he passed them.
Then, too, Monseigneur Rochart was creating a terrible commotion
throughout the official world, and it was said that he had even complained to the Empress herself on the subject. Moreover, the scandal
was doubtless kept alive by a few wily individuals, who were bent
on making the most of it; for orders and suggestions circulated, and
the same complaints were raised at once in every quarter. Amidst
all these furious attacks, Rougon at first maintained a perfectly serene and smiling demeanour. He shrugged his broad shoulders and
spoke scoffingly of the whole matter. At an evening reception at the
Ministry of Justice he even remarked: 'By the way, I never told you
that they found a priest hidden in the convent.' However, when this
sally circulated there was a fresh outburst of anger, and then he on
his side at last became impassioned. People were making him quite
sick with all their foolish talk, he said; the Sisters were certainly
thieves, for silver cups and saucepans had been discovered in their
possession. And he actually showed an inclination to take further
steps in the matter, made inquiries, and threatened to overwhelm the
whole clergy of Faverolles with confusion in the law-courts. Early
one morning, however, the Charbonnels presented themselves before him; at which he was much astonished, for he did not know that
they were even in Paris. As soon as he saw them, he exclaimed that
matters were proceeding most satisfactorily, and that he had sent
instructions to the prefect to compel the public prosecutor to take
active steps. But at this M. Charbonnel assumed an expression of
consternation, and Madame Charbonnel replied: 'No, no! we don't
want that! You have gone too far, Monsieur Rougon. You have quite
misunderstood us.'

Then they both began to sing the praises of the Sisters of the
Holy Family, who were extremely good women, they said; though

they themselves had for a moment gone to law against them, they had never ventured so far as to accuse them of anything base. Such a charge would have produced the greatest amazement in Faverolles, where everyone in society held the Sisters in such high esteem.

'You will do us the greatest injury, Monsieur Rougon,' Madame Charbonnel said, in conclusion, 'if you continue to show such violence towards religion. We have come to pray you to desist from further action. Down yonder people don't understand the real state of affairs, but think that it is we who are hounding you on; so, if you don't stop, they will end by stoning us.... We have made a handsome present to the convent, an ivory crucifix, which used to hang at the foot of our poor cousin's bed.'

'Well, we've warned you now,' added M. Charbonnel, 'and the responsibility rests with you. We have nothing further to do with the business.'

Rougon let them talk on. They seemed to be very much displeased with him, and gradually raised their voices in indignation. As the minister looked at them he felt a slight chill and sudden lassitude, as though some portion of his strength had again been ravished from him. However, he made no attempt to discuss the subject, but dismissed his visitors, promising that he would take no further steps in the affair; and, indeed, so far as he was concerned, he let the whole matter die out.

During the last few days his name had been indirectly mixed up in another scandal. A frightful tragedy had taken place at Coulonges. Du Poizat, obstinately intent upon getting the better of his father, had again one morning knocked at the old miser's door. Five minutes afterwards the neighbours heard the sound of gun-shots in the house, accompanied by fearful shrieks. When they made their way inside, they found the old man stretched at the foot of the staircase with his head split open. Two discharged guns were lying on the hall floor, and Du Poizat told them, with a livid face, that his father, upon seeing him advance towards the staircase, had suddenly shouted, 'Thieves!' as though he were mad, and had fired upon him twice, almost touching him with the muzzle of his gun. In proof of this, he even showed them a bullet-hole in his hat. However, said he, just as his father was advancing still nearer, he had fallen and broken his skull against the bottom step. This tragical death, this mysterious, unwitnessed drama, had given rise to the most unpleasant rumours throughout the department. The doctors said it was clear that the old man had died of an attack of apoplexy. Nevertheless, the prefect's enemies insinuated that he must have given his father a push, and the number of these enemies increased day by day, owing to the harshness of his rule, which oppressed Niort as with a reign of terror. Stern and pale, with his teeth clenched and his hands twitching, Du Poizat had to check the gossips on their doorsteps with a glance from his fierce grey eyes as he passed along the streets.

However, another misfortune befell him. He was obliged to remove Gilquin, who had compromised himself by taking a bribe to procure a conscript exemption from the service. It was his wont to promise exemption to peasants' sons on being paid a hundred francs a head. All that Du Poizat could do for Gilquin in the matter was to save him from prosecution and then disown him. So far the sub-prefect had relied entirely upon Rougon, and had tried to make him more and more responsible for every matter that went wrong. Now, however, he probably divined something of the minister's critical position, for he came to Paris without giving him any intimation of his intention to do so. He felt his own position to be very much shaken, and, fearing the collapse of the power which he had so largely helped to ruin, he was already on the look-out for the support of some influential hand. He contemplated asking permission to change his prefecture in order to escape certain dismissal. Indeed, since his father's death and Gilquin's knavery, Niort was becoming quite impossible for him.

'I just met Monsieur Du Poizat in the Faubourg Saint Honoré,' Clorinde mischievously said to the minister one day. 'Aren't you good friends now? He seems very bitter against you.'

Rougon avoided making any reply. After being compelled to refuse several favours to the prefect, he had become conscious of increasing coldness between them, and they now simply confined themselves to official intercourse. The desertion was becoming general. Even Madame Correur had abandoned Rougon. On certain evenings he again experienced that feeling of loneliness which he had formerly felt in the Rue Marbeuf when his friends were doubting his star. At the close of his busy days, amidst the crowd of visitors who besieged his drawing-room, he felt alone and lost and heartbroken, because his old familiar friends were not there. And he once more began to feel an overwhelming craving for the continuous praises of the colonel and M. Bouchard, for all the vitalising warmth with which his little court had once encompassed him. He even regretted M. Béjuin's silence. And so he made an attempt to win his old associates back again, by showing himself very pleasant and amiable, writing to them and even venturing to call on them. But the ties were broken, and he could never succeed in getting them all around him. If he contrived to piece up the links at one end of the chain, some mischance kept those at the other end broken; the chain remained imperfect in spite of every endeavour; some of his old friends were invariably absent. At last they all abandoned him. This was the death-agony of his power. He, strong as he was, was bound to those foolish weaklings by the long labour of their common fortune; and, as each deserted him, a piece of his being seemed to be ravished away. His strength and abilities remained as it were useless in this lessening of his importance; his big fists only struck the empty air. On the day when his shadow alone showed in the sunshine and he could no longer add to it by an abuse of power and patronage, it seemed to him as if he held but little room in the world; and he began to dream of a new incarnation, a resurrection in the shape of some Jupiter Tonans, with no band at his feet, but ruling by the sole power of his voice.

However, Rougon did not yet feel that his position was seriously threatened. He treated with disdain the bites that scarcely touched his heels. He went on governing with stern decision, unpopular and solitary. His great reliance was on the Emperor. His only weakness was his credulity. Each time that he saw his Majesty he found him kindly disposed and amiable, ever preserving his impenetrable smile; and the Emperor invariably renewed his expressions of confidence, and repeated the instructions which he had so frequently given before. This seemed quite sufficient to Rougon. His sovereign could have no thought of sacrificing him.

His feeling of security led him to venture on a deep stroke of policy. To silence his enemies and place his authority on a firmer footing than ever, he sent in his resignation couched in the most dignified terms. He spoke of the complaints which were being circulated against him, and asserted that he had strictly obeyed the Emperor's commands, but at the same time he felt the need of his Majesty's undoubted approval before further continuing his labours for the public weal. Moreover, he undisguisingly championed a stern policy, posed as the representative of merciless repression. The Court was at Fontainebleau at the time, and the resignation having been despatched, Rougon awaited the result with the confidence of a cool gamester. All the recent scandals, the tragedy at Coulonges, the perquisition at the convent of the Sisters of the Holy Family, would be blotted out, he thought. At any rate, if he were destined to fall, he wished to fall boldly like the strong man he was.

On the day when the minister's fate was to be decided, it so happened that a bazaar was held at the Orangery in the Tuileries gardens in support of an orphanage which the Empress patronised. All the palace circle and the high officials would certainly attend out of respect for their Majesties. And Rougon resolved that he also would go and show them his unruffled face. It was quite a piece of bravado, this idea of boldly confronting the people who cast furtive glances at him, of thus exhibiting his contemptuous unconcern amidst their hostile whispers. Towards three o'clock, while he was giving a final order to his chief subordinate, his valet came to tell him that a lady and gentleman particularly wished to see him in his private rooms. The card which the servant brought bore the names of the Marquis and Marchioness d'Escorailles.

The two old people, whom the valet, deceived by their almost shabby appearance, had left in the dining-room, rose ceremoniously when Rougon appeared. He hastened to lead them into the drawing-room, feeling some emotion at their presence and also a thrill of disquietude. However, he spoke of their arrival in Paris as an unexpected pleasure, and tried to appear as amiable as possible. But the Marquis and his wife remained cold and stiff and sullen.

'Monsieur,' at length said the Marquis, 'you will excuse, I hope, the step we have considered it necessary to take. It concerns our son Jules. We wish him to retire from the administration; we ask you to keep him no longer about you.' Then, as the minister looked at him with extreme surprise, he added: 'Young people are not to be depended upon. We have twice written to Jules telling him our reasons, and desiring him to send in his resignation. As he has not obeyed our instructions, we at last determined to come ourselves. This is the second time, monsieur, that we have come to Paris in thirty years.'

Then Rougon began to protest. Jules had the most promising future before him, said he; they would simply ruin his career. But the Marchioness made a gesture of impatience, and began to explain her reasons with more animation than her husband had shown. 'It is not for us, Monsieur Rougon, to judge you,' said she, 'but there are certain traditions in our family. Jules must not be mixed up in any abominable persecution of the Church. Everyone at Plassans is amazed already. We should embroil ourselves with the whole nobility of the neighbourhood.'

Rougon at once understood what was amiss. He was going to reply, but the Marchioness silenced him with an imperious gesture. 'Let me finish!' she said. 'Our son entered the public service in spite of our protests. You know what grief we felt at seeing him take office under an illegitimate government. It was all I could do to keep his father from cursing him. However, our house has been in mourning ever since, and when we receive our friends, the name of our son is never mentioned. We had sworn that we would trouble ourselves about him no longer; but there are limits to everything, and it is intolerable that an Escorailles should be mixed up with the enemies of our holy faith. You hear me, do you not, monsieur?'

Rougon bowed. He did not even think of smiling at the old lady's pious fibs. She and her husband once more stood before him proud and haughty and disdainful, as in the old days when he had prowled about Plassans pinched with hunger. If anyone else had used such language to him, he would certainly have had them turned out by the lackeys.

But now he felt wounded, distressed, shrunken as it were. He again thought of his youth of sordid poverty, and for a moment could almost have fancied that he was wearing his old worn-down shoes once more. However, he promised that he would use his influence with Jules to make him conform with his parents' wishes; and then alluding to the reply which he was awaiting from the Emperor he just added: 'It is quite possible, madame, that your son will be restored to you this very evening.'

When he was alone again, Rougon felt a thrill of fear. That old couple had succeeded in disturbing his hitherto unruffled placidity. He now hesitated about going to the bazaar where all eyes would read his perturbation on his face. He felt ashamed, however, of this childish fear, and so passed through his study on his way out. Then he asked Merle if anything had come for him.

'No, your excellency,' respectfully replied the usher, who had been on the look-out all the morning.

The Orangery in the Tuileries Gardens, where the bazaar was being held, had been sumptuously decorated for the occasion. Crimson velvet hangings with fringes of gold concealed the walls, and transformed the huge bare gallery into a lofty gala hall. Towards one end on the left, large curtains, also of crimson velvet, were stretched across the gallery, cutting off a portion of it. They were, however, looped up with bands ornamented with huge golden tassels so as to afford free communication between the chief section of the hall, where the stalls were ranged on either side, and the smaller division where a refreshment counter had been fitted up. The floor was strewn with fine sand; and in each corner stood majolica pots containing rare plants. In the middle of the square space formed by the stalls there was a low circular settee upholstered in velvet and with a very sloping back; and from the centre of it a huge column of flowers shot up, a sheaf of stems amongst which drooped roses, carnations, and verbenas, like a shower of dazzling drops. On the terrace overlooking the Seine, in front of the folding glass-doors, which had been thrown wide open, some grave-looking ushers in black dress coats glanced at the cards of the *invités* as they arrived.

The lady patronesses did not expect many people before four o'clock. Erect behind their stalls in the great hall they waited for customers to arrive. Their wares were spread out on long tables covered with crimson cloth. There were several stalls of Parisian and Chinese fancy goods; two of children's toys; a florist's kiosk crammed full of roses; and, lastly, inside a tent, a lucky-wheel, like those to be seen at the fairs in the Parisian suburbs. The stall-holders, in low-necked theatre dresses, assumed all the persuasive graces of shopkeepers, the seductive smiles of *modistes* trying to palm off old-fashioned goods, and they modulated their voices alluringly, as they prattled and puffed their wares. They made themselves quite familiar with everyone who came to purchase of them. A Princess presided over one of the toy stalls, and in front of her, on the opposite side of the hall, a Marchioness sold purses which had cost twenty-nine sous for twenty francs a-piece. These two were rivals, each seeking to make a larger sum of money than the other. They seized hold of customers, called out to the men, and asked the most shameless prices; and, after bargaining as greedily as thievish butchers, they would throw in the tips of their fingers or a glimpse of their bosoms to turn the scale and complete some remunerative transaction. Charity was, of course, their excuse.

Little by little the hall gradually filled. Gentlemen calmly halted and examined the stall-holders, as though the latter formed part of the goods for sale. Fashionably dressed young fellows crowded round certain stalls, laughing and flirting, while the lady-sellers flitted from one to another with inexhaustible complacence, offering all their wares in turn with the same charming expression. It seemed quite an enjoyment to them. Sales by auction could be heard proceeding, interrupted by joyous peals of laughter, amid the low tramping over the sanded floor. The crimson hangings softened the bright light from the lofty windows, and diffused a ruddy glow, which here and there set a pinky touch on the stall-holders' bare necks and shoulders. And in the space between the stalls six other ladies, a baroness, two bankers' daughters, and the wives of three high officials, threaded their way among the public with light baskets hanging from their necks. These darted upon each new arrival, crying cigars and matches.

However, Madame de Combelot met with particular success. She was the flower girl, and sat on a high seat in the rose-crammed kiosk, a carved and gilded affair which looked like a great pigeon-cote. She was dressed in a tight-fitting rose-coloured dress, the corsage of which was very low. And she wore no jewellery, but simply the regulation bunch of violets nestling on her bosom. To make herself as much like a genuine flower-girl as possible, it had occurred to her to tie up her bouquets in public, holding the wire between her teeth and twisting it round a full-blown rose, a bud, and three leaves, which she sold at prices ranging from one to ten louis, according to the appearance of her customers. And her bouquets were in such demand that she could not make them quickly enough, while every now and then she pricked herself in her haste and quickly sucked the blood from her fingers.

In the canvas tent opposite the flower stall pretty Madame Bouchard presided over the lucky-wheel. She was wearing a charming blue peasant-costume, high waisted and with a *fichu*-shaped bodice; indeed almost a disguise which gave her quite the appearance of a vendor of cakes and gingerbread. She also affected a pretty lisp and a guileless air which was very original. Over the lucky-wheel were displayed the different prizes; some hideous trifles in leather, glass, and china, worth four or five sous apiece. And every few moments, whenever there was a lack of patrons, Madame Bouchard called out, in her pretty innocent voice, which suggested some simple Susan fresh from her village: 'Try your luck, gentlemen! Only twenty sous a time! Try your luck, gentlemen!'

The refreshment room, which, like the larger hall, had its floor sanded and its corners decorated with rare plants, was furnished with little round tables and cane-seated chairs. It had been made to resemble a café as much as possible. At one end, behind a massive counter, were three ladies who fanned themselves while waiting for orders. Decanters of *liqueurs,* plates of cakes and sandwiches, sweetmeats, cigars and cigarettes, were set out in front of them, recalling the kind of display which one sees at the buffets of questionable dancing saloons. Every few moments the lady in the middle, a dark and petulant Countess, rose and bent forward to pour out a glass of something or other, seeming quite bewildered amidst all those decanters, and dashing her bare arms about at the risk of breaking everything. It was Clorinde, however, who was the real queen of the buffet. It was she who handed the customers the refreshments they ordered, when they sat down at the little tables. She looked like Juno masquerading as a waiting-maid. She wore a yellow satin robe slashed slant-wise with black satin, a dazzling, extraordinary arrangement which suggested a blazing star with a comet's tail sweeping after it. Her bodice was cut very low, and she sailed about majestically amidst the cane-seated chairs, carrying her glasses on a pewter tray with all the serenity of a goddess. Her bare elbows brushed against the men's shoulders, and her bosom showed conspicuously as she bent down to take their orders, evincing no haste as she did so, but answering every one with a smile, apparently quite at her ease. When the refreshments had been consumed, she received in her queenly hand the silver and copper coins tendered in payment, and, with a gesture that had already become familiar to her, dropped them into a bag hanging from her waist.

At last M. Kahn and M. Béjuin came into the buffet and sat down. The former jocosely rapped the zinc table at which he installed himself just as he might have done at a café, and called: 'Two beers, madame.'

Clorinde hastened up, served the two glasses of beer, and then remained standing near the table, to snatch a little rest, as just then there happened to be very few customers. And while she wiped her fingers on which some beer had trickled, M. Kahn noticed the peculiar brightness of her eyes, the expression of triumph with which her whole face shone. He blinked at her for a moment, and then asked: 'When did you get back from Fontainebleau?'

'This morning,' she replied.

'You've seen the Emperor, then, I suppose? Well, what is the news?'

Clorinde smiled, compressed her lips in a peculiar fashion, and then in her turn looked at M. Kahn. The latter thereupon noticed that she was wearing an eccentric ornament which he had never seen before. It was a dog-collar encircling her bare neck; a real dog-collar of black velvet, with buckle, ring and bell. The bell was of gold, and a pearl tinkled inside it. Upon the collar there were two names in letters of diamonds, oddly twisted and interlaced. And from the ring a thick gold chain fell over her bosom, and then rose again, ending in a gold plate fastened to her right arm, on which were these words: *I belong to my master.*

'Is that a present?' softly asked M. Kahn, pointing to the ornament.

Clorinde nodded assent, still keeping her lips compressed with a cunning, sensual expression. She had desired this servitude and she paraded it with shameless serenity, as though she felt honoured by a sovereign's choice, an object of envy to every other woman. When she had made her appearance with this collar round her neck, on which the keen eyes of rivals fancied they could decipher an illustrious name interlaced with her own, every woman present had understood the truth, and had exchanged significant glances with her acquaintances. However, business in the refreshment room was suddenly becoming brisk. 'A glass of beer, madame, please,' said a fat gentleman wearing a decoration—a general—as he looked at Clorinde smiling.

When she had brought the beer, two deputies asked her for some Chartreuse. A crowd was now pouring into the buffet, and orders were given on all sides for liqueurs, lemonade, biscuits, and cigars. And the men, while staring at Clorinde, repeated in whispers the various stories which were current. For her part she turned her neck in all serenity, the better indeed to show her dog-collar and the heavy gold chain which tinkled as she moved. That she had been a queen of the left hand imparted additional piquancy to her present assumption of the part of a waiting-maid, who, answering every one's beck and call, dragged statuesque feet—which had been passionately kissed by august moustaches—over the floor of a mock café, amongst pieces of lemon-peel and biscuit-crumbs.

'It's really quite amusing,' the young woman said, as she came back and stood by M. Kahn. 'One of the gentlemen actually gave me a pinch just now! But I didn't say anything. What would have been the good? It's all for the sake of the poor, isn't it?'

M. Kahn motioned to her to stoop, and when she had done so, he whispered: 'Well, what about Rougon?'

'Hush! You'll know everything soon,' she replied, in equally low tones. 'I have sent him an invitation card, and I am expecting his arrival.' Then, as M. Kahn wagged his head, she added, with animation: 'Yes, yes, I know him, I'm sure he'll come. And besides he knows nothing of what has happened.'

M. Kahn and M. Béjuin then began to look out anxiously for Rougon's appearance. They could see the whole of the large hall through the opening in the curtains. The crowd there was increasing every minute. On the circular settee several men were lounging with their knees crossed and their eyes sleepily closed, while a continual flow of visitors brushed against their feet as it streamed past. The heat was becoming excessive; and the hubbub grew ever louder in the roseate haze that floated over the forest of black silk hats. Every few moments, too, the grating, rattling sound of the lucky-wheel could be heard.

Madame Correur, who had just arrived, was going slowly round the stalls. She looked very fat, in her gown of grenadine striped white and mauve; and there was a shrewd expression on her face, the calculating air of the customer who looks about her with the intention of making some advantageous bargain. There were plenty of such to be made, she said, at these charitable bazaars, for the ladies often did not know the value of their wares. However, she never bought anything of such stall-holders as were friends of her own, for they always tried to take advantage of her. When she had been all round the hall, moving the different goods about, examining them and putting them back in their places again, she returned to a stall where some fancy articles in leather were displayed for sale, and here she remained for fully ten minutes turning everything over with an air of perplexity. At last, she carelessly took up a Russian leather pocket-book, on which she had really cast her eyes a quarter of an hour previously.

'How much?' she asked.

The stall-holder, a tall, fair, young woman, who was joking with two gentlemen, scarcely turned as she replied: 'Fifteen francs.'

The pocket-book was worth at least twenty. These ladies, who contended with each other in wresting extravagant prices from the men, generally sold their goods to visitors of their own sex at cost price, actuated in the matter by a sort of freemasonry. Madame Correur, however, laid the pocket-book on the stall again, and put on an expression of alarm. 'Oh, it is too expensive,' she said. 'I want something for a present, but I don't wish to give more than ten francs. Have you got anything nice for ten francs?'

Then she began to turn all the goods over again. Nothing, however, seemed to suit her. What a pity it was that the pocket-book was so dear! She took it up again and poked her nose into the pockets, whereupon the stall-holder, growing impatient, at last offered to sell it to her for fourteen francs, and then for twelve. That, however, was still too much, according to Madame Correur, who, after much keen bargaining, succeeded in getting it for eleven.

'I prefer selling things if I can,' said the tall young woman. 'All the ladies bargain and not one of them buys anything. If it weren't for the gentlemen I don't know what we should do!'

As Madame Correur went off she had the satisfaction of finding inside the pocket-book a ticket denoting that the real price was twenty-five francs. Then she strolled about again, and finally installed herself behind the lucky-wheel, by the side of Madame Bouchard, whom she called her 'pet,' and whose side curls she began to arrange.

'Ah! here comes the colonel!' suddenly exclaimed M. Kahn, who was still sitting in the refreshment room with his eyes fixed upon the entrance.

The colonel had come because he could not very well help doing so. He hoped, however, to get off with the expenditure of a louis, though the thought of even that small outlay was already making his heart bleed. As soon as he made his appearance he was surrounded and attacked by three or four ladies, who repeated: 'Buy a cigar of me, monsieur! A box of matches, monsieur!'

The colonel smiled, and politely extricated himself from their skirts. Then he looked round him and coming to the conclusion that he had better spend his money at once, he went up to a stall presided over by a lady high in favour at Court, of whom he inquired the price of a very ugly cigar-case. Seventy-five francs! The colonel could not suppress a gesture of alarm, and dropping the cigar-case he hurriedly escaped; while the lady, flushing red and feeling offended, turned her head away as though he had been guilty of some shocking impropriety in her presence. Then the colonel, desirous of preventing any unpleasant comments, went up to the kiosk where Madame de Combelot was still manufacturing her little bouquets.

These, at any rate, could not be so very expensive; he thought. However, he would not even venture upon the purchase of a bouquet, for he felt sure that Madame de Combelot would put a fairly good price upon her handiwork; so from amongst the heap of roses he chose a cankered bud, the poorest and most insignificant he could see.

'What is the price of this flower, madame?' he then inquired, with a great show of politeness, as he took out his purse.

'A hundred francs, monsieur,' replied the lady, who had been stealthily watching his manœuvres.

The colonel began to stammer, and his hands trembled. This time, however, he felt that retreat was impossible. There were several people watching him. So he reluctantly paid his money and then sought refuge in the refreshment room.

'It is an abominable swindle, an abominable swindle!' he muttered, as he took a seat at M. Kahn's table.

'You haven't seen anything of Rougon in the hall, have you?' asked M. Kahn.

The colonel made no reply. He was casting furious sidelong glances at the stall-holders. Then, hearing M. d'Escorailles and M. La Rouquette laughing loudly in front of one of the stalls, he ground out between his teeth: 'Ah! it's all very well for those young fellows! They manage to get something for their money!'

M. d'Escorailles and M. La Rouquette certainly seemed to be amusing themselves. The ladies at the stalls were struggling to get possession of them. As soon as they had made their appearance, all hands had beckoned to them and they were called on every side: 'Monsieur d'Escorailles, you know that you promised me—' 'Now, Monsieur La Rouquette, do buy this little horse of me! No? Well, you shall buy a doll, then! Yes, a doll: a doll's exactly what you want!'

The two young men were walking arm in arm for mutual protection as they playfully asserted. They advanced radiant, enraptured through the attacking battalion of petticoats, greeted with a caressing chorus of sweet voices. Every now and then they disappeared amidst a wave of bare shoulders, against which they pretended to defend themselves with little cries of alarm. And at every stall they allowed themselves to be attacked. Then they began to affect miserliness and to assume the most comical expressions of surprise. What! a louis for a doll that wasn't worth more than a sou! Oh, that was quite beyond their means! Two louis for three pencils! What!

did the ladies want to reduce them to starvation? The ladies were immensely amused and their pretty laughter rippled on in flute-like strains. They grew keener than ever, quite intoxicated by the shower of gold raining around them, and trebled and quadrupled their prices in their craving for plunder. They passed the young men on from stall to stall with significant winks; and such remarks as 'I'll squeeze them well!' or 'You can stick it on with them!' were bandied about; remarks which the two young fellows heard and acknowledged with playful bows. Behind them the ladies triumphed and boasted one to the other. The cleverest and most envied was a girl of eighteen, who had sold one of them a stick of sealing wax for three louis. However, when they at last reached the end of the hall and a lady insisted upon forcing a box of soap into M. d'Escorailles' pocket, he shook his purse before her face, saying: 'But I haven't a copper left. Shall I give you a promissory note for the money?'

The lady, who was quite excited, took the purse and searched it. Then she looked at the young man, and it seemed as though she was on the point of asking him for his watch chain. However, it was all a trick on M. d'Escorailles' part. On such occasions he took an empty purse with him by way of amusement.

'Come, let's be off!' he said, dragging M. La Rouquette away. 'I'm going to be stingy now. We must try to recoup ourselves, eh?'

'Try your luck, gentlemen! Twenty sous a chance!' called Madame Bouchard as they passed in front of the lucky wheel.

They at once approached her, and went into the business enthusiastically. For a quarter of an hour the lucky-wheel was kept going without cessation. First one, then the other set it spinning. M. d'Escorailles won two dozen egg-cups, three little looking-glasses, seven china figures, and five cigarette-cases; while M. La Rouquette's winnings consisted of two packets of lace, a china tray mounted on feet of gilded zinc, some glasses, a candle-stick, and a box with a glass cover. Madame Bouchard became indignant: 'Come, that's enough,' said she, 'you're too lucky! I won't let you go on any longer! Here, take your winnings away.'

She had arranged them in two big piles upon a table beside her. M. La Rouquette seemed filled with consternation at the sight of them; and asked her to exchange them for the regulation bunch of violets which she was wearing in her hair. But she declined to do so. 'No, no,' she said, 'you've won those things, haven't you? Very well, then, take them away with you.'

'Madame is quite right,' remarked M. d'Escorailles, gravely. 'We mustn't despise fortune, and for my part I do not mean to leave a single egg-cup behind me. I'm getting stingy.'

He had spread out his handkerchief and was tying his winnings up in a neat bundle, which caused a fresh burst of gaiety. And M. La Rouquette's embarrassment was equally amusing. But at last Madame Correur, who had hitherto kept in the background with smiling matronly dignity, protruded her fat rosy face. She would be very glad to make an exchange, said she.

'Oh, no, I don't want anything!' the young deputy hastily exclaimed. 'Take the whole lot; I make you a present of everything.'

He and Escorailles did not, however, take themselves off at once, but began to whisper doubtful compliments to Madame Bouchard. Turning a lucky-wheel was all very well, they told her, but she knew much better how to turn men's heads. Meanwhile Madame Bouchard dropped her eyelashes and giggled like a peasant-girl chaffed by gentlemen. Madame Correur gazed at her in admiration. 'Isn't she sweet? Isn't she sweet?' she exclaimed every now and then, with a rapturous expression.

But Madame Bouchard at last began to rap M. d'Escorailles' fingers, for he wanted to examine the mechanism of the lucky-wheel, alleging that it did not work fairly. Would they never leave her at peace? she cried. As there was nothing more to be got out of them they had better go. And when she at length managed to get rid of them, she again began to call in a coaxing voice: 'Only twenty sous a spin, gentlemen. Come and try one spin!'

At that moment M. Kahn, who had risen from his chair to look over the heads of the crowd, hastily sat down again. 'Here's Rougon coming!' he exclaimed. 'Let's pretend not to see him.'

Rougon was slowly making his way up the hall. He stopped first at Madame Bouchard's tent, tried his fortune at the lucky-wheel, and afterwards purchased a rose from Madame de Combelot for three louis. Having thus contributed to the funds of the charity, he seemed inclined to take his departure. He elbowed his way through the throng, already turning towards one of the doors. But all at once, having glanced into the refreshment room, he abruptly altered his course, and entered the buffet, proudly, calmly, with head erect. M. d'Escorailles and M. La Rouquette had now taken seats beside M. Kahn, M. Béjuin, and the colonel. M. Bouchard also came up and joined them. And all of them trembled slightly as the minister passed by, so big and strong did he seem to them with those massive limbs of his. He greeted them familiarly in a loud distinct voice and seated himself at a neighbouring table. He kept his broad face raised, and turned it slowly to the right and left as though anxious to confront unflinchingly the glances which he felt were fixed upon him.

Clorinde stepped up to him, dragging her heavy yellow train majestically behind her. 'What will you take?' she asked him, affecting a vulgarity of manners not untinged with raillery.

'Ah, that's the question,' he answered gaily. 'I never drink anything, you know. What have you got?'

Clorinde went rapidly through her list of liqueurs; brandy, rum, curaçoa, kirsch-water, chartreuse, vespétro, anisette, and kummel.

'No, no, I won't have any of those. Give me a glass of sugared water.'

She went off to the counter, and came back with the glass of sugared water, still preserving an air of goddess-like majesty. And she lingered in front of Rougon, watching him stir the sugar. The minister continued to smile, making the first commonplace remarks that suggested themselves to him. 'You are well, I hope? It is an age since I saw you.'

'I have been at Fontainebleau,' she quietly replied.

Rougon raised his eyes, and gave her a searching glance. But in her turn she began to question him. 'And are you well pleased?' she asked. 'Is everything going on as you wish it?'

'Yes, quite so,' the minister replied.

'Oh! so much the better.'

For a moment she turned around him with all the attention of a professional waiter. But her malicious flashing eyes were fixed on him, as though she were every moment going to overwhelm him with her triumph. At last, as she was making up her mind to leave him, she raised herself upon tip-toes, and cast a glance into the adjoining hall. And thereupon she touched Rougon's shoulder. 'There is some one looking for you, I believe,' she said, with an animated expression on her face.

Merle indeed was respectfully threading his way between the neighbouring chairs and tables. He made three bows, one after the other, and begged his excellency to excuse him; but, said he, the letter which his excellency had been expecting all the morning had arrived, and, although he had received no instructions, he had thought—

'Yes, yes, all right; give it to me,' interrupted Rougon. The usher handed him a large envelope, and then went off to prowl about the bazaar. Rougon had recognised the writing at a glance. It was an autograph letter from the Emperor in answer to the one proffering his resignation. A chilly perspiration mounted to his brow; still he showed no sign of pallor, but quietly slipped the letter into the inner pocket of his coat, without ceasing to meet the glances that were directed upon him from M. Kahn's table. Clorinde had just gone to speak a few words to the latter gentleman; and the whole band was now watching Rougon with feverish curiosity.

However, Clorinde returned and again stood in front of him, while he drank half his glassful of sugared water, and thought of some compliment to address to her.

'You are looking quite lovely to day. If queens turn themselves into waiting-maids—'

But she cut his compliment short. 'You haven't read your letter then?' she said audaciously.

For a moment he affected forgetfulness; and then all at once pretended to recollect. 'Oh, yes, that letter. I'll read it at once, if it will give you any pleasure.'

He opened the envelope carefully with a penknife, and at a glance read the brief letter inside it. The Emperor accepted his resignation. For nearly a minute he kept the letter before his face as though he were reading it over again. He felt afraid lest he should not be able to maintain a calm expression. A terrible protest was rising within him; a rebellion of his whole strength, which was unwilling to accept this downfall, shook him to his very bones. If he had not sternly restrained himself, he would have shouted aloud, and have smashed the table with his ponderous fists. And with his eyes still fixed upon the letter, he pictured the Emperor as he had seen him at Saint Cloud renewing his expressions of confidence, and confirming his previous instructions with soft words and ceaseless smile. What long devised plan of disgrace had Napoléon been maturing behind that impenetrable expression of his, that he should now so suddenly have crushed him in a night, after a score of times insisting on his retaining office? At last, by a mighty effort, Rougon conquered his emotion. He raised his face again, and it appeared unruffled. Then he put the letter back into his pocket with a careless gesture. But Clorinde, whose hands rested upon the little table, stooped eagerly towards him, and with quivering, eager lips exclaimed: 'I knew it all. I was there this morning—my poor friend!'

Then she went on to pity him in so cruelly mocking a voice that he again looked keenly at her. She had ceased to dissemble now. She had at last reached the triumph to which she had been looking forward for months past, and she spoke slowly and deliberately, savouring the sweetness of being at last able to show herself his implacable and avenged foe.

'I was unable to defend you,' she continued. 'You are doubtless not aware—' Then she broke off, and said with a cutting expression: 'Guess who succeeds you as Minister of the Interior!'

He made a gesture expressive of indifference; but she still kept her eyes fixed on him, and at last let these words fall: 'My husband!'

Rougon, whose mouth was parched, drank some more of the sugared water. Clorinde had thrown into her last two words the expression of all she felt, her anger at having been formerly despised, the rancour which she had so skilfully satisfied, her delight as a woman in having crushed a man who was credited with the highest abilities. And she allowed herself the pleasure of torturing him and abusing her victory. No doubt, said she, her husband wasn't a very clever person. She confessed it freely, and even joked about it; meaning to convey that the first comer would have done equally as well, and that she could have made Merle a minister if the whim had seized her. Yes, indeed, the usher Merle, or any other imbecile that she might have come across. Any one would have done to succeed Rougon. All this went to prove the omnipotence of woman. Then she assumed a motherly, protecting air, and began to lavish good advice.

'You see, my friend, as I've often told you, you made a mistake in despising women. Women are not the fools you imagine them to be. It used to make me quite angry to hear you speak of us as though we were idiots, mere cumbersome paraphernalia, even mill-stones about your neck. Look at my husband now! Have I been a mill-stone to him, do you think? I have been looking forward to show you all this. I promised myself this satisfaction, as you may perhaps remember, on the day when we had a certain conversation together. Now I hope I have convinced you. I willingly allow, my friend, that you are a very clever fellow; but be quite sure of this, that a woman can always topple you over if she chooses to take the trouble.'

Rougon had turned rather pale, still he smiled. 'Yes; I dare say you are right,' he said in a low voice, calling to mind all that had gone before.

He indulged in no recriminations. Clorinde had sucked some of his strength away from him to use it for his own overthrow; she had applied to his own ruin the lessons which she had learnt from him during those pleasant afternoons in the Rue Marbeuf. He was now drinking the cup of ingratitude and treason; but, man of experience that he was, he accepted it with all its bitterness. The only point which troubled him was whether he even now fully understood Clorinde. He thought of his former inquiries about her, his futile efforts to discover the secret workings of that majestic but erratic machine. Decidedly, he said to himself, the folly of man was great indeed. Clorinde had twice left him for a moment to serve other customers; and, now that she had had full satisfaction, she again resumed her stately perambulations amidst the tables, affecting to take no further notice of him. He watched her, however, and saw her approach a gentleman with an immense beard, a foreigner, whose lavish prodigality was at that time quite exciting Paris. He was just finishing a glass of Malaga. 'How much, madame?' he inquired, rising from his seat. 'Five francs, monsieur. Everything is five francs a glass.' He paid the money. 'And a kiss, how much is that?' he continued, in the same tone with his foreign accent.

'A hundred thousand francs,' answered Clorinde, without the slightest hesitation.

The foreigner sat down again, and wrote a few words on a page which he tore from a memorandum-book. Then he deposited a smacking kiss on Clorinde's cheek, paid for it, and went off in the most phlegmatic manner possible. All the people in the café smiled, much amused by the incident.

'It's only a question of paying the price,' murmured Clorinde, going up towards Rougon again.

He detected a fresh allusion in this remark. To him she had said 'Never!' And then, this man of chaste life, who had borne so bravely the stunning blow of his dismissal, began to feel keenly pained by the collar which Clorinde so impudently paraded. She stooped and swayed her neck as though to provoke him still further. The pearl tinkled in the golden bell; the chain hung low, still warm from the hands of the giver; and on the velvet flashed the diamond letters by which Rougon could easily read the secret known to everybody. And never before had he so keenly felt the bite of unconfessed jealousy, the burning envy which he had sometimes experienced in the presence of the all-powerful Emperor.

The young woman probably guessed the torment he was suffering, and it pleased her to inflict yet another pang upon him. She called his attention to Madame de Combelot, who was still selling her roses in the flower-stall. 'Ah! that poor Madame de Combelot!' she said, with a malicious laugh; 'she is still waiting!'

However, Rougon finished his sugared water. He felt as though he were choking. 'How much?' he stammered, taking out his purse. 'Five francs.'

When she had tossed the coin into the bag, Clorinde held out her hand again. 'Aren't you going to give anything to the waiter?' she asked playfully.

Rougon' felt in his pocket and brought out a couple of sous, which he dropped into her hand. This insult was the only vengeance which his parvenu boorishness could think of. In spite of her self-possession, Clorinde blushed. But she quickly resumed her goddess-like demeanour, and went off bowing and saying: 'Thank you, your excellency.'

Rougon did not dare to rise immediately. His legs felt nerveless, he was afraid of tottering, and desired to go away as he had come, with a firm gait and calm expression. He particularly disliked having to pass his old friends and associates, whose straining ears and staring eyes had not lost a point of what had taken place. So for a few moments longer he let his glance wander over the room, feigning perfect indifference. He was thinking over what had happened. Another act of his political life had come to a conclusion. He had fallen, undermined, eaten away and ruined by his band. His heavy shoulders had collapsed beneath the weight of the responsibilities he had assumed, the acts of folly and injustice which he had perpetrated entirely on their account in his braggart craving to be a feared and generous chief. And his mighty muscles only made his fall the more ignominious. The very conditions on which he had held power: the necessity of having behind him a crowd of greedy appetites whose longings he must satisfy, of maintaining himself in his position by dint of abusing his credit, had made his fall merely a question of time. And he now recalled the slow efforts of his band, whose sharp teeth had day by day nibbled away some of his authority. They had thronged around him, hung on to his knees, then to his breast, then to his throat, and finally they had choked him. They had availed themselves of him in every way. They had used his feet to climb with, his hands to plunder with, his jaws to devour with. They had, so to say, used his body as their own, used it for their personal gratification, indulging in every fancy without a thought of the morrow. And now, having drained his body, and hearing its frame-work crack, they abandoned him like rats, whom instinct warns of the approaching collapse of a house, the foundations of which they have undermined. They were all sleek and flourishing, and they were already battening upon some one else. M. Kahn had just sold his railway line from Niort to Angers to M. de Marsy. In another week the colonel would be gazetted to an appointment in the imperial palaces. M. Bouchard had received a formal promise that his *protégé,* the interesting Georges Duchesne, should be appointed assistant head clerk as soon as Delestang entered upon his duties at the Ministry of the Interior. Madame Correur was rejoicing over a serious illness which had fallen on Madame Martineau, and already pictured herself residing in her house at Coulonges, where she would live comfortably, and play the part of a lady bountiful. M. Béjuin, on his side, was certain of the Emperor visiting his cut-glass works towards the autumn; and, lastly, M. d'Escorailles, after being seriously lectured by his parents, was rendering homage to Clorinde and winning a sub-prefecture merely by the look of admiration with which he watched her carrying glasses about the refreshment room. And Rougon, as he glanced at his glutted band, felt as though he had grown smaller, whereas they had attained to huge proportions, and were crushing him beneath their weight. And he did not dare to rise from his seat, for fear lest he should see them smile if he happened to totter.

By degrees, however, he grew more collected and then he at last stood up. And he was pushing the little zinc table aside to give himself room to pass, when Delestang entered the refreshment room on Count de Marsy's arm. There was a very curious story in circulation about the latter. If certain whisperings were to be believed, he had gone to Fontainebleau the previous week, while Clorinde was there, solely to facilitate the young woman's assignations with the Emperor, by entertaining and amusing the Empress, so as to divert her attention. To most people this seemed merely a piquant incident; but Rougon fancied he could detect in it a piece of revenge on the part of the Count, who had leagued himself with Clorinde to bring about his fall, thus turning against him the very weapons which had been successfully employed against himself some time previously at Compiègne. At all events, the Count, since his return from Fontainebleau, had kept perpetually in Delestang's company.

M. Kahn, M. Béjuin, the colonel, indeed the whole coterie, received the new minister with open arms. His appointment would
not be officially notified in the *Moniteur* till the following morning, when it would appear beneath the announcement of Rougon's
resignation, but the decree was signed, and so they were at liberty
to triumph. They greeted him with much vigorous handshaking,
grinning, and whispered congratulation; indeed the presence of the
crowd alone kept their enthusiasm within bounds. It was a gradual
assumption of possession on the part of intimates, who kiss one's
hands and one's feet before making one's entire body their prey.
They already considered that Delestang belonged to them. One of
them was holding him by the right arm, another by the left; a third
had grasped one of the buttons of his coat, while a fourth, standing
behind him, craned forward and breathed words of praise to the nape
of his neck. Delestang, on his side, held his handsome head erect
with affable dignity, preserving the stately yet imbecile demeanour
of some monarch on his travels, such as one sees in official prints,
receiving bouquets from the ladies of petty towns. Rougon looked
at the group, very pale and stung to the quick by this triumph of mediocrity, and yet he could not restrain a smile. He remembered.

'I always predicted that Delestang would go a long way,' he said
with a subtle expression to Count de Marsy, who had stepped up to
him with outstretched hand.

The Count replied by a slight pout instinct with delicate irony.
He had doubtless had much amusement since he had struck up a
friendship with Delestang after rendering certain services to his
wife. He detained Rougon for a moment, evincing the most refined
politeness. Constant rivals as they were, antagonists by reason of
their very temperaments, these two skilful men saluted each other at
the termination of each of their duels, like enemies of equal strength
who looked forward to an endless succession of return combats.
Rougon had previously wounded Marsy; Marsy had now wounded
Rougon; and so it would go on until one or other of them should be
left dead on the field. It is possible that neither would have cared
to see the other absolutely ruined, for their rivalry was at once a
source of amusement and occupation. And, moreover, they vaguely
felt that they were counterpoises necessary for the equilibrium of
the Empire; one the shaggy fist which killed by a knock-down blow,
the other the slender gloved hand which clutched the throat and
strangled.

However, Delestang was a prey to painful embarrassment. He had seen Rougon, but he did not know whether he ought to step up and shake hands with him. In his perplexity, he glanced at Clorinde, who seemed absorbed in her duties and indifferent to everything else. She was now hurrying about the room with sandwiches and pastry. However, her husband thought he could gather instruction from a glance she cast at him, so he at last advanced towards Rougon, nervous and seeking to justify himself.

'I hope, my dear friend, that you don't bear me any ill will,' he said. 'I refused at first, but they forced me to accept. There are demands, you know—'

But Rougon interrupted him. The Emperor had acted in his wisdom, and the country would find itself in excellent hands.

At this Delestang took courage. 'I said all I could in your defence,' he continued. 'We all did. But really, between ourselves, you had gone a little too far. The greatest grievance against you was what you did in connection with the Charbonnel affair; the matter of those poor Sisters, you know—'

M. de Marsy restrained a smile.

'Oh, yes, the perquisition at the convent,' replied Rougon, with all the good humour of his successful days. 'Well, really, among the various acts of folly which my friends led me to commit, that was perhaps the only sensible and just act of my five months of power.'

He was already going off, when he noticed Du Poizat come in and seize hold of Delestang. The prefect pretended not to see him. For the last three days he had been hiding in Paris and waiting. And apparently he was now successful in his request to be transferred to another prefecture, for he began to express the most profuse thanks with a wolfish smile which revealed his irregular white teeth. Then, on the new minister turning round, Merle, whom Madame Correur had just pushed forward, almost fell into his arms. The usher kept his eyes lowered, like a big bashful girl, while Madame Correur spoke warmly in his favour.

'He is not a favourite in the office,' she murmured, 'because he protested by his silence against abuses of authority; and he saw some very strange ones under Monsieur Rougon!'

'Yes, yes; very strange ones indeed,' added Merle. 'I could tell a long story about them. Monsieur Rougon won't be much regretted. I've no reason to love him myself. It was all through him that I was nearly turned adrift.'

Rougon heard none of this; he was already slowly passing down the great hall, where the stalls were now quite denuded of their wares. To please the Empress, who was the patroness of the charity, the visitors had carried everything away; and the delighted stall-holders were talking of opening again in the evening with a fresh supply of goods. They counted up the money they had taken, and different sums were shouted out amidst peals of triumphant laughter. One lady had taken three thousand francs, another seven thousand, and another ten thousand. The last was radiant with delight at having made so much money.

Madame de Combelot, however, was in despair. She had just disposed of her last rose, and yet customers were still thronging round her kiosk. She stepped out of it to ask Madame Bouchard if she could not give her something to sell, no matter what. But the latter's lucky-wheel had likewise disposed of everything. A lady had just carried off the last prize, a doll's washing-basin. However, they obstinately hunted about, and at last found a bundle of tooth-picks, which had fallen on the ground. Madame de Combelot carried it off with a shout of triumph. Madame Bouchard followed her, and they both mounted into the kiosk.

'Gentlemen! gentlemen!' cried Madame de Combelot boldly, standing up, and collecting the men together with a beckoning sweep of her bare arm. 'This is all that we have left, a bundle of tooth-picks. There are twenty-five of them. I shall put them up to auction.'

The men jostled one another, laughing, and waving their gloved hands in the air. Madame de Combelot's idea was hailed with great enthusiasm.

'A tooth-pick!' she now cried. 'We'll start it at five francs. Now, gentlemen, five francs!'

'Ten francs!' said a voice.

'Twelve francs!'

'Fifteen francs!'

However, on M. d'Escorailles suddenly going up to a bid of twenty-five francs, Madame Bouchard quickly called out in her fluty voice: 'Sold for twenty-five francs!'

The other tooth-picks fetched still higher prices. M. La Rouquette paid forty-three francs for the one that was knocked down to him. Chevalier Rusconi, who had just made his appearance, bid as much as seventy-two francs for another one. And eventually the very last, a very small one, which was split, as Madame Combelot kindly announced, not wishing to impose upon her audience, was knocked down for a hundred and seventeen francs to an old gentleman whose eyes glistened at the sight of the young woman's heaving bosom, as she vigorously plied the calling of auctioneer.

'It is split, gentlemen, but it is still a serviceable article. We've got to a hundred and eight francs for it. A hundred and ten are bid over there! a hundred and eleven! a hundred and twelve! a hundred and thirteen! a hundred and fourteen! Come, a hundred and fourteen! It's worth more than that, gentlemen! A hundred and seventeen! A hundred and seventeen! Won't any one bid any more? Sold, then, for a hundred and seventeen francs!'

Pursued by these figures, Rougon left the hall. He slackened his steps when he reached the terrace overlooking the river. Stormy-looking clouds were rising in the distance. Below him, the Seine, greasy and dirty green, flowed sluggishly past the pale quays, along which the dust was sweeping. In the Tuileries gardens, puffs of hot air shook the trees, whose branches fell languidly, lifelessly, without a quiver of their leaves. Rougon took his way beneath the tall chestnuts. It was almost quite dark there, and the atmosphere was damp and clammy like that of a vault. As he emerged into the main avenue, he saw the Charbonnels sitting on a bench. They were quite transformed, magnificent. The husband wore light-coloured trousers and a frock-coat fitting tightly at the waist, while his wife sported a light mantle over a robe of lilac silk, and her bonnet was ornamented with red flowers. Astride one end of the bench, however, there was a ragged, shirtless fellow, wearing a wretched old shooting-jacket. He was gesticulating energetically, and gradually drawing-nearer to the Charbonnels. It was Gilquin. Administering frequent slaps to his canvas cap, which kept on slipping off his head, he exclaimed: 'They're a parcel of scoundrels. Has Théodore ever tried to cheat any one out of a single copper? They invented a fine story about a military substitute in order to ruin me. Then, of course, as you can understand, I left them to get on as they could without me. Ah! they are afraid of me! They know very well what my political opinions are. I have never belonged to Badinguet's gang. I only regret one person down there,' he continued in a lower tone, leaning forward and rolling his eyes sentimentally. 'Ah! such an adorable woman, a lady of society! She was fair, I had some of her hair given me.' Then, edging himself up to Madame Charbonnel, he broke into a loud voice again, and tapped her on the knee. 'Well, old lady, when are you going to take me with you to Plassans to taste those preserves of yours—the apples and the cherries and the jam? You've got your nest pretty well lined now, eh?'

But the Charbonnels seemed to be much annoyed by Gilquin's familiarity. 'We are stopping in Paris for some time,' replied Madame Charbonnel, stiffly, while gathering up her lilac silk dress. 'We shall probably spend six months here every year.'

'Ah, yes,' added her husband with an air of profound admiration, 'Paris is the only place!' Then as the gusts of wind became stronger, and a troop of nurses with children passed hastily through the garden, he resumed, turning to his wife, 'We had better be getting home my dear, if we don't want to be soaked through. Fortunately, we have only a step or two to take.'

They were now staying at the Hôtel du Palais Royal in the Rue de Rivoli. Gilquin watched them go off, shrugging his shoulders contemptuously. 'So they leave me in the lurch too!' he muttered. 'Ah, they're all alike.'

But then he suddenly caught sight of Rougon, and, rising with a swagger, he waited for him to pass. 'I haven't been to see you yet,' he said, again tapping his cap. 'I hope you're not offended. That mountebank Du Poizat has told you some fine stories about me, I dare say. But they are all lies, my good fellow, as I can prove to you whenever you like. Well, for my part I don't bear you any ill will; and I'll prove it by giving you my address, 25 Rue du Bon Puits, at La Chapelle, five minutes' walk from the barrier. So if I can be of any further use to you, you see, you have merely to let me know.'

Then he walked away with a slouching gait. For a moment he glanced round as if taking his bearings, and then, shaking his fist at the Tuileries, which showed grey and gloomy beneath the black sky at the end of the avenue, he cried: 'Long live the Republic!'

Rougon passed out of the garden and went up the Champs Elysées. He experienced a strong desire to go and look at his little house in the Rue Marbeuf. He intended to quit his official residence on the morrow and again instal himself in his old home. He felt tired but calm, with just a slight pain in the depths of his being. He already dreamt hazily of some day proving his powers by again doing great things. Every now and then, too, he raised his head and looked at the sky. The rain did not seem inclined to come down just yet, though the horizon was streaked with coppery clouds, and loud claps of thunder travelled over the deserted avenue of the Champs Elysées, with a crash like that of some detachment of artillery at full gallop. The crests of the trees shook with the reverberation. As Rougon turned the corner of the Rue Marbeuf the first drops of rain began to fall.

A brougham was standing in front of the house, and Rougon found his wife examining the rooms, measuring the windows and giving orders to an upholsterer. He felt much surprised, but she explained to him that she had just seen her brother, M. Beulin-d'Orchère. The judge, who had already heard of Rougon's fall, had desired to overwhelm his sister, and after informing her of his approaching assumption of office as Minister of Justice, he had again tried to create discord between her and her husband. Madame Rougon, however, had merely ordered her brougham to be got ready, so that she might at once prepare for removal into their old house. She still retained a calm, pale, nun-like face, the unchangeable serenity of a good housewife. And with faint steps she went through the rooms, again taking possession of that house which she had indued with such cloistral quietude. Her only thought was to administer like a faithful stewardess the fortune which had been entrusted to her. Rougon felt quite touched at the sight of her spare withered face and all her scrupulous attention.

However, the storm now burst with tremendous violence. The thunder pealed and the rain came down in torrents. Rougon was obliged to remain there for nearly three quarters of an hour, for he wanted to walk back. When he set out again the Champs Elysées was a mass of mud, yellow liquid mud, which stretched from the Arc de Triomphe to the Place de la Concorde like the bed of a freshly drained river. In the avenue there were but few pedestrians, who carefully picked their way along the kerbstones. The trees stood dripping in the calm fresh air. Overhead in the heavens the storm had left a trail of ragged coppery clouds, a low murky veil, from which fell a glimmer of weird, mournful light.

Rougon had again lapsed into his dreams for the future. He felt stiff and bruised, as though he had come into violent collision with some obstacle that had blocked his progress. But suddenly he heard a loud noise behind him, the approach of galloping hoofs which made the ground tremble. He turned to see what it could be.

It was a *cortège,* dashing through the mire of the roadway beneath the faint glimmer of the coppery sky, a *cortège,* returning from the Bois and illumining the dimness of the Champs Elysées with the brilliance of uniforms. In front and behind galloped detachments of dragoons. And in the centre there was a closed landau drawn by four horses and flanked by two mounted equerries in gorgeous gold-embroidered uniforms, each of them imperturbably enduring the splashing of the mire, which was covering them from their high boots to their cocked hats. And inside the dim closed carriage only a child was to be seen, the Prince Impérial, who gazed out of the window, with his ten fingers and his red nose pressed to the glass.

'Hallo, it's the little chap!' said a road-sweeper, with a smile, as he trundled his barrow along.

Rougon had halted, looking thoughtful, and his eyes followed the *cortège* as it hurried away through the splashing puddles, speckling even the lower leaves of the trees with all the mire it raised.

XIV

TRANSFORMATION

ONE day in March, three years later, there was a very stormy sitting in the Corps Législatif. The privilege of presenting an address to the Crown had been conceded by the Emperor, and, for the first time, this address was being discussed.

M. La Rouquette and M. de Lamberthon, an old deputy, and the husband of a charming wife, sat opposite one another in the 'buvette' or refreshment room, quietly drinking grog. 'Well, shall we go back into the Chamber?' said Lamberthon, who had been straining his ear to listen. 'I fancy things are getting pretty warm there.'

Every now and then indeed one heard distant shouting, a sudden roar like some squall of wind, but afterwards complete silence ensued. M. La Rouquette continued smoking with an air of utter indifference. 'Oh, we needn't go just yet,' he said; 'I want to finish my cigar. They'll let us know if we are wanted. I told them to do so.'

La Rouquette and Lamberthon were the only members then in the 'buvette,' a sort of smart little café established at the end of the narrow garden at the corner of the quay and the Rue de Bourgogne. Painted a soft green, covered with bamboo trellis-work, and having large windows that opened right on to the garden, the place looked like some conservatory transformed into a refreshment room for a garden party. It was panelled with mirrors; the tables and counter were of red marble, and the seats were upholstered with green rep. One of the windows was open, and through it there came the soft air of the lovely spring afternoon, freshened by the breezes from the Seine.

'The Italian war filled the cup of his glory,' said M. La Rouquette, continuing a conversation that had been interrupted. 'Today, in conferring liberty on the country, he displays all the greatness of his genius.'

He was speaking of the Emperor, and he went on to extol the provisions of the November decrees,[1] the more direct participation of the great state bodies in the policy of the sovereign, and the creation of ministers without departments for the purpose of representing the government in the Chambers. It was a return to constitutional government, he said, in all its most wholesome and desirable features. A new era, that of the liberal Empire, was beginning. Then he knocked the ash from his cigar in a transport of enthusiasm.

But M. de Lamberthon shook his head. 'I'm afraid the Emperor has gone rather too fast,' he said. 'It would have been better to have waited a little longer, there was no pressing hurry.'

'Oh, yes, I assure you there was. It was quite necessary to do something,' replied the young deputy with animation.

'It is just in that respect that his genius—'

Then he lowered his voice, and with a profound expression began to explain the political situation. The charges issued by the bishops on the subject of the Pope's temporal power, which was threatened by the government of Turin, were greatly disturbing the Emperor. On the other hand, the opposition was growing more active, and an uneasy thrill was passing through the country. So the moment had come for making an attempt to reconcile the different parties, and win political malcontents over by wise concessions. La Rouquette now considered that the despotic Empire had been very defective; whereas the liberal Empire would be a blaze of glory, illumining the whole of Europe.

---

[1] November 24 and 27, 1860. These decrees gave the right of presenting an address; promised the Legislature full explanations on questions of home and foreign policy; and made certain provisions to enable the deputies to present amendments to Government bills.—*Ed.*

'Well, I'm still of opinion that he has gone too fast,' repeated M. de Lamberthon, again shaking his head. 'It's all very well to talk about the liberal Empire; but the liberal Empire is the Unknown, my dear sir; the Unknown, the Unknown—'

He thrice repeated this expression, each time in a different tone, and waving his hand in the air. M. La Rouquette said nothing further; he was finishing his grog. However, they still sat where they were, gazing blankly out of the open window, as though they were looking for the unknown fate of the liberal Empire across the quay, in the direction of the Tuileries, where hung a thick grey haze. Behind them, beyond the lobbies, the hurricane of voices rose afresh, with the uproar of an approaching storm.

M. de Lamberthon turned his head uneasily. 'It's Rougon who is going to reply, isn't it?' he asked after a pause.

'Yes, I believe so,' replied M. La Rouquette with an air of reserve.

'He was very much compromised,' the old deputy continued. 'The Emperor has made a singular choice in appointing him as a minister without department, and commissioning him to defend his new policy.'

M. La Rouquette did not immediately express an opinion, but slowly stroked his fair moustache. 'The Emperor knows Rougon,' he said at last.

Then in quite a different tone he exclaimed: 'I say, these grogs were not up to much. I'm dreadfully thirsty. I think I shall have a glass of syrup and water.'

He ordered one, and, after some hesitation, M. de Lamberthon decided that he would have a glass of Madeira. Then they began to talk of Madame de Lamberthon, and the old deputy chided his young colleague for the rarity of his visits. The latter was lounging back on the settee, furtively admiring himself in the mirrors, quite pleased by the soft green tint of the walls, and the general freshness of the buvette, which seemed almost like a Pompadour arbour reared in some princely forest for love assignations.

However, an usher suddenly came in, almost breathless. 'Monsieur La Rouquette, you are wanted immediately—immediately!' he gasped.

Then, as the young deputy made a gesture of vexation, the usher stooped and whispered that he had been sent by M. de Marsy, the President of the Chamber, himself. And he added in a louder tone, 'Everybody is wanted; so come at once.'

M. de Lamberthon at once rushed off in the direction of the Chamber and M. La Rouquette was following him, when he appeared to change his mind. It had indeed occurred to him that it might be advisable to hunt up all the deputies lounging in different parts of the building, and send them back to their places. So he hastened first into the Conference Hall, a beautiful apartment lighted by a glazed roof and boasting a huge chimney-piece of green marble, ornamented with two white marble female figures, nude and recumbent.

Despite the warmth of the afternoon, a great wood fire was burning there. At the large table sat three deputies with sleepy eyes, which wandered over the pictures on the walls and the famous clock, which was only wound up once a year. A fourth deputy, who had installed himself at the fire, so as to warm his back, seemed to be gazing with emotion at a plaster statuette of Henri IV. which at the other end of the room stood out against a trophy of Austrian and Prussian standards captured at Marengo, Austerlitz, and Jena. As M. La Rouquette went from one to the other of his colleagues, bidding them at once hurry to the Chamber, they started up as if suddenly awakened, and hastened away in procession.

In his enthusiasm, La Rouquette was already rushing off to the library, when it occurred to him that it would be as well to glance into the lavatory. There he found M. de Combelot, who, with his hands plunged in a large basin, was gently rubbing them, and smiling admiringly at their whiteness. He did not show the least excitement, but said that he would return to his seat in a moment. Before doing so, however, he lingered for some time wiping his hands on a warm towel, which he then replaced in the copper-doored stove. And finally he took his stand before a lofty mirror, and carefully combed his handsome black beard.

There was no one in the library, which La Rouquette next visited. The books were slumbering on their oak shelves; the two huge tables with covers of green cloth stood severely bare; and the book-rests attached to the arms of the chairs were folded back, and covered with a slight coating of dust.

'There is never any one here!' exclaimed La Rouquette in a loud voice which sounded quite strange amid all the silence and solitude; and having closed the door with a bang he went on searching a series of passages and halls. He crossed the Distribution Hall, floored with marble from the Pyrenees, where his footsteps echoed as though he had been walking through a church. And an usher having told him that a deputy he knew, M. de la Villardière, was showing the palace to a lady and gentleman, he obstinately set about finding him. He hastened into the severe-looking vestibule known as General Foy's Hall, where the statues of Mirabeau, Foy, Bailly, and Casimir Périer invariably command the respectful admiration of country visitors. And, near by, in the Throne Room, he at last discovered M. de la Villardière, with a fat lady on one side of him and a fat gentleman on the other, an influential elector and notary of Dijon and his wife.

'You are wanted,' said M. La Rouquette. 'Quick to your place, eh?'

'Yes, I'll go at once,' replied the deputy. But he could not make his escape. The fat gentleman had taken his hat off, much impressed by the magnificence of the hall, with its glittering gilding and mirrored panels; and he clung firmly to his 'dear deputy,' as he called him, and would not let him go. He was asking for some explanations of Delacroix's paintings, the great decorative figures representing the seas and rivers of France; *Mediterraneum Mare, Oceanus, Ligeris, Rhenus, Sequana, Rhodanus, Garumna, Araris.* These Latin words seemed to puzzle him.

'Ligeris is the Loire,' M. de la Villardière explained.

The Dijon notary briskly nodded his head to signify that he understood. Meanwhile his wife was examining the throne, an armchair slightly higher than the others, placed on a broad platform. She stood some little distance away from it, contemplating it with reverent emotion. Presently she summoned up sufficient courage to go nearer, and then, furtively raising its covering, she touched the gilded wood, and felt the crimson velvet.

However, M. La Rouquette was now scouring the right wing of the palace, with its interminable corridors and offices and committee-rooms. He returned by way of the Hall of the Four Columns, where young deputies dream of fame while gazing at the statues of Brutus, Solon, and Lycurgus. Then he cut across the large waiting hall, and hastily skirted a semi-circular gallery, like a sort of low crypt, as dim and as bare as a church, and lighted, day and night, by gas. Finally, quite breathless, and dragging after him the little troop of deputies whom he had gathered together, La Rouquette threw open one of the mahogany doors decorated with gold stars. M. de Combelot, his hands quite white, and his beard neatly combed, followed him, M. de la Villardière, having made his escape from his constituents, came on close behind, and they all rushed together into the assembly hall where the other deputies stood erect in their places, furiously shouting and waving their arms at a member in the tribune who seemed altogether unmoved by their cries.[1]

'Order! order! order!' they shouted.

'Order! order!' cried M. La Rouquette and his friends, still louder than the others, though they knew absolutely nothing of what was going on.

The uproar was frightful. Some deputies were ragefully stamping their feet, while others kept up a noise like that of a fusillade by violently rattling the lids of their desks. Screaming and yelping voices rose, fifelike, amidst others which were gruff and full, and rumbled on like an organ accompaniment. Every now and then there was a slight lull in the din, and then jeers could be distinguished in the subsiding clamour, and some words even were plainly heard.

'It is detestable! intolerable!'

'He must withdraw it!'

'Yes, yes! withdraw it!'

However, the cry that was stubbornly repeated, which ever and ever went on to the rhythmical stamping of heels was that of 'Order! order! order!' coming hoarsely, huskily, from a hundred dry throats.

The deputy in the tribune had crossed his arms, and was gazing calmly at his furious colleagues with barking faces and brandished arms. Twice, when the tumult seemed to subside, he attempted to continue his speech, but each time that he opened his mouth there came a renewal of the tempest, a fresh outburst of frantic rage. The din in the Chamber was fairly ear-splitting.

M. de Marsy, erect in his place, with his hand upon the button of his bell, was ringing a continuous summons to silence amidst the hurricane. His long pale face remained perfectly calm. For a moment even he ceased to ring; quietly drew down his wristbands, and then applied himself to his bell again. A faint, sceptical smile, which was almost habitual to him, played round his thin lips, and whenever the shouters grew weary he contented himself with repeating 'Gentlemen, allow me, allow me!'

At last he obtained comparative silence; and then he resumed:

---

[1] Jules Favre.—*Ed.*

'I call upon the member in the tribune to explain the words he just made use of.'

Thereupon the deputy in question, bending forward, with his hands resting on the edges of the tribune, repeated his words, emphasising them by a determined movement of the chin. 'I said that what took place on the second of December[1] was a crime—'

He was not allowed to proceed further. The storm broke out afresh. A deputy with flashed cheeks called him a murderer. Another applied such a filthy term to him that the shorthand writers smiled and refrained from reporting it. There was a cross-fire of exclamations which mingled together. However, M. La Rouquette could be heard repeating in his shrill voice: 'He is insulting the Emperor! He is insulting France!'

M. de Marsy made a dignified gesture and then sat down. 'I call the speaker to order,' he said.

A long interval of agitation followed. This was no longer the drowsy Corps Législatif which five years previously had voted a credit of 400,000 francs for the Prince Impérial's baptism. On a bench to the left were four deputies who applauded the language which had been used by their colleague in the tribune. There were now five of them who attacked the Empire.[2] They were already shaking it by their continued efforts, refusing to recognise it or to vote for it, with an obstinate persistency which was destined to gradually rouse the whole country against it. These five deputies kept erect, tiny group though they were, amidst an overwhelming majority; and they replied to the threats and fists and clamorous browbeating of their colleagues without the least sign of discouragement, steadfast and fervent as they were in their desire for revenge.

The very hall itself, echoing with all the feverish excitement, seemed to have been changed. The tribune beneath the President's desk had been set up again. The cold marbles and pompous columns round the amphitheatre appeared to gather warmth from all the ardent oratory; while the light that streamed from the ceiling window set the long tiers of crimson velvet seats ablaze amid the tempests of momentous debates. The massive presidential desk, with its se-

---

[1] An allusion to the Coup d'Etat of Dec. 2, 1851.—*Ed.*

[2] Jules Favre, Ernest Picard, Henon (of Lyons), Emile Ollivier, and Alfred Darimon. Unhappily the two last subsequently sold themselves to the Empire.—*Ed.*

vere panels, acquired life from the irony and impertinence of M. de Marsy, who with the slim figure of a worn-out man of pleasure showed like a thin line against the *bas relief* behind him. And only the symbolical statues of Public Order and Liberty, in their niches between the pairs of columns, preserved inanimate countenances and pupil-less stony eyes. However, that which more than anything else imparted increased life to the hall was the much larger number of spectators, all excitedly leaning forward and eagerly following the discussions. The upper tier of seats had now been revived, and the newspaper reporters had a special gallery to themselves. High aloft, near the heavily gilded cornice, numbers of heads were craned forward, a swarming, invading throng, which occasionally made the uneasy deputies glance aloft, as though they fancied they could hear the rushing tramp of the populace on some day of insurrection.

However, the member in the tribune was still waiting for an opportunity to continue. 'Gentlemen, to resume my argument,' he said, amidst the noise which still rolled on. Then he paused, and in a louder voice, which made itself heard above the tumult, he exclaimed: 'If the Chamber refuses to hear me, I shall leave the tribune with a protest.'

'Go on! Go on!' cried several deputies; and a thick husky voice growled out the words: 'Go on; we shall know how to answer you.' Then, all at once, there was complete silence. From all the seats and galleries, deputies and spectators craned their heads forward to look at Rougon, who had just made this observation. He sat in the front row with his elbows resting on the marble tablet before him. His broad bent back remained motionless save when now and then he slightly swayed his shoulders. His face was buried in his hands and could not be seen; however, he was listening. His *début* was awaited with great curiosity, for he had not yet spoken since he had been appointed a minister without portfolio. He probably divined that many eyes were fixed on him, for at last he turned his head and glanced round the Chamber. Opposite to him, in the ministers' gallery, sat Clorinde, in a violet dress, with her elbows resting on the red velvet balustrade. She gazed at him with her wonted tranquil boldness. For a moment their eyes met, but they exchanged no smile of recognition. It was as though they had been perfect strangers. Then Rougon reverted to his previous position, burying his face in his hands, and again listening to the opposition deputy.

'Gentlemen,' said the latter, 'I resume my argument. The liberties conceded by the decree of the twenty-fourth of November are perfectly illusory. We are still far away from the principles of '89 which are so ostentatiously inscribed at the head of the Imperial Constitution. If the government persists in arming itself with exceptional laws, if it continues to force its own candidates upon the country, if it refuses to free the press from arbitrary control, if, in a word, it still keeps France at its mercy, all the seeming concessions which it may make will be lying ones—'

At this the President intervened. 'I cannot permit the speaker to use such a term,' he said.

'Hear, hear!' cried the deputies on the right. The deputy in the tribune took up his phrase again and softened it. He now strove to be more temperate in his language, speaking in carefully rounded periods of great purity of style, which fell from his lips with a solemn rhythm. But M. de Marsy angrily objected to almost every expression he used. And then the deputy launched out into abstract oratory, vague sentences overladen with long words, which so veiled his real thoughts that the President was obliged to leave him alone. However, all at once the orator returned to his old manner.

'To resume what I was saying. My friends and myself refuse to vote the first paragraph of the address in answer to the speech from the throne—'

'We can get on very well without you!' cried a voice; at which loud laughter sped along the benches.

'We shall not vote in favour of the first paragraph of the address,' quietly continued the representative of the opposition, 'unless our amendment is adopted. We cannot join in returning exaggerated thanks to the Chief of the State when so many restrictions are imposed. Liberty is indivisible. It cannot be cut up into fragments and distributed in rations like alms.'

At this fresh shouts arose from every part of the Chamber. 'Your liberty is license!'

'Don't talk about alms! You yourself are begging an unwholesome popularity!'

'You'd be cutting off heads if you had your way!'

'Our amendment,' continued the deputy in the tribune, as though he had heard nothing of these cries, 'asks for the repeal of the Public Safety Act, the liberty of the press, freedom of elections—'

Here there was another outbreak of laughter. One member exclaimed, loud enough to be heard by his neighbours: 'Ah, my fine fellow, you'll get nothing of all that!' and another made mocking comments on every sentence that dropped from the speaker's lips. The greater number, however, by way of amusing themselves, punctuated their colleague's sentences by stealthily rapping their paper-knives on their desks, thus producing a rattling sound something like a roll of kettledrums, which quite drowned the speaker's voice. Nevertheless, he struggled on to the end. Drawing himself up, he thundered forth his concluding words in such wise as to be heard above all the uproar. 'Yes, we are revolutionists, if by revolutionists you mean men of progress, resolved upon winning liberty. Refuse the people liberty, and one day the people will seize it!'

Then he descended from the tribune, amidst a fresh outburst. The deputies were no longer laughing like a lot of school-boys. They had risen to their feet, turning towards the left, and again shouting: 'Order! order!' The member of the opposition, who had regained his place, remained standing among his friends. There was a deal of surging, and the majority seemed inclined to throw themselves on those five men who stood there so defiantly with pale faces. M. de Marsy, however, angrily rang his bell, glancing as he did so at the gallery, where several ladies were drawing back with an appearance of alarm.

'Gentlemen,' he said, 'it is scandalous.' And then, silence being restored, he continued in a loud and keenly authoritative voice: 'I do not wish to call the hon. member a second time to order. I will content myself with saying that it is disgraceful in the extreme to proffer from this tribune menaces which dishonour it.'[1]

A triple burst of applause greeted these words from the President. The members of the majority cried 'bravo!' and again rattled their paper-knives, but this time in approbation. The opposition deputy wanted to say something in reply, but his friends restrained him. Then the tumult gradually subsided till there only remained a buzz of private conversation.

'I now call upon His Excellency Monsieur Rougon,' resumed M. de Marsy in a quiet tone.

A thrill, a sigh of satisfaction as it were, ran through the Chamber, followed by earnest attention. With slouching gait Rougon had ponderously made his way into the tribune. He did not at first turn

---

[1] A second call to order would have carried with it expulsion and suspension for five days, according to the rules then in force.—*Ed.*

his eyes upon his audience, but laid a bundle of notes in front of him, pushed the glass of sugared water out of his way, and stretched his hands over the narrow mahogany table as though he were taking possession of it. Then at last, leaning against the President's desk behind him, he raised his face. He did not seem to grow any older. His square brow, his large well shaped nose and his long cheeks, on which not a wrinkle showed, still had a pale rosy tint, the fresh complexion of some country notary. It was only his thick hair that had undergone any change. It had begun to grizzle and grow thinner about his temples, exposing his big ears. With eyes half-closed he glanced round the Chamber as if looking for some one; then his glance encountered the attentive face of Clorinde, who was leaning forward, and he began to speak in a heavy laborious way.

'We too are revolutionists, if by that term is meant men of progress who are resolved to restore to the country, piece by piece, every reasonable liberty—'

'Hear! hear!'

'What government, gentlemen, has ever surpassed the Empire in according a generous measure of liberal reform, such as the alluring programme you have heard sketched out? It is not necessary that I should refute the speech of the honourable member who has just spoken. It will be sufficient to prove to you that the Emperor with his genius and noble heart has forestalled the demands of the most bitter opponents of his rule. Yes, gentlemen, of his own accord, our sovereign has restored to the nation the power with which it entrusted him during a period of public danger. A magnificent spectacle of which there are few parallels in history! Oh! we can easily understand the discomfiture experienced by certain lawless individuals. They are reduced to attack our intentions, to carp at the measure of liberty which has been restored. But you have fully understood and appreciated, gentlemen, the great act of the twenty-fourth of November. In the first paragraph of the address it has been your desire to express to the Emperor your deep gratitude for his magnanimity and his confidence in the discretion of the Corps Législatif. To adopt the amendment which has been proposed to you would be a gratuitous insult. I will even say, an act of baseness. Consult your own consciences, gentlemen, and ask yourselves whether you do not feel that you are free. Liberty has been granted whole and entire—that I formally guarantee.'

A prolonged outburst of applause here interrupted him. He had gradually drawn to the edge of the tribune, and now, bending forward with his right arm outstretched, he raised his voice which rang out with wonderful power. Behind him, M. de Marsy sat back listening and smiling vaguely like a connoisseur admiring some brilliant tour de force. And amidst the loud cheering of the Chamber, deputies kept bending forward, whispering or looking surprised with lips compressed. Clorinde's arms rested listlessly on the crimson, velvet balustrade, but she seemed very serious.

Rougon continued. 'To-day,' he said, 'the hour for which we were all so impatiently waiting has at length struck. There is no longer any danger in making prosperous France free France also. The anarchical passions are dead. The energy of the Sovereign and the solemn determination of the people have for ever annihilated all abominable epochs of public perversity. Liberty became possible on the day when the faction which had so obstinately ignored the fundamental bases of sound government was defeated; and for this reason the Emperor has deemed fit to lay aside the stern strong hand, to decline excessive prerogatives as a useless burden, rightly considering his rule to be so unassailable that discussion may be freely allowed. And he has not shunned promises for the future, he will carry out his task of enfranchisement to the end, giving back one liberty after another at such times as shall seem fitting to his wisdom. Henceforth it is a programme of continual progress that it will be our duty to support in this assembly.'

'You, yourself, were the minister of the fiercest oppression!' interrupted one of the five deputies on the left, indignantly rising from his seat. And another passionately added: 'The purveyors for Cayenne and Lambessa have no right to speak in the name of liberty!'

An outburst of murmurs followed. Several deputies, who did not quite catch what was said, bent forward and questioned their neighbours. M. de Marsy pretended not to have heard, and contented himself with threatening to call all interrupters to order.

'I have just been reproached—' Rougon resumed; but shouts now rose from the right and prevented him from continuing.

'No, no! Don't reply!'

'Such insults are unworthy of your notice!'

Rougon pacified the Chamber by a gesture, and with his big fists resting on the edge of the tribune, he turned to the left with the expression of a wild boar at bay. 'I will not reply,' he calmly said.

What had gone before was merely the exordium of his speech.

Although he had stated that he did not intend to refute the assertions of the deputy of the left, he now entered upon a minute discussion. He began by clearly stating the whole of his opponent's arguments, enumerating them with an air of fairness and candour which had an immense effect; for it was as though he disdained these arguments and could destroy them by a breath. However, as he went on, he appeared to forget them entirely, and, without replying to any of them, he attacked the weakest with indescribable violence and quite overwhelmed it beneath a flood of words. Applause burst forth, he triumphed. His huge body seemed to fill the tribune; his shoulders swayed in rhythm with his periods. His oratory was of a mediocre, inartistic order, bristling with legal points and trite commonplaces, which he bellowed forth in thundering tones. He shouted and brandished trivialities; and his only real oratorical gift was his immense, inexhaustible fund of breath, which enabled him to pour forth magniloquent sentences for hours together, careless of what they might contain.

After he had spoken for an hour without a break, he gulped down a mouthful of water, and panted a little while rearranging his notes in front of him.

'Take a rest!' cried several deputies.

But he did not feel at all tired, and wanted to finish. 'What is it, gentlemen, that is asked of you?' he resumed.

'Hush! Hush!'

Every face was now again fixed on him with silent straining attention. At certain bursts of his oratory the Chamber quivered from one end to the other, as though a gale had swept through it.

'What is asked of you, gentlemen, is that you should repeal the Public Safety Act. I will not now recall the ever-accursed hour which made that act a needful weapon. It was necessary to reassure the country, to save France from a fresh cataclysm. To-day the weapon is sheathed. The government, which invariably used it with the greatest prudence—I will even say with the greatest moderation—'

'Quite true!'

'The government now only uses it in certain altogether exceptional cases. It inconveniences no one except those sectaries who still cherish the guilty madness of wishing for the return of the basest days of our history. Search through our towns, search through our villages, everywhere you will find peace and prosperity. Inquire of all orderly citizens, and you will not find one who feels in any way oppressed by those exceptional laws which are imputed to us as great crimes. I repeat that, in the paternal hands of the government, they simply continue to shield society against all hateful attempts, the success of which, moreover, is henceforth impossible. Honest, well-disposed men have no occasion to trouble themselves about their existence. Leave them to their slumber, until our Sovereign shall feel justified in doing away with them himself. But what else is asked of you, gentlemen? Freedom of elections, the liberty of the press, every kind of liberty that can be imagined. Ah! Let me pause for a moment to glance at the great things which the Empire has already accomplished. All around me, wherever I turn my eyes, I see public liberties increasing and bearing splendid fruits. I feel the profoundest emotion. France, once fallen so low, is now fast recovering, and giving to the world the example of a nation winning its own freedom by its good behaviour. The days of trial are now over. There is no longer any question of a dictatorship, or of despotism. We are all workers in the cause of liberty—'

'Bravo! bravo!'

'Freedom of elections is asked for; but is not universal suffrage on the widest basis the primordial source of the Empire's existence? Doubtless the government recommends its candidates. But does not the revolutionary party support its own with shameless audacity? We are attacked, and we defend ourselves. Nothing could be fairer. Our opponents would like to gag us, bind us hand and foot, reduce us to the condition of dead bodies. That is a thing which we can never allow. Our love for our country requires that we should advise it and tell it where its true interests lie. It still remains the absolute master of its destinies. It votes and we bow to its wishes. Those members of the Opposition who belong to this assembly, where they enjoy entire liberty of speech, are themselves a proof of our respect for the decrees of universal suffrage. The revolutionary party must settle the matter with the nation, for it is the nation that supports the Empire by overwhelming majorities... In parliament all obstacles to free control have now been swept aside. Our Sovereign has been pleased to accord the great bodies of the state a more direct participation in his policy, and a conspicuous proof of his confidence in them. Henceforth you will be able to discuss the measures of the government, you will be able to exercise the right of amendment in the fullest degree, as well as to express all your desires. Every year the discussion on the address will form, as it were, an interview between the Emperor and the representatives of the nation, at which the latter will be able to say whatever they please with perfect freedom. It is by free and open discussion that powerful states are formed. The tribune is restored to you, the tribune which so many orators, whose names history has preserved, has made illustrious. A parliament which discusses is a parliament that works. And, to tell you the real truth, I am glad to see here a group of opposition deputies. There will always be amongst us opponents who will try to find us at fault, and who, by doing so, will make our good faith show conspicuously. We solicit the most generous treatment for them. We fear neither passion nor scandal, nor abuse of the freedom of speech, dangerous though these things be.

'As for the press, gentlemen, under no government determined upon making itself respected has it enjoyed greater freedom than it does at present. Every great question and every serious interest has its organs. The government only opposes the propagation of dangerous doctrines, the dissemination of poisonous ideas. For the honourable portion of the press, which is the great voice of public opinion, I assure you that we entertain the most absolute respect. It assists us in our task; it is the tool of the age. If the government has taken it into its own hands, this is only to keep it from falling into those of its enemies.'

Approving laughter arose. Rougon was now drawing near to his peroration. He gripped the frame-work of the tribune with the stiffened fingers of his left hand, and throwing his whole body forward he swept the air with his right arm. His words flowed forth like a sonorous torrent. And suddenly, amidst his glowing praise of the new liberal policy, he seemed overcome by wild excitement. He shot his fist forward like a battering ram, as though aiming at something yonder in empty space. This invisible enemy was the spectre of the Red Revolution. In a few dramatic sentences he depicted that red spectre shaking its blood-stained banner and waving its incendiary torch as it rushed on, leaving streams of mud and gore behind it. His voice rang out like the alarm-bell of the days of revolution, while bullets whizzed by, and the Bank of France was sacked and the money of respectable citizens was stolen and shared. The deputies turned pale in their seats as they listened. But then Rougon calmed down, and concluded by speaking of the Emperor in warm bursts of laudation, which suggested the swaying of a censer. 'God be thanked!' said he. 'We are under the protection of the Prince whom Providence in its infinite mercy selected to save us. We can safely rest beneath the shelter of his wisdom. He has taken us by the hand, and is leading us step by step through the breakers, to the safety of the harbour.'[1]

Vociferous applause resounded. For nearly ten minutes the proceedings were interrupted. A crowd of deputies rushed to meet the minister as he returned to his seat, with perspiration streaming down his face and his figure still quivering from such an expenditure of breath. M. La Rouquette, M. de Combelot, and a hundred others poured forth their congratulations, and stretched out their arms to try and grasp his hand as he passed them. The whole Chamber was heaving with excitement. Even the occupants of the galleries shouted and gesticulated. Beneath the sun-lit ceiling-window, amidst the gilding and the marble, all the severe magnificence characteristic both of a temple and an office, there raged commotion such as one might find in a public square on some day of demonstration—bursts of doubting laughter, loud exclamations of astonishment and of wild admiration, all the clamour, in a word, of a passion-swayed multitude.

And as the eyes of M. de Marsy and Clorinde met, they both nodded their heads in confession of the great man's triumph. The speech which Rougon had just delivered was his first step up that splendid ladder of fortune which was to carry him to so great a height.

However, a deputy had mounted the tribune. He had a clean-shaven face, a waxy complexion, and long yellow hair, with sparse curls which fell over his shoulders. Standing stiff and rigid, he consulted some big sheets of paper, the manuscript of a speech, which he finally commenced to read in an unctuous voice.

'Silence, gentlemen, silence!' cried the usher.

This deputy had certain explanations to ask from the government. He showed great irritation at the dilatory attitude of France in presence of the threats of Italy against the Holy See. The temporal power of the Pope, said he, was really the ark of God, and the address ought to contain a formally expressed hope, a command even, that this power should be maintained in all its integrity. The speaker launched out into historical references, and showed that the forces

---

[1] Sedan.—*Ed.*

of Christianity had established political order in Europe many centuries before the treaties of 1815. Then, in periods that breathed fear and consternation, he said that he beheld with the greatest alarm the olden society of Europe vanishing in the midst of popular convulsions. Every now and then, as he indulged in too direct an allusion to the King of Italy, murmurs sped through a part of the Chamber; but the compact group of clerical deputies on the right, nearly a hundred strong, listened most attentively, accentuating his slightest references by an expression of approval, applauding, too, every time that he named the Pope with a slight reverent inclination of the head.

A chorus of bravos greeted his last words: 'It distresses me,' he said, 'that proud Venice, the Queen of the Adriatic, should become the obscure vassal of Turin.'

Rougon, though his neck was still wet with perspiration, his voice hoarse and his big frame exhausted by his previous exertions, insisted upon replying at once. It was a remarkable sight. He made a parade of his fatigue, exhibited it ostentatiously, dragging himself to the tribune, where he began by stammering faint words. He bitterly complained that men of position, hitherto so loyal to the Imperial institutions, should now be among the adversaries of the government. There must surely be some misunderstanding. They could not wish to swell the ranks of the revolutionists, and weaken a power which made constant efforts to ensure the triumph of religion. And, turning towards the deputies on the right, he addressed them with pathetic gestures, spoke to them with a humility full of craft, as though they were powerful foes, the only foes that he really feared.

Meantime his voice gradually recovered all its previous force, and once more he filled the Chamber with a bellowing roar, striking his breast the while with his closed fist.

'We are accused of irreligion,' he cried. 'It is a falsehood! We are the reverent children of the Church, and it is our happiness to be faithful believers. Yes, gentlemen, faith is our guide and our support in this task of governing, which is often so heavy a burden. What, indeed, would become of us if we did not trustfully place ourselves in the hands of Providence? Our only pretension is to be the humble executants of its designs, the docile instruments of the will of God. It is this which enables us to speak out freely and to accomplish some little good. And, gentlemen, I am happy that this opportunity presents itself for me to bend the knee with all the fervour of a true Catholic heart before the sovereign Pontiff, before that august and venerable old man whose watchful and devoted daughter France will ever remain.'

Before he had well finished, the Chamber resounded with applause. His triumph was becoming an apotheosis. The very walls shook.

When they were all leaving, Clorinde watched for Rougon to pass by. He and she had not exchanged a word for the last three years. When he made his appearance, looking younger and lighter, having in a single hour given the lie to all his previous political life, ready to satisfy, under the fiction of constitutionalism, his rageful craving for power, she yielded to an impulsive feeling and stepped towards him, with hand outstretched and moist caressing eyes. 'Ah!' said she, 'in spite of everything, you are a wonderfully able fellow!'

THE END

Emile Zola's "Les Rougon-Macquart"

La Fortune des Rougon (1871) - The Fortune of the Rougons

La Curée (1871–72) - The Kill / La Curee

Le Ventre de Paris (1873) -
The Fat and the Thin / The Belly of Paris

La Conquête de Plassans (1874) - The Conquest of Plassans

La Faute de l'Abbé Mouret (1875) -
Abbé Mouret's Transgression / The Sin of the Abbé Mouret

Son Excellence Eugène Rougon (1876) - His Excellency

L'Assommoir (1877) - L'Assommoire / The Dram Shop

Une Page d'amour (1878) - A Love Episode / A Page of Love

Nana (1880) - Nana

Pot-Bouille (1882) - Pot-Bouille / Pot Luck

Au Bonheur des Dames (1883) - The Ladies' Paradise

La Joie de vivre (1884) - The Joy of Life / Zest for Life

Germinal (1885) - Germinal

L'Œuvre (1886) - The Masterpiece

La Terre (1887) - The Earth

Le Rêve (1888) - The Dream

La Bête humaine (1890) - The Human Beast / Beast in Man

L'Argent (1891) - Money

La Débâcle (1892) - The Debacle

Le Docteur Pascal (1893) - Doctor Pascal

Printed in the United States
128431LV00003B/74/A